THIS DARK TIME
CHRONICLES OF BEAR – VOLUME 1

Tim Hanner

THIS DARK TIME
CHRONICLES OF BEAR – VOLUME 1

Acknowledgements

There is no way this work could have taken place without the help and constant attention of Cathy, my "Sis." Still, there is someone else who stood by and watched as this novel unfolded. It's been said many times that behind every successful man there is a great woman. I couldn't agree more. My woman is Cathy. However, in this case, in addition to her, there is a caring, loving and understanding man—her husband Dan.

Dan has understood and supported her dedication, steadfast attention to and assistance with everything I have written. Both of these wonderful people are loosely represented by characters in this book. There is no way I could ever write characters as solid and devoted as they are in real life.

Dan, I have to thank you for allowing me to impose upon your marriage and have your lovely lady keep me on the path time and time again. Without your help and understanding, this work would have never been completed.

PART ONE
LOSS

"Change is the constant, the signal for rebirth,
the egg of the phoenix."

Christina Baldwin

CHAPTER ONE

Rafe awoke from a fitful sleep, laden with dreams of hellish shapes chasing him. He always remembered his dreams, but it was rare for him to have nightmares; and he especially hated remembering them after waking up.

Kim slept peacefully beside him. Her short blond hair looked as if she were posed for a picture with every strand in place. The outline of her ample breasts rose and fell beneath the sheet with her slow rhythmic breathing. Kim had worked for him a little less than two years as a receptionist at his medical clinic, and they were involved for about half that time. Following last night's Halloween party, they decided to stay at Rafe's apartment, since it was closer, even though it was her turn to have him over.

As Rafe swung his legs over the side of the bed, stretched and looked at the sun shining through the window, the dream began to fade from his memory. Soon it would be lost, the same as many of the others.

At forty-eight years, Raphael Edmonds was in remarkably good shape. The twenty-four years he spent in the U.S. Navy had treated him well. Seventeen of those were working with the SEALs. The last four was as an instructor at the SEAR School, as an aggressor. After retiring, he went back to school and earned a Master's Degree and two Doctorates in alternative medicines.

While trying to establish his medical practice, he opened a karate school, which had since grown enough to expand into a second branch. Not only did he still exercise five days a week, but he also worked out with his students daily.

Looking at the clock, he was surprised to see no display. In fact, it looked like a blob sitting on the table beside his bed. He went to the front door and peered out the peephole. The hallway outside was dark, which meant the whole building was out. *Figures. Bet there's not enough hot water left for a shower either.*

In the dark bathroom, he turned the hot water on and was relieved to find there was indeed some left. A few seconds after climbing in the shower, the curtain slid open enough to allow Kim to step into the tub with him. She stood six inches shorter than his five-foot-ten inches. When she stared at him with her beautiful green eyes and pressed her body against his, he had to remind himself the warm water wouldn't last long.

"There's no electricity so there won't be much hot water," he told her, not wanting her to think he wasn't in the mood.

Instead of having a long, luxurious shower, they took a quick one, and she helped wash his long, brown hair. As a small rebellion to his military background, he had let his hair and beard grow after retirement. Stepping from the shower, they did get to enjoy some time slowly drying each other with oversized towels. They found the clothes and dressed-there was still no electricity.

"Would you like some breakfast?" He asked.

"Let's go to Daryl's," she said.

"Sure. That diner makes the best breakfast in town. Maybe they'll have the electricity back on by the time we get back."

"I hope they've got power."

"I'll bet they do," he said. "They're far enough away this outage probably won't affect 'em. Hang on, I'll check."

He removed a small battery-powered radio from the closet, turned it on, but no sound came from the instrument. In fact, the thing felt warped. "It must have gotten too hot in the closet sometime this summer," he said, tossing it into the trash.

They left his apartment and headed toward the parking lot. Reaching the access gate, Rafe noticed there were more cars in the lot than normal for this time of day. "Looks like everyone's home for the Halloween weekend."

"I doesn't look like anyone's working," she agreed.

Instinctively, he glanced around and noticed a group of men about half way down the lot, talking.

He hurried her toward his car, opened the door, and let her in. He went and climbed in the driver's side. Inserting the key in the ignition, he turned it, expecting the engine to turn over. Instead, there was nothing. He tried again with the same results. "What the hell's going on?" It was more of a statement than a question.

As he started to get out, he noticed a couple of men from the group wandering toward him.

"Stay in here," he said not wanting to have to worry about her safety. He stepped over to meet the other people.

"Car won't start?" A man asked with a heavy Spanish accent.

"Nah," Rafe answered, eyeing the men closely.

Before he could say anything else one of the other men said, "None of 'em will. They're all dead. Wait until you look under the hood."

"What do you mean?" Rafe asked. He knew his car was okay last night. He and Kim had used it to return home from the party.

"Take a look," the second man answered. "Every one of 'em, so far, has their wires fried. Pop your hood, you'll see."

Rafe turned back to his vehicle, motioned to Kim who pulled the handle for the hood release. The hood popped loose, and he pulled it up. The others joined him as he raised it.

The first man pointed and said, "Yep, the same as all the rest."

Burn marks and fried wires lay all over the engine compartment. The distributor cap was melted in place with all its wires now nothing but melted rubber. Rafe frowned. *This shit only happens with a power surge. What the hell would cause a surge of electricity strong enough to burn only the wires and plastic and still not be enough to set the rest of the vehicle on fire?* He ran his hand through his hair.

"They're all like this," the man continued. "No power at all. It's the same as in the apartments. Did you notice the burn marks on your walls?"

"I didn't notice anything out of the ordinary." However, he thought about the slightly warped radio.

"You check, I'll bet you see burn marks where the wires run."

Another man spoke up and said, "It's like this all over. I've checked for about two blocks. Plus, look around. Do you see or hear anything moving?"

Rafe stopped and listened. The guy was right. It was only then he realized he didn't even hear the sound of the power station across the river. The station that supplied all the power for the Austin area now sat silent.

One of the men said, "You don't hear it do you. The generators aren't running. That's nothing, earlier; there was smoke pouring out of it."

Kim climbed out of the car. "Is everything okay?"

"I'm not sure," Rafe answered. "If these gentlemen are right, then no, something's wrong."

Kim walked over to Rafe and put her arm around his waist. "It looks like a mess."

"They all are," the second man answered.

Rafe was sure the men knew nothing about what had caused the situation. "Thanks gents," he said to them, and then to Kim, he asked, "Wanna take a walk?"

"Sure," she answered.

They left the lot, heading for Interstate 35, which ran through Austin. As they walked along Riverside Drive, Rafe concentrated on his surroundings using all his senses as he did while in the military. With very few people stirring, he easily noticed any movement. The silence was something he had never heard in the city before. Even at night, there was the constant sound of life. However, it afforded him the opportunity to detect the sound of strapped on his western holsters and stuffed a 9mm pistol in a shoulder holster. On top of all this, he donned a black duster and cowboy hat. Over his shoulder and hanging on the other side, he carried his "possibles" bag for all his black powder guns.

He gave Kim a 20-gauge shotgun, which she slung over her shoulder. He showed her how to put on a shoulder holster, which held another 9mm pistol. She also carried a "possibles" bag on the other shoulder, and Rafe put a container in the bag. "This is breakfast," he said. "We'll eat on the edge of town." He strapped a web belt on her hips with two canteens of water on it. "I know it's heavy, but we will need it later."

"It's not bad," she assured him.

Quickly and quietly, they slipped out of the apartment building and into the parking lot.

***

They traveled east along Riverside drive. Rafe told her it was the opposite direction from their destination, but the horses were to the east and would save them precious hours later. "If cars and trucks wouldn't work, we'll revert to traveling by horseback," Rafe said.

Kim trusted him and was sure he knew what he was doing. Besides, she was sure there was no way she could survive something like this without his help. *The longest I've been without electricity is a couple of hours. I never would have expected things to turn bad so soon. It's like the bad guys realized there wasn't help available to regular citizens and are taking full advantage of it.*

people he might not be able to see. He couldn't smell the familiar odor of exhaust from the thousands of vehicles of the city. It was as if the impurities of the city were carried away on a cool, clean Texas breeze.

No cars moved anywhere. This particular part of the Interstate was never without traffic. Never that is, until today.

They talked to small groups of people in various places along the way, but nobody had any idea what had happened. During the conversations, Rafe noticed that they seemed to fidget as they talked and glanced around as if expecting trouble. They seemed to be anxious and not comfortable being outside.

As Rafe and Kim turned from the interstate, back toward the apartment, he looked at his digital watch. The face was blank. Uneasiness was rapidly settling on him as well, covering him like a blanket.

"What's going on here?" Kim asked. "I've never seen I-35 empty like this. Look over there." She pointed at a couple of vehicles in the distance. "The only cars on the Interstate are stopped. None of them are moving."

Rafe instinctively thought back to his training in the military. "The only thing I can think of, which could kill all electricity, including houses, cars, and even the power plant is an EM pulse from a nuclear weapon."

Fear rushed onto Kim's face.

"Don't worry," Rafe quickly assured her. "If there were a nuclear burst, we wouldn't be able to walk around here like this. Also, there'd be massive destruction and there's not."

14

She relaxed a little. There *was* something different though. He wasn't sure if it was his nerves or real, but the air felt different. He couldn't put his finger on what it was. Maybe it was the stillness-maybe not-but the air felt heavier, thicker-like it had more substance than it should.

"Let's get back to the apartment and give this a while to get straightened out," he said and took her hand.

Back at the apartment, he lit a match to ignite the gas burners on the stovetop. Luckily, he could still cook for them since the range was gas and not electric. When he finished cooking, they stepped out on his balcony and sat in a couple of chairs. As they ate, he observed the actions of the people he saw passing by.

"Everything looks normal," Kim observed. "Except for no cars and no electricity anywhere."

"Yeah, it does," he answered. "But, did you notice that the buildings were not only closed, but there were no lights on in them either? Most of the businesses with coolers or freezers will have back up power just in case."

"I didn't really notice," Kim admitted. "I was too busy watching people in the house watch us."

"You noticed too, huh?"

After a while, the sun dipped low enough to the horizon to put a chill on the air.

"We're supposed to have a front pass through tonight. I imagine it's gonna get cold even inside." He went back inside, and she came in as he lit the kerosene lamp he kept stored on a shelf. The air inside the apartment was already as chilly as outside, and the front was still a ways away. "Would you please close the sliding glass door?"

He lit all four burners of the stove as well as the oven for warmth, figuring the temperature would dip into the low to mid-forties. It was then he heard the sounds of the first shots outside.

"What was that?" Kim asked nervously. "Those weren't gunshots were they?"

"Yep," he answered, "That's what it was."

Leaving the lamp in the kitchen, he went to the glass doors of the balcony and peered out through a small slit in the curtains. All he could see was the movement of dark silhouettes near the road. Figuring it would be safer to stay out of the window, he made sure the curtains overlapped so no light could escape and returned to the kitchen.

"We're gonna have to keep those curtains closed." He constructed a pallet of pillows and blankets for them in the kitchen.

"I know it's not as comfortable as the bed, but it's the only room with any heat at all," he said almost apologetically.

"Don't worry about it," Kim said. "I understand."

He looked at the strained smile on her face. "We need to talk about what to do if this hasn't changed by tomorrow."

"I was wondering about that myself."

More gunshots sounded outside.

"Those tell me if nothing's changed, we need to get outta town," he said. "I can't and won't try to make decisions for you, but I'm not gonna stay here. This place is gonna get very crazy and very dangerous very fast."

16

"Surely the police will get things under control soon," she countered.

"How? If things are the same, they can't drive cars and remember the radio didn't work this morning."

"What are you saying?"

"Think about it," he said, "police always call for back-up even when they have cars that work. Do you actually think they would go on patrol if they don't have cars, radios, or any other way to get back-up?"

"You're scaring me." Kim's voice quivered slightly.

"Good," Rafe answered. "I don't mean to be cruel, but fear means you're not in denial either. We'll simply have to see what things are like tomorrow."

The night turned into an uncomfortable, long ordeal. As he expected, the cold crept into the apartment and slowly overtook the warmth of all the rooms other than the kitchen. Kim snuggled up close to Rafe, but by the way she jumped at the sound of the guns outside, he knew it was from the cold and fear rather than any physical desire. He wasn't sure how long she could keep up her brave facade, but he had to give her a ton of credit for trying. The *pop-pop-pop* of guns echoed throughout the night until immediately before morning. Once there was even the sound of guns firing downstairs in their building.

CHAPTER TWO

When he awoke the next morning, Rafe knew he was leaving town. Outside, from his balcony, he counted five bodies. This part of Austin was lower-middle class, but the body count only confirmed the seriousness of the situation. The few people he saw carried guns and constantly glanced around, obviously uncomfortable being in the open. As best he could tell, it was about eight in the morning, and there was no need to waste any more daylight around here.

He returned to the kitchen where Kim still slept on the floor. He gently shook her shoulder. "Hey young lady, it's time to get up."

Her breathing continued rhythmically, and her eyes moved beneath their lids.

He shook her a little harder and repeated his message for her to wake up.

Slowly, her eyes opened, and she blinked uncomprehendingly. Rafe knew she was trying to acclimate herself. It wasn't often a person woke up on an unfamiliar kitchen floor.

With a slight jerk, she muttered, "What, who, huh... " Her eyes locked on Rafe, and he could see recognition slip into them. Kim looked around. "Are things back to normal?"

Rafe shook his head. "I'm sad to say no. In fact, it seems it was a bad night. There are bodies out on the lawn."

"Bodies?" She repeated and started to stand.

"You don't need to look. I'm afraid you'll see enough of them before this is over. Rafe ran his hand through his hair, took a deep breath and let it out. "I think it's time we left town. I won't try to make the decision for you, but I'm leaving. I can't help but believe this place is gonna get real crazy real quick." He paused for this information to sink in. "You're welcome to come with me. In fact, I think it's best if you do. Of course, it's up to you."

She rose to her feet. "If things are turning bad, I don't have any reason to stay here," Kim said. She paused looking as if she was deep in thought and then continued. "If it's that dangerous, how will we get out of town without getting killed? I don't know what's going on, but this feels like more than a simple loss of electricity. If that's all it is, we can come back later."

"We're not too far from the east edge of town. I figure we can go out on Ben White, and I know where there are some horses about a mile from the airport. I figure we can get them and use them for transportation." He paused as a small knot formed in his stomach. There's definitely more going on here than just a simple loss of electricity. Too many things don't fit."

Kim nodded and looked toward the bedroom. "I don't have the right type of clothing for cold weather."

"Not a problem. I've got some clothes you can use." He grinned. "They may not be at the pinnacle of fashion, but they're functional; and they'll keep you warm."

Rafe entered the bedroom and walked over to his closet with Kim close behind. The closet was dark, and Kim's eyes widened when he walked out with an arm full of western clothes for her.

"I'm a member of a Wild West gunfighter's group called the Hays County Regulators. You've seen us perform once or twice. Here are some of the clothes from the shows. I've got half a closet full."

"I remember. They're the people that gave you the nickname Bear. She took the clothes from him. I'm not sure they'll fit me though. You're not quite my size."

"These are some smaller ones I wore a few years ago. I wasn't always this size. Actually, I got the nickname Bear when I was in the military." Her hands shook as she held the clothes up to look at them. *She's doing her best to hold it together.*

Kim chose a pair of pants and a shirt. "These look smaller. Maybe they'll work."

Rafe reentered the closet and emerged carrying a couple of the outfits he regularly wore. Kim pulled up some trousers and tucked a shirt into them. "Do you actually expect me to wear these? There's no way these pants will stay up." When Rafe started to smile, she quickly added, "And I don't wanna hear anything about how easy they'll be to get off later."

Rafe grinned and produced some suspenders. "This is how we keep our pants up in the ole west, Ma'am."

After helping Kim adjust the suspenders, he went back into the dark closet. When he stepped out, he was carrying numerous black powder weapons they used in the shows.

Rafe loaded his black powder pistols. However, this time he added a lead ball to each cylinder. He

Many of the shops already showed signs of looting and vandalism with smashed windows and some of their contents were scattered outside. Windows of homes were also missing, and Kim could see curtains fluttering through them. Car and truck windows were smashed, and some of the vehicles looked like someone had taken a sledgehammer to them. "What the hell's going on? Are people really this easily changed? How can they turn so cruel so fast?"

"We'll talk about it later," Rafe said. "Right now, our main concern is to get out of here."

When Kim saw the bodies, she stopped dead in her tracks, horror-struck. There was a body lying near the road and two more in a front yard. It seemed insanity had already struck in all its ugly forms in such a short time.

Rafe wrapped his arm around her. "People are instinctively slipping into survival mode. You have to realize-to some, this will be to protect home, property, and loved ones. To others, it will mean aggression is the answer. They'll reach out and attack anyone or anything not a piece of their little portion of the world. Those people pose more of danger to a traveler than the first. People strictly defending themselves will be more willing to ask questions, negotiate, and let a traveler pass than the thugs and gangs looking to expand their territory. Still, if this situation didn't change soon, it will all degrade into a deadly dog-eat-dog attitude very quickly."

Kim gazed up at him. "I simply can't believe what I'm seeing. People really are capable of becoming complete animals.

"I know what you're going through." Rafe removed his hat and ran his hand though his hair. I'm sorry to say I've seen this and more before. You never get used to it. It never becomes easy to see things normal people consider atrocities. But you do acquire the ability to rebound from it quicker. I'm sorry to say that I'm at that point." He replaced his hat and continued down the road.

As they traveled, Rafe took a closer look at the condition of the growing number of bodies they found. Even from a distance, she could see that most were the result of being shot, stabbed, or beaten. A great many, however, looked as if a disease of some sort did the job. They had sores on their skin with eruptions, which once oozed a combination of puss and blood. The skin stretched tight across the corpse and started to swell as if they had been dead and exposed to the elements for a long time. Twice she had to turn away and fight the urge to vomit.

Rafe stepped away from Kim for a minute, leaving her at the edge of the road as he inspected a couple of corpses laying in a yard. He returned to Kim and told her what he had found. "They're in about the same condition as the others we've seen. But these bodies look like they've been exposed to the elements for at least a week."

"If they were out here that long, wouldn't someone have seen and reported them?"

"You're right. Rafe sighed and shook his head. "Something else has to be going on here."

"What do you mean? You don't think all this is causing a disease of some sort do you?"

"I don't know." He was quiet as he looked around. "However, without transportation or communication, it's doubtful anyone would do anything about the bodies; even if they knew about them. With all the shots we heard last night and the condition of the buildings after a night of looting, the people of the city now have to be in a defensive mode."

"You've done nothing to bolster my confidence," Kim said, trying to smile. "I have to agree, it's literally time to head for the hills. I just hope we can make it."

Rafe put his arm around her. "We'll make it. There're not many living people out right now, and we've only got another mile or so before we're out of the city."

Another twenty minutes of walking, and they came to the edge of town. Rafe guided Kim onto a small road, which they followed a while before stopping under a couple of trees. They opened their food, which was in the form of military MREs or Meals Ready To Eat. Rafe showed Kim how to add the water to the heaters to heat her food. She ate in silence. She wasn't sure how she could accept what was happening. *There's no electricity. People are killing each other. There's looting and the evidence of violence everywhere. I'm not like Rafe; I never thought I'd ever have to see a dead person anywhere but a funeral home.* Tears filled her eyes, and she wiped them away.

She barely remembered eating the food and wasn't even sure she could keep it down, but she would try. She didn't want to be a hindrance to

Rafe. After eating, they buried their trash and continued toward where the horses were.

***

About an hour later, they arrived at the pasture where Rafe had seen the horses. Looking around, he saw nothing of them.

Beside him, Kim said, "I don't see any horses. Are you sure we're at the right place?"

"Damn sure didn't remember this pasture being this big." He looked at Kim and grinned. "Of course, it wouldn't look this big from a car." He motioned toward a structure on the other side of the field. "They're probably in the barn over there."

Half way across the field, Kim grabbed his arm and stopped. "What if someone's in the there?"

Honestly, he hadn't thought of that. She was right. There might be an owner for those horses-not only an owner, but possibly an owner with a gun to protect what was his. With no other buildings or trees in the pasture, the owner could have been watching them as they approached.

There was a small rise of dirt a few yards away. "You stay here," he said. "If you're right, there's no reason to put you in danger. I'll check out the barn, and if it's okay, I'll let you know."

"I don't wanna just stay here," she objected. "I can... "

"Wait here," Rafe interrupted sternly. "I need to know where you are if I have to use a gun."

Kim frowned but slid behind the rise and waited, fear and concerned etched on her pretty face.

Rafe smiled. "It'll be okay," he assured her and turned toward the barn.

Reaching the closest corner of the barn minutes later, he stopped and listened. He heard no sound other than the wind as it rustled the high grass around him. Slowly, he made his way to the front of the structure. One of the large double doors was open and secured against the wall.

Sticking his head around the edge of the door, he peered into semi-darkness. Inside, he could hear the breathing and an occasional snort of a horse. There was no other sound to mark the presents of anyone or anything else.

Pulling his 44-caliber pistol and cocking it, he stepped through the edge of the opening and into the darkness. Leaning against the wall, he waited for his eyes to adjust, once again listening. After what seemed to be hours, but in reality was no more than thirty or forty seconds, he was able to make out some details of the barn.

Thankfully, he and the horses were alone. There was no owner inside with a gun waiting to shoot the first person to walk through the door. The four horses stood in their stalls as if waiting patiently for their feed, which served to reinforce his belief that no one else was in the area.

Rafe slowly let the hammer down on his pistol and returned it to his holster, wondering softly to himself what he would have done had he come face-to-face with the horse's owners.

As he left the barn, Kim rose from her position in the tall grass. He motioned, and she trotted over to him.

"The horses are inside. There's no one else around." He turned and walked inside with Kim beside him.

"I was wondering," she said, "what would you have done if the owner was in here?"

"I'm not sure. I don't know if I would have been willing to shoot a person simply for defending what was theirs. I could never kill someone in cold blood. I think I would have tried to explain. Thank God I didn't have to find out." Something deep inside told him he needed to find the answer to this question. The same something said his life would depend on the answer sooner or later. An involuntary shudder briefly ran through his body.

Following a short search, they found feed for the animals and gave it to them along with some hay. He was glad they didn't have to chase the horses to hell and back to catch and saddle them. Each stall was marked with a horse's name and across the barn, all the tack was marked with a corresponding name on the wall behind it. Rafe showed Kim how to put on their bridles. As she did, he saddled them. He figured he and Kim could ride two and lead the other two, using them as packhorses. After leading the horses outside, Rafe mounted one named Dusty, and Kim was on Ranger. They turned back toward Austin. He knew they would have to skirt the city if they were to avoid trouble.

We're going back through Austin?" Kim asked.

"We're gonna skirt the city as much as possible," he explained. "But there's a place we need to visit before leaving completely."

"Where are we going?"

"We need to go to a small gun shop a friend of mine owns named 'Guns and More.' I need to see about the availability of black powder and possibly food." His friend, Pete, was a member of the Army Special Forces until a grenade took four inches of his left leg in a training accident. He had supplied Rafe with the powder used for many of the shows in which he previously performed. Pete was also a survivalist, and unknown to most people, he stashed a stock of supplies away in a cellar. Because of their backgrounds, an instant friendship developed between them and grew over last five years. Rafe knew he could rely on Pete for any extra provisions he might have.

After traveling south about an hour, they found an abandoned house with a privacy fence around the back yard four blocks from the gun shop. Rafe checked the inside the house for any signs of recent occupancy and finding none, he and Kim led the horses into the back yard.

"I need for you to stay here with the horses," he told Kim.

"Not a chance," she snapped. "I'm coming with you."

"If you come with me," Rafe explained, "then who will keep the horses safe? Who'll make sure they're still here when we get back?"

Kim must have realized he was right. "I don't like it. I understand, but I don't like it."

Rafe smiled, leaned over, and kissed her. "I won't be gone long," he said as he opened the back gate.

"I'll be here," she said as he turned away.

CHAPTER THREE

Arriving at the back of the shop, Rafe wasn't surprised to see Pete walking out the door with an arm full of supplies. "Yo, Fracas," He said, startling the man enough to make him struggle with his load. "Looks like you're stocking up for the winter."

The big man looked at Rafe with an equally big grin and said, "Yeah, and it looks like it's gonna be a long winter too." Pete set the load down in the back of his truck and offered his hand to Rafe, which he gladly shook. Rafe again noticed the Masonic ring on Pete's right hand. It was the same type he wore.

"Well, what do you think?" Rafe asked, looking around.

"Shit has definitely hit the fan," Pete replied. "There's nothing natural about this, and you can bet everything you own, it's a bad sign. Somebody really fucked up this time."

"Think it'll get straightened out any time soon?"

"Not before it gets a hell of a lot worse," Pete answered. "Last night it was like a firefight around here. Guns were popping all night. Hell, two rounds came through my guest bedroom window."

"Looks like you're heading out," Rafe said motioning to the truck.

"Sure am, in a day or two, and I'll bet you are too." A slight smile played at the corner of his mouth. "Otherwise, why would you be here?"

"You're right, I wanted to see if you might have any extra supplies,"-Rafe glanced at the truck-"and by the way, why the hell are you loading that truck? The thing won't run."

"Damn sure will!" Pete snorted. "Seems like everything relying on electricity is down and dead-this truck is diesel. It doesn't have to have a spark plug to run. All I have to do is have a hill to roll it down, and it'll start. Found that out early this morning. Didn't know what was going on when it wouldn't start. I popped the hood and of course, you know what I found. There was a hell of a mess under there. However, with some tinkering, I was able to get the damn thing running. I simply rolled it down the hill by my house, and when I popped the clutch, it ran like everything was hunky-dory. When I'm loaded, I'm gonna roll it down the alley, and away I go. Gotta be careful though. I was shot at twice coming here."

"Well, kiss my ass," Rafe said slowly. "At least something's still working."

"In answer to your question about supplies... I do have some extra you can take. May even have some surprises you might like."

Pete took him into the shop and down a back staircase to the cellar. On the sidewall of the cellar, there was a door Rafe had never noticed in the twenty or thirty times he was down here in the past. The door opened into another smaller room stocked with MREs, ammunition, and weapons of every kind and description.

After considerable discussion, Rafe removed five M16's, five more 9mm pistols, and a thousand rounds of each type of ammunition. They also loaded four cases of MREs, various types of knives, canteens, mess kits, and other items both men considered essential. They hauled all the supplies up and out of the shop and loaded them in the back of Pete's truck. He insisted on taking the items to where Rafe's horses were.

Approaching the house from the alley Rafe said, "I've got a surprise for you."

Pete looked at him and raised an eyebrow.

"There is a friend of mine waiting there," Rafe explained. "Her name is Kim. She's the receptionist for my clinic."

"... and you left her here alone?"

"She's tough and doesn't panic in a tight situation."

Pete grinned. "It doesn't surprise me you have some piece of tail with you."

"We're good friends. The only reason she's here is because we were together when the power went out. I'm taking her to Rollingblock."

The truck pulled to a stop. "I have to leave the engine running," Pete said. "It's too flat here."

Rafe climbed from the vehicle. When he opened the back gate, Kim greeted him with a pistol in his face.

She quickly stepped back and lowered the weapon. "I'm glad it's you. People have been shooting all around the area."

"We need to hurry," Pete said from behind Rafe.

Following a quick introduction, they began loading the horses. They divided the supplies as equally as possible so the two extra animals could handle the weight and bulk.

As Rafe mounted his horse, Pete took hold of the reigns, looked up at him and said, "Listen Brother, some of the people out there are acting real crazy. I don't know what, but something is wrong with them. Watch yourself and don't trust anyone straight off. If they don't act right avoid 'em, if you can't do that, kill 'em. This is serious shit, now. The same goes for friends too. I hate to say it, but it even goes for Brothers. Don't let a ring or an emblem or a sign fool ya. There're crazies out there, and some of them may be people we're supposed to be able to trust."

Rafe could tell the man meant exactly what he said, and figured as unsavory as it seemed, it was probably sound advice. "Look Pete, you never told me where you're going. Do you have any idea where you'll be?"

"Not yet," he answered. "All I know is it'll be somewhere there ain't lots of people. I'll take another day or two and get things tied up here. Gotta seal the rest of the gear up in the cellar, in case I need it later. Then I'll head out."

"Tell ya what, if you decide to head over toward Rollingblock, that's where I'll be," Rafe said. "You know you're damn well welcome there. You and anyone else you think might be right. I or someone else I trust will come to the square every day at 1700 hrs. If things are as crazy as we think they are, the town will probably be empty within two or three days. If you don't see anyone in town, paint a red X on a white bed sheet and raise it on the flagpole. We'll see it and should be able to get to you within a couple of hours."

32

"Okay," Pete answered. "Only, to be on the safe side, when they walk up, have them ask 'Are you a traveling man, or traveling from the east?' I know it sounds crazy, but you can never be too careful, and I don't want to kill one of your friends."

"Doesn't sound crazy at all. In fact, if you don't answer with 'I'm lookin' for a lodge to meet in,' then you'll be shot. I think you're right. Things have changed. Someone messed up bad enough to set us back at least a century."

Pete looked down at his ring and then back up at the other man and grinned. "Sounds good to me."

The men shook hands. Rafe turned his mount with Kim following and headed for the hill country. He was unsure what the future held, but knew he had an ally in the Pete if needed.

***

Rafe and Kim continued until the sun sank in the west, and the cold began to set in. They skirted the edge of Austin and continued toward Rollingblock, staying away from the populated areas and keeping to the seldom-used roads and streets until they reached a convenience store at the end of Loop 1.

There, they unloaded and fed the horses, took all the supplies into the building, and staked the horses out with enough rope so they could graze. They started a fire in the building's fireplace and laid out two of the three sleeping bags Pete had stuffed into one of the duffle bags. Also, as a surprise, he packed four hand grenades in one of the duffels. Rafe could only smile and shake his head.

"What's wrong," Kim asked.

"Nothing," Rafe answered. "Pete knew I wouldn't have taken these,"-he held up the grenades-"so he slipped them without telling me. "I'm beginning to see how valuable a man like Pete can be in a situation like this. People have called him loony and insane for years. I'll bet their singing a different story now, though. In fact, I'll bet most of them are either dead or dodging bullets right now." He looked at Kim. Actually, his last thought wasn't all that pleasant. For all he knew, they might all be dodging bullets in the future. "Sorry, I didn't...
"

"It's okay," she interrupted. "The rules are different now. We have to face facts. It's dangerous, and things probably won't get better for a while."

They quietly ate MREs and lay down to sleep. Even though they snuggled up close, weariness took over, and they were soon asleep.

CHAPTER FOUR

The sunlight gently woke Rafe, its rays warm and pleasant on his face. Since only embers remained from the fire, the air in the building was cold and crisp. The scene was so tranquil he forgot for a few minutes how much his world had changed, including the events of the last couple of days. He rolled over and put his arm over Kim.

She made a soft mewling sound and pushed her hips back against him. Instantly aroused, he kissed the hair on the back of her head. He gently pulled the hair back from her neck and jerked away, "What the... " he exclaimed scrambling from under the blankets to his feet.

It rolled toward him. "Hello lover," a gravelly voice said.

He looked at the thing he was just lying beside. It no longer resembled the woman he knew as Kim Winters. The brown reptilian skin on the thing moved and rolled as if the blood and tissue beneath was boiling. The face peered at him through red eyes with cat-like pupils as a small muzzle reshaped its mouth.

The creature started to rise but only made it halfway up before falling back to the floor of the restaurant. Rafe looked to his left for a weapon and saw nothing, and then looking to his right, spied a 9mm on a table about six feet away.

The thing on the floor must have read his mind. It leapt to its feet, and in a flash, stood between Rafe and the weapons. "Don't you still want me?" The creature managed to growl. The words slipped from a misshapen mouth, through large canine teeth in a guttural slur.

Rafe tried to circle around the animal, but it cut him off making a sound no longer intelligible to him. As it lunged forward, Rafe's martial training took over. He released all thought and entered a state known in Japanese as Satori. There was no thinking, no planning, only relaxed muscles and reactions. Muscle memory took the place of conscious thought increasing speed and agility. Even though he taught it to all of his students, only a handful of them were able to develop their minds to the point they could separate thinking and actions.

As the creature lunged, Rafe redirected its momentum to his left. At the same time, he stepped to his right and around behind it; and placing one hand beneath its muzzle and one on the back of its grizzly head, he then twisted as quickly and as far as possible.

The head spun around with cracking and popping sounds as the bones of the spinal cord ground together. He saw the inhuman face turn toward him before it dropped to the floor.

Instinctively, he stepped back as the thing thrashed and wriggled on the floor. With its head twisted around, the grotesque face twitching, and guttural sounds coming from between snapping jaws, it was all Rafe could do to keep from running out of the building.

He quickly retrieved one of the 9mm pistols and aimed at the creature's head. As he did, it shuddered and exhaled. Its red eyes darkened to almost black, and it lay still.

Rafe found a nearby chair and sat before his legs gave way. Never in his life had he seen anything even vaguely resembling the animal before him. While in the navy, he traveled all over the world. He heard numerous myths about various creatures and had seen many things including strange animals, but nothing prepared him for this.

He actually watched someone shape-shift before him-change from being a loving person to a grotesque creature with malevolent intent in seconds. He wasn't sure if he could wrap his mind around this. The night before Kim had said the rules are different now. There was no way for her to know how different they really were. In the blink of an eye, a woman he cared for changed, and he had to take her life. Even he wasn't ready for something like that.

Rafe took a deep breath and released it to steady himself as he rose to his feet. With trepidation, he reached down and took hold of the body, dragged it through the back door, and put it in the tool shed behind the convenience store. He thought about burying the animal. After all, it was the remains of a friend, but he quickly discarded the thought. He didn't want to spend any more time around the thing than was necessary.

Returning inside the business, he started what he figured would become a regular morning routine. He stoked the fire, took a very quick field bath, fed the horses, and fixed his breakfast. He was lucky enough that some of the freezers and coolers were closed, so the food inside was still good. After eating, he loaded the horses and headed out for Rollingblock.

This time he was alone.

***

Mike got out of the truck, slammed the door and stomped off, feeling sorry for himself. He walked about five miles up US 281 and came up on an Exxon station sitting a short distance off the road. He was in the hill country outside San Antonio.

Since he had seen no one, he figured most people had headed into the heart of the city. He started up the driveway to the convenience store. As he approached the door, a man emerged holding a shotgun.

"What the fuck you want?" The man held the weapon leveled at Mike.

"N-Nothing, Sir," Mike stuttered. "I was only looking to see if there was someone here and maybe something to eat or drink."

"They is, and they ain't nutten' ta eat er drink," the man answered. "Now git yore pasty ass outta here b'fore I blow it off."

"Y-Yes, Sir." Mike quickly sidestepped away from the building. "I'm going-don't shoot-I'm going." Mike was almost running as he reached the highway and headed further off into the hills. His heart kept racing even after he put a mile between the gunman and himself.

The sun was near the hilltops surrounding him, and soon dark would descend. *I'm going to have to find some place to stay for the night. But I have to be careful not to get myself into any more close situations. These people are crazy around here.*

After walking another two or three miles, and with the light rapidly fading, Mike noticed a building about a hundred feet off the road. He was able to see a light showing through one of its windows, and he stood a few minutes, trying to decide if he should go up and knock on the door or keep going. Finally, the encroaching darkness and the thought of how he had barely escaped when some inhuman monstrosities killed a group of bikers in a house earlier that morning made the decision for him. He slowly walked up to the front door and knocked.

From inside a voice called out, "Who is it?"

"Excuse me," Mike called back. I'm just looking for some help. I'm not from around here and need some food, if you have any to spare-and maybe a place to sleep."

How many are with you?" The voice asked.

"Only me-I'm alone," he answered, and then quickly added, "I mean you no harm. I just need some help."

"Step back away from the door."

Mike stepped back a few steps.

"Farther," The disembodied voice demanded. Mike took five or six steps backward.

The front door opened to reveal a figure silhouetted by lamplight. The person clearly carried a rifle of some sort.

"Like I said..." Mike started.

"Let me see your hands," The voice interrupted.

Mike raised his hands with his palms forward.

"Turn around slowly. Let me see all of you."

Mike slowly turned, being sure to make no fast movements.

"Slow and careful now, walk forward," the voice said.

As Mike walked forward, the figure moved backward and to the side. Mike entered the house about five feet when the front door closed. Looking behind him, he saw a woman in her mid-twenties-in front of him stood a teenage boy. The boy obviously knew how to use the rifle he pointed at the stranger standing before him. "Check him for weapons," the boy said to the young woman who quickly ran her hands over Mike's upper body and waist.

He doesn't have anything on him," she said when she finished. The boy lowered his rifle to his side. What's your name, mister?"

"Mike. Mike Slater." Mike said, taking a step forward and extending his hand.

Immediately, the boy stepped back and raised the rifle. "Hold right where you are."

Mike stopped and withdrew the offered hand. "What's your name?" He kept his movements slow and deliberate as he again raised both hands in the air.

"Keith," the young man answered, "and behind you is Amanda."

"Nice to meet you both," Mike said. "May I lower my hands? Like I said, I mean you no harm. I just need some help."

"Yeah, you can put 'em down, but don't do nothing funny," Keith said. "Where're you from?" He asked moving over to an overstuffed easy chair. He motioned with the rifle for Mike to sit on a sofa situated along the wall.

Mike walked over and sat on the sofa. It felt good to get off his feet. This was the most walking he had done in one day since he was a teenager. Salesmen no longer went from door to door trying to sell items to housewives. Most sold to large chains through a single contact in some corporate office, and Mike knew someday he would be as good at it as any one of them. Of course, that was after he survived his current situation.

Amanda disappeared into the next room

"Well I'm actually from Virginia Beach, Virginia. But I was on a business trip when all this happened-somewhere in New Mexico or West Texas when the plane lost power and went down. The last thing I remember was a loud noise, then flying around the cabin; and the next thing I know, I'm coming to-outside the plane, which was pretty tore up. There were only about fifteen passengers onboard, and only about five were still there, all of them dead. I don't know what happened to the rest. They must have wandered off or something."

"You've been walking since then?" Keith lowered the barrel of the rifle to the floor and rested its butt against his chair.

"I'm not sure," Mike answered. "I know I was walking for a while. Then I got sick, or maybe it was exposure or something else. I'm not sure what. Anyway, I came out of it-whatever it was-yesterday."

"How'd you make it here?" The boy inquired.

"Late last night, I went to sleep on the second floor of an abandoned house," Mike explained. "This morning, I woke up, and there were people on the first floor. A short time later, some creatures

41

busted into the house and began fighting. As it was, I had to kill some of the bikers and a couple of the animals in self-defense."

"Muties," Keith interrupted the story.

Mike looked at him and nodded. *It's as good a name as any.* He paused for effect. "I hate killing. Anyway, I left the house and found a truck parked on a hill. When I tried starting it by coasting down the hill and popping the clutch, it worked. I was able to drive the truck around and to the north end of San Antonio. Then, after a couple of hours, I found this place."

"Like I said, those things that killed those people were Muties," Keith told him. "Something has happened to a bunch of the people around here. They've turned into animals of some kind." Keith described the animals, then added, "Watch out for them-they'll stalk you. Kill any you come across."

Mike hesitated a second. "I didn't know they were once humans. But if you must, you must." *There is no way I could kill them-especially if they were once humans.* "I don't want to have to kill anything else."

"Well, it's up to you, man. But remember they'll kill and eat you. And once you're dead, it's too late to change your mind."

Amanda came into the room carrying a large bowl of stew. "Hope you're still hungry, Mr. Slater," she said, setting the bowl on a table in the adjoining dining room.

"Yes, I am. I'm starving. Like I said, I haven't eaten in over twenty-four hours. And please, call me Mike," Mike said, rising to his feet.

"Well there isn't much, but you're welcome to eat with us," Amanda told him.

"There's a spare bed in the other room," Keith said motioning to an open door. "You're welcome to it tonight, if you want."

"Thank you," Mike responded gratefully. "I'll take you up on the offer-if you're sure it's not too much trouble."

"No trouble, now let's eat," Keith answered, moving toward the table.

Mike noticed Keith left the rifle leaning against his chair. *Well, at least he's starting to relax a little.*

As if reading his mind, Keith picked up the weapon, sat at the table with Amanda, and leaned the rifle against the back of his chair. "Nothing against you, Mike. You never know when you'll need it for a Mutie or something."

"I understand." Mike sat at the same time as Amanda and heard a clunk from the other end of the table. Amanda pulled a pistol from the back of her pants and placed it on the table next to her.

"Thing digs in when I sit," she said and smiled.

They ate in silence for a few minutes. Mike had no idea what animal these young people killed for the meat in the stew, and he didn't really care. It was too good to question, plus he might not like the answer. After a few minutes, he asked, "How did the two of you wind up here? Is this your home?"

"No," Amanda answered. "We both lived a couple of miles from here. I was a schoolteacher in Bulverde, and Keith lived at home with his parents. I met Keith at the karate school I go to and found out he lived less than half a mile from me."

Keith looked at her sharply when she mentioned the karate school. He frowned and then continued eating.

"When all the power went out, I waited a couple of hours, then decided to walk to town and see if I could get help for my car. I was walking down the road when I heard a shot followed by a loud scream, then another shot. The scream sounded like a mountain lion or something. Then Keith came out of the trees. He shot one of the Muties, as he calls them. It had evidently been stalking me. If it hadn't been for him, I'd be dead now."

Keith kept eating during the story and now looked up. "They're hard suckers to kill," He said in a matter of fact tone. "Ya have to hit 'em in the head for a quick kill. Otherwise, they might have enough left in 'em to get to you."

Mike watched the young man during the story. *Kid has a lot of nerve-either a lot of nerve or no feelings.* This boy's emotionless talk of killing and apparent lack of feelings for their current predicament made Mike uncomfortable.

Again, as if reading his mind, Keith looked at Mike and said, "It's not that I don't have feelings about what's going on-I do. But I can't get emotionally involved in the situation if I'm gonna be able to take care of us. I can feel later when things are worked out. Until then, I have to stay alert." He got up and took his bowl into the kitchen.

"He feels responsible for me," Amanda said, "and I'm grateful for it. I'm not sure I could have made it this far on my own. I'm fairly resourceful, but he's amazing."

Mike could surely believe her last statement. Keith seemed to have the situation with the two of them well in hand, and frankly, it made him feel very inadequate.

Keith came back in the room from the kitchen and said, "I hate to rain on the party, but we need to get some rest. No telling what'll happen tomorrow." He went over to the sofa Mike previously sat on and removed the cushions. Grabbing hold of a strap, Keith pulled out the bed hidden inside. "I'll be out here," he told Mike. "Please don't wander around during the night."

Amanda took the other bowls and the plate of bread to the kitchen. Over her shoulder she said, "There's sheets on the bed and a bathroom connecting to your bedroom. We'll see you in the morning. I'm going to wash these. Then I'll turn in." She then disappeared into the kitchen, leaving Mike standing next to the dining room table.

As Mike approached the door, Keith said, "Use the lamp on the table beside you. Like she said, there's a bathroom next to you. It doesn't work, but it's there."

Keith stood next to the couch, grinning. "If you must go, do it now or wake me up. But don't go outside alone, okay?"

"Trust me, I won't." Mike picked up the lantern and entered the room, hoping for a good night's rest.

***

Rafe knew of a place where more horses were located. When he found them, there were six he could see. He was lucky enough to find bags of feed in a barn next to the field. *I'll have to come back for these later.*

After traveling all day, he moved away from the road and made camp next to a stream to spend another night out on the trail. He staked all the horses out, carefully giving them enough rope to be able to reach grass and bushes to eat. He used Kim's horse to carry food and water for him and all the other animals.

Staking the animals out, rubbing them down, feeding them, and then setting up camp took a little over an hour and wore him out. He made a fire as a necessity, to ward off the cold of the night. He used a heater to warm up an MRE, and then sat back against a tree with his legs crossed and ate.

As the dark descended, he listened to the call of a Whippoorwill. Most of the other birds were settling down for a night's sleep. What little breeze there was went away and left the night quiet and peaceful. The only other sound was the stream beside his camp. It was soft and soothing like a melody playing in the background.

Rafe finished his meal and buried his trash. He rolled out a sleeping bag and crawled in, leaving both his pistols beside his head. It took very little time for sleep to overtake him, and he slept soundly until near the middle of the night.

A noise in the dark pulled Rafe from his sleep, dragging him back to the reality of his current situation. From training, he was wide-awake instantly, but instead of moving, Rafe lay where he was and listened. He could hear the horses at their tethers. All seemed to be nervous, shifting and snorting as if they too sensed something was amiss.

46

With very little movement, he looked around the camp but could see nothing to cause this feeling of unease. Slowly he retrieved his pistols, rose, and put them in their holsters. Still unable to see anything out of the ordinary, he went over to try to calm the horses.

As he reached the first horse, he heard something like another animal moving in the dark, barely outside the reach of the light. He scanned the darkness but could make nothing out. Again, he heard the rustle of something moving. He could tell more than a single critter made the noise. There were at least four animals out there, and by the sound of it, they were stalking him.

He picked up the 30-30, lever action rifle, levered a round into the chamber and moved away from the embers of the fire. There was no longer a flame but enough of a glow to silhouette him and mess up his night vision.

Another rustling off to his left and a single yellow glow appeared in the darkness. Rafe knew the yellow color and height of the glow meant he was seeing the eyes of deer. *I must be at least partially surrounded by a herd of deer.* He relaxed enough to lower the rifle to his side.

There was another rustling different from the first. This one sounded like something moving fast in the dark. Two sets of red eyes appeared much higher than the yellow ones. They bobbed as if the animals were running, and in less than a second, converged on the deer. There were two distinct thumps, and the deer's eyes ceased to glow.

The movement seemed to continue in one direction for a couple of seconds then there was only silence. Rafe could swear the deer's eyes had disappeared-yanked to the side. It was as if something struck the animal before it could blink-before it knew what happened to it.

He stood still and listened to the rest of the herd bound rapidly away from the camp. *Something weird just happened. Something isn't right with this.* He put some wood on the fire, took a piece that flamed up, and went over to where the deer once was.

There was nothing there. The light from his torch didn't illuminate enough of the area to be able to see clearly. Figuring he would check it out better the next morning, he returned to the camp.

He sat up for another fifteen or twenty minutes, listening to the night. All seemed to be back to normal. The horses stood relaxed at their ropes, no longer skittish or nervous.

Surprisingly, it only took him a few minutes to go back to sleep. This time, however, he slept lightly and kept one of his pistols inside the sleeping bag-in case.

CHAPTER FIVE

After traveling two days, the idea of having to spend one more night outside was unacceptable. He knew deep down inside the animal last night was what Kim turned into, and he didn't want to take another chance of coming face to face with one again anytime soon.

Rafe pushed himself until he arrived at the outskirts of the small town of Rollingblock, Texas, which was nestled in the Hays Valley surrounded by forests and thick underbrush. With few roads, only individuals wanting to escape the confines of large cities populated most of the area. Only a few other small towns, ranches, and homesteads occupied the rest.

Most people in the hill country valued their privacy and didn't allow commercial endeavors to encroach too closely. The homesteads varied from less than one acre in size to about fifteen. Only a few ranches numbered a hundred acres or more and one of these was his destination. The afternoon was almost gone as he skirted the village and cautiously headed over to where the Lazy R Ranch was located.

As he approached it, he saw Kyle and Lynn feeding the horses at the stables.

The ranch consisted of about one hundred-fifty acres. Bear scanned the area. To the south, hidden from view by trees, the buildings in the main area were converted into an old "Wild West" town, and went by the name of Sagebrush. There were several businesses with facades that looked as if they were built in the 1800's. This was the resort area and in summer, housed the majority of the tourists visiting Rollingblock.

The stables were a short distance from the resort area ahead of him. His friends Kyle and Lynn Jennings operated the stables used by the ranch for its guests. They owned the horses and all the equipment used to take guests on trail rides. In addition, Lynn trained people in English and Western styles of riding. For the use of the stables, they paid a percentage of each ride or lesson for any of its guests to the resort. Everything looked normal, as if nothing out of the ordinary had happened.

As Rafe approached the perimeter of the area, he called out to his friends, "Hello, the stables."

Both Kyle and Lynn turned, Kyle reaching toward the gun strapped on his hip with Lynn simultaneously moving toward a rifle propped against the building. Then both waved. Kyle motioned Rafe and the string of animals had in tow toward the gate.

By the time Kyle got to him, Rafe dismounted and waited to be let in. The two men shook hands and hugged, patting each other on the back. They led the horses into the holding area containing a feeding shed and two large hay rolls.

Kyle, like Rafe, wore both of his black powder pistols used in the shows they put on. Even though he couldn't see it, Rafe knew his friend had at least one other pistol hidden somewhere else on his body, probably in the back of his pants. Kyle's duster covered his western wear, and his flat brimmed hat sat squarely on his head, true to the style of the old west and would serve him well in the cold, wet months to come. He reminded Rafe of the old pictures of Wild Bill Hickok. The only thing ruining the effect was his British accent. He was born and raised in Great Britain and was unable to adopt a southern drawl.

Looking to his left, Rafe saw Lynn approaching with a big smile on her face. With her were her three boys, Carl, Will, and Paul. She walked up, and gave Rafe a big hug. "Kyle and I were talking about you not more'n ten minutes ago. We were wondering if you were okay. We weren't sure if you would come here or go somewhere else."

The boys stepped up and each, in turn, shook Rafe's hand. Carl was seventeen, Will thirteen, and Paul was eleven. The two older boys were tall and lanky for their ages, and Rafe noticed Paul had gained weight since he last saw him. All knew their way around the stables and could handle a weapon as well as most adults.

"It was time to get out of the city, and this was the best place I could think of," Rafe responded. "Any family I have is at least a couple of months travel from here by horse, and I've already seen what happens to a diesel vehicle. You'll get your ass shot off in one of those."

"Diesel," Kyle repeated. "What about diesel?"

"It looks like a diesel engine is the only thing working right now," Rafe explained. "I talked to Pete at 'Guns And More' in Austin. He has a diesel rig, and it'll run if you give it a push start. Seems like everything that's happened has to do with electricity, diesels run off compression... "

51

"Right, they don't need a spark," Kyle cut him off. "But what do you mean about getting your ass shot off?"

Lynn called to her sons to help with the horses as the group started leading the animals back toward the tack room. On the way, Rafe related the story Pete told him and then added, "Plus, I was shot at twice, riding here on horseback. There're some crazy people out there right now."

"We've heard shots coming from over near the square," Lynn told him. "In fact, the night before last and yesterday morning sounded like a war going on. There was constant gunfire and some explosions. We figure folks are probably protecting anything they own about now. Of course with it being Halloween weekend, the town was full of more tourists than usual."

"Even so," Kyle said, "There was almost no one down at the cabins yesterday."

"Have you seen any other members of the Regulators?" Rafe asked.

"Ben came by yesterday morning. He left to go and see about some relatives on the other side of town," Lynn told him. "He should be back today or tomorrow. Kyle saw Hal Sloan in town yesterday morning as well. He had come to town gathering information. He said he was heading home to get Sandy and should be back today or tomorrow. He was on foot, and you know how far out they live. I doubt we will see them before tomorrow afternoon."

Lynn assigned each of the boys a couple of horses to take care of. Everyone pitched in, led the horses to the stables, and started removing the gear

52

from them. "How the hell did you bring a string of seven horses in with you?" Lynn asked.

"Wasn't easy," Rafe answered. "I was forced to travel a lot slower than I thought I would have to, but attaching one horse to the other by rope worked. Plus, the fact they all seemed to get along, helped out a lot. There were a couple of times I divided them and made more than one trip because of obstacles."

As they finished feeding and watering the animals, a voice called to them from the other side of the exercise area. Looking over, Rafe saw Ben Williamson standing inside the tree line. It seemed western clothes were the order of the day. He, too, was dressed in the same getup he wore for the gunfights-his old western hat, shirt, jacket, blue jeans with chaps, and a 45-caliber pistol strapped around his waist. The old man was an outstanding actor, storyteller and writer. *I wonder if he's able to switch characters and accents at the drop of a hat after all this.*

Even at sixty with a slight paunch, Ben was still extremely active. Other than looking a little drawn and haggard, he looked much the same as he had the last fifteen years Rafe knew him. Of course, with all that had happened, it was no wonder. *I'm glad to see he's okay.* Rafe grinned in spite of himself.

***

Immediately switching into an ole time southern drawl, Ben said, "Well I see we've been joined by that infamous outlaw 'The Brazos Bear.'" The Brazos Bear was the name Rafe used in the gunfights. His friends had shortened it to Bear. He said it was fine with him since it was his nickname in the Navy as well. Ben befriended Bear when he first moved to Rollingblock about five years before. They stayed in contact when Bear moved to Austin and even acted in a couple of plays together.

"Hell yeah," Bear answered in the same accent, "wouldn't miss this shindig for nutten."

Ben went over, gave him a big hug and a pat on the back. "It's good to see you, man," he said, turning serious. "Wasn't sure what happened to you since the power was turned off. Ain't this a hell of a note? Looking over at the extra horses and motioning toward them with a point of his thumb, he continued, "By the looks of the extra mounts, I'd say Rollingblock isn't the only place that's lost its electricity." He shook hands with Kyle and gave Lynn a hug.

"Nope," Bear answered. "Everything between here and Austin appears to be in the same shape."

"What about your relatives, Ben?" Kyle asked. "Did you find them okay?"

"Well," Ben started. "I found 'em alright. They were all at home, but every one of 'em was down with some sort of bug. They're all throwin' up and carryin' a high fever. A couple of 'em had some discolored splotches on their skin. Don't know what it was but... " -he looked up at the others, a concerned look on his face-"it weren't good. They seemed to be gettin' worse in the couple of hours I was there.

"Figured I might try to find a doctor and get some help. I looked for another couple of hours, but none of them was home; or at least none of them answered their door. By the time I got back to my aunt's house, my cousin and a friend there with them had gone into a coma. This morning they were dead. By noon, all of them were dead. None of them survived whatever it was."

"Died!" Kyle repeated, shocked at the delivery of the news.

"Oh Ben, I'm sorry," Lynn said putting her arm around his shoulders.

Ben looked up at his friends. "They're gone now, but I'll tell you the truth. I think their sickness was a result of whatever it is happening around here. I've seen a lot of sick folk in my time, but I never saw any get so bad so fast. Before they went, all of 'em had big sores all over their bodies and talked out of their heads. I may be wrong, but I think we're in for a heap of trouble before this is over."

"I've seen what he's talking about," Bear said and took a deep breath and hesitated.

The others waited for an explanation.

"I think my Bookkeeper, Kim, died of the same thing." He ran his hand through his hair and then told them the story of Kim's death. When he finished he took a deep breath and shook his head.

"Right-okay," Kyle said, "enough with the bullshit."

"You can kiss my ass, Kyle," Bear growled. "Do you really believe I would lie about something as serious as this... Especially at a time like this?"

"No," he answered, "I guess not. It's just that what you're describing is more than a reasonable person can believe."

"You should have lived it," Bear answered.

"What else happened?" Lynn asked.

"What do you mean?" Bear asked.

Lynn simply looked at him.

Taking another deep breath, he said, "She attacked me, and I was forced to kill her."

"How," Kyle asked.

"Thinking back about it, I think it was a miracle," Bear answered. "I couldn't get to a weapon when she attacked, and I managed to break her neck. But I don't think I would have been able to do it if it was fifteen minutes later. Her muscles were developing at a phenomenal rate. Any longer and I wouldn't have been able to."

Bear turned his gaze to Ben. "Listen-is there anything we can do? "What about their bodies? Do you want us to go with you and help you bury 'em?"

"No... thanks," Ben answered. "The neighbor that died with them was digging a new septic tank. I put all 'em in it together and covered 'em with a layer of dirt. It'll have to do for right now. There is no way to dig through this rock without the proper equipment. Maybe later... " Tears threatened to flow from his eyes.

"Ben, go get Trace," Kyle said. "Bring him in. We've got food and hay for him." Trace actually belonged to Hal and Lynn. He was the horse Ben used when he came out for his weekly ride.

"He'll like that," Ben said as he turned to get the horse. "I fed him this morning but didn't have enough left for this evening. Be back in a second."

"Shame to hear about his family," Bear said to Kyle and Lynn, looking at Ben as he walk off. "Has to be hard on him,"

"Sure is, but I think he is right," Kyle agreed. "We're going to be seeing a lot more death in the near future if things stay the way they are. Now, what about you, Bear? Are you okay now? Was this your destination, or were you heading on for somewhere else?"

As Lynn had left to get food for Ben's horse, Bear looked at Kyle and said, "Well, it really depends on what happens here and who else comes. I've read enough of those horror and fantasy stories to know if this situation stays the way it is, there is a logical progression society will follow. Cities will turn into battlegrounds between gangs. Decent people will have to fight to defend what they think is worth saving. For a while, anything moving will be a target. I damn sure don't want to be in the middle of that. On the other hand, I'm not sure that after a short time the same thing won't happen out here in the small towns. Of course, some people will try and escape the madness in the cities and come to the hills. Without meaning to, they'll add to the problems out here."

"You may be right," Kyle conceded. "Like Lynn said, it's already happened here. I'd bet there's not a handful of people left in Rollingblock itself. I think those of us here need to get organized somehow."

"That's what I'm talking about," Bear started. "If we can put together some type of organized group around here, we'll stand a better chance. Right now though, I'm gonna be very careful where I stay and sleep. I may be wrong, but with those mutants around, I think any house with a light in it at night will be asking for trouble from them and maybe from humans. Besides, except for those with gas in 'em, it gets as cold in a house now as it does outside. Not to mention, outside, at least you can build a fire and sleep around it. Put out watches, and you'll probably be pretty safe." Bear thought back about the night before but said nothing. He had relayed enough bad news as it was.

A yodel came from the direction of the road Bear used a short time before. "That's gotta be Spyder," Kyle said with a grin.

They both looked over at the fence line and sure enough, it was Spyder standing there with Ginny beside him. Bear knew Spyder and Ginny were actually only business partners and very good friends. However, many people outside the group thought they were married since they fought like they were husband and wife for years.

"Spyder, Ginny," Kyle yelled. "Get your asses over here" Back to Bear he said, "Thought something happened to 'em. Haven't seen hide nor hair of either of them since the day before the blackout."

Lynn came from the storage room carrying Hal's Sharps rifle. "Who is it, Kyle?" She asked, looking around.

"Spyder and Ginny's here," Kyle answered.

Spyder was the only member of the Regulators who didn't have to change his style of clothing to look the part of the old west. He was about 5'11", with light brown hair down to the middle of his back and a beard to match. The only things added to his normal attire were the four guns he wore on his body. His regular occupation was as an electrician. He could work on new construction or fix about any

58

existing circuit if needed. In the past, he had been in a number of scrapes with the law due to his involvement with a motorcycle group and being one of the highest members of the Ku Klux Klan in Texas.

Ginny, his "little tea cup," as he called her, fit her role as well. She was the right height for and was always dressed as a saloon girl in the shows. She was pleasant and easy-going, which only went so far. It appeared she was comfortable with the style and habits of the women of the old west, including the foul language, and anyone underestimating her was in for a rude awakening.

They made it to the stables at the same time Ben came up from the opposite side. Following hugs and handshakes all around Ginny asked, "Where's everyone else? We might as well put on a show. Almost everyone is here."

Kyle and Lynn related what they knew about Hal and Sandy Sloan. Then Lynn asked Spyder and Ginny if they had heard anything about what was going on or anything information about their other friends.

Spyder answered, "Hell no, we don't know what's goin' on. Best we can tell, the only thing different is there's no electricity-and the fact that it's sent some of the people around here off their rocker. Shit, Gordy Crocker took a shot at me this morning-and that's after I told the pecker-head who I was. Crazy bastard almost hit me too."

"We heard some shots while walking over here," Ginny said, "and we saw someone running off into the woods in their shorts, didn't we?" She looked at Spyder for confirmation.

"Hell yeah," Spyder snorted. "Some goofy son-of-a-bitch was running off through the trees, toward Woodcliff. Silly fucker was screaming and running like he didn't have good sense. Probably didn't, running around in his underwear with the temperature around forty. Dumb ass." Spyder made the statement as if it was only the cold, and not the man running around in his underwear that was strange.

"Where'd you get all the horses?" Ginny asked, noticing the extra animals standing around.

"Bear brought eight with him," Lynn answered. "It's a good thing too. We might wind up needing the extra mounts."

"Why?" Ginny asked. "This can't last too long. They'll get the power back on soon."

"Well, maybe and maybe not," Kyle said. "Bear said all the power's gone in Austin too. Hal didn't have any over at his place. This seems to be pretty wide spread."

"Has anyone seen any airplanes? They're always flying overhead en route to somewhere-I haven't," Bear threw the question out to the group. "All this tells me this thing's a lot bigger than we might think."

"You know," Lynn said thoughtfully. "I haven't. Bear's right. They fly over all the time, and that damn helicopter usually flying over every afternoon hasn't been by either."

"I figure within a week we should see a sign of some sort of authority, if there's any such thing left in place," Bear said, a doubtful tone to his voice. Because of his military training, he believed something really bad had happened, and everyone had better get used to their current situation and expect it to last for a long time.

The group exchanged stories of where they spent the last few nights and the strange people they ran into. Most of the group were in their various homes, and it seemed like a lot of the people around were starting to act real strange-some even dangerous.

After listening to the others, Bear threw out an observation. "Speaking of places to stay, it's getting dark quick. You better think of a place for the night. I'm going to the Chuck Wagon Area and start a fire there. It's protected from the wind, and it's hard to see a fire there with all the trees and the stage barn. Anyone wanting to join me's welcome."

"Sounds good to me," Spyder said. "Not sure what I'll sleep on, but it sounds like the right place for Ginny and me to be."

"I'll join ya," Ben answered. "Can't be no colder than my house."

In a few minutes, the group all agreed to stay there with Bear. The Chuck Wagon Area was where they performed shows when a group contracted with Spyder and Ginny to have a special dinner catered. It was located at the far end of a rutted loop created by the constant rides on an authentic replica of a stagecoach used by the resort for sightseeing. There was a barn so the stage could be stored out of the weather. Beside the stagecoach barn, there was an old covered wagon, a fire pit, a barbecue pit, and some tables for the customers.

"One thing I am worried about," Lynn said. "I don't like leaving the horses here unguarded. I mean Bear stole those. What's to stop someone from stealing these?" Looking at Bear she said, "No offense Bear."

"None taken," Bear said with a sheepish grin. "We'll just take 'em with us. We can set up a line between some of the trees out there and keep 'em up close. I'm like you, I don't want to leave mine where someone can walk up and take 'em. Nope, he goes with me."

"Good idea," She said.

"We're taking them with us then," Kyle said. "Let's get going, boys and girls. It's going to get cold fast."

Everyone began gathering the items Bear had brought and saddled his horses. By the time they finished, Kyle and Lynn moved all their supplies from the tack room. They were survivalists and had even more than Bear.

It didn't take long to saddle all the horses and load them with the food, tack, and weapons on hand. Kyle and Lynn informed them it was only about half of the total on hand. They could get the rest from inside the building later. Things were looking up for the small group of survivors, for the time being anyway.

Trees surrounded the area on three sides and the fourth looked out over part of the Hays Valley. The slope there was almost vertical which would make it almost impossible for someone to approach from that direction. It made for a good sheltered, private area. They all agreed that if it started to rain or got too windy they could break the lock on the door at the end of the stage barn, push the stagecoach out and sleep in there.

"Stake the horses out over there," Kyle said pointing to an area away from the barn. "We can set up camp here." He climbed from his mount in an area Spyder and Ginny used for cooking.

They were able to get a fire started and a line run for the horses before dark completely descended. Spyder, Ginny and Ben arranged all the supplies against the stage barn and fixed supper while Bear, Kyle and Lynn tied the horses to the line.

"I hate to get all military on everyone," Bear said, "but I think we need watches tonight."

To his surprise, no one argued or objected.

I figure Kyle, Ben, and I can take three hour shifts, which should cover the night," Bear said.

"Bite me," Lynn said staring defiantly at the man.

"What's wrong?" He asked innocently and braced himself for the tirade he was sure would follow.

All she said was, "I'll take the first watch because I have to be up early to feed the horses. The rest of you decide on the order after that. I figure two hours on watch will let everyone get enough sleep and still cover the night.

Bear looked at Kyle who was grinning in the firelight, a hand-rolled cigarette between his lips. "Welcome to my world."

Bear shook his head and grinned back. "Lynn will take first watch; then she'll wake Kyle up. Ben is next and then me." He pulled a watch from his pocket. "Here's a windup pocket-watch." He handed it to Lynn. "We can pass it to the next person on watch. That way we only do two hours each."

They all sat around the campfire for a couple of hours, talking and remembering past times before slipping into bedrolls or between blankets as they tried to retreat from their reality into the escape of sleep.

PART TWO
CONFEDERATIONS

"The more people gathering firewood,
the higher the flames will grow."

Chinese proverb

CHAPTER SIX

In the short time since the blackout, Keith taught himself to wake to the sun hitting his face. He opened his eyes and looked around. All seemed to be, as it should. The house was quiet except for the faint sound of snoring coming from the room in which their new guest was sleeping. *Probably needs the rest.* Keith thought. He sat up, swung his legs over the side of couch, and stretched. Still blinking sleep from his eyes, he dressed and went into the kitchen.

There was a gas stove located in the corner. He lit one of the burners and put a teakettle of water on it for coffee. Outside, there was a chill on the air that was cool but not unpleasant.

He fished a pack of cigarettes from his pocket, and lit one. Despite the insistence of his parents to quit, he only smoked about three a day. He even continued throughout his athletic training in high school, swearing that if it ever caused him a problem, he would quit.

Keith was in his senior year in school when the world shrugged off its electrical charge. He was a star at football and track and on the honor roll. His one true passion though was karate. He had been studying for three years now and loved every minute of it. He had no idea where his parents were. They were away at his Grandmother's funeral in Utah when these circumstances descended on him and the rest of the world. With no brothers or sisters, he knew he was on his own.

Keith loved this part of the day and used it to meditate or simply contemplate the time ahead.

Another day, but without another dollar. Now, if I could only get someone to pay me. He grinned to himself. *How long is this Mike character gonna be with us? I don't mind looking after Amanda, but I sure don't want the responsibility of someone else- especially if I don't know 'em.*

What if she starts to rely on him? After all, he looks to be in his thirties. He's probably more appealing to her than I am. What if she likes him more than me? He could wind up being a real pain in the ass.

His mind shifted.

Now what would Sensei say in a situation like this?

The answer that came wasn't what he wanted.

We are here to serve others as well as ourselves. We must always be sure our own WANTS don't overshadow the NEEDS of others. It's the only way to ensure one's actions are not self-serving.

These thoughts did little to satisfy his concern about Amanda, but his Sensei's wisdom had definitely served him well in the past. He knew he would follow those teachings. It didn't mean he would like it, though.

Keith heard the whistle of the teapot from inside the house. As he entered the building, it ceased.

In the kitchen, Amanda stood in front of the stove. As was her routine every morning, she wore only a long button down shirt and nothing else visible to him.

That's all I need. Keith thought to himself. *If he sees her dressed like that, I'll lose her for sure.* His

67

Sensei's teachings rapidly rushed to the back of his mind.

Amanda looked up and smiled. "So, how was your night?"

"It was okay," Keith answered, trying not to look at her. He could feel an erection growing even though he stood all the way across the kitchen. He concentrated on the sink and said, "Nothing happened."

"What about Mike?" She asked, as she poured hot water into the cups containing instant coffee.

"What about him?" Keith answered bringing his gaze back up to her face. Since the blackout, he had discovered she taught junior high school teacher in Bulverde, Texas, but she was originally from Okmulgee, Oklahoma.

He couldn't help having feelings for her. She was a beautiful young woman with her long, coal black hair and green, penetrating eyes. She was 5'6" with an hourglass figure she worked hard to maintain. Right now, she seemed more beautiful than usual to him. Her perfectly shaped legs, now emphasized by the short length of the shirt she was wearing, were almost more than he could stand.

"Is he up yet?" She asked.

"Not yet," Keith said. "I figure he'll sleep for a while. He seemed pretty tired when he went to bed last night."

"You're probably right." Amanda picked up both coffee cups and offered one to Keith as she walked by him.

Taking the cup, he said, "I thought I'd let him sleep until he wakes up on his own."

"Good idea," She answered over her shoulder as she headed for the front door. "I'll be outside for a little bit."

Keith knew she only wanted to get some fresh air. She did this same thing every morning and would stay close to the house. He also realized his amorous feelings this morning for Amanda were more to do with the competition from another male in the house. He went into the front room, made sure she left the front door open, and sat in the armchair to relax and enjoy his coffee. She needed her time alone, but he wasn't willing to let her be outside without him being able to tell if she needed him quickly. From his chair, he could see out the front door, and his rifle was at his side.

CHAPTER SEVEN

Kyle awoke to a nudge on his shoulder.

"Get your old body out of the bed," Bear said with a grin, "and if you must, bring your ugly face with it."

"Kiss my ugly ass," Kyle replied, in his usual British accent, as he sat up. "What's the time anyway? It feels like it's only been a few minutes since I turned the guard duty over to Ben, at two this morning, and climbed into bed."

"It's somewhere around six o'clock. Lynn wouldn't let me get you up any earlier. She and Ben have fed the horses, and Ginny is fixing breakfast. Guess she figured you could stand some rest."

"She's good about those things. Think I might keep her around for a while."

"Probably should," Bear said, moving toward the fire. "She's the most useful of the pair of you."

Kyle rose and joined Bear. Soon the rest of the group gathered around the warmth to eat. The entire breakfast of eggs, bacon, and bread disappeared in only a few minutes.

"This brings something to mind," Spyder said. "If this predicament continues, we're going to need fresh food. We can get some canned goods, but those will only last a short time. Sooner or later, we're going to need real food."

"I agree," Bear said. "The same for the horses. I've been thinking about this very thing, and I've got a solution. But I have to tell you, it's against the law."

"What law?" Kyle interjected. "As I see it, right now we're going by the law of the fittest. I mean I won't go out and kill someone. But if it comes down to my family starving, I'm willing to do about whatever's needed."

Everyone nodded and mumbled their agreement.

"Okay," Bear continued, "I suggest we make a raid on Country Boys. Hit a couple of the feed stores and maybe some of the restaurants. We can do it at night and cover most of the town in one night."

"Sure," Lynn said. "We can use the horses and my two wagons to haul everything. It's quiet and doesn't require fuel."

"Good idea," Ben spoke up. "I bet we can probably take four or five horses through the back way into town and take a look at the feed stores before night fall. Then we can use the wagon strictly for our food."

This suggestion from Ben came as a shock to Kyle and by the looks on their faces, the rest as well. He never believed Ben would agree to the plan. Ben was a very honest, moral man and never indicated he was even capable of thinking such things.

Ben must have read Kyle's face and said, "Hey man, this seems like a matter of survival. If everything straightens out soon, we can make restitution. If not, we might have a jump on other people when they get hungry." Then he turned very serious, "and they will get hungry. Then you can bet, if they get hungry enough, they'll get dangerous."

Even though his logic made good sense, it still seemed out of character for the man. Of course, most people's characters were undergoing a change or soon would be.

"So, we look for food for the horses and ourselves tonight," Bear stated. "There's another thing I think we need to do. We know Hal and Sandy Sloan are either at their home or on their way here. Also, because all this hit on Halloween, David and Cindy Alexander are probably out at their house. Since all of them are members of the Regulators, and none have any family around here, I think we need to go looking for 'em."

"I agree," Spyder said. "But how we gonna get that done and get the food tonight?"

"We may not," Bear admitted. "But I think our friends should come first. If we send two people in each direction with each one leading a horse, we should be able to get it done fairly quick. That'll also give every person a horse to return on."

"Right," Kyle said. "Bear, why don't you and Spyder go for David and Cindy? But take an extra horse. David has a lot of weapons and probably some powder. In fact, both groups should take an extra horse to pack any possible supplies back. Ben and I can go to Hal and Sandy's. Plus I want to stop at the 'Stop and Go', over at the 'T' and raid any supplies they may have there."

"Good thinking," Bear responded. "The more supplies the better."

"Sounds good to me," Spyder said. "If I remember right they all live about the same distance, only in opposite directions."

"If we hurry, we still might be able to get the food tonight," Lynn pointed out."

"Wait a minute," Ginny said. "There are enough diesel trucks around here, so we should be able to find at least two and cut the time down to at least a couple of hours."

"It might take as much time to find the vehicles as it would to get to their houses," Kyle argued. "Not to mention drawing attention to us with the sound of a truck and possibly getting shot at."

"There's two here on the ranch," Ben told him. "If need be, we can use the horses to pull the trucks to the hill at the main gate of the ranch and get them started."

"That's the way to do it," Lynn agreed. "Not only will it be quicker, but the trucks can haul more. We can use Princess and Poncho to pull the trucks."

"I don't think so," Kyle said. "There's still the matter of the noise of a truck."

"We use back roads and travel as fast as is safely possible," Bear said.

"It'll also make hauling extra supplies from the 'T' easier," Ben added.

Kyle only hesitated a second. "Okay, let's get it done. But we all have to take care and watch for crazies."

***

Hal and Sandy both wore backpacks with MREs and a change of clothes inside. As well, they were dressed in layers of western clothes and both carried rifles. They were about a quarter of the way into town when they saw a truck round a curve in the road. As the truck approached, Hal raised his rifle and aimed at the cab. The truck slowed to a stop about thirty feet away, and the passenger door opened.

Both Sandy and Hal were born and raised in Tyler, Texas and were not only married but also best friends as well. Hal, a sign painter, worked on billboards, road signs, and business signs made from all sorts of materials. He could make a sign of almost any design depending on the needs of the customer.

One of Hal's best-kept secrets was his artistic ability. He had produced numerous paintings, both oil and watercolor, and everyone fortunate enough to have seen them wondered why he didn't sell them. It seemed, to all those around him, he minimized his ability.

Kyle stuck his head out and said, "You're blocking the road. Move your ass to the side, and we won't have to run over you."

"That's a helluva thing to say with a rifle pointed at you," Hal returned.

"Nah, not really," Kyle said climbing from the cab. "I've seen you shoot, I'm safe."

Both men laughed as Ben climbed from the truck on the other side.

"Ben!" Sandy exclaimed and hurried over to hug him.

Sandy was as talented as Hal in another way. She was an artist in her own right with a sewing machine. Her specialty was western clothing, which she sold in various stores and at cowboy shooting matches she and Hal attended. All her clothing was authentic and based on the styles of the old west. As well, she was single-handedly responsible for supplying all the Hays County Regulators with the rugged clothes they wore in their shows.

"Damn," Kyle said. "He gets a hug from her, and I get you with a rifle pointed at me."

Hal smiled. "We get what we all deserve." The two men shook hands and patted each other on the back.

"Glad to see you're both okay," Kyle said hugging Sandy.

It's been quiet," Hal said. "Shoot, there aren't many people living around here anyway."

"We're here to get you and anything you want to bring with you," Ben said.

There's not much at the house but my weapons, some ammunition and the black powder stuff," Hal said.

"We can use all of it," Kyle said.

"What about canned or non-perishable food?" Ben asked.

"Sure, we have some," Sandy answered. "We just didn't have a way to bring it with us. I've also got flour and cornmeal."

"Hop in, and we'll go get it," Ben said climbing back into the truck.

"How the hell did you get a truck to run?" Hal asked. "I tried everything I could to get mine running."

Ben started the truck toward Hal and Sandy's house.

This is diesel," Kyle answered. "We bypassed all the electrical system, made a few adjustments, and rolled it down a hill. It doesn't take a spark to run."

Hal understood and nodded. "Of course, mine runs on gasoline. That's why it wouldn't start."

Back at Hal and Sandy's house, they loaded all the supplies there, which turned out to be more than Sandy expected.

"I'm bringing all my tools for fixing weapons," Hal said.

"We were thinking about raiding the store at the 'T' but I'm not sure if we have room for anything else," Ben said.

"We could make two trips," Hal said.

"I guess we could," Ben answered.

"What about our truck?" Sandy asked.

"It won't run, honey" Hal said.

"Why can't we pull it?" She asked. "We've got a chain. Then we could use it as a trailer and make only the one trip."

Kyle looked at Hal and they both broke out laughing. Neither had thought of the most obvious solution.

When they reached the store at the "T" they found others had already hit it and not much was left. They put what was there in the back of their truck, unhooked Hal's truck, and headed toward the ranch to unload.

***

As Spyder drove up the long driveway, Bear saw David, Cindy, and their daughter Deborah, loading a homemade wagon with what appeared to be weapons and supplies.

David pick up a rifle leaning against a tree. He kept the weapon pointed at the truck until Bear

76

brought it to a stop, then put the weapon back against the tree, and came forward to greet his friends.

At forty-five David was a self-taught computer genius. When the scare over the change of the millennium and the possible computer shutdowns happened, he and his partner worked with several cities and a couple of state's computer networks to ensure a smooth transition. The trick of it was he did it all from home using his computer to program all those needing to be corrected.

He greeted both men as soon as they climbed out of the vehicle. "I sure didn't expect to see either of you out here-especially driving one of those," he said pointing at the truck.

Diesel works with the right amount of coaxing," Spyder said as Cindy and Deborah gave both men a hug. "We were coming to see what you all were planning to do. By the looks of things, you're heading out for somewhere."

"We were going to see if anyone was at the stables," David said. "If no one was there, we were going to Colorado. I've got family there."

"Well, Ginny, Lynn, and her boys are back at the Chuck Wagon Area on the Lazy R Ranch," Bear said. "Kyle and Ben are on their way to see if Hal and Sandy want to come in, or if they're staying at their place."

"I'm not wanting to pry," Spyder said, "but Colorado would be one helluva long trip. What makes you want to move from here? It's secluded and your neighbors are at least a half mile away. A trip all the way to Colorado would be dangerous at the very least."

77

"I love this house," David said, "but it's all electric. It's cold at night, and we have to go outside to cook anything. Of course we have the barbeque pit, but it won't work if it's raining or snowing, and there's no water within two miles." He paused and shook his head. "If things return to normal, we'll come back, but it's a death trap now."

"Tell him," Cindy said from beside her husband.

He looked at her and hesitated.

"These are our friends," she said. "They'll believe you-tell them, David."

He shook his head and looked from Spyder to Bear.

"We had a couple of friends here from Houston, one was named Suzie. A couple of days ago, they all came down with some sort of fever. Two of 'em died the next day, but after two days, Suzie seemed to completely recover except for some splotches on her skin. They seemed to harden and scab or scale over." David hesitated, took a deep breath and looked at his wife again. When Cindy shrugged, he said, "Then, during the night she became violent. She began throwing things-furniture, silverware, anything she could get her hands on-at all of us and eventually ran outta the house screaming and cursing. The last we saw of her was when she entered the trees and ran off into the woods."

Bear immediately thought of Kim but didn't say anything. He could see the story made Cindy and Deborah nervous. As well, his experience with Kim told him David's story was the truth.

78

"I've seen some crazy things," Spyder said. "I've got no cause to disbelieve you."

"Now you know the other reason we have to leave here," Cindy said. "The incident with Suzie was last night. I have no doubt she'll come back."

"Do you want to ride back with us?" Bear asked.

"Hell yeah," David answered. "Now, I don't have to steal the horses over the hill. We can load our supplies in the back of the truck."

"You can also hook your horse trailer up, and we'll take your two horses with us," Spyder said.

"I know you hate to leave the house." Bear looked around the property. "I've house-sat for you so many times, I almost feel like I live here part-time. But it's time to leave it behind-at least for now."

With Spyder and Bear's help, they easily transferred all their belongings to the truck, hooked up David's horse trailer, and headed out for the campsite. The large truck was equipped with duallys and easily pulled the trailer.

As they pulled away, Bear noticed Cindy looking back at her home. "With any luck, you'll be back soon," he said.

She simply nodded and said nothing as tears welled up in her eyes.

Spyder pulled the truck out of the driveway and onto the cul-de-sac. Bear sat on one side with a rifle, and David sat on the other with his rifle. Both windows were still up for warmth and also because they operated electrically, but neither man would hesitate to smash his out if needed.

They drove only about a mile when a hole appeared in the top of the cab and a bullet slammed into the headrest of the front passenger seat, and bits of padding flew into the air. The truck swerved dangerously from side to side as Spyder reacted to the impact and jerked the steering wheel sharply to the left. The trailer, with the horses in it, sluggishly followed the erratic movement of the truck.

"We've got incoming," Bear called out. "Cindy, you and Deborah get on the floor." He was barely understandable over Cindy's screams as she reacted to what had happened. She continued screaming as Deborah pulled her to the floor.

"Son of a bitch," Bear exclaimed and slid as far down as he could.

"I don't see anything," David searched the dense trees as they passed by for the shooter.

Another shot struck the truck at enough of an angle that it didn't penetrate the cab but ricochet away.

"I doubt you'll ever see 'em," Bear said. They're at a distance and up high."

"How the hell do you know?" Spyder asked.

"We made a curve, and he hit us with a second shot, and the angle of the first bullet," Bear answered keeping his head down. "He's also on my side."

Three more shots struck the truck in rapid succession. One again glanced off the truck, the other penetrated the cab, smashing the front passenger window out, and the third caused a blow-out in the rear left dually.

With the tire wobbling and giving off a thumping sound, Spyder accelerated and rounded a sharp bend in the road putting a hill between them and the road behind. "This fucker's handling like a tank now. It's sluggish as hell. We should be okay from here on though. I think I can get us back to camp."

"That is if no one else takes a shot at us," David said.

"You can bet your ass this is the last truck I drive," Spyder declared.

"I'm with you on that one," Bear grumbled.

***

Back at the campsite, the group pushed the stagecoach from its barn and packed all their supplies inside to protect them from the weather.

"I'm glad to have you with us," Bear said. "If this is anything near what I think it is, we'll need your wood-working and gunsmith abilities."

"Just what do you think this is?" David stared inside the barn and then looked back at Bear. "It's gonna be like this for a while isn't it?

I'm afraid so," Bear answered. "In fact, I'm not sure it'll ever return to what we knew before."

"I realized that last night. But I'm not sure Cindy could handle information like that. She's been crying off and on since she realized this was more than just a loss of electricity at the house. I know she's very supportive and interested in whatever I do. But I'm realistic enough to know emotional strength isn't her forte. Actually, that would be when she's a hostess."

"I remember all the parties she's put on for the Regulators."

On the other hand," David continued, "I'm sure Deborah's strong enough to do whatever is needed. Shoot she's able to handle all the stuff she does in high school plus keep an A+ average."

"I know Deborah's a remarkable young lady, but she's only a sophomore, and I wouldn't put too much on her yet. I don't think we need to add any more stress to an already volatile situation. People are slowly coming to a realization that this is more serious than just a power loss.

"There are fourteen of us," David said, looking at the others. "We're gonna have to rely on each other if we're gonna make it through this."

"There'll be more," is all Bear said as he turned to the fire to warm his hands.

***

"We need everyone over here," Kyle yelled to the others at the camp. "We need to discuss some things."

"It's four o'clock and we need to take a look at getting more supplies," Kyle said as everyone gathered around the fire. Some sat while others stood.

"We're gonna need food for us and feed for the horses," he said. "I realize taking things without permission, or without paying for them, might not set right with many of you-but it's what has to be done." He paused to let this information sink in.

"There are two feed stores in town and Country Cousin's Supermarket. "I figure we can hit all three tonight without much trouble."

"It'll take longer than you think," Hal said. "There's no way we can use the trucks. They make entirely too much noise."

"After today, I ain't ridin' in or drivin' no truck," Spyder stated.

"Agreed," Kyle said. "We can divide into two groups of three. One group can use the wagon for the supermarket. The other can use six packhorses for the two feed stores. At least the feed stores are straight across the street from each other and not across town."

"Even though they're close together, the group getting the horse feed will have to make a bunch of trips," Bear said. "The feed is heavy and traveling at night can be hazardous for the animals."

"We can use the back streets," Kyle said. "That way we can stay on pavement most of the time."

"One thing," Hal said rising to his feet. "If anyone encounters a problem at any of the three places, he or she will have to abandon the attempt and return here immediately."

"If we give up at the first sign of resistance, we might as well not even try," Kyle said. "I have no doubt... "

"I agree with Hal," Bear interrupted. "In fact, I insist on it. No one here wants the death of another person, whose protecting their possessions, on their conscience. No one is to be killed over this."

"I must say I agree," Ben said. "I won't kill a neighbor over this."

Kyle shrugged. "Okay, if that's the way you want it. That's the way it'll be." He silently disagreed. *I hope you wimps don't regret this decision. Bear makes entirely too much noise about killing in battle. I may have never done it, but I have no doubt that I can without any problem. I guess that's the difference between them .*

After dark, they discovered vandals had ransacked the supermarket. However, it was mostly for perishables like milk and frozen dinners. The raiders, as they now thought of themselves, collected most of the rest of the supplies and took them back to the camp. Kyle was surprised to see Ben even thought of detergent and brought a packhorse load of nothing but that.

They worked throughout the night and were able to get everything they felt they needed by five in the morning. Kyle made a special trip to Harry's Hardware and picked up all the ammunition he could carry for the weapons stockpiled at the campsite.

By dawn, the raiders returned, set out guards, and bedded down for a rest.

CHAPTER EIGHT

Andy opened his eyes and blinked, trying to remove the drowsiness from his mind as well as his eyes. Davata was only half awake, slouched in a chair beside him. When he shifted in the bed for the first time in over a day, she sat up.

It's okay," she assured him, placing a hand on his shoulder. "Welcome back to the world of the living. You've been out for two days."

Davata met Andy two days following the blackout. They had moved from New Orleans to a large home in one of the Louisiana bayous, looking for safety out of the city.

"How are you feeling?" she asked.

"My chest is numb now. At least it doesn't hurt like it did before." Andy shifted into a sitting position and leaned back against the headboard. "Two days, huh." He ran a hand over his face and then across his chest. He held his arm up and looked at it. Red streaks ran from his shoulders to his elbows. He quickly looked at the rest of his body. "The striations mean I've been poisoned somehow. But what are the splotches of gray skin?

Davata sat and silently moved her mouth, but produced no sound.

"What is it, Sweetheart?" he asked. "What is it you can't say?"

"We've got some new people here, and one of them is a doctor." She rose from her chair. "I'll get him." Before Andy could react, she hurried from the room.

A minute later, a man of about sixty followed her back into the room. "I'm Doctor Hamilton. How do you feel, Andy?"

"Okay," he replied. "Better than I did a couple of days ago. Now Doc, tell me what's going on. Why is Davata acting so strange?"

The doctor sat in the chair Davata previously occupied. He took a deep breath and let it out in a long sigh. "Since the decay of civilization, I've dealt with eight or nine people scratched or bitten by one of those mutated animals. Not only have the people changed in appearance, they have mutated biochemically also. Every one of them carries a virus. The virus they carry has mutated also. It is unlike anything I have ever seen." Dr. Hamilton paused and looked at Andy.

"Go ahead Doc," he said. "Telling me about it can't change the outcome."

Dr. Hamilton bowed his head and hesitantly continued. "Once a person is scratched or bitten, he or she will do one of two things. He or she will go totally insane or die. The insanity takes about five days and results in them mutating. Death takes about four and is extremely painful. There is no antidote or medicine to change the course of the virus. Symptoms are the same until about day three."

"Do you have anything for pain?" Andy asked.

Doctor Hamilton wore a grim look on his face as he nodded and handed Andy a bottle of pills. "Two should ease any pain, but any more than four would be dangerous." He turned and left Andy and Davata alone.

"You heard everything," Andy said. "There's no way I'm gonna go through that."

"I know," she said and sat on the bed beside him. Reaching out, she moved a strand of hair off his forehead. Tears welled in her eyes. She leaned over and kissed him.

He put his arms around her and pulled her toward him. Kicking her shoes off, she slid onto the bed next to him. She held him close, comfortable in the darkness of the room, even though she knew Andy's inevitable fate.

Andy lay in Davata's arms as he quietly drifted into his final sleep.

CHAPTER NINE

Four days later, the doctor and his party waited on the road to New Orleans. Davata remained behind briefly to gather some things, but more than that, she wanted to say goodbye to Andy. She stood over his grave, big tears in her eyes.

"Goodbye," she said as her fingers gently touched the wooden cross marking his grave. "I love you, Andy." She turned slowly and left, quietly leaving the grave in the warm sunshine and at peace.

As she walked from the house across the yard to highway 90, tears streamed down her face, yet a smile softly played on her lips. Her heart filled with a mixture of sadness and joy. She was sad to lose Andy. However, something deep inside told her this chapter of her life wasn't finished yet. Davata turned left on the highway and headed toward New Orleans with the hope of a future and a new life.

Davata joined her group of new acquaintances about a hundred yards down the road from where they buried Andy a couple of days before.

The group now consisted of four people Dr. Sydney Hamilton, Carl "Melon" Snyder, Winston "Wind" Jefferson, and Davata. Two days ago, Dr. Hamilton announced that he was leaving for San Antonio, Texas in a couple of days, and everyone was welcome to join him if they wanted to. Following a very short discussion, the rest decided San Antonio was as good a place as any.

As they walked along highway 90, Davata threw a question out to nobody in particular. "I know there were more of you before. May I ask what happened to the others?"

"A group of men caught us by surprise while we were eating," Wind spoke up. "Being an African American in the South, I've experienced their types all my life and can tell them at a glance. By the looks of their clothes and the way they talked, they seemed to be a bunch of rednecks who probably banded together to bully the people of the local area. After some threats and demands, they attacked us." To Davata, it looked as if Wind was reliving the incident. He took on what her daddy (who had been in the Vietnam War) called a *thousand yard stare*.

"We lost three of our friends before managing to get away by running off, into the surrounding woods." Melon continued the story. "The jerks were evidently more interested in the truck and its contents than pursuing us. Plus there was no way they could keep up with Wind."

The four of them took up most of one lane of the highway they now walked. Davata reached over and rubbed Wind on his shoulder. Slowly he looked at her and appeared to return from his thoughts. "Are you all right?"

"Yeah," Wind answered. "I'm okay. It's just that I saw Angie and Rick get shot before I got away-ran away." He spat out the last two words.

"Man, don't say it that way. There was nothing you could have done about them," Melon said. "If it hadn't been for you coming back, we would have probably never made it ourselves."

Wind looked appreciative but doubtful.

Looking back at Davata, Melon continued, "We definitely found out why his nickname is Wind. In only a couple of seconds, he disappeared ahead of us; and in less than a minute, he was back, pointing the way he just came. Then he took off in another direction, making enough noise to draw the killers away from the rest of us. We found the main road a mile or so later and went down it a couple of hundred yards. In only a few minutes, he came running back and told us the others gave up." Melon stopped and looked at Wind, "Something just occurred to me. We thanked you for coming back and saving our asses, but you never told us why."

"Why what?" Wind asked.

"Why did you come back? You were safe. There's no way they would have ever caught up to you. As far as you knew, Doc Hamilton and I were either close behind you, or they had caught us."

Wind wore a look of mild surprise on his face. "Mamma always taught me that you take care of friends when you can. You folks are my friends."

"I'm glad you did," Melon said. "But-and please pardon how this question may sound-why would you risk your life for white men when other white men were trying to kill you?"

"My Mamma always said it's not the color of a person's skin, but what's in their heart that counts. Color meant nothing. My friends were in trouble, and I couldn't leave them to fend for themselves when I could do something to help."

"You're a hell of a man, Winston Jefferson." Melon patted him on his shoulder.

"I'll second that, my young friend." Dr. Hamilton reached over and shook hands with Wind. "A hell of a man."

The group resumed their way down the road, walking in silence. A short time later, Davata said. "You never did explain who gave you the nickname Wind?"

"It was given to me by a track coach," Wind answered. "I won state in high school track for the quarter mile, and he said I ran like the wind. I guess it kinda stuck."

"Speaking of nicknames," Davata looked at melon. "How did you get the nickname of Melon?"

He grinned, "From the time I was born, my head was too big for my body. It started out as Melon Head, and later, shortened to Melon when I was in the Army. I got a lot of teasing when I was a kid, but when I finally grew enough for my body to match the size of my head, the name just stuck."

"Kids can be cruel," Davata agreed.

"I'm used to it now and actually prefer going by it," he answered.

"Your Army training has certainly come in handy," Dr. Hamilton said. "If it hadn't been for Melon here, we would have gone hungry many days. He knows how to hunt, trap, and all sorts of other things."

"Sounds like you're a handy man to have around, Mr. Melon," Davata said.

Melon continued walking. She could tell by his smile he was happy to be able to help and especially to be appreciated.

"Tell me again why we're going to San Antonio," Wind said to nobody in particular. "Why can't we simply stay around here?"

"Because there's a better possibility of hurricanes here and probably more mutants than in a city," the doctor answered. "Not only will people be banding together in the larger cities, but they should be pushing the mutants out by sheer numbers, if nothing else. That probably means that when the creatures left the city, they probably stayed nearby, on the outskirts."

"Not necessarily," Davata interjected. "Remember, I told you about the mutants in New Orleans. They're in at least some parts of the large cities as well."

"But San Antonio," Melon complained, "it'll take us months."

"Not if we use those," Davata said pointing in the direction of a group of fishing huts ahead. One of which had a number of bicycles leaning against the front of it.

"You know," Dr. Hamilton said, "you may just have the best idea yet."

All the bicycles were in reasonably good condition, and with no one around to protest, each of the travelers had their choice.

"Time to ride," Melon said, mounting one of the bikes. They each took one they liked and started peddling west, along Highway 90.

***

After riding what seemed like days rather than three hours, they came to the end of the swamp.

Davata knew New Orleans lay ahead. She also knew there were crazies and mutants in the city. She pulled her bike to a stop at an intersection and called the others over.

"Look, I was in the city before with Andy. Believe me; you don't want to spend a night in there. I suggest we stay here tonight. Then get through New Orleans tomorrow. We don't have to go all the way through the city. We can take major roads for a little over fifteen miles. There's a bridge across Lake Pontchartrain we can use. It'll take us over to the Interstate. It's a long one, but we're going to have to cross a long one whichever way we go. The other bridge is across a swamp, and we couldn't make it through New Orleans and over it in one day. I'm not too crazy about being stuck on it during the night either."

Since the others didn't know the area or the city, they agreed to follow Davata's suggestion and pulled over to spend the night. They located a suitable house and moved in for the night.

After eating, they gathered in the living room. "Who's washing the dishes?" Melon asked. "I did 'em last time."

"I left them for the maid," Wind answered. "She'll do 'em tomorrow."

Davata looked at the two young men. "The two of you are weird, you know."

"But it's so much fun," Melon answered.

A barrage of gunfire sounded in the distance. Everyone looked around uncomfortably, and Dr. Hamilton extinguished the kerosene lamp. They shortly drifted off to separate rooms for much needed rest.

All through the night, Davata could hear the faint sound of gunfire. It was obviously a long way away, but it still sounded like there was a battle zone in the distance. She knew it was only a matter of time before the violence worked its way out here. They would have to make it across the Pontchartrain Bridge tomorrow.

***

Following breakfast the next morning, they sat in the living room to discuss the situation.

The doctor started. "After the noise I heard night, I'm not sure we should go any nearer the city than we already are."

"We have to go in the city a short distance, if we want to go west," Davata told him. "Either that or backtrack fifty miles."

"There's got to be another way," Melon said. "But, I agree. I'm not going through that city under any circumstances."

"Look," Davata replied, "there is a road a mile or so ahead we can use to go north until we hit I-10. We then go west to the Pontchartrain Bridge. It travels north to Interstate 12. From there we go west again. We will only be in the city about an hour and a half, and most of the road there is elevated. It should be safe if we don't stop until we're on the Bridge."

The doctor stroked his chin and said, "Well, none of us knows the area as well as you, Davata. I don't think we have a choice. Gentlemen, I vote we follow the lady."

94

"I'm with you," Melon chimed in. "I don't like being here now. So the sooner we get out, the better it suits me."

They all looked at Wind who remained quiet throughout the discussion. He looked back at them with a gaze more mature and knowing than his years should allow. "I'll go with you under one condition. We have to find some guns or something else to protect ourselves. The only thing we have is the rifle and shotgun of Davata's. If I'm gonna be in danger, I'm gonna be able to defend myself."

No one disagreed. Davata had said this was a dangerous undertaking, and by the looks on their faces, they believed her.

"I'm sure I can find guns," Wind told them. "But, I don't know about ammunition. Davata, you'll need to show us the way to the Interstate. I'll let you know when I see something."

Davata found the road she wanted and turned north. About three blocks later, Wind called for them to pull to the side of the road. He climbed off his bike and led them to a run-down Quickie-Mart. They had to break the front window of the store, but once inside, Wind led them to the front and looked underneath the counter.

When he stood up, he held a sawed off shotgun. "There should be at least one in every store like this."

Before leaving, they rummaged through the store and loaded up on supplies. Wind even found a .38cal. pistol in a desk in the office. Soon they climbed on their bikes and headed further along the road.

After a couple of blocks, Melon pointed at another convenience store a little way ahead and shouted, "There's another one!"

"Melon," Wind called to him.

Melon stopped shouting and looked at Wind. "What?" He responded still excited, but considerably quieter.

"That's good. But look over there," Wind said pointing across the street.

There sat a gun shop. The windows were broken out, but the wrought iron covering them was still intact.

"Now we can do some shopping," Wind said with a grin.

They all peddled over to the front of the store, dismounted, and propped their bikes against its wall.

"How do we get in?" Dr. Hamilton asked, finding the front door locked.

"Wait here," Wind answered and disappeared around the end of the building.

In only a couple minutes, he appeared inside the front door. Twisting the dead bolt, he let his companions inside.

"How did you get in?" Davata asked.

"Trade secret," Wind answered. "Don't you know? All us colored folk know how to break into places like this. It's in our blood." Wind was wearing a huge grin.

"Not funny," Davata answered fighting to hide a smile of her own. Still, she wondered how he did it.

They each took one pistol and one rifle and all the ammunition they could carry in makeshift bags they attached to their bikes. When they were loaded, they continued on their way.

It took all day for them to reach and cross the Pontchartrain Bridge and then make it to Interstate 12. After a short search, they found an abandoned house and settled in for a well-deserved night's rest.

CHAPTER TEN

Bear woke up and looked around. The sun was almost straight overhead. He tried to blink the sleep away and sat up. Most of the other survivors were up and moving around. *Must be somewhere around noon. I could have done with a few more hours' sleep.* However, there was no doubt in his ex-military mind; his days of sleeping late were over, at least for a while anyway. He got up, stretched, and wandered over to the campfire.

"Well, look who's up," Hal said with a grin. "You know, Bear, you can't help being ugly, but do you have to bring it out in public? I mean, can't you wear a sack over your head or something?"

"Now, Hal," Sandy said to her husband. "You'd better hush. There's no law left to prevent him from shooting you."

"As bad a shot as he is-I don't need no law," he answered, still grinning. "I've seen him shoot."

"Hal," Bear said with a smirk, "if you're asleep and feel water hitting your face, just think of it as rain. Don't mind me standing above you."

Hal gave him a wary look. "You would too, you son-of-a-bitch."

"She's the only thing stopping me," Bear said flicking a thumb toward Sandy.

"Now do I have to separate the two of you and put you each in a corner?" She asked.

Both men looked around the camp as if to ensure there were no corners at hand. "She'll find one," Hal said.

Sandy and Bear had, over the last five years or so, come to think of each other as brother and sister. Bear knew Hal recognized the relationship for what it was-a very close friendship. Because of his feelings for Sandy, Bear thought of Hal as a brother and would accept his playful insults in step and never think twice about them.

"Now, is there anyone else around here who might, at least, be worth talking to?" Bear asked no one in particular.

"Hell, yes," Ben answered a short distance away. "I'm thinking about appointing myself Mayor of Rollingblock. Is that important enough?"

"No shit, Ben. That's great. Why don't you wander your ole self down to the square and give us a speech," Bear suggested with a grin. "Let everyone know you're running for office."

"Nah," Ben responded. "I figured I'd select you as my campaign manager and let you get the campaign started for me."

"Sounds good, Ben," he said. "Now let me tell you what you can do while you're waiting for me to get that done." Bear grinned.

"Consider yourself elected," Cindy spoke up. "I don't think anyone would vote against you, Ben."

"All right," Ben answered. "I'll do it, and as my first proclamation I declare this place to be named 'Rebel's Revenge.'"

"Sounds great to me," Cindy said, "but what about any Yankees that might come here and want to live?"

Ben immediately went into his *old man* routine, placing his hands together, twiddling his thumbs, puckering up his face, and hunching his shoulders.

"Well Darlin', ifin they wanna stay, they gonna hafta agree to our terms. We give in to 'em afore, but not this time. We gonna win this un."

Everyone around the camp was grinning. Ben was always good for the spirits and the situation being what it was, they all needed some help with their spirits.

Everyone gathered around the fire and loaded their plates with food. Sitting down to eat, their conversation slowed.

"Mighty good grub," Ben said. "Ginny, I think we're gonna have to keep you on as cook."

"I'll stay on," Ginny said, "as long as I don't have to kill or dress any of the food. I draw the line at that. You bring it in ready to cook, and I'll take care of the rest."

"That's my 'Little Teacup'," Spyder spoke up. "She can cook anything that ain't movin'." Looking around he added, "So fellers, I wouldn't suggest you sit in one place too long."

***

It was a long night of gathering supplies, the bulk of which were haphazardly stuck in the stagecoach barn.

"I'll help Ginny with arranging the food," Ben said. "I assume she's gonna be in charge of it if she's gonna do all the cooking."

"Carl, Will, you two and Paul come over here and help us get this stuff straightened out," Lynn called to her sons.

Bear and Hal headed to positions at the north and northeast respectively to keep watch while the others worked. As well, David and Kyle situated themselves as lookouts on the south and east sides of the camp.

Five hours later, Carl set the last of the supplies in place. "Take a break," Lynn said to her sons. She pulled three sodas from a box and handed one to each. "We don't have many of these so enjoy 'em while we do."

"Now all we have to do is keep this as orderly as it is now in the future," Ben said. "That means you'll have to be strict about using and stocking supplies." He nodded at Ginny.

"I didn't expect to have this much room left over after arranging everything," Ginny said.

"Boys, let's go feed the horses," Lynn said.

Cindy approached Ginny. "I'll help you with supper if you want."

"Thanks," Ginny said. "Even with two of us it'll take a couple of hours to get the pots and pans cleaned up before we can even start making another meal."

"I'm gonna go out and see if I can locate our guards." Ben turned away grinning. He could tell by Cindy's face she had forgotten about the task of cleaning the cooking utensils from the meal before.

He located them with no problem and all returned except Spyder who volunteered to stay out until everyone else finished eating.

***

Since sitting on watch was the first time for him to be by himself since the blackout, Spyder relaxed and let his mind wander. *Well, it's a hell of a mess we've got ourselves into this time. Somebody really went and fucked the monkey on this one. At least we got enough resourceful people involved here to be able to take care of things as long as we're all willing to work together. Damn, hadn't thought of that. We may have too many chiefs and not enough Indians if we ain't careful. You can bet your ass we better find a job for everybody or the natives will damn sure get restless. It's for damn sure this situation ain't a short-term thing.* He let his gaze wander through the forest. Even though the sun was setting, there was enough light left to be able to detect anyone or anything if it approached. *We're gonna have to completely change the way we think and act. This here's probably the best people Ginny and I could possibly join up with though. However, I wonder if they know what might be required for us to make it. Bear, Hal, and Kyle do. But I don't think the rest have any idea how dangerous it is now.*

A short distance away, Spyder heard the bushes rustle as Ben came to relieve him on watch.

"Think you might could eat something?" Ben asked the other man.

"I could eat the north end of a south bound skunk," Spyder answered.

"Well, I don't think they cooked anything up as gourmet as all that," Ben said with a grin. "But why don't you get yourself back there and see can you choke down what they do have? I've got this under control."

Spyder gave him a slap on the shoulder and headed off through the woods in the direction of the camp.

102

Back in camp, he found everyone sitting around the fire relaxing except Cindy and Lynn. Cindy gathered what was left of the dishes, and Lynn filled a large plastic trash barrel with water heated on the fire.

"There should be plenty left over there for you Spyder," Cindy told him motioning toward the fire. "There's a plate there, so eat all you want."

Spyder went to the fire, picked up the plate, and filled it from the grill. "Damn, we're eating mighty good for all the problems we have, ain't we?" The question not directed to anyone in particular.

"We have to finish all the perishables before they go bad," Kyle answered. "We won't be eating this good for much longer. In fact, we're gonna need to start planning on doing some hunting and trapping if we're gonna eat this winter."

The last statement produced a sobering effect on the others.

The sun was below the hills in the distance, which formed The Spine of Hays Valley. As darkness settled around them, the temperature began to drop and reminded the survivors of the severity of the situation engulfing them.

***

Ben leaned against a tree and scanned the brush and foliage around him. As he watched for approaching danger, he thought about the events of the preceding days and the problems they now faced.

We're in deep trouble. Probably more than any of us realize. There are things going on here none

103

of us have ever faced before, not for any great length of time, anyway. Some have been without electricity for a while but never without the possibility of ever having it again. Some have lived away from civilization. However, they even came into town every couple of weeks or so to get supplies and find out what was going on in the area.

There's also the problem of leadership. It's becoming more and more obvious we'll grow in size, which will require a strong leader. There are some that can handle the task. Not too damn sure who'll be best though. There's people, like Bear who know how to survive and defend themselves. There's people like David who know how to run a business-organize people and such. Then there's Kyle who wants to be a leader-be in charge, but we need more than that. We need someone who can put it all together and make it work. All of them have owned a business of their own, but we need someone with a more level head-someone who won't be too quick to act one way or another but will sort the situation out before making a decision.

"Ben," a voice softly called from the direction of the camp.

Ben turned and watched as Carl came into view.

Kyle had sent Carl to relieve Ben on watch. Even though Carl was only seventeen years old, Ben knew he would stay awake and be watchful for however long he was asked to do so. Carl had proven himself many times on hunting expeditions and would do about anything not to let his father down.

CHAPTER ELEVEN

Ben walked into the firelight from the edge of the trees. "Thanks for sending Carl," he said to Kyle. "It's all quiet out there. I haven't even seen or heard an animal in the last thirty minutes. He moved over near the fire and sat on a stump to listen to the ongoing conversation.

Hal was speaking. "... and with only two or three days of perishables left, it won't be long before we'll be digging into the supplemental items. We're gonna need to add meat to the stores, or we'll eat all the canned goods and have nothing left."

"I agree," David said. "We're gonna have to stretch those as long as we can, until we can grow some next spring and summer."

"Bear, you ain't said nothing," Spyder observed. "What do you think?"

Before he was able to answer, a gunshot rang out from the direction of the resort area.

"Sounds a bit too close to me," Kyle said rising to his feet. "Maybe we'd better go over and take a look."

Everyone quickly rose. "I don't think we need to let anyone get any closer," David agreed. "We damn sure don't need anyone locating us yet."

"Well, don't just stand here," Spyder snorted. "Let's get goin'."

Bear, David and Kyle were the first to move over to the edge of the firelight with Spyder.

David looked at the others and said, "This is all we'll need for now. The rest of you arm yourselves, get outta sight and keep an eye on things here. If someone other than us shows up, don't take any chances. Hal if you have to, shoot first and ask questions later," he turned and as if on command, the four men disappeared into the trees.

***

David, leading the way, stopped and turned to the other three. "Look fellas, I don't want to hurt anyone unless it's a necessity. Let's see what's going on and then decide what we need to do."

"I agree," Kyle answered. "But if whoever's there is armed, don't take any chances. Try and stay outta sight if we can. Take a look and then get back to the stables."

"I don't like it," Bear interjected. "If there's someone in Sagebrush, they'll see us coming. The stable is open ground, same as the area near the stagecoach station. I damn sure don't wanna get caught crossing any of them. I say we go down the stage tracks to the edge of the stables-then stay in the trees over to the lodges."

Another gunshot sounded in the dark followed by a series of shots then silence.

"He's right," David agreed. "If we're gonna stay outta sight, then we need to circle both places."

"Okay, we go that way and return by the trees along the edge of the stables," Spyder said.

"Let's do it," Kyle said looking at the others.

The four men moved off into the night as another series of shots rang out.

Back in camp, Hal, Ben, and Lynn threw some dirt on the fire, checked their weapons and slipped into the bushes, out of the now dimming firelight.

Cindy, armed with the pistol she used in the shows, waited with Deborah and Paul inside the stagecoach barn. Both kids could safely use black powder and modern firearms, and both were good shots.

The fire's embers cast weak but strange shadows, which moved and danced across the quiet scene. A light, cold breeze blew through the trees, causing a faint whispering sound, and everyone nervously waited.

Bear and the others made their way down to the lodges without seeing anything out of the normal. There were faint sounds coming from the area in the center of Sagebrush, where a restaurant was located. Quietly, the four men moved along the buildings in a leapfrog manner as learned in their military training. Bear was the first one to the front porch of the old saloon, located on southwest corner of the only intersection in Sagebrush. A curio shop stood on the northeast corner with a livery stable beside it, and across the street from those, on the northwest corner, was the printing shop for making fake wanted posters. Southwest and across the street from the saloon, he could see a faint flicker of light through one of the River's Bend restaurant windows. He motioned the others up and waited for them to make their way to him.

Before they could arrive, the door of the restaurant was yanked open, and two men stumbled out. From their actions and the way they swayed,

Bear figured them to be not simply drunk but smashed.

Spyder and David plastered themselves against the wall of the livery across the street. Kyle was along the wall of the saloon, about twenty feet behind Bear. All four men waited to see what the drunks in front of them were going to do.

One of the men stepped away from the door, unzipped his pants, and relieved himself there on the street.

"Ain't nothing better than taking a piss outside," he said.

"Obviously you ain't never got laid outside," the other drunk slurred back. When the first finished his business, he zipped his pants and turned back toward his friend. As he did, a shadow from the doorway not five feet from Bear rushed out and crossed the street in a few giant strides.

The creature, moving with incredible speed, reached the drunks almost before they knew what was happening.

"Kill the fucking thing," one of the drunks yelled.

The animal grabbed the man by the neck with its left paw as it struck the other in the face, crushing his skull with its massive right. The second man immediately collapsed, his face a bloody mass, his lifeless body twitching on the ground.

The man caught in the creature's vice-like grip was unable to make a sound as his neck snapped like a dry twig. The creature quickly turned its attention toward the place where Bear crouched.

As Bear rose to his feet, the thing started for him. He was barely able to get his pistol pulled before shots rang out. The creature spun to its left. More shots followed, and it sank to the ground.

Bear looked at his companions and realized none of them had fired a shot. As with him, they had barely cleared leather when the shots rang out. Instinctively, he backed up against the wall of the saloon. He could hear voices coming from his right. He motioned the rest back and waited.

In seconds, three men came into view. At the same time, five or six more emerged from the restaurant. All the strangers gathered around the body of the thing lying on the street. At the same time, Bear and the rest of his group melted into the shadows, all feeling they needed to put some distance between themselves and the others. They made their way quietly, but quickly back to the trees, then the stables, and finally the campsite.

As they approached the camp, David called out in a loud whisper, "Don't shoot, it's us."

"Come on in," Ben called back.

"Hold you're fucking voice down," Kyle snapped back. When he and the rest were in the area, he explained. "We're not alone here. There are people down at Sagebrush."

David immediately started to describe what took place only minutes before.

When he got to the part about the animal they had seen, Bear interrupted. "What the fuck was that? Have any of you ever seen anything like it? Come on now. This is bullshit. Somebody tell me what the hell it was."

"You got me." Spyder answered. "I ain't never seen nothing like that shit."

"Me neither," Kyle chimed in.

"What did you see?" Lynn asked. "What was it? What did it look like?"

"I don't even know how to describe it," Bear answered, looking to the others for help. "It was big... and fast."

David proceeded, with the help of the others, to describe the creature they saw as best he could.

"There's something bad wrong here," Spyder said when they finished. "The damn thing moved faster'n anything its size oughta."

"He's right," Kyle said. "I don't know what it was, but if there are many more around here, we're in deep shit."

"Look guys," Lynn started. "I know things are a little weird-but come on. An eight-foot animal, which lays in wait, then attacks people for no reason-and is faster than a person? Think about what you're all saying. If that was true, then where did it come from? And why haven't we seen it before now?"

"We have," David said. "Remember, I told you about our friend running off in hysterics? Her skin had started to change. Her whole body was changing."

"He's right," Cindy agreed. "I noticed it before but thought it was only my imagination. But she was taller and broader across the shoulders. What you saw was once human."

Everyone looked at her as if she just announced she was an alien from Saturn. This was simply too incredible for them to believe.

Then Spyder added, "That would explain why a few of us have seen some acting crazy and avoiding other people. We saw crazy son-of-a-bitch running

110

off into the woods before we arrived at the stables. Now that I think of it, he wasn't only acting crazy; he ran kinda funny too."

"He's right," Ginny said. "I knew there was something wrong with him. I just thought it was the sickness-whatever it is."

"Remember what I told you about my bookkeeper Kim?" Bear asked. Then without waiting for an answer he continued, "While I was on my way here, I saw something in the dark attack a deer." He explained what had happened and included the tracks he found the next day. "I know how crazy it sounds, but I'm convinced something's happening to some people-something beyond anything any of us have ever seen."

Ben spoke up, looking more serious than most of the group had ever seen him. "Well, this adds another log to the fire. If what the rest of you say is true-and I got no cause to doubt you-we've got a big problem now added to the existing situation."

"This means we gotta keep the fire low tonight. Tomorrow, we're gonna have to decide what to do about those others down there," Bear stated flatly. "Plus keep a keen eye out for those creatures. We damn sure don't want to be surprised by any of them."

After establishing shifts for standing watch, they settled in to get some rest. Things had certainly taken a crazy twist, and none of them had the slightest idea what they should do next.

CHAPTER TWELVE

Davata left her room and went to the kitchen, where she found Dr. Hamilton making a cup of tea.

"Tea?" she asked.

"Yeah, would you like some?"

"Sure, if it's not too much trouble," she answered.

"Couldn't find any coffee, and I need my caffeine to get started in the morning."

"Me too. Andy and I would always sit and relax, every morning, over coffee." Realizing what she was saying, she quickly took a drink. "Sorry," she said looking into her cup.

"Don't be," Dr. Hamilton told her. "You've suffered quite a loss in addition to everything else that's happened. It's natural to grieve."

"I don't mean to pry, but what brought you to Louisiana if you're from Texas? I mean-it's none of my business, so you don't have to tell me if you don't want to. Just tell me to mind my own business and I will."

"It's actually rather a boring story." He took a sip of tea and sat back in his chair. I moved to San Antonio after completing medical school and opened a private practice. My wife and I were very much in love and tried to have children for several years with no success. One day, she came in and announced to me we had tried enough, and it was time to enjoy each other. Shortly thereafter, she took over the operations of the office and ran it until killed by a drunk driver. She was on her way to meet a friend for lunch, and I found out about it when two police officers showed up at my office shortly afterward.

"I closed my practice a couple of months later and moved out east, feeling the need to make a geographical change in order to get a new perspective on life. Three years later, everything changed for everyone, and I'm now on my way back to where the love of my life rests. I didn't have nor do I now have any idea what I'm going to do once I get there, but I felt a need to come back.

"Not only natural but expected," Wind said as he entered the room. "My hat's off to the both of you, and if you ever need me, I'll be here. You can count on it."

They all sat at the kitchen table, and Dr. Hamilton reached over and patted her hand.

"Thank you." Davata smiled. "I thank you both."

"Now," Dr. Hamilton said. "We have over five hundred miles to cover. If we use the bikes, it will take us around two weeks to get to San Antonio."

"Of course, we're supposing we don't run into trouble on the way." Melon said, from the doorway behind them. "It also supposes no problems with the bicycles."

"Right," Davata said. "Everything is based on nothing going wrong."

"Something I've been thinking about," Melon continued, "if Davata and Andy saw all the problems in New Orleans she has described to us, why should we expect anything different in San Antonio? All the gunfire we heard last night wasn't from mutants or individuals in their homes. Before I

113

met up with you guys, I went through Jackson, Mississippi where I ran up on Wind. There, gangs had taken over. They were in charge of the entire city. I figure it's probably happened in most big cities."

"He may be right," The doctor said. "It's possible the cities have been taken over by gangs. Which means we'll have to be careful when we get near the Texas state line-there are large cities near there."

"Now, we get back to my question the other day," Wind said. "Why go to San Antonio? Why not simply stay here? We're not in the city now."

"I lived in the San Antonio area for over twenty years and know that part of Texas pretty well," Dr. Hamilton answered. "The climate is temperate. There are no hurricanes, it rarely freezes for more than a couple of days, and there are good people living outside the city. If it's been taken over by anyone or anything, we'll be safe on the outside of the city." He sat his teacup on the table. "Look, I'm not trying to convince anyone to go with me, but it's where I'm going; and I welcome any or all of you to come."

Wind stood up and said, "Well now, Doc, That's the kind of answer I like. Now, I know why I'm on my way to the land of the cowboys." A look of concern appeared, and then he asked, "I'm not going to have to start wearing cowboy boots-or a hat, am I?"

"I think you'd look great in a ten gallon hat, boots-and on a horse," Melon said, grinning. "I'm with you too, doctor. Besides, where the hell else do I have to go?"

"Well, it looks like all four of us are off to Texas," Davata agreed and then added, "Wind, I think you would be as cute as you could be in a cowboy hat."

"Don't count on it, lady," He declared. "Not even for you. Next you'll want me to start singing with a twang."

Davata grinned. "For me? You'd do that for me?"

Wind gave her a look, which left no doubt in her imagination the answer was a resounding no.

"Okay, the decision's made. We'll go to San Antonio together," she said. *It's nice to have a purpose rather than simply follow the doctor across the country.*

When they were ready to leave, Davata stopped them in the living room. "One thing we might consider. If we come across a diesel truck, we should take it. We can load the bikes in it and carry them with us."

"Wait a minute, we've been that route before," Melon said. "We were almost killed, and the truck was taken away from us."

"I understand. I just think that if we could get a truck, we could get there sooner," Davata explained. "We could actually get there in a day or so. That could also cut down on our chances of being attacked. Not to mention the fact the weather could get real cold at any time."

"She's got a point," Dr. Hamilton said, "and it could cut down on a lot of problems. We have Beaumont and Houston ahead of us; and it's like I said before, we still have over five hundred miles to cover. Besides we'll be traveling on the interstate and not on small back roads."

"Then let's keep our eyes open for a vehicle," Melon said.

"Yeah, we probably should," Wind agreed.

"I'm glad you both agree," Davata answered. "I saw a Dodge truck just around the corner from here when we arrived yesterday. I vote we try it."

"Doc," Wind said with a grin, "we've been set up. You keep an eye on this woman, otherwise she'll have us men pulling the son-of-a-bitch behind the bikes while she sits inside and steers."

Dr. Hamilton grinned and said, "Let's go gents." Then to Davata, "You didn't happen to see if it was parked on a hill or not did you?"

By the time they returned, she made them a breakfast of eggs, cheese, and toast. "Did you find a truck?" she asked.

"Not only did we find one, we found tools to get it running and even some diesel in a tank behind the house two doors down. It's sitting on a small hill, so we should be able to get it started by pushing it," Melon explained.

"Now, where the hell did you come up with the cheese?" Wind asked, looking at the table and then back to her.

"If you trim off the green stuff on the outside, it leaves only the good cheese from the middle," Davata answered with a smile. "Now, since we have transportation, I suggest all you big strong men eat up so you will have the strength to get the thing started."

Wind looked at her doubtfully but ate as much as the rest. After eating, they gathered their things and prepared to leave. Then Wind said, "Don't think feeding us makes us forget how sneaky you can be, girl."

"Darn," Davata exclaimed, "you saw right through me."

With the entire group in a lighter mood, they all climbed into the truck, pushed it down the short hill, and entered the west lane of Interstate 12. The was an extended cab and provided ample room for all of them to ride in comfort.

They figured they would reach San Antonio at least by noon the following day. They also planned to circle Beaumont and Houston, staying out of the main part of the cities, as much as possible.

They made good time traveling about 70 miles an hour on the interstate until they rounded a sharp curve and came face to face with a four-car pile-up.

"Goddamn!" Wind exclaimed and swerved to his left. The four vehicles only left a small opening between a car and an eighteen-wheeler.

Wind flew into the small space, and Melon shouted, "Son-of-a-bitch."

It felt as if Wind had slammed on the brakes, and there was a loud squeal as metal scraped metal on both sides of the truck. When they popped from the opening, they were barely traveling twenty miles per hour.

Wind guided the truck to the side of the road, put it in neutral, set the parking brake, and put his head on the steering wheel.

Davata climbed from the cab and walked to the front of the truck. "You've gotta come out here and see this."

Dr. Hamilton and Melon climbed from the vehicle and walked toward her. As he did, Melon slowed down and looked at the side of the truck.

When he reached Davata, she said, "Look there," and pointed at the truck's side.

"It's the same on the other side," Melon said. "We scrapped both sides getting through. He lifted his chin toward the small breach in the pile-up.

Wind finally opened his door and climbed out.

"Look at the side," Melon called to him.

"That was a helluva demonstration of driving," Dr. Hamilton said.

"You may be a good driver," Melon said, "maybe even a great driver, but that was pure luck, my man."

"More than you'll ever know," Wind answered. "I've got no idea how we made it through there."

"I hate to be this way," Dr. Hamilton said, "but we need to be going. I also think you should keep driving." He said the last sentence to Wind. "I know it's hard, but like they say, you have to get right back on the horse."

"I don't mind driving," Wind answered, but you can bet your ass we won't be doing any seventy miles an hour."

Climbing back into the severely scarred truck, they continued their trip much more slowly. Occasionally, they would see people along the road. Most of the ones they spotted would move away from the highway or attempt to hide. Very few were willing to remain in the open and take a chance on the occupants of passing vehicles being friendly.

Shortly after circling Beaumont, Dr. Hamilton noticed a group of mutants as they exited a building in the distance. The creatures took no precautions to remain unseen. They didn't withdraw and try to hide themselves like many the other ones they saw.

"Look," the doctor said, pointing in the direction of the animals. "They're not acting like the others we've seen before. The others were shy and timid. These aren't."

"Not the ones I saw," Davata told him. "The ones that killed Andy were never shy or timid. They came looking for us in broad daylight and then attacked under the cover of darkness. There was nothing fearful about them. They were brutal and their attack was well planned and executed."

"You make it sound like they planned it," Melon said.

"They did," she answered. "There was nothing accidental or incidental about it."

Melon looked at her but said nothing.

As they continued driving, the creatures turned to follow their progress as the vehicle passed. A couple of them raised their heads and appeared to be sniffing the air.

The group circled Houston with no major problems, and Melon took over the driving. However, about half way between Houston and San Antonio, they saw a commotion on the road ahead of them. The sun was barely above the horizon and allowed them to see there were faint, flickering lights, which looked as if they were from torches all grouped together about a half mile ahead. Melon pulled to the side of the road to avoid discovery while discussing their situation.

"Looks like there's a gathering of people up there," Melon said. "Wonder what it's all about?"

"There's no telling," Davata said, squinting to see better through the growing darkness. "But we have to find out what's going on if we're to continue on the interstate."

"Well, either one of us is going to have to go up there and find out what's going on," Dr. Hamilton said, "or we go back about eight miles and take a road back there, which will take us over near Austin. From there, we can cut across through the hill country and get to about anywhere we want to be. The only thing is-it will add about twenty miles to our trip."

"I vote we go back and go the Austin route," Melon said. "It may be longer, but for all our immediate safety, I think it's best."

"What do you think, Wind?" Davata asked, looking at the young man.

"I've got no idea what's going on up there," he said, "but, whatever it is, it don't concern me at the present time. I think we need to turn around, go back, and read about whatever it is up there in the paper tomorrow."

Melon turned the truck around and headed back the way they previously came in order to take the alternate road. "You can have my paper delivered to my hotel room along with room service," he said, accelerating to get more distance between them and the other group.

***

A half mile ahead of where the small group turned around, a group of eight mutants waited for the vehicle they could see and hear in the distance

120

to arrive. They lit torches to draw any possible travelers to their location. After all, it had worked many times before.

CHAPTER THIRTEEN

The next morning, Kyle awoke early. He went to Spyder and shook him. A bleary-eyed Spyder rolled on to his back and looked up. "Shhh," Kyle hushed, looking around to make sure no one could hear them. "Come on," he finished in a whisper and motioned for the other man to follow.

Spyder climbed from under his blankets, rose, glanced at the others who were still sleeping, and followed Kyle away from the campfire. The two of them moved about fifty yards away from camp, to the far side of a stand of trees before squatting

Kyle was the first to speak. "Wanna do some recon?"

"Sure," Spyder answered, "whatcha wantin' to do?"

"Let's check out what our friends are doing down there," Kyle said, tilting his head in the direction of the resort area.

"Think we oughta let somebody know where we're going?" Spyder asked.

"Nah," Kyle answered. "We'll be back before any of them are up. Besides, we don't need more than two of us stomping around making a bunch of noise."

Both men stood up, turned, and found themselves face to face with Lynn.

"Gentlemen," Lynn said her arms crossed under her breasts, "now, exactly what the hell do you think you're gonna do?"

"We're gonna do some looking around," her husband answered. "Make sure everything's okay."

"No you're not," she said, firmly. "We're supposed to have a meeting in camp after breakfast. Then we'll decide what to do next."

"We'll be back shortly," Kyle told her.

"No you won't-you'll go back now, or I'll wake the whole camp up and send 'em after you."

"Shit!" Kyle said, walking toward the campfire. "There's no sense arguing with her Spyder. Let's go."

"Hell, I wasn't gonna argue with her in the first damn place," Spyder said as he turned to follow the other man.

***

When Spyder, Lynn, and Kyle arrived back at camp, the others, except for Ginny and Cindy, were waking up. Earlier, the two women fed the horses and started fixing breakfast for the rest of camp.

The camp known as Rebel's Revenge started to come to life and move around. Each person performed his or her own particular morning ritual to prepare them to face the day. A while later, after having breakfast and cleaning up, the members gathered around the campfire to discuss their situation and look at possible solutions.

The discussion started out with everyone telling what they individually knew of the current situation. Each gave accounts of the loss of electricity.

"I woke up and put my hand on a melted blob that was once my alarm clock," Bear said.

"My problem was my truck," Spyder said. "It wouldn't start when Ginny and I tried to get away after the trailer caught fire. The thing that pissed me off was it caught fire before I could have my coffee."

It was obvious everyone was trying to keep his spirits up. After a lull in the conversation, David stood up and said, "Look folks. We all have some idea of what happened. We don't know why, but we do know the results."

They all nodded in agreement and mumbled among themselves. David continued, "We have some supplies, weapons, and a considerable amount of talent." He paused and looked at all the people around him, letting what he said sink in. "Now, if things are really as bad as we think they very well may be, I think it's time for us to stop playing games and get serious."

"David, I don't know about you," Kyle stood up to speak. "But, I'm not playing games. I'm as serious about this as a heart attack."

"Kyle, I'm not saying anything as an insult," David told him. "But, it's time for us, as a group, to look at handling this thing as a long term problem. We're gonna have to look at defense, gathering food, growing food when we can, and in the long run, getting things back to as normal as possible."

"Plus, keeping whatever that creature was we saw last night at a distance," Bear added. "I don't know about anyone else, but I'm not ready to have to defend myself against a group of those things."

"Bear," Kyle said, "you're overreacting to what you saw."

"Bullshit, Kyle," Bear answered. "You can shove your macho garbage up your ass. If we, as a group, ever have to face just two or three of whatever those were, we're dead."

"Bear, look," Kyle, still standing, now began to pace, "It was only some type of animal. It wasn't armed. It was simply big."

"Kyle," David said. "I saw that thing last night too, and I agree with Bear. The thing was not only big, but it looked like it was hunting those men. It knew where to wait-hiding in the shadows-and when to attack, which would mean it has intelligence or is one hell of a natural predator."

"I think you're both worrying about something before it's really a problem," Kyle answered. "We have enough problems with the people around here, some of whom are armed. I think they're who we need to worry about."

"Well, gents," Spyder started. "I don't know about everyone else here, but I think you both have a valid concern. We definitely need to keep our eyes open for any of those things we saw last night. At the same time, we need to be real cautious of anyone approaching the camp. We shouldn't let just anyone in that comes up. One other thing I'm seeing is the need for us to decide on a leader. There're too many chiefs and not enough Indians.

CHAPTER FOURTEEN

"Morning," Keith said, seeing Mike enter the room.

"Morning," Mike returned.

"There's instant coffee on the stove if you want some."

"Thanks, man." Mike proceeded toward the kitchen.

"What do you plan to do from here on?" Keith asked, sipping his coffee.

"I'm not sure. What about the two of you? What are you going to do?"

"We talked about it the other day," Keith said, "and both realize we're not in the best of situations here. With what I've seen of the bunch down the road-you know, the ones you met yesterday-things seem to be getting worse."

"I have to agree," Mike said. "But I don't know where to go any safer."

"As much as I hate to admit it, this isn't the right place to be waiting this thing out," Keith said.

"Do you know this area very well?" Mike asked.

"I was born and raised here," Keith answered. "I know almost all this part of the hill country up to the north part of Lake Brazos, at least. Beyond there, I'm kinda sketchy."

"What kind of area is this?"

"There's a lot of hills and tourists along with the locals," Keith explained. "There's no real industry except in San Antonio, Austin, or along I35."

"Are all the locals like the ones I met down the road?"

"By now, I imagine so," Keith answered. "Let me put it this way. I wouldn't bet my life on how anyone will act now."

I imagine that's smart thinking." After a pause, Mike asked, "What have you heard about Austin?"

"Nothing," Keith answered. "I haven't seen anyone I cared to talk to about what's happening. Amanda and I have mostly holed up here and waited to see if things would improve."

"The only real possibility I see for surviving this is for us to find a town or even a city, which will afford us protection. I don't think any one of the three of us is capable of keeping ourselves safe on our own. No insult intended, Keith. You've proven yourself up to now. But I think it would be safer with a group of people than with only the three of us."

Keith noticed how Mike included himself with him and Amanda as he spoke. He also realized what Mike said made sense. However, whether it made sense or not, he knew his chances with Amanda were slowly slipping away.

Mike gave him a strange look. "Is there something wrong? You look a little uncomfortable. Is it because I'm here?"

"Being honest, yes. You've only been here one day, and you're already trying to make decisions for Amanda and me. I've done okay for her and me, and we don't need someone we don't know coming around and telling us what to do.

Mike was quiet for a moment and then said, "Keith, can I ask you to keep a secret?"

Keith looked at him cautiously and answered, "As long as it doesn't include Amanda."

"Well, in a way it does," he said. "Look, I've dealt with some real problems with this situation, and I'm not looking for any more responsibility. I had to kill some bikers and some of those mutants, and I don't want anyone else to rely on me right now. Before all this, I made decisions from a desk in an office. I'm used to running a corporation and the problems that come with it. I'll kill if I have to, but I don't want to be in the position of making that type of decision, at least for a while. I'd rather leave it up to someone else for now."

Keith nodded and visibly relaxed. This was the kind of information he was waiting for. This new addition to his life might be help in a physical sense, but he had no training in survival and no idea how to handle a situation of a life threatening nature-no matter what he said or claimed. *For that matter, I doubt he's killed anything in his life. Otherwise, he wouldn't have been such a wuss last night. This will also mean that I'll be making all the decisions about our safety.*

Mike continued, "I'm good with a gun but prefer to use my hands

"Don't worry about it, Mike. If you're willing to do what I say and work toward all our safety, we will do fine." Keith knew something was wrong. He was a black belt in karate and had watched how Mike carried himself. It was doubtful he knew martial arts. However, for right now Keith was satisfied to wait and watch.

128

***

The front door opened and Amanda came in. Seeing the two men in the room, she smiled and said, "We have to talk."

Both men looked at her and waited.

Amanda was outside thinking about their situation and thought she had an answer. Keith was her *guardian angel*, as she now thought of him; and with the addition of Mike, she thought there was a better than average chance of the three of them getting to Fracas. Her aunt and uncle there were self-sufficient and would be equipped to handle this situation.

She entered the house, went into the kitchen, refilled her coffee cup, and came back to the front room with Keith and Mike. "I have a couple of relatives in Fracas, Texas, north of here, and I think they'll be willing to help us if we can get there," she said as the two men watched her attentively. "I know, we've been pretty safe and secure here, but I don't think this will last forever. Mike, no offense to you, but I know what Keith is capable of handling and feel safe with his decisions. You are new to both of us, and even though I imagine you want to be as safe as possible, I would feel safer with Keith being in charge. I don't want to insult you or make you angry, but I feel it's for the best if Keith is the leader here."

Keith and Mike looked at each other. Suddenly, a big grin spread over Mike's face, and both he and Keith broke in to laughter.

Amanda looked at the two men, slightly confused.

A moment later, Mike said, "We were just talking about that very subject."

"We were trying to figure out how to break the news to you that we had reached the same conclusion," Keith explained. "Now, you say you have come up with the same decision as us two geniuses."

"Sorry to laugh," Mike said. "But, we seem to all be thinking on the same wavelength."

Amanda let out a sigh of relief. She worried she might be adding a problem to an already touchy situation.

"Now tell us about those relatives of yours," Mike said, leaning back on the couch.

"Well, they're my Aunt Mae and Uncle Clifton," Amanda explained. "They have a farm with goats, chickens, pigs, and cattle. The last time I heard from them, there were also three or four horses. I believe if we can get there, we will be set for food and Uncle Clifton has a bunch of guns he collects, so we should be pretty safe."

Mike looked at Keith who asked, "They're in Fracas?"

"Right," Amanda answered.

"Where's this Fracas?" Mike asked.

"It's about forty miles from here," Keith answered. "We can get there in a couple of days."

"What about the area and country between here and there?" Mike pressed.

"It's kinda rough," Keith told him. "But, if we're careful, we can make it okay. We'll simply go up highway 281 to 409 and across. There's a road from there to RR133 called Hell's Acre Road. From there we take RR26 through Rollingblock and on to Fracas."

"There's a shortcut my family uses," Amanda interjected. "If we take it, we can cut at least ten miles off our trip; and we still use 409 to get to it."

"I vote we do it," Mike said without hesitation.

Amanda nodded and Keith said, "We leave first thing in the morning. Today, we need to gather supplies and get ready."

Mike stood up and said, "Me and my backpack are ready to go. What else do we need to do?"

After refilling their cups, they sat down to discuss what they would need for the trip.

CHAPTER FIFTEEN

Davata and her group backtracked, followed County Road 125 to Highway 290, and reached the outskirts of Austin Texas. Using a map they found, Dr. Hamilton pointed out a farm-to-market road across to the town of Flat Top. He told them that before the blackout, Flat Top was a town of a couple of hundred people located on Interstate 35. Now, they found only empty houses. Not a single soul appeared to be in the small community, which suited Davata just fine. Situated on the edge of the hill country, it gave them a place to rest before venturing off into the hills and trees before them.

"There is a road leading to the west connecting to Ranch Road fifteen, which will take us to highway 281," Dr. Hamilton told the group as they settled down in a nice two-story house for the night. "Two eighty-one will allow us to go directly to San Antonio or north up into the hill country."

"What's between San Antonio and us?" Wind asked, laying some of their supplies out on the kitchen counter.

"A lot of hills and trees," Dr. Hamilton answered. "We could go straight down I35 and get to San Antonio quicker, but I have friends on RR15; and maybe they can tell us how safe the area is. They may have information on what the safest areas are. With what we've seen, I doubt San Antonio is any better off than any of the other larger cities. I guess it was only wishful thinking. Before the blackout, its population was about one million people."

Davata came in from investigating the rest of the house. You aren't going to believe what I found." As the three men watched, she went to the kitchen sink and turned the handle. "Water," she said as a stream poured from the faucet. "There's a water tower about three blocks away, which must still have water in it. You can see it from a window upstairs. There's not a lot of pressure, but there's enough for us to be able to use."

Everyone gathered around the sink to see the water pouring from the faucet. Only a short time ago, water from a faucet was expected and taken for granted. Now, it was a miracle. Obviously, the pumps were shut down, but the weight of the water, high above the level of the town, was enough to supply water to the houses.

"Guess who's taking a shower," Melon said with a grin. "No sponge bath for me tonight."

Then Dr. Hamilton interrupted, "Now, hang on folks. I'm going to have to test the water and make sure it's all right to use. The tests will only take an hour or so-same as all the others I've done-but they have to be done. Remember the batch we found in Louisiana."

"What about Louisiana?" Davata asked.

"We found some water in a ground level storage area with microbes in it," Dr. Hamilton explained. "If we had drunk any of it, we would have been dead within forty-eight hours. That's why I've been testing all the water we use since you joined us."

133

"I sure didn't know that," Davata answered. Then she added, "Test doctor, test." She looked over at Melon and smiled. "You're not the only one who wants to take advantage of a good thing."

Dr. Hamilton took a small bag in the next room along with a sample of water from the tap. The rest of the group gathered around the kitchen table, sat down, and relaxed.

"What did you do where you come from?" Davata asked looking at Wind.

"Not much," Wind answered. "I was in my first year of college on a track scholarship when all this happened."

"A track scholarship?" Davata questioned.

"Yeah," Wind answered. "I was in the hundred meter dash-never got to prove myself though. The world fell apart before I got a chance to run in even one meet. It was the only way I could afford to get to college. My father ran off when I was three, and my momma raised my sister and me by herself. She did her best, but I still worry about turning out like he did. I'm not sure I made Mamma as happy as I could.

"I'm sure you're wrong there," Melon said. Then looking at Davata he said, "It's like I told you, when we ran into trouble back there in Mississippi, he showed what he was made of. He passed up a chance to get away and instead, came back for the rest of us."

Wind looked down at the table, and Davata looked over at him.

"Not only did he show what his mother taught him right, but he showed what an athlete he was. I've never witnessed anyone move as fast as he did."

134

Wind was still looking at the table, when Davata asked him, "What happened to your mother and sister?"

"I don't know," he answered. "I was at school when all this happened. I left the school, and two days later made it home. No one was there. I looked around for three days but never found them. I went down to South Mississippi to a relative's house, and they were gone too. That was when Melon and I met up."

For a while, they sat in silence, lost in their own thoughts. A little over an hour after starting the water tests, Dr. Hamilton came out. He had no problem gaining everyone's attention as he looked at each of them in turn with a look that indicated a problem.

"Well here's the part where he says there's good news and bad news," Davata said. "I don't need any bad news for a while so just give us the good, okay?"

Dr. Hamilton cleared his throat and said, "The water is completely usable for bathing and drinking."

"Okay, now that's news I can live with," Davata said, smiling.

"No shit," Wind agreed.

The doctor stood there waiting until everyone calmed down. Then, he said, "Now for the bad news."

Everyone went somber, looked at him and waited.

"There are two bathrooms in this house and only enough water pressure to support one, and there's no way to heat it. This means some will have to stay dirty a little longer than the others."

Everyone burst into laughter, the tension relieved. "I'll rassle you fer it," Wind said to Melon.

"Rassle?" Davata repeated.

"Well if I'm in Texas, I might as well talk like Texans do," Wind answered.

"Well, while you two rassle, I'll be upstairs taking a shower," Davata said.

"Now just what makes you think you're getting the first shot at inside falling water?" Melon asked, with a sly smile. "Unless of course, you want rassle for it."

Instantly, Wind grabbed her from behind, and Melon reached down and grabbed her feet. Davata, caught off guard, could only wiggle in their grip.

"Do ya give up, ma'am?" Wind asked.

Laughing, Davata said, "I give up, I give up. You win. But remember it took two of you to beat me."

Laughing, the two men put her back on the floor, feet first. "Well, I guess it's between you and me, partner," Wind said.

"Where's the doctor?" Davata asked looking around alarmed. None of them saw or heard the doctor leave the room.

A door closed upstairs. Without checking, they all knew it was Dr. Hamilton shutting the upstairs bathroom door. All they could do was look at each other and laugh even harder.

***

136

Wind was awake a little before sunrise. He climbed out of bed, dressed, and wandered into the kitchen. He put on a pot of water on the gas stove to make coffee. While waiting for the water to boil, he walked down the block to an intersection and saw a large building with "library" painted on the front. Across the street, there was a building with "Laundr-O-Mat" painted on the window. Beside it was a used car dealership. *Those are about as useless as warts on a pickle.*

He looked up and saw a group of figures a little over a block away. They crossed from right to left, heading in the general direction of the house now occupied by his three friends.

Oh shit. They're only about two houses down from the others. Wind thought fast and started walking down the middle of the street toward the group. He only walked about ten steps when someone in the group saw him.

A man yelled, and he and the rest started running toward Wind. He waited, letting them get closer. They were yelling and cursing as they moved closer.

When they were about fifty yards away, Wind turned and headed out. He went straight down the middle of the street for two blocks and then turned left. A half-block later, he turned right and up an alley. As he turned, he looked back. The group was unable to keep up, so he slowed down a little. He wanted them to stay within sight so they would keep after him. They entered the alley about forty yards behind him. Knowing he could run off and leave them at any time gave him an extra boost of confidence.

137

He turned left at the next street and accelerated, looking back to see how far the mob was behind him. When he looked forward again, he saw three figures standing in the street at the next intersection.

Wind instantly knew these weren't humans. *I'm in deep shit.* He skidded to a stop as the three figures started moving swiftly toward him.

He looked at the creatures then at where the mob would soon be. *Screw this. I'm taking my chances with the crazy humans.* He turned and raced to where they would exit the alley. As he approached the spot, the mob came out into the street.

He moved to the center of the street and as the mob approached him. He could tell they saw the creatures running toward them by their screams, shouts, and curses. The two groups, the three creatures and the mob, would meet each other where he stood.

Wind turned back toward the creatures, pointed and yelled, "Get 'em, get 'em."

It must have been the right thing. The mob turned their full attention to the figures moving toward them and angled their attack away from him.

At the last moment, Wind sprinted to the side. The two groups ran together in a mixture of grunts, growls, and screams. Not waiting for the outcome, he headed back to the house.

He jogged three blocks out of his way, in case any of those left behind saw where he had gone, although he doubted it. They were engaged in a life and death struggle of their own.

Arriving back at the house, he found all his friends up and searching the grounds for him.

"What the hell happened to you?" Dr. Hamilton asked.

"There isn't time to explain," Wind answered, panting. "I'll tell you later. Now, we need to get everything gathered up and get the hell outta here-and hurry."

It took them less than five minutes to get all their things thrown together and in the back of the truck. The men pushed while Davata steered. When she popped the clutch, the truck roared to life. They all climbed in and headed out.

Dr. Hamilton gave directions how to get to the road they needed. Luckily, the road was in a different direction than where Wind's pursuers were.

About five miles out of town, Melon asked, "Now, what the hell was that all about?"

Wind explained what had happened and how he escaped from both groups. He told them about the group of humans and mutants clashing and how he managed to get away without detection. "By the way, did anyone turn the fire off under the boiling water?"

They all looked at each other shaking their heads "no."

"Well there's going to be one hell of a fire, then," Wind said.

***

As they traveled down the road from Flat Top, the group was constantly on the lookout for any movement of people or mutants. They saw none. When they were a couple of miles from the village

139

of Rollingblock, Davata announced they were going to need fuel.

"Do you know anything about this place?" Wind asked the doctor.

"It's probably changed considerably since I was last here," Dr. Hamilton answered. "This area was growing rapidly, and I'm sure the population has doubled or tripled since then."

What about going into town?" Davata asked. "Should we take the truck?"

"I don't think so," the doctor answered. "Back then the buildings were clustered close together. If anyone is left there now, I don't think we want to draw any more attention to ourselves than we absolutely have to."

"How close to town are we now?" Wind asked.

"About a mile if I remember correctly," Dr. Hamilton answered. "In fact, let's park over there," he said, pointing to a building on the left side of the road.

The building displayed a sign proclaiming it an auto body shop. Davata pulled into the spacious parking She backed into a partially secluded area in the corner of the lot, situating the truck so it could be started by pushing it down the slope of the parking lot.

Climbing from the cab, they each took at least two weapons along with some ammunition and began walking toward town. About half a mile along, the road split. They took the right fork and continued along a tree-lined street with buildings standing on each side. Some buildings appeared to be small businesses and some private residences, and all appeared abandoned.

As they approached town, the buildings became more congested. A short distance away, the street curved to the left. Dr. Hamilton pointed ahead. "If I remember correctly, around the curve up there is the *square*. There are lots of retail businesses all around it, so keep your eyes open."

"Let's get out of the middle of the street," Wind suggested. "I don't like being this exposed."

They moved to the left side of the road, and heeding Dr. Hamilton's advice, continued more cautiously. Upon reaching a building, Wind or Melon would carefully check for any signs of life. All of the structures stood empty and appeared to be pieces of a jigsaw puzzle of a ghost town. As they reached a gas station on the edge of the square, a shot rang out. Four more followed the first in rapid succession.

Across the square, a man carrying a rifle ran toward them. His limp indicated he was hit by one of the shots. Still he kept running, approaching where they crouched, concealed by flower planters alongside a gas station lane.

On the opposite side of the square, two other men chased the first, both armed with rifles of their own. Every few steps they would either fire from their hips at the fleeing man or take the extra time to pull the weapon up to their shoulder before shooting.

The lone man was now in the street separating the square from the gas station. It looked like he would make it to where the group watched the situation unfold. To Davata, time seemed to slow down. The man ran in slow motion. His limp didn't allow him to sprint to safety. Instead, determination etched itself on his weather-aged face as he limped to get out of the line of fire. Then a shot hit him in the back, sending him sprawling on the gas station drive.

Wind stepped out and fired three rapid shots from his 9mm. Davata knew how he felt. He wasn't willing to allow another person to be killed for no apparent reason. He wasn't trying to hit the others just give them something to think about.

Immediately, Melon joined him and fired two shots of his own. The move worked, and the pursuers turned and sprinted for a building on the opposite side of the square.

As the men tried to escape, Melon and Wind hurried to the downed man, grabbed him under each arm and dragged him back to where Davata and the doctor waited.

Wind kept a watchful eye on the door where the men entered the building. Dr. Hamilton looked at the injured man's back. A few seconds later, he looked up at Davata and shook his head, indicating the man was beyond his assistance.

When they rolled him over and his eyes fluttered open. His face showed signs of a hard life. Deep creases lined his features.

Even in death, the lines add character to him, Davata thought.

The injured man's lips moved as he tried to speak. Taking a deep breath, he whispered, "Behind the Silver Spoon." His breathing, ragged and shallow, caught in his chest as he tried to draw air into his lungs. He struggled to reach into his coat and removed part of something from his coat. Taking another jagged breath he said, "Flag pole."

142

Davata reached down and pulled the rest of a folded up bed sheet from under his coat. Inside one of the folds, she saw a piece of paper. Written on it were the words, *"Are you a traveling man or traveling from the east?"* with the answer, *"I'm looking for a lodge to meet in."*

The man took another breath and said, "Bear-1700." The breath escaped his body in a long sigh as life left him.

"Did any of this make any sense to you, Doctor Hamilton?" Davata asked.

The doctor reached down and closed the half-open eyes of the man before them. "Yes it does," he answered and looked at the ring on his finger. "I know what it means, but I don't know how or when to use it."

"Where are those other men, Wind?" Davata asked the young man standing guard at the corner of the building.

"It looks like they left through the back of the building they were in and ran off between those other buildings away from us," Wind told her.

"What was all that stuff he said?" Melon asked.

"There's more than what he said," Davata unfolded the sheet and saw a red cross painted on it in magic marker.

"We can't just sit here," Melon said. "There may be more where those others came from."

"He's right," Dr. Hamilton answered. "The road curves right over there," He pointed over to the edge of the square.

"I'm not too crazy about crossing that open space with the possibility of those guys having friends," Wind interjected. "If the road curves right, then I suggest we go behind those buildings across the street." He pointed at a group of low structures on the opposite side of the road they used to enter the town. "If we stay behind those, we can stay out of sight and hopefully reach the road on the other side of the curve."

"Will that work?" Davata asked, looking at Dr. Hamilton.

"It should," he answered, "and I agree. I want to stay out of open spaces for right now."

The group reluctantly left the body of the man close to the gas station and quickly crossed the street. Once on the other side, they went between two buildings and found themselves on a riverbank.

***

Lush vegetation added visual impact to the peace and quiet of the area surrounding the river. The only sound was the water as it flowed around and over rocks occasionally protruding above its surface. Large Cypress and Spanish Oak trees were plentiful here and served as homes to numerous species of birds.

Davata stopped behind a building and waited for the others to gather. "We need a lookout up at the front of the buildings," she said.

"I've got it." Melon hurried between two structures and disappeared around the front of the building.

Davata spread the sheet on the ground and sat beside it. She unfolded the note she had found.

"What was it he said?" Dr. Hamilton asked. "Something about a Silver Spoon."

144

"Behind the Silver Spoon," she repeated, "and Bear-1700. What is it-an address?"

"Nope," Wind answered. "It's five o'clock in the afternoon."

"How do you know?" She asked.

"No, I agree with him, Davata," the doctor said. "In the U.S. it's known as military time. But in the rest of the world, it's the way they tell the time of day."

"Then, if that's right, he might be meeting this Bear at five o'clock or 1700 hours," Wind said, recognizing a pattern. "... or a bear passes by here at the same time every day, which I'm sure is not the case-and look at the note. If this man was in the military, or was in the past, then this note is probably something like a password."

Davata read it aloud, "'Are you a traveling man, or traveling from the east?' 'Just lookin' for a lodge to meet in.'"

"You're pretty good at this," Dr. Hamilton said to Wind. "I know what that last part means. Don't worry about it for now."

"Thanks," Wind said, "but what does the sheet have to do with it?"

"When he pulled it out, he said the word 'flagpole,'" the doctor answered.

"Of course," Davata said. "We have to raise this on the flagpole to signal someone-maybe this Bear person." She looked at up at the men. "Now the question is who wants to volunteer to go raise a flag with those nuts out there?"

"I think I may know a way to do it," Wind answered.

"Before we do anything," Davata interrupted. "Do we want to?"

"What do you mean?" Dr. Hamilton asked.

"Well," she took a deep breath and let it out with a sigh. "How do we know they're the good guys? I mean all we saw was two men chasing one. How do we know they weren't chasing someone who was a danger to them and maybe even us?"

"You could be right," Wind said. "But how do we make sure?"

"If the dead man meant us harm, I don't think he would have used his last breath to give us information," Dr. Hamilton answered. "The last part of the note also tells me we can trust him."

"You may be right," Davata said. "I just wanted to throw out the possibility. Most people who know they're dying will speak the truth. Not always, but most will."

"I have a gut feeling about this one too," Wind said. "I know this is stupid, but for some reason, the guy looked honest."

"Wind, you said you might have a way for us to get the flag up," Davata said. "I think we agree we need to do this. Of course, Melon should have a vote too."

"Let me tell you what I've thought of and if we agree, we can talk to him about it."

"Agreed," Dr. Hamilton answered and looked at Davata.

Davata simply nodded her agreement and waited.

"Well, there are four of us and four sides to the square," Wind explained. We make sure this side is clear. We then split up, each taking a different side,

146

and make sure the other buildings are empty. Once we see it's clear, Dr. Hamilton can go out and raise the flag. Then we all return here and wait." As he explained, he used a stick to draw a picture of the square and their position in relation to it.

"That looks like it might just work," Dr. Hamilton said when Wind finished.

"It seems to be a good way of covering all the sides quickly and safely." Davata said.

"Why don't I go tell Melon what we've talked about and see what he thinks?" Wind suggested.

Dr. Hamilton and Davata nodded, and Wind moved off to Melon's location.

"If our plan was to get to your friend's house, why are we doing this?" Davata asked the doctor after Wind left.

"Look at Wind's reaction," the doctor answered. "People need other people, for the most part. If there are other people here and they are friendly, it'll be a huge boost for all of us." He hesitated then added, "I also now have a debt to repay."

"Makes sense to me, except for the debt part," Davata answered. "Last night, I was thinking about something as simple as laughing. I didn't remember how long it's been since I was able to laugh, and I realized how much I missed it."

They heard a sound at the corner of the building, and Wind appeared. "Looks like it's a go," he said, sitting next to Davata.

"When do we do this?" Davata asked, looking at Dr. Hamilton.

"I was thinking about that too," Wind answered before the doctor could say anything. "We have no

147

way of telling time and neither does this Bear person. I suggest we do it as soon as possible. Then we can wait out of sight until someone makes contact."

"We need to get ready to move," the doctor said and smiled.

"Oh, and Doc," Wind said. "I could see there's still a rope on the flagpole, which means you can run it all the way up."

"We might as well get this done," Davata said, standing.

Dr. Hamilton folded the flag, and then he and Wind followed Davata to Melon's location. There, they found Melon sitting on a large log near the corner of the building. He sat with his back against one wall, chewing on a sliver of grass.

"Have you seen anything?" Davata asked.

"Not a thing," he answered. "Not a movement of any kind."

"Is everyone ready?" Wind asked. When the others nodded, he said, "We all go at the same time. Be careful and don't rush. We have to be quick, but don't overlook anything."

As one, they all moved out, each taking a different route to an assigned location. They worked their way to positions where they could watch for the approach of others while the doctor ran the sheet up the flagpole.

With everyone in position, Dr. Hamilton emerged from the side of the building and quickly moved to the flagpole. He attached the flag and ran it to the top of the pole in less than twenty seconds, and waved to the rest. They retreated to where they began only a minute before.

"All the buildings were clear on my side of the square," Wind reported.

"Same here," Melon said.

"I didn't see anyone or anything," Davata said. "However, I can't be sure no one was watching from somewhere else."

"None of us can be sure of that," Dr. Hamilton said. "Why don't the rest of you take a break, and I'll keep watch."

**

A while later Davata relieved the doctor on watch.

"Have you seen anything?" She asked, handing him a bottle of water.

"Nothing," he answered and took a drink.

"What time do you think it is?"

"It looks to be about four."

"Why don't you take a break and get some rest," she suggested.

"I think I'll do that," he said, rising to his feet and stretching. "Thanks for the water." He gave her a smile and disappeared around the corner.

About ten minutes later, Davata hurried around the corner. Dr. Hamilton, Wind, and Melon immediately rose to their feet. "There're five men coming into the square from the other side," she said.

The men gathered their weapons and followed Davata to where she previously kept watch.

Looking out from between the buildings, they saw five men walking to the center of the square. They didn't seem to worry about the possibility of

149

attack. Their only movement of caution was that they kept scanning the surrounding buildings for possible danger.

Their attitude seemed to be a challenge to anyone or anything around. They were all dressed in ragged clothes, which resembled torn and filthy military uniforms, carried rifles, and wore pistols on their hips. As they talked among themselves, they cursed and laughed loudly.

They didn't seem to notice the flag even though they stood directly below it.

One of the men asked, "Are you sure Rat said they shot the bastard on the square?"

"That's what he said," another answered. "Said he hit him, then some other assholes started shooting back, and they left the body behind."

From the north side of the square came the sound of a loud whistle. The men at the flagpole turned toward the sound. It came from the bend in the road off to Davata's right. A couple of seconds later, three men strolled into view.

The three looked as if they had just stepped off the set of a western movie. They were dressed as cowboys, in western attire with guns strapped to their hips. Each carried a rifle of some sort, and none of them demonstrated any signs of fear or nervousness.

One wore a flat, brown cowboy hat and a brown duster. He actually looked like Wild Bill Hickok as depicted in old photographs. The second had a western hat with the front of the brim pinned up and looked as if he would make the perfect *sidekick* for some cowboy hero. The third wore a dirty white duster and dark brown cowboy hat. His hair coursed down to the middle of his back and his beard was almost as long. As he pulled his duster back, he exposed a row of at least four pistols in various positions and holsters.

One of the cowboys said, "Now take it easy, boys. There's no reason for a problem here."

Immediately, the five at the flagpole began laughing and threw insults at the men standing across the street from them. "If it ain't Wyatt Earp and his brothers," one man said.

"Hell, no," another exclaimed, "It's Marshal Dillon, Festus, and Gabby Hayes. Better watch out boys, they might try to arrest us."

As the cowboy looking like Wild Bill Hickok spoke again, Davata noticed his raspy voice and a strong British accent. "Fellas," he said, "we're just looking for a friend that should be here, that's all. We don't want any trouble."

The men at the flagpole mumbled among themselves, then one of them wearing a beret said, "He wouldn't be the one we killed a couple of hours ago, would it?"

The other four laughed at this.

"I hope not," the cowboy said. "Like I said, we're looking for a friend of ours, and if you shot him, we'd have to take exception to it."

"I didn't say we shot him, asshole," beret corrected. "I said we killed him."

The others again laughed at this statement, one slapping the other on the shoulder. The cowboys looked casually at each other. As the man with the beret and his group turned their attention back to the cowboys, White Coat nodded, and in unison, they all pulled their pistols and fired.

The quiet of the day erupted in explosions from their side arms. Blue smoke spat from each pistol. Davata and her group could see the smoke pushed out of the barrel of each pistol by a tongue of flame.

The men at the flagpole never had a chance to raise their weapons. They stumbled, as hot lead balls slammed into their bodies. Trying to stay on their feet, the men at the flagpole stumbled backward before hitting the pavement. One went airborne as two balls hit him at once. He flew backward about six feet before landing flat on his back.

The shooting stopped as abruptly as it started. Blue smoke filled the entire area between the two groups. The three men walked slowly toward the bodies on the ground before them. Cautiously, they looked around for any help the five might have in the area.

Upon reaching the bodies, they checked for any signs of life. There was none. "Change cylinders and we'll reload back at camp," British Accent said.

It took two of the men less than thirty seconds to remove one cylinder and exchange it with another. While they were doing so, the one in the dirty white duster holstered his weapon, pulled a pair of modern 9mm pistols, and kept watch-his shotgun on the ground. When the other two finished, he reloaded his empty pistol. They holstered their weapons, and stripped the bodies of weapons, which they slung over their shoulders.

As the cowboys removed the guns from the bodies, Davata looked at her friends and whispered, "Wait here." She rose and moved forward.

"Bullshit," Wind said grabbing her by the arm. "You don't know what they'll do."

"I think they were looking for the man we saw shot. They have to be the ones he was looking for." She pulled loose and stepped forward before Wind could say anything else.

"She's got more balls than I do," he said watching Davata walk into the open area.

"I hope not," Melon answered with a smile. "I like her better without them."

As she stepped out, one of the cowboys watched as she emerged from between the buildings. "Heads up," he said to the others as his pistol cleared its holster. Immediately, the other two men placed a hand on their weapons and turned.

Davata raised both hands and stopped. There was a brief pause, and then she said, "Gentlemen, I'm looking for someone named Bear. I'm not armed," she said, pulling her coat open and slowly turning around.

"What about those gents back there behind you?" White Coat asked.

"They're friends and don't want any trouble," Davata answered. "We just didn't want to all step out and possibly cause you to start shooting."

"What have you got to do with these here fellas?" White Coat asked.

"Nothing, in fact," Davata said, "I think they were looking for us. When they were chasing and shooting at the other man, we shot back and ran 'em off."

"Where's the other guy you're talking about?" British accent asked.

"They told you the truth. They shot him while he was running. He died a few minutes later."

"Did this guy have a limp?" White coat asked.

"Yes, he did, come to think of it," Davata responded. "Look, I'm Davata Sanders. We don't know the name of the man who they killed. But before he died, he gave us the flag up there"-Davata pointed at the flag-"and said some things we don't fully understand."

The man with the British accent stepped forward saying, "Kyle Jennings ma'am. Pleased to meet you."

The sidekick came forward, took Davata's extended hand, and introduced himself. "Hal Sloan," he said, a friendly smile on his bearded face.

The last one stepped forward and said, "I'm Spyder, ma'am." His long hair and beard made him look like a mountain man returning to civilization.

Three men emerged from between two of the buildings. Spyder stepped away from the group, motioned with his hand, and yelled, "Come on in boys."

Wind, Melon and Dr. Hamilton walked toward the group at the center of the square. When they arrived, Davata introduced each of them.

Following the introductions, Kyle said, "I think we ought to get outta here. I'm sure these guys have friends somewhere around. Where's Pete's body?"

"He's over behind the gas station," Wind said pointing, "but Dr. Hamilton here checked him out, and he's definitely dead."

"I don't doubt it mister," Spyder said. "But, we can't leave him there. Come summer, what's left of a body might cause disease or something."

They went over to the body. Kyle checked it for anything usable. Finding nothing, he said, "We need to get back to camp." We can come back here later with a wagon and pick him up."

Hal indicated the direction they had come, and the group began walking. After a short distance, Dr. Hamilton pointed at a restaurant with a sign saying, "The Silver Spoon."

"Wait a minute," he said. "Before he died, the gentleman back there said, 'Behind the Silver Spoon.' I wonder if he meant that."

"Behind the Silver Spoon?" Hal repeated. "There's a group of businesses back there."

"Time to check it out, boys and girls," Kyle said leading the way to the back of the building.

Behind the Silver Spoon Cafe was a group of small buildings as Hal promised. They sat in a row along the edge of the creek where Davata and her group rested earlier. As they walked around the end of the last building, they saw a truck.

In the back of the truck, they found weapons, ammunition, and numerous boxes of MREs, as well as tools for fixing guns of all kinds.

"Pete was using his head," Hal said. "There's a slope from here to the road. Let's get this thing going."

"No, wait, "Kyle said, "We don't know how close any friends of those guys might be. We need to get outta here and come back later for the truck and the body."

"Not a chance in hell," Spyder said. "We leave the truck here, and it'll be gone by the time we get back-we take it."

"Spyder, we... " Kyle started.

"There's no sense arguing with him," Hal said. "When he makes up his mind, it's a done thing. Besides, it makes sense. It probably would be gone."

Everyone grabbed hold of the truck and pushed. Following a short roll, Davata released the clutch and again, the vehicle fired into life. They quickly climbed into the truck with Hal behind the wheel. They drove to the camp known as Rebel's Revenge.

Along the way, they traveled beside the slowly meandering Buffalo River, along whose banks grew the same type of large Spanish Oaks, Cypress, and Oak trees Davata's group had previously seen. Even though the banks were still green, patches of brown spread throughout its grass.

After a ride of about five minutes, Hal pulled off the main road and onto what appeared to be only two ruts in the ground. After two hundred yards, he turned again and drove into the trees to the right.

A short distance later, a man stepped out of the bushes and stood in front of the vehicle. Hal stopped and waved as he walked up to the truck.

"David, we got some visitors," Hal said. "Everybody, this is David Alexander." Knowing the man was not alone, he looked around and asked, "Who else is here?"

"Carl is over there," he said, pointing to the right side of the truck, "and Ben's behind me. Where'd you get the truck?"

"Pete brought it," Hal answered.

"Which one's Pete?" David asked, looking at the occupants inside and outside the truck.

"He's dead," Hal told him. "We'll tell you about it later. Now, we need to get this thing unloaded and outta here."

"Okay," David answered and stepped back. "See you in a while."

Hal drove on up, over a hill. As they cleared the trees, the newcomers saw a clearing open up before them. It was almost a hundred yards across with an old western style covered wagon, a place for a large campfire and a long tin building with horses tied to one side.

A couple of people moving around the camp turned to look as the truck rolled up. Hal drove to the end of the long tin building and stopped. He engaged the emergency brake, left the vehicle running, and got out. The rest piled out and grabbed items as they hit the ground.

A short woman came out of the building and pointed to various places they could store things. It only took about ten minutes to unload the truck, and then Hal climbed back inside and drove off.

***

All the members of the camp gathered around and introduced themselves to the new arrivals. After exchanging all their names, Sandy invited Davata and her group to the fire for some coffee. As an afterthought Sandy said, "The rest of you are welcome too. I just want these new people to understand we're not all as strange as we may seem."

157

"Good luck on that," Spyder said with a grin.

Sandy watched as Davata took in her surroundings. The entire group wore western outfits based on styles from the eighteen hundreds-and all of them, including the women and one of the kids, wore pistols strapped to their hips. Sandy read the concern on Davata's face. "We're really not as strange as we must look to you. Most of us were members of a gunfighters group. We used to put on shows depicting scenarios of the Wild West. The clothes we wear are more durable and practical than modern clothes. Nobody worries about style anymore."

"Makes sense," Davata answered. "We saw why the guns are worn. Plus, we've been attacked a couple of times between Mississippi and here."

"What do you mean 'you've seen what the guns are for'?" Sandy asked.

"We saw Hal, Spyder, and Kyle in action."

Sandy looked around and noticed all three men stood away from the rest. They were on the edge of the clearing, each standing or sitting alone.

"What happened?" Sandy asked Davata as she watched her husband.

Davata explained about the five men in the square. She told how Hal, Spyder, and Kyle tried to talk their way out of the confrontation, but in the end, they were forced to shoot and kill the other five men.

"Oh damn," Sandy said, looking at Hal. Spyder and Kyle had joined him, and the three of them talked quietly. Sandy could see by the look on their faces, the men were dealing with what happened.

She turned back to Davata. "That's the first human killing any of us have had to do."

"I'm sorry. I guess I should have let him tell you. I just wasn't thinking."

"No. It's okay. He'll need some time to himself. Actually, I need to thank you. Now, I know how to act around him when he comes back."

"You may not want to hear this," Davata said. "If so, stop me-but it was like watching a western movie. The three simply walked into the square and said why they were there. None of them showed any fear or concern even though the others were talking loudly, cursing, and badmouthing them."

"That says the other men were nervous about what was happening," Sandy explained.

"That's what I thought afterwards," Davata continued. "When they saw they weren't going to be able to talk their way out of the situation, they looked at each other. Then the one called Spyder nodded and immediately, all three drew their guns and began firing. It was over in a couple of seconds. I've never seen anything like it in real life."

"Now look at them," Sandy said, lifting her chin, motioning in the direction of the men. "They're trying to deal with what happened. Believe me. No one here wants to hurt anyone else, but if it comes to it, they'll never hesitate."

"Here they come."

The three men walked into the center of the camp. Without hesitation, Spyder walked over to Wind and stopped before him.

"Oh damn," Sandy said.

Davata looked at her and then back to where Spyder stood.

159

Quickly, Sandy said, "At one time, Spyder was real high up in the KKK." She looked back at the man. "I have no idea what he's up to now."

As Spyder stopped, Wind rose to his feet. Both men stood less than three feet from each other. Spyder eyed the other man for a second then said, "What kinda pistol you got there, son?"

Wind looked down at the weapon then back at Spyder. "Nine millimeter."

"Let's take a look at it." Spyder said, holding his hand out.

Wind simply looked at the other man and asked, "What do you need to see it for?"

Spyder held Wind's gaze and said, "Young man, around here, when someone asks to see your weapon, you give it to 'em."

Wind smiled and said, "Okay, fine. Let me see yours."

The entire camp stopped what they were doing to watch. Everyone knew there was the very real possibility of a problem developing here.

Spyder slowly pulled his duster back exposing three pistols. Two in holsters on his hips and one tucked in his belt. "Which one?"

"The one stuck in the back of your pants," Wind answered in an even voice.

Spyder reached around to his back and produced a thirty-eight-caliber colt revolver. "This one?"

"Yes sir," Wind answered. "That's the one."

In a blink, Spyder spun the pistol so the butt was facing Wind. "It's loaded," was all he said.

Wind picked his pistol up and in the same fashion, spun it and held it out butt first to Spyder. "It's loaded too," Wind told him.

As the men exchanged guns, the tension eased a little. However, the rest of the Regulators watched as the rest of the encounter unfolded.

Spyder pressed the clip release, caught the clip and ejected the round from the chamber. He held the gun up and looked down the barrel, placing his thumbnail to reflect what was left of the sunlight down the shaft.

While Spyder was looking at the 9mm, Wind pushed the cylinder release and rotated it out. All six cylinders were loaded and noticeably clean. He closed the cylinder and held the weapon out to Spyder.

Spyder was sliding the clip back in the handle. He looked at Wind and asked, "How much do you know about weapons like this?"

"I know enough to be able to use one," Wind answered.

"This thing needs to be cleaned," Spyder told him. "Do you know how to do that?"

Wind shook his head slowly and said, "No, probably not the right way."

Spyder handed the pistol back to him and said, "Every one of us here has the right to ask anyone else to see their weapon, at any time. It's a safety thing. Now, young man, if you don't have anything else pressing at this time, I'll teach you how to clean this weapon of yours."

Wind grinned, took his gun and said, "I've got nothing going on right at the moment. Lead the way, sir."

Spyder turned and headed for a table. As he passed Hal, he winked and said, "I think I'm gonna like this guy."

Davata turned back to Sandy, not sure why everyone was worried about what just happened. "Where's this Bear person we've heard about?"

"He's out hunting."

"By himself?" Davata asked, surprised. "Don't any of you worry about those weird animals running around?"

"You mean the mutants?"

"I guess it's as good a way to refer to them as any. Aren't any of you worried about them?"

"Sure we do. But, we haven't experienced any trouble with them in the daylight-only at night."

"We were in Flat Top last night," Davata started to explain, "and this morning, Wind got up and wandered around the area for a little bit. While he was out, a group of men chased him, and they ran into some of those mutants. Obviously, he was able to get away from both, but it was shortly after sunrise when he saw the mutants."

"I guess we've been lucky then," Sandy said. "We've only seen one since all this started. We didn't figure there were very many out roaming around."

"We've seen groups from as few as three to over ten at a time, "Davata explained. "There have also been single ones. The only thing I know they have in common is they're all aggressive. I even saw one driving a yacht in Louisiana."

"Driving a yacht?" Sandy said, shocked.

Davata told her about Andy, and how he died because of a mutant attack. "There's something else. No one but Dr. Hamilton knows, but I'm pregnant."

"Is it your friend Andy's?"

"Yes," Davata answered, "it's his."

"How far along are ya?" Sandy wore a big grin.

"About four or five weeks." After talking to Sandy for only a short time, she was sure she was right and could trust this new friend to keep her secret.

"When are you planning to tell the rest?"

"As soon as we settle down."

"Are you all planning to go somewhere from here?" Sandy was concerned about the young woman being pregnant and facing the hardships of being with a small group.

"I'm not sure. Dr. Hamilton has family somewhere around here-somewhere on a highway 15."

"Ranch Road fifteen," Sandy corrected. "Hal and I lived on that road before all this."

"You may know the doctors relatives."

"It's possible," Sandy said. "I'll have to talk to him. Anyway, you should know you and your group are welcome here."

"That's very kind of you."

"I say you are welcome to stay, but it will actually depend on a vote by everyone here. I didn't mean to mislead you. But I don't see any problem with you joining us."

"I understand," Davata answered. "It's nice to see there are people still trying to work together. In every city we passed, we saw fighting, looting, or heard gunshots all through the night."

From a short distance away, they heard a voice shout, "You can kiss my black ass, you redneck son-of-a-bitch." It was Wind.

Everyone in camp hurried to where Wind and Spyder sat at a table, cleaning their weapons. As people started gathering around them, both men looked up surprised.

"What the fuck are you looking at?" Spyder asked in a gruff voice.

"What's going on here?" David asked as he came from the edge of the clearing. Ben followed on his heels. Both men wore expressions of concern.

"Nothin's going on," Wind answered. "This redneck here was saying that, with my past, he shouldn't have to show me how to clean anything. He said my people have been cleaning things ever since they came to this country."

"Spyder, goddamn," David said. "We don't need trouble here."

"Shit, it's true," Spyder argued. "Not to mention, this peckerhead said that if it wasn't for his people, my people wouldn't even be around because his ancestors did all the work, and we couldn't take care of ourselves."

David looked at both men. "Both of you can kiss my ass." He abruptly turned and walked toward the fire.

Wind looked at Spyder. "Touchy sort, isn't he?"

"Always has been," Spyder answered and picked up another part of a pistol to clean. "Always wantin' to fix something."

When everyone realized Spyder had discovered a new friend and everything was okay, they each

164

returned to various parts of the clearing, leaving the two men working at the table.

CHAPTER SIXTEEN

It was shortly after sunrise when Mike awoke. He sat up and looked around. It took him a couple of seconds to become oriented. Then, he remembered where he was and what was happening.

Yesterday, he, Amanda, and Keith rounded up four horses and traveled all day, trying to get to Magnum, Texas. Late in the afternoon, they found a mobile home where they spent the night.

He climbed out of bed, dressed, and went out into the hallway. He could smell the fresh coffee brewing before he reached the kitchen. Entering the room, he saw Keith bent over looking through the cupboards below the sink.

"Where the hell would they have kept their pots and pans?" Keith asked as he saw Mike come in the room.

"Beats the hell out of me," Mike answered.

Keith opened another cupboard door and said, "Bingo," as he pulled out a frying pan and placed it on the stove.

"What the hell's that for?"

"These." Keith unfolded a towel and produced eight eggs. "Do you like 'em scrambled?" He asked as he set the eggs on the counter.

"Where did you get those?"

"Well, while I was feeding the horses, I heard a bunch of chickens at the next house over."

"The next house over," Mike repeated, sharply. "When did you go and get them?"

"A few minutes ago," Keith answered defensively, hearing the change in Mike's voice.

"You mean you left the two of us alone, unguarded and went looking for food? Are you fucking crazy?"

"Now hold on, Mike... "

"Hold on, my ass," Mike interrupted. "With both of us asleep, you take off and leave us open to attack? What the hell were you thinking?"

"Neither of you were ever in any danger."

"How the hell do you know?" Mike stepped toward the younger man.

"Knock it off," Amanda demanded from the corner of the adjoining hall and kitchen. She entered the room looking at both men. "Both of you calm down."

"Calm down? There's no way I'll calm down as long as this little twerp is willing to leave us open to danger," Mike barked.

"Neither of you were ever in danger," Keith repeated.

"Keith," Amanda interjected. "There's no way you could have known that if you were off down the road. I know you were only trying to do something special for us, but you put us in danger by what you did."

"There wasn't anyone around," Keith argued. "I checked before I left. Then I was only gone about fifteen minutes before I came back."

"Listen to me," Amanda talked in a soothing voice, trying to get the young man to calm down and listen to reason. "How long would it take someone to get in here if you missed seeing them in the trees? They could be in here before you even reached the chickens."

Keith knew she was right, and he shouldn't have taken the chance even to get her the eggs. However, he didn't like having to admit he was wrong in front of Mike. It was a sign of weakness, and Mike was sure to try to take advantage of it. He might be a wimp, but that didn't mean he was stupid-plus, he was one of those corporate types.

"Mike, I know he made a mistake," Amanda said. "But we're all safe. So let's use this as a learning experience. There's nothing to be gained by everyone yelling at one another."

Mike only nodded, sighed, and walked out the front door.

***

In a couple of minutes, Amanda walked outside with two cups of coffee. She offered one to Mike.

"Thanks," he said.

"Keith knows he messed up," Amanda said. "He's just young and didn't think things through. He came outside, heard the chickens, figured there were eggs, and went to get them."

"I know, and everything worked out okay this time; but that doesn't mean it will next time. If we're going to rely on each other, then we all have to use our heads."

"I agree. Right now though, I think our attention should be on getting to Magnum."

Mike looked at Amanda and smiled. "You're right and we might as well get to it."

They both turned and went back into the mobile home. Inside, they could smell the mixture of coffee and eggs. It smelled great, and Amanda told Keith that they needed to gather their things and get on the road.

Keith looked at both of them and said, "Not a chance in hell." He paused for effect then smiled and continued, "Not until both of you sit down and eat this meal I've been slaving over for the past ten minutes."

Mike could see the young man was doing his best to work things out, and if Keith could make the effort, he damn sure could. "Smells great," he said, walking to the kitchen. He held his hand out to Keith who shook it with a smile.

They all filled their plates then sat down and ate. When they finished, Amanda asked, "Who's going to volunteer to do the dishes?"

Both men looked up surprised. Then Mike said, "Well, since Keith made breakfast, just put your dishes in the sink, and I'll do them later tonight."

It took about thirty minutes for them to gather all their things and load the horses. They took down the rope the horses were tied to, mounted up, and headed out.

They traveled about five hours, stopping only a couple of times at creeks, to allow the horses to drink. At the top of a hill, Keith pointed out an intersection ahead. "That's where we turn to the right."

At the intersection of highway 281 and 409, there were the remains of two convenience stores sitting across the road from each other. They stopped and cautiously checked both buildings but found nothing of use.

"Why can't we cut across country from here?" Mike asked as they continued down 409.

"You'll see in a few miles," Keith answered. "There are deep ravines and gorges. The only guaranteed way across them is to use the bridges on this road. Otherwise, we might have to travel ten or fifteen miles out of our way."

About five miles later, Keith was able to show Mike what he meant. The group came up on a bridge spanning a deep gash in the ground. It was about two hundred yards across and at least a hundred deep. Their side of gorge was a sheer drop to a small river at the bottom. The other side wasn't much better.

After crossing the bridge, they moved off the road to give their horses a break. After eating, they sat and talked, resting.

Keith excused himself from the other two, saying nature had stopped calling and was now shouting. He was only gone a couple of minutes when he hurried out of the bushes. He went to his horse. After quickly rummaging through a pack, he produced some binoculars.

"Come look at this," he said to the others, "but, don't make any noise."

Mike and Amanda followed him to the edge of a cliff where he dropped to his stomach and sighted the binoculars in. "Holy shit! Look," he held the binoculars out to Mike.

Mike took them and looked at a black spot beside the river where he saw a movement. There, squatting on its haunches and eating something, was a creature like the ones before. The ones Keith called Muties.

From its profile, Mike could tell there were some human features and thick, dark brown hair covered most of its body.

The Mutie stopped eating, held its head up and sniffed the air, looking from side to side. It rose and looked warily around. As it stood, its left paw-like hand dropped to its side, and he could see what it was eating-a human arm from the shoulder down.

The Mutie turned and looked at the bottom of the precipice where they lay. Its eyes scanned up the cliff and stopped as it came to the top. Mike was looking in the eyes of a predator, and it felt like the thing knew he was there.

"Let's get the hell outta here," Mike said quickly and quietly.

"What's wrong?" Amanda asked.

"It saw us," he answered.

"It couldn't have," Keith argued.

Mike was already up and moving fast toward the horses. He caught his and mounted fast. Reaching over, he took hold of the lead rope on the packhorse and as soon as the other two mounted, headed out, down 409 at a lope.

A mile or so later, Mike pulled his horse up to give it a rest. His right arm ached from hanging on to the lead rope. Keith and Amanda pulled up beside him.

"What makes you think it saw us?" Amanda asked.

"It looked right at me," Mike answered. "I could tell it saw us, and I realized what it was eating... It was eating an arm."

"An arm?" Amanda repeated.

"Yes, a human arm," he answered, "a human arm from the shoulder down."

Amanda groaned and looked away. Keith turned his head and looked at the countryside and said, "Then we don't need to stay around here any longer than we have to."

"True," Mike agreed, "but remember, these things are all over the place. Like I told you before-I ran into a group of 'em down south."

"The ones that killed the biker gang," Keith said.

Mike looked up and frowned.

"Let's keep moving," Amanda said, pressing her heels into her horse.

They traveled another couple of hours and found a house on the side of the road with a corral behind it. They unloaded the animals and put them in the pen.

Inside, they found the stove was electric. "It's cold food tonight," Amanda said.

"Not necessarily," Mike answered. "I saw a grill outside. We can use that."

"I don't know about you," Keith said. "But, I don't think we need the smell of smoke or food outside with the possibility of Muties out there."

"You're damn sure right there," Mike answered. "Sorry, I wasn't thinking."

Keith smiled and said, "It can happen to anyone."

"There's a stream about twenty-five yards to the north," Keith said. I'm gonna take a bath and wash my clothes in it. What about the two of you?"

"Let me get my robe," Amanda said.

172

A couple of moments later, she reentered the room and handed Keith her clothes. "I'll need some water to bathe with," she told Keith.

As he left the house with two five-gallon buckets, Mike joined him, chattering non-stop.

***

Sunrise the next day found Mike sitting on the front porch of their overnight accommodations. He took the last watch so Amanda and Keith could rest for today's trip. He figured he had a little over six hours sleep and would be fine.

After eating some fruit, they loaded the horses and started down the road.

"There's a shortcut a little ways up ahead," Amanda said. "We used to use it when we went to Rollingblock for a giant flea market they have there every month or so. There's a sign for a church camp we can follow."

About five or six miles up highway 409, they found the road they wanted snaking off into the thick woods ahead of them.

"There it is," Amanda said.

"You sure this is a shortcut?" Mike asked.

"It cuts off about ten miles."

"That's a shortcut," Keith agreed.

They followed it until reaching the church camp. It was only about two o'clock, and they were sitting in what must have been the main house of the camp. It was spacious and comfortable, and as luck would have it, there was a gas stove in its kitchen. They would have hot food tonight.

"I can make supper tonight," Mike offered.

"I can do it," Amanda said. "Why don't you go out and help Keith?"

"Are you sure? I can cook fairly well."

"I'll do it," she said and turned her back on him.

Mike went outside and found Keith in a barn behind the house. There were stalls inside, and they found hay and more feed in different rooms. They put the horses in the stalls and poured feed for them.

"Let's take a look," Mike agreed.

They went to the back of the barn and saw what appeared to be a corral a short distance away. They went toward the corral but stopped as they approached it.

"Holy Shit!" Mike exclaimed.

Keith stood quietly gazing at the carcasses of three dead horses inside. Tearing his attention from the desiccated animals, he looked around.

Keith climbed between the planks of the fence to get a closer view of the dead animals. "They've been dead for a while, and they've been partially eaten."

Mike climbed through the fence and joined Keith beside the dead horses. He knelt beside one corpse for a closer look.

"There's no way of telling if it was one of those creatures we've seen or some other wild animals."

"Those were caused by something other than Muties," Keith said.

"How can you tell?" Mike asked.

"These animals were chewed on in various places. No parts are missing, and you can see small bite marks on the edge of the wounds. This was probably done by a pack of dogs, wolves, or coyotes-maybe even a big cat."

"Well, whatever the case," Mike said. "It's getting dark soon, so let's get back to the house."

They returned to the house where they found Amanda finishing with the food preparation. All three sat down and hungrily dug in. As Keith put the last bite into his mouth, a heavy knock sounded at the front door.

All three looked up in surprise. Keith rose to his feet, picking up his rifle from beside him. He cautiously walked to the door and looked out a window beside it.

Outside, standing about ten feet from the porch was a man. He was dressed as if he just stepped out of one of those Wild West books you saw on the bookracks at the supermarkets. He wore a beard, a black cowboy hat, and a black duster. The duster, pulled back on both sides, revealed a pistol in holsters on both hips.

Keith slowly opened the door. Pushing the rifle barrel out ahead of him, he cautiously came in full view of the cowboy standing before him.

The cowboy held both hands out away from his body and said, "How you doing, sir?"

Keith didn't say anything but held the rifle on the man in front of him.

"Sorry to bother ya," the cowboy said. "But I was surprised to see anyone here and just wanted to let you know I was in the area. Don't want you mistaking me for someone or something else and taking a shot."

Mike and Amanda stepped up beside Keith and couldn't believe what they saw.

175

The cowboy, upon seeing Amanda, slowly reached up and tugged on the brim of his hat. "Ma'am."

"Where're you from?" Mike asked.

"I'm from Rollingblock," the cowboy answered. "My name's Raphael Edmonds, but most folks call me Bear. We have a camp on the edge of the village."

"What are you doing out here?" Keith asked, still holding the gun level.

"Just doin' some huntin'," Bear answered.

"How did you get here?"

"My horse is tied over in those trees." He pointed to a grove of trees across the yard. "I don't mean to bother you folks. Like I said-I simply wanted you to know I was in the area for the night."

Amanda stepped near the edge of the porch and asked, "Do you have anything to eat, mister?"

"Bear," the man corrected, "and yes ma'am, I've got some grub with my horse."

Then Keith surprised them all. "Well, why don't you put your horse in the barn and come inside?"

"A house would be nice," Bear answered. "But, like I said-I don't wanna be a bother."

"No bother," Amanda said. "We've got food already fixed, and you're welcome to what's left."

Bear reached up, tipped the brim of his hat again and said, "Thanks much ma'am."

As he turned and walked toward his horse, Keith told the others, "I'll go with him. He seems friendly enough, but you never know."

When he stepped off the porch, Mike and Amanda returned into the house. Half way across the yard, Keith met the other man. He held out his hand and introduced himself. "Keith Watson."

Bear took his hand a shook it, "Rafe Edmonds," he repeated. "But please, call me Bear. Nowadays, I prefer that."

Keith could see how the man got the nickname of Bear. He was sturdy built and even with the neatly trimmed beard, it gave him a hard look.

As they walked on to the barn, Keith asked, "I don't mean to insult or anything, but what's with the getup?"

"You're not insulting at all. Before the power went out, I was a member of a gunfighter group. We put on shows about the old Wild West-comedy mostly. But we've found these clothes hold up better to hard wear than today's clothes do. So, we've kinda stuck with them. The guns are black powder, and we're able to carry more ammo in less room than with bullets. What's that you're carrying-a thirty-thirty?"

"Yeah. It's powerful. But unless you hit it in the head, it still takes two or three shots to kill a Mutie."

"A Mutie?" Bear asked.

"Yeah," Keith answered. "Those things some people have turned into."

"I think I know what you're talking about. We ran into one the other night. So you call them Muties, huh?"

"Don't know what else to call them."

Bear unsaddled his horse and got some hay from across the barn. When he started rummaging through his saddlebag, Keith said, "There's some feed over in those bins. Help yourself."

177

"Thanks man." Bear went over to the bin and dipped a coffee can into the feed. He poured the feed in a trough in front of his horse, Dusty, and stepped back.

"Come on up to the house," Keith said. "Amanda did the cooking tonight, so supper is actually worth eating." Grinning, he walked over to the door and waited.

The two men left the barn and strolled toward the house to join Mike and Amanda. About half way there, Bear stopped.

"What's wrong?"

Bear held up his hand with his palm toward Keith, motioning him to be quiet. He listened for a second and then said, "Move slowly toward the house. We're being watched."

"How do you know?" Keith asked as he started slowly walking toward the house.

"I heard something over to the left," Bear answered. "Also, take a whiff. You can smell it from here, and trust me, that's not the smell of a human."

The two men walked about twenty feet when they both saw a shadow moving rapidly toward them from the left. Keith swung his rifle up, but before he could even get it level, he heard two explosions come from Bear's gun. There was a slight pause; then the weapon roared again.

Temporarily blinded by the flash from the pistol, Keith hoped the man had killed the Mutie. In less than a minute, his night vision started to return.

He saw Bear standing over the dead animal. The man looked at the creature on the ground. As

Keith approached, Bear holstered his pistol and said, "You're right, it does take a head shot."

Seemingly unfazed, Bear turned and walked toward the house. Keith followed the man, still surprised at how quickly this cowboy had pulled his weapon and shot the Mutie. Hell, it was as if they were in a western movie, and the man had drawn against some desperado.

Both, Mike and Amanda heard the shots and met them at the back door. Amanda carried her pistol by her side and stepped back as the men entered.

"What the hell happened out there," Mike asked once they were inside.

"Oh, one of those things-those mutants made a run at us," Bear answered. "Keith and I took care of it though."

Keith was surprised the man included him in the incident as if he had done anything.

"Are you both all right?" Amanda asked, looking at the two men.

"We're fine," Keith answered. "But, I didn't have anything to do with killing the Mutie. Bear was the one who shot it. Hell, he even knew it was there before it charged us."

Bear stepped over to the table, sat down, and slid his hat off the back of his head, the stampede string holding the hat against his back. He removed the cylinder from his forty-four and pulled the caps off. He produced a leather pouch from under his duster. From the pouch, he took a metal powder horn and some lead balls. He refilled the spent chambers with black powder and packed them down with the plunger on the pistol. Placing a lead ball on

179

the top of each chamber, he again used the plunger and pushed the ball in so it was below the level of the cylinder. He repeated this process two more times, then replaced the caps on each of the chambers, and holstered the pistol.

"It takes a lot to load one of those things," Mike commented.

"It does that," Bear answered. "But, I have four other cylinders stored away, which can be loaded in less than twenty seconds-ten, if I'm in a hurry and don't fumble it."

Amanda placed a plate of food before Bear. "There's more if you like and by the way, my name's Amanda-Amanda Green," she said.

"No ma'am-uh, Amanda," Bear corrected. "I don't think so." He looked at the full plate in front of him. "This is more'n I eat in an entire day, times being what they are."

As Bear ate, Mike said, "Mr. Edmonds, you said you were from Rollingblock. Are things better there?"

"I don't know," he answered, "and please call me Bear. Mr. Edmonds reminds me of my Grandfather. I came to Rollingblock from Austin when the power went out. Things were getting bad quick there. I figure there's problems all over the place by now."

"What did you do before all this?" Amanda asked.

"I was a doctor," he said, "a Naturopath. I did a lot of acupuncture, auriculotherapy, laser, and herbal therapy-that sort of stuff. Before that, I retired from the military."

"What did you do in the military?" Keith asked, anxious to know more about this man.

"A lot of training," he answered flatly. It was obvious by the answer, he didn't want to talk about it.

"How far are we from Rollingblock?" Mike questioned.

"About three hours by horse," he said. "That's to our camp, and if you cut across country-about an hour longer if you follow the road."

"Earlier, you said you were hunting. Did you get anything?" Keith asked.

"I've got some deer meat in the river over there."

"In the river," Keith repeated. "Why in the river?"

"The water'll keep it cool enough to stop it from spoiling overnight. I have it in some plastic bags to keep it dry."

"Natural refrigeration," Mike mused.

"Works for a day or so-then it'll turn." Bear answered. "Do you three live here?" Now, it was his turn to get some information.

"No," Keith answered. "Amanda and I used to live near Bulverde. Mike joined us a few of days ago. Then we decided to go see some relatives of Amanda's in Magnum, and here we are."

"Well folks, I appreciate your hospitality, but it's time for me to get some shuteye," Bear said, rising from the table.

"You're welcome to stay in here with us," Amanda said as he stood.

"Thanks just the same ma'am, but I feel a little more secure where I can move around," he answered. "If it's all the same to you, I'll roll out a bed on the porch."

"Are you sure," Mike asked. "There's room here."

"I'm sure," Bear insisted. "I don't like the possibly being trapped inside. I can also keep a watch at the front of the house for ya if you'd like."

"Don't you need sleep?" Keith asked.

"Oh, I'll get some sleep," Bear assured the young man. "Nowadays, I sleep real light. You folks lock this back door, and I'll take care of the front." He started toward the front door and once there, he turned and looked back. "I'll be away from the porch for a couple of minutes. I need to get my bedroll from the barn; then I'll be back."

As Bear left through the front door, Keith was sure they had a new friend. For some reason, he knew they could trust this man dressed in the western outfit.

***

Bear went to the barn and gathered his bedroll and a 30-30 rifle. Returning to the front porch, he spread the bedroll the same as every night since leaving Austin and leaned the rifle against the wall next to him. Reaching into his left breast pocket, he pulled out a pack of cigarettes.

He knew the damn things were bad for him but still smoked all the same. He usually kept at least two packs on him unless he was going to be gone for a while. At those times, he would put a carton in one of his saddlebags. He also knew the Muties, as his new companions called them, could probably smell the smoke for miles. *But who plans to live forever.*

He let his mind wonder a little to evaluate his new acquaintances. *The kid's pretty much aware of what's going on. The other one-Mike is going to be a problem. He's scared and has no idea how to handle his present situation. The woman-Amanda has her hands full with the two men. She has the ability of being totally self-reliant, but she has to walk a tightrope between the ego of Keith and the fear of Mike. These two things have put her in a bad spot, which she's handling rather well.*

Keith walks and handles himself as if he has martial arts training. He would probably do well in camp defense, as a scout and a hunter.

Mike's strictly a businessperson and would require someone to watch over him for at least six months. He'd probably do well with keeping records and maybe an inventory.

Amanda would probably be like Sandy Sloan and Lynn Jennings. Once taught she'd be competent at any task or chore required of her. She doesn't seem aggressive, but she would defend herself and others when required to.

Bear heard a rustling of weeds to his right. Quickly, but quietly, he rose to his feet and stepped softly into a shadow to wait-pistol in hand.

A couple of seconds later, Amanda walked around the corner of the house. She stopped and looked around.

It was obvious she was looking for him, so he stepped out of the shadow, intentionally scrapping one of his spurs on the boards of the porch as he did so.

Her head snapped around, and she saw him standing near the middle of the porch. There was less than half a moon, but still enough to allow her to pick his shrouded figure out even without him moving.

"Where the hell did you come from?" She asked startled.

"What are you doing out here alone?" He answered with a question.

"I didn't expect to be alone," Amanda explained, "and as it turns out, I'm not."

A foolhardy move. Then to her, he said, "Is the back door unlocked?"

"No. I locked it when I came out."

"Why are you out here?"

She stepped up on the porch and said, "I couldn't sleep and thought I'd come out and keep you company for a little while."

He walked over to the front steps and sat down. As she joined him, he said, "Don't take this wrong, Amanda, but you took a big chance coming out here by yourself."

"I didn't think of it as much of a chance since I was only walking around the house, and you were out here."

"Well, there's no harm done," he said, paused a couple of seconds and said, "Looks like a cold front's coming in. It'll turn cold in the next day or two."

"I was hoping the cold would hold off for a while. I only have this one coat."

"We have some clothes back at Rebel's Revenge."

"Rebel's Revenge?"

"It's the name we gave our camp," Bear explained. "Actually, Ben Williamson was the one who named it. If you three come back with me, you'll get to meet him. Speaking of that, I know all of you were going to Magnum, but I doubt you'll make it before the front hits. It's up to you, but I suggest you stay with us until the weather passes."

"I'll have to talk to the others, but I think they'll agree," she said. "Besides, it's my relatives we're on our way to see."

"Our only requirements at the camp are that everyone helps out however they can."

"I don't think there'll be a problem."

"How old is Keith?" Bear asked.

"Nineteen," Amanda answered, "and I'm twenty-eight."

"Were either of you married before the blackout?"

"No," she answered, looking at him.

"I don't mean to be nosey," he explained. "I'm simply trying to get some information about the people who might be coming home with me."

"I understand."

"What about Mike?"

"I don't know," she answered. "He's only been with us a couple of days. He's nice enough, but there's something about him I can't figure out."

He's spineless. He wasn't absolutely sure why, but it was what he felt. To Amanda he said, "We give everyone an equal chance back at camp. He'll either work out, or he won't."

"What about you? Are you married?"

"Nah," Bear answered. "Nobody'll put up with me.

"I doubt that's true," Amanda said, leaning back against the wall of the house. "How many are there back at this camp of yours?"

Bear looked at her knowing she was only curious, but at the same time, he wasn't willing to feed her this type of information. "You'll find out soon enough. Besides, the number changes from day to day."

"When do you plan on leaving? Tomorrow?"

"As soon after sunup as I can. How is it going between those two?"

Amanda looked as if she didn't know what he meant.

"It's obvious there's some sort of friction there. I don't know how much, but there's some."

"It seems like they're doing better. Believe me, this is nothing compared to what it was like the first day. I think everything will be okay."

"Good," Bear answered, "because if the three of you come with me, there's going to be a very large change in the dynamics."

"Well, if we're going to go with you, I need to get to bed," she said, rising to her feet.

"You sleep well, young lady," Bear answered opening the door for her.

"I will," she answered. Then she smiled and said, "Goodnight."

"This time lock the door." Once she disappeared inside, Bear lay down on his bedroll and relaxed. It only took him about five minutes to get to sleep. Tonight, he would sleep light and be aware of his surroundings.

***

186

Keith awoke in time to see the sunrise out his bedroom window. He climbed out of bed, dressed, and went into the living room. The house was quiet with no one besides himself moving around inside.

He decided to go out and see if Bear was up yet. As he walked out the front door, he saw Bear's horse standing, tied to a bush in the front yard. Bear sat in a chair on the porch. A pot of coffee sat on a stand with a lit sterno can under it.

"Morning," he said without looking up.

"Morning," Keith responded. "Everything okay out here?"

Bear raised his head and slowly looked around the property. "Everything's quiet for now."

"I wanted to thank you for saving my hide last night," Keith spoke a little more quietly. He meant what he was saying. He wasn't sure he would have been successful in killing the Mutie the night before.

"You're more than welcome," Bear said. "We all have to help each other the way things are now, but you did fine. You stood your ground and were moving to defend yourself." Then after a couple of seconds he asked, "What style of martial arts do you study?"

Keith looked at the other man, shocked. "How did you know I took karate?"

"It shows in your movements. Looks like you had a good teacher. He or she taught you to be aware of your surroundings-which is important."

"Thanks. The style is Shotokan. Have you heard of it?"

"Anyone in karate knows of Master Funikoshi's style."

"Okay then, what style do you study?" Keith asked, interested in finding out more about Bear.

Bear knew he had tipped his hand with his previous question. He also felt this young man was serious in his training, and he was just curious and not interested in trying to prove himself.

"I studied some Shotokan, Shorin Ryu, Kajukembo, and Kenpo-Ryu," Bear told him. "We also learned some close combat in the military."

"Sounds like we need to compare notes sometime," Keith suggested. "I'm always looking for new techniques."

This last statement confirmed his feelings about Keith. The young man was open to learning and demonstrated no need for false bravado. "I guess it depends on if you folks come back to camp or not," he said casually. "Which reminds me-if you would-please go in and wake your friends. If you three are going back with me, we need to hit the trail."

A little surprised, Keith looked at Bear and then said, "I'll be right back."

"When you come back," Bear said to the man's back. "You might bring some cups if any of you want to try some of the worst coffee in the world."

Keith smiled and went into the house.

The group remained in the house talking about Bear's invitation. It didn't take much discussion about whether or not they wanted to take him up on the offer. They definitely wanted to go.

"Hey, I'm willing to go where people can protect each other," Mike said.

"As far as I'm concerned, it's up to you," Keith said. "My closest family is in Utah. It's where my parents were when this happened."

"I think we should go with him," Amanda said. "My Aunt and Uncle have resources, but I'm not completely sure they're still at home. They were supposed to be in Phoenix sometime this month."

They all walked out of the house carrying coffee cups, and Keith announced their acceptance of Bear's offer of company. As they poured the coffee, Amanda said, "I've got to see what the world's worst coffee tastes like."

Bear stood faced them and said, "One thing I have to tell you is that you are welcome to come to the camp. However, whether or not you'll be welcome to stay will be up to a vote by all the people there. If that gives any of you second thoughts, now's the time to change your minds."

Amanda spoke up, "If they decide for us to go, at least we'll have company for a couple of days."

Bear looked at the other two and grinned. "Then I suggest you all drink that gourmet coffee, gather your things, and get your horses loaded. They've already been fed and watered this morning."

The other three looked down at their cups, and in unison dumped the liquid in the yard. As they headed back in the house to get their belongings, they heard Bear say, "No appreciation for the finer things in life."

Thirty minutes later, they were all packed. Bear checked the pack animal and found it properly loaded. It wouldn't cause the horse any discomfort or be cumbersome.

189

***

Bear led the way, traveling through trees to the edge of a ridge. They rode along the ridge about a hundred yards then cut left toward the sound of running water.

Descending a small hill to the Buffalo River below, they found it was about thirty feet wide and was running smoothly along. Bear led them along the bank a short distance, then stopped, and dismounted. He located a rope tied to a small tree, knelt down, and fished three plastic bags from the water. He gathered the bags, coiled the rope, and handed one bag each to Mike and Keith. After loading the third bag on the packhorse, he climbed back up on Dusty.

"How deep is the water here?" Mike asked, watching it flow past him.

"I don't know," Bear answered. "But you're welcome to climb down, jump in, and find out."

"Very funny," Mike snorted. "I think I'll stay up here."

Bear nodded and spurred Dusty forward.

After traveling about three hours, Bear saw Ben sitting under a tree. Ben faced to his right to keep his good ear away from the camp. Ben was deaf as a post in his left ear, and the hearing in the right was fading. In the tree above him, Bear saw a slight movement. He smiled and continued on.

Bear and his group rode up within thirty yards of Ben before the lookout heard them. He stood up holding a forty-five caliber, black powder rifle across his chest. Recognizing Bear, he waved and called out, "Come on in, Bear. We was wondering what had happened to ya."

"Aw, I found some people over at Crystal Crossing." Bear turned in his saddle and pointed to people as he introduced them. Ben, this is Keith, Amanda, and Mike. Folks this here's Wild Ben Williamson, and the one up in the tree is Will Jennings."

"Hey folks," Will called down the greeting.

The presence of the young man sitting in the tree shocked the people behind Bear. None of them were aware of him until he was pointed out.

"We're gonna head on in," Bear said to Ben. "These folks have decided to stay a while."

"I'll see you in a couple of minutes," Ben returned. "They're just now eatin', and someone'll be out soon to relieve me'n my ears up there in the tree."

"Anything new happened?" Bear asked as he turned Dusty's head toward the camp and urged him along.

"Yup," Ben answered, "got some other new folks the day before yesterday."

Bear waved in acknowledgment as he continued on. The other three rode past Ben, and as Amanda went by, Ben reached up and touched the rim of his hat. "Ma'am," he said and watched as they followed Bear.

Ben looked up at Will and said, "Damn, it's starting to get crowded around here."

"I agree," Will said. "The more people we have here, the less chance we have of being attacked by some weirdo's or any of those creatures."

191

"We need more people to keep Ben in line," Bear shouted as he disappeared over a small hill.

A hundred yards down the trail, Keith, Amanda, and Mike followed Bear into a clearing where they saw a number of people sitting at four picnic tables eating.

Kyle rose and asked, "Hey Bear, everything okay?" The man, except for his British accent, still reminded Bear of Wild Bill Hickok.

"Yep," Bear answered and turned to sit sideways in his saddle. "Met up with these folks last night," he called each one by name and slid off Dusty at the same time David reached him.

The two men shook hands. Looking up at the others, still on their horses, Bear said, "This here's David Alexander. The rest, you'll have to meet on your own."

Carl stepped up beside Bear. "I'll take your horse, Bear."

"You sure?" Bear asked.

Carl took hold of the reins and said, "Sure, I've already eaten," then he turned to the others and said, "I'll take yours too if you want."

"Hang on a second, Carl," Bear told him. "There's meat on those three. You need to take your things off them, otherwise you're gonna have to carry all of it back up here."

After the horses were unloaded, Carl led the animals off to unsaddle and feed them.

Ginny, Deborah, and Cindy picked up the meat in the plastic bags. "We'll take care of these," Cindy said, heading toward the stage barn.

192

Bear went to the cook area and got a plate of food. As he turned to find a seat, Spyder yelled out, "Get your decrepit ole ass over here and plant it."

Bear grinned, walked over and sat down beside the man. "I heard there're some other new people that came in while I was gone."

"Yeah, four came in day before yesterday."

"Look like they're okay?" Bear asked.

"Seem to be. One of them, a guy named Melon, went to San Marcos with Hal this morning to raid a clothing store. They took one of the trucks and should be back this evening. Hal said he would stop by Boggs's and see if he could get more powder and weapons."

"What about the others?"

"There's a woman and two men," Spyder answered. "The woman, Davata, seems to be a strong and willing to do what it takes to help out. One of the men is a doctor. The other is a ."

"Spyder, that shit is over," Bear said sternly.

"Oh no," Spyder interrupted. "I only meant he's black. He's as good as anyone here and maybe better'n some. Trust me. If you need to trust someone, he's gonna be your man."

Bear was impressed with the other man. For years, Spyder espoused the uselessness of any race other than white, and now here he was with an African-American as a friend.

All the members of the "Hays County Regulators" had at one time or another, seen Spyder treat people of other races as well as he treated his friends. Most of the Regulators recognized Spyder's attitude as a product of his upbringing. The man never pushed any of those beliefs on another person.

In other words, Spyder was full of shit, and it was nice to see him finally drop the facade.

The other remarkable thing about this man was that he was an ordained Methodist Minister. His religion was the only belief he was willing to push and was not willing to compromise on.

"Sounds like a good man," Bear observed.

"He is," Spyder answered. "You might want to put him in your defense classes."

"I'll take a look at it. Eventually, I want everyone to be trained in self-defense. You never know when it'll be needed."

"That's a fact," Spyder said. "David and Hal are planning to work with everyone on shooting. They're gonna to set up some targets and train everybody in using all the weapons we have here."

A woman walked up and stood beside the two men as they talked. Bear looked at her, and she held her hand out.

"Davata Sanders," she said, shaking the man's hand. "Sorry about your friend."

"What friend?" Bear asked. He looked around at the people gathered at the tables. No one appeared to be missing.

Davata looked at Spyder. "Sorry, I thought you told him."

Hell no, lady," Spyder snorted. "I hadn't got to it yet. Shit," Spyder said shaking his head. Looking at Bear, he continued, "Sorry about this shit man but... Pete was killed two days ago. He was shot by some assholes at the square."

Bear looked at his friend and without missing a beat said, "Fuckers gotta die, Spyder."

"They're already dead," Spyder told him. "Hal, Kyle, and me killed them right before we found her and her group." He motioned at Davata with his thumb. "Before he died, he gave them enough information to contact us here. We found five of the assholes at the square and was forced to kill 'em."

"Okay, it's done," Bear said. "I guess it's time to get on with the situation at hand." It was easy to say, but he knew Pete's death would be with him for a while.

"He was trying to get in touch with you," Davata continued. "It was because of him we ran the flag up the flagpole."

"I understand," Bear answered. "Pete and I shared some common events in our past, but other than that, he was simply an acquaintance. Bear got up and walked away, leaving Spyder and Davata at the table.

***

"Cold isn't he," Davata observed.

"Not really," Spyder answered. "He has to look to the future. Pete was simply a friend. People like him learn that friends can be used against you. He's kept most people at a distance the whole time I've known him. There are only a couple of people he allows close enough to worry about. Most of them are original members of the 'Regulators.'"

"Hard man. He must be lonely. It has to be a hard way to live, not being able to trust the people around him. I can't imagine living like that."

"When it's what you've done all your life, it comes natural," Spyder said as he rose from the table.

Bear turned and looked at her as if he were able to hear her over the hum of conversations and other noises of the camp.

CHAPTER SEVENTEEN

Now in a satellite jail annex, Gabriel faced a mutant standing in one of the cells. He backed away from the cell before him and as he did, the mutant in the adjacent cell quieted down.

He looked at Chico standing a couple of feet away. "If that asshole over there,"-he pointed at the noisy animal-"makes any more noise, shoot the fucking thing."

As Gabriel stepped toward the cell, the mutant in the next cell stood up. The mutant before him turned his head and grunted. The movement of its head and the grunt were almost imperceptible, but they were there, nonetheless. The other mutant slowly sat down.

It was obvious the creature in the cell before him was the senior of the two. Gabriel thought about it. *If it's a leader, then there is more intelligence there than I thought. Also, if it could understand what I was saying to Chico, then we're in for a lot of trouble. If they ever get organized, there'll be almost no way to fight them.*

This last thought was the one that bothered him most. The mutant creatures were stronger, faster, and more cunning in their movements than any humans Gabriel knew. If they proved to be anywhere near the intelligence of humans, he saw no way he and his organization could beat them short of making them allies. Gabriel knew he must find out just how smart this leader was. He called to

Karl, the head of his personal escort, and told him to get the car ready to go.

A number of Gabriel's men were able to modify virtually any diesel car they saw. Those men had been able to fix up several vehicles for the organization's use. Gabriel walked down to the street where his personal car waited.

Arriving at the jail housing the mutants, he went to the wing with the cells. He looked at Karl. "I want everybody outta here. You included, Karl."

He started to say something else but thought better of it and ran everyone out of the area. "I'll be right outside the door here," he said then closed it.

Gabriel pulled a chair up and sat down about five feet from the bars of the cell. The mutant he thought of as a possible leader sat on a metal bed attached to the wall. He looked at the mutant for a couple of minutes then said, "I know you can understand what I'm saying." He paused to let this sink in and see if there was any sign of it being willing to communicate.

There was none. The creature simply sat and looked at him without the slightest hint of understanding.

"Look, I don't want to hurt any of you. Hell, maybe there's even a way we can work together," Gabriel suggested.

Still there was no change in the animal.

"I saw you look at the man I was talking to the other day. Not only did you know who I was talking to, but you understood what I said."

The mutant sat, looking at Gabriel, motionless.

"There is no reason for you to be locked up like this if you will simply communicate," he said. "All you have to do is let me know you understand."

The mutant simply sat and stared. There was no change in its position or its gaze, which remained locked on the man on the other side of the bars from him.

"Look, you piece of shit," Gabriel said, his voice growing louder and deeper. "Either you communicate with me in some way, or I'll blow the head off one of your friends here."

The mutant's eyes seemed to narrow slightly, and Gabriel knew he had seen a reaction. Minute as it was, it was still there. "You let me know you understand me in the next ten seconds, or one of your friends die."

Gabriel rose to his feet and pulled his pistol from its holster. It was a .45 caliber semi-automatic and would only take one shot to the head to kill the mutant. Gabriel waited.

Ten seconds later he said, "Okay. If that's the way you wanna play it, let's play." He walked over to the end cell, raised his pistol and shot the mutant in it above the right eye.

Immediately, the two remaining mutants erupted in a cascade of howls, screams, and growls. Gabriel's men came rushing into the hallway even though he motioned them back outside.

"Everything's all right," he said, pointing at the mutant leader. "I just had to make a believer out of this asshole."

His men gave him a strange look as they turned, and once again, left the hallway. Gabriel walked over to the cell where the mutant leader was and sat back down in the chair.

"Now if you're ready, we can continue," he said after both animals quieted some. "Maybe this time you'll believe me when I tell you, the other one will die next if you don't cooperate. Do you understand?"

It only took a couple of seconds until the mutant in front of him nodded. Its eyes locked on the man before it.

"I knew it," Gabriel said, almost shouting. "You understand everything I've said."

The mutant continued to stare without moving.

"If you can understand me, then you can talk too, can't you?" Gabriel spoke excitedly.

The mutant sat and stared at the human before him. After a couple of seconds, Gabriel put his hand on his pistol in its holster. The mutant's eyes followed the move, and then it shook its head-indicating no.

"You can't talk, but you can understand me, right?" Gabriel clarified.

This time the animal shook its head yes.

It took about thirty minutes and a long series of questions and answers for Gabriel to find out some of the mutants were more intelligent than others. He also found out that, because of a change in facial muscles and the structure of the tongue, they were unable to form words. One thing never communicated, but Gabriel knew, was that the mutant's thought processes were at least equal to those of humans.

The intelligent mutants made up about five percent of the mutant population. The less intelligent ones were still stronger, faster, and more fearless than most humans. All mutants, once they were in a pack, were fiercely loyal to the pack.

Gabriel also found that, even though it was unable to talk, it could hold a pencil in its fist and write words. Even though the writing was in large, distorted letters, he learned the mutant's name when it wrote *Bo*. It seemed, along with the change in musculature, the part of the brain controlling the ability to perform intricate tasks was no longer functioning as it did before.

He also found out the mutants now carried an instinctual hatred for humans. The mutant in front of him, Bo, was totally unwilling to consider an alliance with the humans. Gabriel told the creature he would remain behind bars as long as it took to get an alliance between the mutants and humans.

Gabriel left the room, leaving Bo to think about his situation. In the outer room, he told the guards to make sure both mutants were fed and made comfortable.

CHAPTER EIGHTEEN

As everyone else sat around the campfire waiting on Kyle and Melon to return, Bear sat on the perimeter of the clearing, looking across the valley to the hills known as Satin's Spine. Most of the Regulators spoke with the new arrivals, hoping to discover all they could about the situation in other parts of the country.

Bear heard a sound behind him and looked around to see Davata approaching.

"Mind if I join you?"

"Have a seat," he said motioning beside him.

"If you don't mind, I've got to ask you-why Bear?" She asked as she sat on a rock next to him.

"Excuse me?" He answered.

"The name Bear, how did you get it?"

He grinned, "I got it in the military. Bears aren't known for diplomacy or stealth, and neither was I. Back then and even now, I tend to charge into things head on."

Davata smiled. "Reminds me of someone else I once knew." She looked across the valley at the hills. "What a beautiful view."

"This has been one of my favorite places since I first saw it. Those hills are called Satin's Spine. A road runs along the top of it with beautiful views from over there. A couple of years before all this happened, I used to live in Rollingblock and would come here and eat lunch. It was quiet and secluded."

"I know what you mean," Davata said. "There was a place like this along the Mississippi River, in

New Orleans I love. Actually, it was north of the city."

"I spent a lot of time in New Orleans when I was stationed in Gulfport, Mississippi," he said looking at her, "I really enjoyed the whole area. Of course, anything's better than where I grew up in the Texas panhandle." He paused looking at the hills. "As far as I'm concerned, the only thing better than that,"-he motioned toward the hills in the distance-"is the ocean."

"I don't mean to sound pushy," Davata said. "I guess I wanted to know if you're the leader here?"

Bear chuckled. "Hell no. I'm just a member of this group who managed to get together. Actually, we don't have a designated leader. I guess the closest one to being the leader would be David."

"Why David?"

"David has leadership qualities and knows survival tactics. As former president of our gunfighter's group, he's probably the one person respected by everyone. Then there's the fact that he'll let people do what they do best and not try and force them to change according to his will."

"Sounds like you respect him."

"I do," Bear answered. "I don't agree with all his views, but I think he's the one to hold us together and keep us working as a team. The only other possible leader would possibly be Hal Sloan."

"Well, why not him then?"

"I really don't think Hal would want the position. He's trained in fixing weapons and construction, but I don't think Hal would have the job. He'd rather be in the background and get things

203

done rather than telling others what to do. If he would take it, though, he'd be my choice."

"Then why doesn't the group get together and make a decision to put either Hal or David in charge?"

"It's coming." Bear said. "Up until now, there didn't seem to be a need for any single leader. Give them another couple of days, and they'll see it. I've already heard some rumblings." Bear looked at the valley and ridge beyond it.

***

It was four in the afternoon, and everyone was concerned about Kyle and Melon. They left early in the morning to see if they could find more clothes at some of the stores in San Marcos. They expected to return by noon and people were now worried. Dr. Hamilton approached David and said, "Something doesn't seem right here. I've seen both Kyle and Melon in action, and they might have been a couple of minutes late but not four hours."

"I'm afraid you're right," David answered. "We ought to go look for them. But it'll be dark soon, and it would put even more of us in jeopardy."

"Do you have any idea what route they would have taken?" The doctor asked.

"I know how they'll go into and come back from San Marcos," David answered, "and if they only go where they planned, I know where the stores are."

"Then why don't we wait until first thing tomorrow morning to go and check on them?"

204

"That's probably what we're gonna do," David answered. "We'll just have to check with the rest of the group."

Dr. Hamilton knew the other man was right. If they were going to protect the integrity of the community, everyone would need to have a voice in what was to take place. There were also Lynn's feelings to consider.

The only discussion on the matter was about who would be on the search team. Eventually, it was decided it would be David, Bear, Hal, and Lynn. A couple of people voiced opposition to Lynn, but David stopped the discussion when he said, "Okay, whoever thinks they're big enough to stop her from going, step right on up."

No one was willing to risk having his or her butt kicked, so Lynn was on the team. They planned to leave at first light the following morning.

***

As the meeting broke up, Davata caught up to Bear and tapped him on the shoulder. "Can I ask you a question?"

"Sure, but I have to go on watch right now."

"Mind if I join you?"

"No, not at all," he said and continued walking toward the stables area.

"I don't want to sound too nosey," Davata started, "but why are you always the one to volunteer to go out and put yourself in danger?"

"Someone has to, and out of all the people to choose from, I'm the most qualified."

They walked to where he would post himself for perimeter watch. He sat on a rock situated in the middle of some brush. Davata sat down beside him and pulled her coat around her.

"It's gonna get cold real quick," he said.

"I won't take up much of your time. But, there are some things I'd like to know."

"I'll tell you anything you want. All you have to do is ask."

"First, we met the man named Pete over by the square. He gave us this." She pulled out the piece of paper Pete had given her and handed it to him. "None of us could figure it out completely."

He looked at the paper and said, "It was a phrase he was to use when he got to the square. The other sentence was how they were to answer. If those two things weren't said, then he was to run or shoot the person."

"Something about it made Dr. Hamilton say he now had a dept to repay."

"He must have recognized parts of it referring to the Freemasons," Bear said. "I'll have to check with him and see."

"When I asked you if you were the person in charge, it was because I heard your name from Pete and then again a bunch of times around the other people here."

"I do a lot of hunting," Bear explained. "I tend to bring in a lot of food and like I said, I was one of the original Regulators."

"Don't you ever worry about those mutants running all over the place?"

"Sure I do," he answered. "But, I'm pretty well armed and take precautions against sneak attack.

206

I've seen quite a few of 'em running around and when I do, I simply avoid 'em."

"I know it's none of my business," Davata continued. "But, I've seen something in you that frankly confuses me."

He looked straight into her eyes and waited.

She let her gaze linger a couple of seconds and then said, "You seem to be very contemplative and at the same time, from what I understand, you'll act quickly without hesitation. Those two things don't seem to be compatible with each other."

"I don't know any other way to be. I'm not trying to impress or surprise anyone. I just do what I think is right."

"I didn't mean for it to be an insult."

"I didn't take it as one," he assured her. "I'm just saying I handle things as they come along.

"Aren't you afraid of being killed?"

"Not really. I had a heart attack back some time ago and died for almost a minute. It was probably the most peaceful, quiet, relaxing, and comfortable period in my life. Granted, it didn't last long, but it was great while it lasted."

Davata was staring at him and when she caught herself, she looked away embarrassed. "Sorry. It's only-I've never heard anyone talk about death as matter-of-factly before."

Bear turned toward her, "I was taught death is a part of life. Once a person accepts and starts believing it, then it's one less thing to have to worry about. In a life and death situation, a person can then focus on the problem at hand and not worry it might turn out differently than they expect."

207

Davata continued to look at him. She was trying to fathom how a person could possibly not worry about dying in a dangerous situation.

"Did you ever follow any type of sport?" He asked.

"I used to love watching the women's floor exercise in gymnastics. I even did some in high school."

"Perfect," he said. "When you were on the mat, doing a tumbling run, what was going through your mind?"

"Nothing," Davata answered. "My mind was blank. I just did what I had to do."

"What happened when you thought about what you were doing?"

"I usually made a mistake," she answered.

"That's exactly what I'm talking about," Bear explained. "The state of complete non-concentration you were in is what the Japanese call Satori. It is a state of being. There is no thought process going on, you're simply reacting to the situation. If you are able to do it in a life or death situation, then you have a better chance of survival. However, if you're worried about death or being harmed, then you may make a mistake or miss something that could get you killed. It's what was meant when they say the Samurai always held their deaths in front of them."

Davata was still looking at him but in a different way. It seemed she could actually understand what he meant. "How does a person learn to accept the possibility she may die and be okay with it?"

"It's a matter of faith. What do you think happens to a person after they die?"

"If they've lived a good life, they go to heaven," Davata said. "If not then they go to hell."

"Have you lived a good life?"

"I think I have. For the most part, I've tried to treat other people the right way. Sure, I've slipped up a couple of times but never anything serious."

"Okay," Bear said. "Then when you die, where do you think you'll go?"

"I hope I'll go to heaven," she answered.

"What's waiting there for you?" Bear continued.

"God," Davata answered emphatically.

"Are you sure?"

"Yes, very sure."

"Do you want to see and be with God?"

"Sure, doesn't everybody?" She answered.

"Then, why are you afraid to die and go see him?" Bear asked ignoring her last question. "What is there to fear if that's really where you want to be?"

Davata was thunderstruck. Everything Bear said made sense, and she could only wonder why she didn't think of it before.

"I'm gonna take a walk around," Bear said. "I suggest you go back and get some rest." He stood up and strode away with Davata still sitting by the tree in deep contemplation.

CHAPTER NINETEEN

General Clark looked over the ranks before him. The group called themselves "The New South Militia." It was comprised of over two hundred men, women, and children and slowly growing every week. Every member of the militia carried weapons and was extremely quick to use them. The workers were people from the area the group had captured and forced to work for them. Most were Hispanic along with a few African-Americans and Asians. They were comprised of men, women, and children. Even though the workers numbered over fifty, they were crowded into and kept in the single barn because of the number of weapons possessed by their captors. A fence topped with barbed wire surrounded the barn.

They had already killed over twenty of the workers by either shooting or beating them to death. It appeared slavery was back in America.

The general was explaining how it was imperative they find out who killed five of their people on the square in Rollingblock. "It was an ambush. Otherwise, there's no way they could have been beat in a straight fight. There had to be at least nine or ten people."

"Then you're saying there's another group around here somewhere," one of his men said.

"There has to be," General Clark answered. "They weren't killed by only one or two people."

"How we gonna find 'em?" another man asked. "We've got our hands full keeping our workers here. Hell, we've lost three in the last week."

"First of all, we don't know if they ran off or were taken off by those damn mutant animals," the general answered. "We'll break up into groups of two or three and search the area around Rollingblock. They have to be there somewhere."

He paused for a second and then added, "I want everyone back in camp before dark. We don't want another incident like the one Captain Campbell and his group experienced over there. Remember, one of those creatures alone took out two of our men before they could kill it."

"Captain Campbell." The general barked the man's name as if it were a command.

"Sir," Campbell responded.

"I want a total of five groups of three each. You choose the people, and I want everyone well-armed. You will be ready to head out at first light tomorrow and be back before sunset. NOW MOVE OUT!"

As the Captain turned and began picking the men he wanted for the detail, the general went back in his house.

General Clark wasn't really a general. Before the blackout, he spent twenty years in the Marine Corps and retired as a gunnery sergeant. After retirement, he used the money he saved while in the military and bought twenty acres of land.

On the land, he essentially set up a pseudo-military compound. It was in this compound he and his *New South Militia* set up operations.

The beliefs of the group were simple. If you weren't white, you weren't good for anything other

211

than serving those who were. The group was heavily armed with semi-automatic and automatic weapons and had stored them in an armory until the present crisis.

Clark's organization was dedicated to preserving what he thought the beliefs of the Pre-Civil War south were. Most of the people now with him were members of the organization before the electricity went out. A few others joined afterwards, and almost all were twisted and full of hate in their thinking.

With the loss of electricity, Clark gave himself the rank of general, appointed a number of his people as officers and senior enlisted, and formed the militia.

***

Captain Campbell gathered the people he needed and headed north to Rollingblock, while selected members of Rebel's Revenge traveled to San Marcos in search of Kyle and Melon.

David, Hal, Bear, and Lynn were using one of the diesel trucks. Hal drove to the main road, turned left and after taking a couple of other roads arrived in San Marcos. Once in San Marcos, they stopped by Carter's Gun Shop and found the store virtually empty. All of the weapons, powder, and reloading equipment was gone. There was nothing of use left.

"I wonder if Kyle and Melon got any of the stuff." David said.

"I'd bet the place was already empty," Lynn said. "This was simply a gun shop. They didn't have anything else."

"Makes sense," Hal agreed.

They left the gun store and went to The Sportsman's Supply. Hal pulled up to the front door of the business. The front door was nothing but a metal frame with all the glass broken out.

"This one doesn't look good either," Hal said.

They climbed out of the truck, and with their weapons ready, slowly entered the shattered door. Inside, they found a mess. All the common sizes of clothes were missing. There were no tents, and all the sleeping bags were gone.

Searching the store for anything useful, Lynn called out, "Hey guys, back here."

The men hurried toward the sound of her voice. They found her standing outside a door leading to another room.

"You won't believe what's back here," she said.

Upon entering the room, they found a storeroom for the business. As with the front, the room was in ruins.

"Looks like the rest of the store," Bear said.

"I know this does," Lynn answered. "But, come over here." She led them to a door standing partially open.

Inside was a rack of clothes with bright, reflective stripes on them. They were obviously for hunters not wanting to be mistaken for some sort of prey while they were in the woods.

"These probably won't help keep us warm. Most of them are only safety coverings," David said.

"I know," Lynn answered, "and I think this rack is why everything else is still here."

"What are you talking about?" Bear asked.

213

"Look closely, Gents," Lynn answered. "Does anything look strange to you?"

After shining his light around the edges of the rack, Hal asked, "Okay, what's behind the rack?"

"Hal wins the prize," Lynn said and pushed one end of the rack.

The rack of clothes pivoted to the side, revealing another storeroom filled with boxes.

With a big grin, Lynn said, "I figure when the electricity went out someone was moving this rack around and rather than mess with it, left it here in the door until the lights came back on."

"Makes sense," David agreed. "Then when the store was looted, someone pulled the door open and seeing only the rack of reflective clothing, turned back to the room they were in."

"I would have missed it myself," Lynn explained. "But, I looked to see if there was another rack behind this one and saw the rest of the room."

They entered the box-filled room and found multiple sizes and styles of hunting clothes.

They gathered numerous sets of camouflage clothes and boots along with cooking kits and as many sterno cans as they could find. Hal found some individual hunting suits similar to the used by snipers in the military. Bear located an area with individual and two-man tents. They also took three crossbows with numerous bolts for them.

They removed most of the items from their boxes to save room and loaded them in the truck. They moved the rack of reflective clothing back in place to try to fool others who might be looking for supplies.

Climbing back into the truck, they left the building and continued looking for Kyle and Melon. They went by two other stores the men were planning to check out. The looted businesses showed no signs of Kyle or Melon ever being there.

"Does anyone know of anywhere else we need to look?" Hal finally asked.

"There's no telling where they could be," David answered. "Maybe we should drive around town and see if we can locate them."

"Look Guys," Lynn said. "I appreciate what you're trying to do. But if they're not at any of these locations, something's happened to them."

Everyone knew she was correct. They just didn't want to give up on the other two-especially since she was with them.

She continued, "I think we should get back and check along the way to see if we can find them."

After a moment of silence, the men nodded and reluctantly started back toward Rollingblock and their camp. As they drove through the deserted streets, they saw few signs of life. Once in the distance, they heard the pop, pop, pop of gunfire.

"Still sounds like a place I don't want to live in," Bear observed. "I never did like this damn town anyway."

They continued out of the small city to the road they figured Kyle and Melon used to return to Rebel's Revenge. Once they left town, they traveled at about ten miles per hour, looking for the other truck the two men had used. About half way back, they saw a man and a woman crouching in the brush about twenty yards from the road. They stopped the truck. Leaving their long guns behind, they each

215

carried a pistol beneath their coats and stepped away from the vehicle.

"Hello there," Lynn called. "We were wondering if you could help us." She waited a couple of seconds then said, "We mean you no harm. We only want some information."

"We don't know nothin'," the man answered.

"Mister," Hal called. "We're looking for a couple of our friends. We could sure use some of your help. We've got food to trade for the information."

There was a long pause, and then the man shouted back, "What kind of help?"

"Just some information on my husband and a man with him," Lynn answered.

Another long pause then, "Are you all armed?"

David called back, "Yes sir, but we don't use them unless we have to."

Bear started walking back to the truck.

"Where's he going?" The man asked.

"I'm gonna go take a piss if it's all the same to you," Bear answered.

"Bear!" David said sternly to the man. "We need his help."

"Fuck him," Bear muttered and continued toward the far side of the truck. "I'm tired of talking." He started unzipping his pants as he disappeared from sight.

"We don't want no trouble," the man called out.

"We don't want any either," David answered.

The woman said something to the man. They couldn't tell what she was saying, but based on her tone, she seemed to be trying to convince him to come up and talk to them.

He sharply snapped something back to her then said, "Where's that other fella. Git him back out here."

"He's no problem. Look if you're not willing to help us," David answered, "We need to get going. We have to find out about our friends and get back to camp before sunset."

"Then you might as well git going. I don't mean to be unsocial. But we can't take no chances," the man yelled back.

"Neither can we," Bear said.

The man swung around and was looking down the barrels of two forty-four caliber pistols.

"Now if you'll lay your weapons on the ground," Bear said sternly. "We can go talk to my friends. Then we can be on our way, and you can be on yours.

The man hesitated, sizing Bear up; the man's rifle pointed toward the other members of the group. He laid his rifle on the ground and started to stand.

"All your weapons," was all Bear said. Then motioning to the woman, "Hers too."

The man started to reach under his coat.

"Slowly," Bear growled.

Slowly the man produced a pistol held between his thumb and forefinger and dropped it on the ground beside the rifle. He didn't have to be told not to make any threatening moves.

"Now yours," Bear said looking at the woman.

"I don't have one," she said looking at the man on the ground next to her.

Bear cocked the hammer on the pistol in his left hand.

"She don't have nothing," the man said quickly. "Honest, mister."

Bear stepped back and motioned with the pistol for them to stand. "Get up."

The rest of the group had walked down to where Bear and the two strangers stood, both of whom wore a worried look.

"My name's Ben and this is Janet," he said motioning to the woman.

"I'm David and this is Lynn."

Hal stepped forward and held out his hand. "I'm Hal he said, and I think you've already met Bear."

The man turned and saw Bear holding the rifle out for Ben to take. Ben hesitated a second and Bear said, "Well, take the damn thing. I'm not gonna hold it all day."

Ben took the rifle, and Bear handed him his pistol back. "Like we said-we just want some information if you have it."

Ben and Janet looked as if they weren't sure how to take the group. First, they take their weapons away only to give them right back.

"We told you we didn't want any trouble," David said. "Do you have food?"

"Not much," Janet answered, "but a little."

Everyone walked back to the truck with David leading the way. From inside the cab, they produced some fried meat from the night before. They also gave the couple bread for sandwiches.

Ben and Janet gratefully accepted the food and ate hungrily. By their appearance, they hadn't eaten for some time.

As they ate, Lynn asked, "Have you seen two men driving a truck?"

"We've seen a couple of trucks on the road," Janet answered. "But we couldn't see who was in them."

"One stopped about a mile up the road there," Ben said motioning along the road toward Rollingblock.

"Why didn't you check it out and see who was there?" Hal asked.

"Because it might have been some of those militia boys and girls," Janet told him.

"What militia?" Bear asked, noticing the nervousness in her voice.

"The New South Militia," Ben answered. "Their headquarters is over by Lake Brazos."

"We've never heard of 'em," David said. "What can you tell us about them?"

"They're real trouble," Ben explained. "They've pulled together a bunch of red necks and are trying to rebuild the south as it was before the civil war, including slaves and all."

"Slaves." Bear spat the word out. "What the fuck are you talking about?"

"They have a lot of people locked up and use them as slaves," Janet explained.

"The truck over there," Lynn started. "What about it? When did it pull up?

"Yesterday about this time," Ben said.

"Is it still there?" Lynn asked.

"As far as we know, we didn't see it leave," Ben stated. "It could have left during the night-but we probably would have heard it."

"We need to check it out guys," Lynn said to her companions. Then back to the others she asked, "Can you point it out for us?"

"We'd like to be helpful," Ben answered. "But if it's a group from the militia, then we could be in big trouble."

"Why don't you all stay here for a little bit, and I'll go and check the truck out," Bear suggested.

"I'll go with you," Lynn offered.

"No," Bear answered. "I travel better and faster alone."

"I'm going, Bear!" It was a statement and not a suggestion or request.

Bear simply shook his head and looked at Ben.

"About a mile down this road, there's a dirt road off to the left," Ben explained. "It only goes a quarter mile or so, and there's no other outlet to it."

"Okay," Bear said. "We'll be back soon."

"We'll give you an hour," David said. "Then we'll come looking for you."

Bear shrugged and walked off with Lynn beside him.

They walked down the side of the road their truck sat on until the dirt road came into view.

"We'll cut across here," Bear said.

Lynn nodded and followed him as he cut south through the trees, and after about five minutes, a truck came into view. However, it wasn't the one Kyle and Melon used.

"We might as well check it out," She said walking toward the truck.

"Easy," he cautioned. "Keep an eye out for anything."

There was nothing in the back or the truck's cab. On the ground, beside the passenger door, was what appeared to be a bloodstain.

"That doesn't look promising," she answered. She looked along the dirt road and noticed the bumper of another vehicle around a bend about fifty feet away. She tapped Bear on the shoulder and pointed at the fender.

Holding his finger up against his lips for her to keep quiet, he motioned to the right side of the road. He moved to the left side, and staying even with each other, they both moved along the road toward the vehicle.

As they approached, he could tell the vehicle, like the first, wasn't the one they were looking for. Approaching the door of the truck, he saw two more trucks parked further around the bend.

This time there was blood smeared over both doors as well as inside the truck. Bear pointed at the other trucks and moved forward. When he got close enough to see around the next truck, he saw the one they were looking for.

He motioned for Lynn to join him. She quietly came to where he stood and looked ahead as he nodded to indicate the direction. She looked, and to his surprise, she didn't rush forward or make any noise. Instead, she kept her cool and nodded. Together, they moved cautiously forward, checking the vehicle closest to them as they did. Again, as with the last, there was blood on both doors and inside the cab.

As they approached the next truck, Bear saw articles of clothing in the back of it. *Well, they made it to San Marcos*. But the thought did little to set him at ease.

The cab was empty except for some spent ammo casings, and as before, there was blood all over the inside. Bear looked across the cab at Lynn. She showed no emotions, although she was obviously aware of the implications of the scene before her.

Lynn looked away from the truck and scanned the area.

She's checking the area to make sure it's safe.

Looking back at him she whispered, "There's two more vehicles up ahead. Let's check them out and then get the hell outta here."

"Are you sure you wanna continue?" He asked. "We can beat feet if you prefer."

"No, let's finish what we're doing," she whispered. "Besides, we're gonna have to take this truck with us. It still has supplies in it.

Bear damn sure didn't expect that answer. He realized then how strong a woman Lynn really was. She essentially just found confirmation of her husband's death and was still thinking of the needs of the group.

They finished checking the other two vehicles with the same results. When they returned to the truck with the clothes in it, they realized they would need another vehicle to help get this one started.

It only took about twenty minutes to get back to where David and the others waited.

"We were about to go out and find you," he said as they walked up. "Did you find anything?"

Lynn explained what she and Bear had found and what they needed to do so they could get the truck started and carry the clothes back to camp.

"Well," David said, turning back to Ben and Janet. "It's time for us to be going. Both of you are

222

welcome to come back to camp with us for a day or two."

"We thank you all the same," Ben said. "But, we don't plan to stay around the area any longer than we have to. I think we're gonna head for the coast."

"It's up to you," Hal told them. "We just wanted you to know you're welcome to come back with us if you want to."

The group bade Ben and Janet goodbye, started the truck, and headed out to get the other truck started so they could return to camp before dark.

CHAPTER TWENTY

Captain Campbell had chosen fifteen people to search the Rollingblock area and taken the afternoon to prepare. He laid out his plans for the search figuring it would take two days for them to complete it.

Ron Campbell spent four years in the Marine Corps and held the rank of sergeant when discharged. He became a roughneck, working offshore for six years before the loss of electricity. He was on a vacation, visiting his brother, when the power went out and found himself stuck in Texas.

Ron's brother, a member of the militia, took him to a meeting the first week he was there. The group had impressed him enough he told his brother that if he lived in the area, he would join up.

About two weeks after the loss of power, his brother died and Ron went to the only other people he knew in the area. General Clark invited him for lunch and by the end of the meal, made Ron a Sergeant in the militia.

Between General Clark, Ron, and Capt. Wilkerson, they completely reorganized the group. They set up new rules and regulations and made every man, woman, and child swear allegiance to the militia and their way of life. Since then, they were able to weed out all the people not willing to follow up and carry their weight. Some were simply run out while others received a death sentence.

During one of the conflicts with a group near the Brazos Dam, Capt. Wilkerson died. Ron immediately received the rank of captain and assumed command of Wilkerson's people. Since then, he had proven himself to be an able leader, and The General had come to rely heavily on his knowledge.

Ron assembled all his people. "Listen people," he said, scanning the group before him, "this isn't gonna be a simple walk in the park. There're people out there who killed five of our brothers. Remember, there are still a shit load of those creatures as well, and they're still as dangerous as they ever were." He paused and looked at the group. "We're not out there to try to capture these people. We're only gonna locate them and report back. You all know your assigned sectors. No heroics people. If you find them, get back here, and report. Now let's go."

They all loaded into three vehicles and headed for Rollingblock. The small convoy met no resistance all the way to the drop off point-a new shopping center on the outskirts of the village. There they dismounted and headed toward their various starting points.

They were to sweep the downtown area of the square first. Three groups would then work down the main road of the town and all the businesses there. The other two groups would check the outlying businesses and homes. Following all of that, they would all meet at the north end of the village and return together.

As they started at the edge of town, Ron heard a vehicle coming their way. He barked an order, and everyone moved to the side of the road and hid. As a truck passed, he saw four people in it. He was sure this was part of the group they were looking for. He also figured they would now either find the other group on their own or simply wait and follow this vehicle to them when it returned.

Knowing they were on the right track and there was a very good possibility of finding their enemy, Ron sent one of his people back to headquarters to report. He figured there was a good chance the general would send reinforcements, and then they would be able to get this out of the way soon.

***

David drove along Ranch Road 26 about forty miles an hour, followed by Bear in the truck they previously found. Upon entering Rollingblock, David had a funny feeling. He felt as though they were being watched. He scanned the area around the trucks but saw nothing. Still, his gut told him there were eyes on him-following the two trucks' progression.

"Keep your eyes open," he said to Lynn. "Something's not right."

"I know, I feel it too." She scanned the area.

They crossed the bridge spanning the Buffalo River and entered the downtown area of the village. There was nothing in sight to cause them any trouble.

After passing through the square and crossing the Cypress Creek Bridge, they turned left onto River Road. About a half-mile later, they turned right beside the Lazy R Resort and then the entrance to the camp.

Wind was on guard and stood as they drove up. David only paused long enough to tell him he thought someone was behind them and to get out of sight. He drove to the camp, and both he and Lynn, jumped out of the truck.

As he moved away from the truck, David said, "Everybody take cover. I don't think we're alone. Spyder, get over to where Wind is."

The entire camp began moving in quick time. Lynn ran to the other end of the camp to reinforce the guard there. She found Ben and told him about the situation.

"Do you expect anyone to come around here?" Ben asked.

"There's no way to tell," Lynn answered. "However, we need to keep an eye out and make sure no one circles around and surprises us from behind."

David was with Spyder and Wind at the entrance. "Have either of you seen anything of Bear and Hal?" He asked.

"They drove past a few minutes ago and turned right on Half Mile Road," Wind said.

"Turned right?" David repeated, raising his eyebrows. Then, realizing what Bear was probably doing he said, "It felt like someone was following us back there. Looks like Bear realized it too. He and Hal have probably dropped the truck and are circling around on foot to get behind whoever it was."

They only had to wait about fifteen minutes before hearing a group of people coming up the road. The group wasn't trying to hide themselves or keep their voices low. Instead, there were eight of

227

them, with Hal and Bear in the middle, as they walked up the road. Both men's hands were tied in front, and they were led by ropes looped around their necks.

"That's what you get for trying to be a hero," Wind said.

Spyder looked at the man and said, "Watch your mouth boy. Those are friends of mine."

"Some friends," Wind muttered. "Got their asses caught and now we gotta... "

Before he could say another word, Spyder had his Bowie Knife out with the point against Wind's throat. "I said watch your mouth, son," Spyder warned. "I'll open your throat from ear to ear. Them boys out there's part of us-more'n you'll ever understand. Now shut the fuck up and get ready."

David watched the situation unfold. He knew better than get in it with Spyder when he was in this frame of mind. When Spyder put his knife back in its sheath, David said, "Wind, you cover us." As he rose, Spyder stood with him.

Will and Davata snuck through the brush and were now kneeling with Wind. All three had their weapons ready.

David and Spyder stepped out and slowly walked toward the group of men who held their friends captive. Both men wore their pistols holstered and carried lever action rifles.

Davata sent Will back to the camp to get more reinforcements. Will, was off like a deer. He could move through brush and trees almost at a dead run without being detected. His father had trained him well.

David and Spyder stepped onto the road about thirty yards ahead of the approaching group. Both men wore western wear including dusters, which were pulled back exposing a pistol on each hip. They were also sporting rifles, which both pointed upward with the butts resting on the front of their belts. As the militia group stopped, one of the men raised his rifle. The move was more from fear and caution than a threat

"How you boys doing?" David asked, as both he and Spyder stopped with less than fifty feet between them.

"We're okay," one of the men answered stepping forward. "We found these two running around out there, armed to the teeth. For the time being we relieved them of their weapons-can't be too careful these days."

"You boys okay?" Spyder asked looking at Hal and Bear.

"I could do without this," Hal said holding his tied hands up.

Spyder nodded. Then David said, "You can let them go. They mean you no harm. As for the weapons, it's like you said, you can't be too careful nowadays."

"Sounds like they're friends of yours," the other man said.

"They are," David answered.

"We had a couple of our men ambushed in the square here in Rollingblock," the man said. "We figure these men were probably in on it. I figured we'd take them back to our headquarters for questioning."

229

"I can guarantee you neither of those men had anything to do with an ambush," David explained. "We wouldn't put up with something like that."

"Well, that's what you say," the other man answered. "I don't mean no disrespect, but how do we know you weren't involved yourself?"

"Look," David said. "It seems we're getting off on the wrong foot. My name's David Alexander. This here's Spyder, and we sure don't want any problems. We only want our people back, and we'll be on our way."

"Marty Carpenter," the other man said. "We're members of the New South Militia."

"Well if all we've got here is a misunderstanding," David said. "Then we should be able to work it out without any grief to any of us."

"Don't think we can do that," Marty answered. "This one here," he said, grabbing the rope around Bear's neck, "bit the finger off one of my men when we captured him. ... and he'll have to answer for it."

David could see a blood trail from Bear's mouth. He could also see a cut above his left eye, which oozed blood down the side of his face.

"Looks like you've already made him pay for it," David said lifting his chin toward Bear.

"I'll tell you what," Marty said. "We'll let you have the other one. But this one," he tugged on the rope again, "refuses cooperate. I think we'll take him on back and teach him how to act when he meets one of our army."

"Okay, let us have Hal, and then we can talk about Bear." David answered. David knew the situation was going south fast. All he could hope was that the others were waiting, out of sight, in case needed and he was beginning to believe that they would be soon.

***

Bear knew what was happening. If it took getting them back one at a time, then that's what they would do. He also knew if any member of Rebel's Revenge had the diplomatic skills to pull this off it was David.

Marty turned, slipped the rope off Hal's head and pushed him forward. "The Militia always keeps its word. Here's your man. Now, we'll be on our way."

Hal stopped, turned, and looked at Bear who motioned with his head for Hal to go on. Hal then looked at Marty and said, "I'll be needin' my pistols, mister."

Marty grinned and said, "Once the Militia takes a weapon from someone, we never give them back unless you join up with us."

"Now, hang on a second," David said. "We can't give up one of our men and our weapons."

"That's exactly what you're gonna do," Marty answered. "It's our rules and since we're now the law around here, you'll do as I say."

Spyder tossed his rifle to Hal and pulled a sawed-off shotgun from under his duster. "I don't think you understand," he said. "You're not leaving with Bear."

Quickly Marty stepped over to Bear, pulled a pistol and placed the barrel against the man's back. Then he repeated, "Like I said, we'll be on our way now."

231

David looked into Bear's eyes and saw he had no intention of going with the men.

"I don't think you'll be taking him with you," Spyder said to Marty matter-of-factly.

David could see Bear was shifting his weight to the left. He didn't know what was about to happen, but he was damn sure going to follow the man's lead.

Marty stepped back, and Bear resisted. Marty stepped back up to Bear and from behind his head asked, "Do I kill you here, or do you come quietly?"

Immediately, Bear raised his right foot and smashed his heel against the man's knee causing it to invert, damaging ligaments and cartilage. As Bear started to drop out of the line of fire, Marty pulled the trigger.

The bullet ripped through Bear's back, barely missed the lung and exited through the left side of his lower chest. As he hit the ground, he heard guns firing from all directions. One of the Militia hit the ground in front of him, shot through the neck. Blood poured from the wound and gathered in a quickly spreading pool, on the ground.

The group around him broke and began running. Marty made it to his feet, across the road and into the bushes. He turned just in time for Bear to pick up the pistol of the downed man beside him. Before Marty could point his own pistol toward him, Bear shot the man once in the chest then in the head.

David, Spyder, and Hal were walking down the middle of the road. All three had guns in hand, firing at the retreating men. Even though bullets whizzed around them, they were determined to reach their friend and cause as much damage as possible to the others in doing so. The roar of weapons sounded all around them, not just from the men they faced.

In less than a minute, all of the Militia, except two, lay either in or beside the road. The majority of Rebel's Revenge emerged from the bushes.

The two remaining members of the militia took off running through the trees trying to get away as quickly as possible. Spyder looked at Carl and said, "Track those two. Stay outta sight and see where they go."

"Got it," Carl said and disappeared into the brush.

Dr. Hamilton hurried to where Bear lay. He looked at David, "Get something to carry him back on and be quick about it. He's losing blood fast."

***

Within ten minutes, Bear was carried back to camp. At the direction of Dr. Hamilton, Spyder kept pressure on the wound. They carried him into the stagecoach barn, the only place affording protection from the wind and debris in the area while the doctor operated.

Once in the stage barn, Dr. Hamilton ushered everyone out except Sandy and Davata. He looked at Bear. "I don't have anything for the pain and believe me, this is going to hurt." Turning to Davata, he pointed to a rod and said, "Go put that in the campfire. Get it as hot as possible and bring it back."

Bear called Sandy over. "Get David to come over here, and have him bring some acupuncture needles with him." Sandy went out to get David and in a couple of minutes, they both returned.

"David, you're gonna have to numb me in front and in back," Bear told him.

"You'll have to talk me through it. I don't know the points for that," David answered. For months, David learned acupuncture from Bear and had become almost as adept at it as his teacher.

"I'll tell you where they are," Bear answered. "Sandy, I need you over here too."

"Sure," Sandy answered walking to his left side. "What can I do?"

"Just stand there and be pretty," he answered. He then started showing David where to place the needles by pointing to the acupoints on Sandy. However, after only a couple of points, he burst into a coughing spasm. His body shook convulsively and he passed out.

A few minutes later, Davata returned with the metal rod glowing red-hot. David left the building saying something about some books Bear had brought with him.

Dr. Hamilton swabbed down the wound and said, "He's in shock from loss of blood. We have to work fast. We take too long, and he dies."

Bear lay totally still as the doctor cauterized the wound to stop the bleeding. He had to apply the rod to both holes as well as sticking it inside the wound. Bear, even though unconscious, lay in a pool of sweat, breathing heavily by the time the doctor finished.

"All we can do is wait," Dr. Hamilton told them. "He may have lost too much blood, and there's still some minor internal bleeding."

Sandy wiped Bear's face as Davata covered him with a blanket. The man was very pale. He was shivering and his breathing labored.

"Will he be okay?" Sandy asked.

"It's too soon to tell," Dr. Hamilton answered. He lost a lot of blood. The bullet passed all the way through though. It depends on how much internal damage it caused. All we can do now is keep him warm and still for now."

As Davata put another blanket on Bear, David entered the stage barn, book in hand. "There's herbal formulas in here about building a person's blood back up. The only problem with them is they all take two to three weeks to work. Dr. Hamilton,"- David turned to the doctor-"isn't there any way we can get blood from some of the rest of us and give it to him?"

"There's no way to match the blood properly. There's more to it than simply having the same type," the doctor answered. "The main problem now is keeping him from losing what he has left. I was able to stop most of the bleeding, but he's still bleeding internally. Ordinarily, it wouldn't be a problem. It would stop on its own. But with the blood he's already lost, he can't afford to lose much more."

"Doctor," Davata called out. "He's coming to."

The other three moved over beside the makeshift operating table. Bear's eyes were barely open and when he talked, it only came out in a whisper. As his lips moved, Dr. Hamilton leaned down and put his ear near the Bear's mouth.

Bear whispered something and again passed out. The doctor checked his eyes and pulse, and then he turned to the others.

"What did he say?" Sandy asked.

"It didn't make any sense," Dr. Hamilton answered. "All he said was something about 'dragon bone and a cattail.'"

"He must be hallucinating," Davata said.

"Probably," Dr. Hamilton agreed.

"Nope," David said excitedly paging through the book in his hands. "They're in here, dragon bone and cattail. They're both substances used in Chinese Medicine to stop bleeding."

"Can we get what we need anywhere around here?" Sandy asked. "Maybe there's something in the health food store on the end of town."

"No need," David answered. "It says here dragon bone is nothing more than the bones of animals ground into a fine powder. The only requirement is that it is old. It can't be a fresh kill. Cattail grows around wet areas."

"What about that old cow skull over by the chuck wagon?" Davata asked. "It looks like it's been there for a while."

"It's been here as long as I have," David answered. "Now all we need to do is grind it up into a powder."

"What about the cattail?" Davata asked.

"It's also known around here as pussy willow. We need the pollen growing in groups on the plant," David explained.

236

"Okay, hold on folks," Dr. Hamilton said holding his hands up toward them. "This is all well and good. But there's no way I'm gonna let you put that stuff on his wounds. There has to be all kinds of germs on that skull."

"What if we soak it in alcohol?" David asked.

"Not unless you soak it long enough to completely saturate the entire skull. The germs will be all through the bones," the doctor answered.

"Let me ask you this, Doctor. What happens if we don't use these?" David asked. "What are his chances?"

"I really don't know," Dr. Hamilton answered. "I would guess it to be somewhere around eighty-twenty against recovery."

"That's good enough for me," David stated. "Sandy, get the skull. Totally wipe it down with the alcohol we got at Country Boys. I'll take care of the cattail."

"I told you it won't be enough to kill all the germs," Dr. Hamilton said. "You may be putting him in more danger. Besides, the bleeding is internal. I will have to open him up to get to where it is."

"We understand," Sandy answered. "But it gives him a better chance than if we sit back and do nothing."

"I'm not gonna just sit by and watch him die," David said. "He wouldn't do that if it were me."

"I understand how all of you feel," Dr. Hamilton said. "But, I simply can't allow you to put this man in that kind of danger, and I won't be a part of opening him up so you can pour contaminated voodoo powder inside him."

Before the doctor could fully realize what was happening, he was looking down the barrel of Sandy's pistol. "Doctor," the woman said, a grim look on her face, "that man is closer to me than any brother ever has been. If you'll step aside, we'll take over from here."

David moved toward the door. "I'll take care of getting the stuff ready," he said and called for Spyder as he left the structure.

Dr. Hamilton looked down at the pistol then up into Sandy's eyes. He could see she meant what she said and the pistol in her hands was more than an idle threat. He couldn't help but admire the closeness of the group. He also knew if it were any other member of the group, they would be just as loyal.

He could see the interdependence and loyalty among these people, which had grown since the development of this impossible situation. Each depended on the other for emotional, physical and mental support. Dr. Hamilton had seen no real disagreements or dissatisfaction. Each person played their individual part in the survival of the entire group. With this in mind, he knew the rest of the group would support the decision made by those in this building.

"Well," he said still looking into Sandy's eyes. "If I can't convince you otherwise, I might as well support you and give him the best chance I can to survive."

Sandy smiled, and put her pistol back in its holster. "One of the things you'll learn about us, doctor, is that we no longer stand passively by and simply let things happen. We all believe in what some might call a code. We help each other, care for each other and make things happen. We won't push our beliefs on anyone else, but at the same time, we won't allow anyone else to push us around."

The door to the stage barn opened and Lynn walked in. "Is everything in here okay?" She asked.

Sandy looked at the doctor. "Everything seems to be fine," she answered.

Lynn looked at Bear, "David is boiling that cow skull out there, and Spyder left, saying something about he knew where some-I have no idea what he was talking about. But David said it might be a good idea for me to come in here and keep an eye on Sandy. He said we couldn't afford to lose the doctor."

She turned to the doctor and asked, "Are you planning on leaving us?"

"Not at all, young lady-not at all." He went over to his patient and checked the wound.

Lynn shrugged and sat down on a stack of boxes to wait and watch.

**

As Spyder left to get the cattail, Wind walked up to him and asked, "Where you headed, man?"

"I've got to get some plants," Spyder answered. "If you're free, I could use the company."

"Cindy relieved me on watch. Let's go. What kind of plants are we getting and why?"

"They're for Bear. They're supposed to stop his bleeding."

"... and you know where to find 'em?"

239

"Hell yeah," Spyder answered. "They're all around the river over by Post Oak Mesa."

"Okay," Wind said, "lead the way."

Spyder and Wind went to where the horses were. After saddling up, they started toward the river.

"Keep your eyes open," Spyder told the other man. "At least two of those fellers got away. I figure they're headed back to their camp, but you never can tell."

They rode to the main intersection of Sagebrush and turned right. "About earlier," Spyder started. "When we had our discussion about Bear being captured... "

"Don't worry about it," Wind answered. "I understand what you were saying. I wasn't using my head. It was more frustration than anything. If it was one of my friends there, I would have felt the same way."

They made their way to the river then followed it toward Post Oak Mesa. As they rode along Wind asked, "What the hell are we gonna do? It sounded like those assholes have friends back where they came from. You know they're coming back, and we're gonna have to deal with 'em."

Spyder was rolling a cigarette. "Yeah, looks like there's trouble ahead." He stuck the cigarette in his mouth and lit it. "Those sons-of-bitches will be back, and if they're as stupid as they seem, we're gonna have to kill 'em."

Wind was quiet for a minute then asked, "Doesn't it bother you to think you may have to kill another person?"

"Hell yes, it bothers me," Spyder answered. "But the thought of them trying to kill us bothers me more."

They rode along in silence a little way then Wind said, "You know, I was always involved in school and church. My momma always saw to it that my spiritual education was equal to my schooling. She told me even the smartest man must let God lead him through his life."

Through his thick beard, Wind could see a big smile on Spyder's lips. "I hope you don't think I'm being stupid. I think she was right, and I'm not sure I can kill another person."

"Your momma sounds like a good woman, Wind," Spyder answered his expression now serious. "I also think she was right. Look man, one of the things I have seen about you is that all through the short time I've known you; you haven't once blamed the white race for anything. It's true, in the past; the whites treated your race like shit. Hell, I even done it in my earlier years. It's no secret. I was high up in the Klan when I was in East Texas. That don't make it right, and I'm willing to apologize for what I was like then. Now, don't get me wrong. There's some things still irk me. I still don't like seeing interracial marriages. Up till now, I thought each race should stick to their own kind. Looks like now God has taken the ability to make that decision away from all of us."

"Spyder, I didn't mean... "

"Hang on," Spyder interrupted. "There's three things you should know about me. One is I think your Momma was very a smart woman. It seems like she instilled a sense of pride and responsibility

241

in you. You don't go around blaming other people for what goes on in your life. You take responsibility for all the consequences, both good and bad. Most people don't. I quit the Klan because they didn't let people be individuals. They judged a person by the color of their skin and not by their actions. I can't abide that.

"Second, I'm a member of the same group as you. Now, in the Bible, God says one man shouldn't murder another. It doesn't say 'kill.' It originally said 'murder', or so I was taught. I believe that's right. I won't go out of my way to harm nobody. I also won't allow any of my family to be hurt. Since all this happened, I lost all my blood family as far as I know. This group is now my family. Everyone in it is, and I ain't about to let nothin' happen to any of them if I can help it. If it means killin' some other feller, then that's what it means. The rules have changed, and if we're gonna survive, we have to change too."

Spyder went silent and scanned the area for danger. He looked over and noticed Wind was still looking at him.

"What's number three?" Wind asked.

"What?"

"You said there were three things. What's the third thing?"

"Oh," Spyder answered with a smile. "I guess that'd be that I'm an ordained Methodist Minister."

Wind only showed a slight surprise to his answer. "Spyder," Wind said. "I don't guess there's anything that will surprise me about you. I may never figure you out, but you don't really surprise me."

The two men arrived at a marshy area in the river. "We're here." Spyder dismounted. Wind climbed down from his horse and started helping the other man gather the plant they needed.

***

Inside the barn, Bear had stopped shivering and was lying quietly beneath two blankets.

"This could be either good or bad. On one hand, Bear's body might be working on healing itself. On the other hand, he might be losing the battle and slipping into a coma. That would almost definitely kill him," the doctor said.

Sandy and Lynn were talking with Davata who wanted to know more about the man lying there before them.

"I have blinders on when it comes to him," Sandy said. "He and I have been through a lot. Even before we lost electricity, he and I were close. I don't guess there's anything I wouldn't do for him. The thing I think is great is that I know he feels the same way. Even though he has told me, he doesn't have to. I just know it."

"What does your husband think about it? I don't mean to imply anything. It's just a close friendship like that doesn't always set well with a husband."

"I know what you mean," Sandy answered. "I'll tell you what happened once. Bear wanted to go to Tyler to go on a date with a woman who happened to be my cousin. I wanted to go around the same time, and Hal wasn't able to take off from work to go with me. He suggested I call Bear and ask if I could go with him. I called and he said 'of course, you don't even have to ask.' We went on Friday and returned Sunday. He met my mother before she passed away, plus we sat up and talked almost all night both nights we were there. Hal knows he's the love of my life, my best friend. I want to be with him for the rest of both our lives-and he knows it. I also want Bear to be in my life as much as he can be. It's nothing sexual with either of us. We're just good friends, and Hal knows and understands it."

Davata smiled as she listened to Sandy. "Not too many women are as lucky as you are. You have a remarkable husband and a good friend. I was talking to Bear before and couldn't quite figure him out. He is friendly and obviously cares about everyone here. But at the same time, he seemed very lonely. One thing he did do was to give me a new way to try and look at life."

"He is lonely," Sandy stated. "Cindy, Lynn, and I have been trying to fix him up with a good woman for years now. He has male friends, but he needs a woman in his life to care about. He's even told me that."

"We talked about all the chances he takes." Davata said. "I know he doesn't seem to worry too much about being hurt or even killed, but I thought that was the dumbest thing I ever saw out there on the road. Not to mention, it got him shot-and he still may die. He told me about not being afraid to die and how he was able to achieve that feeling, but still... "

Sandy gave her a stern look.

"He spent over twenty years in the military," Lynn answered. "What he did out there was for our benefit. I didn't see it, but from what everyone has told me, he knew he was in deep trouble if he went with those men. He probably figured he was dead either way. He also knew we would try to rescue him. That would have probably gotten some of us hurt or killed."

"He once told me his military and martial arts training taught him to accept his own death," Sandy explained. "I don't pretend to fully understand what he meant, but it has something to do with Samurai Warriors in Japan's history and not being afraid to die."

"That's what he tried to explain to me," Davata said. "He said it was something called Satori. I thought I understood it until I saw him today. I could never accept my death that way. What Lynn says makes sense, still how could someone simply not care?"

"To change the subject," Lynn said, obviously not comfortable with the talk of death. "Tell us more about you. How the heck did you wind up here if you're from Louisiana?"

Davata told them about Andy and how she met Dr. Hamilton, Wind, and the others. When she told them about the mutants and the information of how a scratch from their claws or a bite caused death, Lynn stopped her.

"You mean to tell me just a bite or scratch will cause death?"

"Yes," Davata answered. "Dr. Hamilton said he had seen other cases of it. Evidently, there's a germ in or on their body that's deadly to humans. He also said that if it doesn't kill the person, it will change them into a mutant themselves."

"Whoa," Lynn exclaimed. "You're saying they may be able to create more mutants simply by scratching a human?"

"That's what the doctor said," Davata answered.

"We've got to get this information out to everyone," Sandy said, a frown creasing her brow. "We could be in more trouble than we thought. If you two will stay with Rafe, I'll go tell Kyle what we just found out." She stood and walked out of the barn.

"I'm sorry," Davata said. "I thought you already knew about this."

"Don't worry about it Davata," Lynn told her. "Now, that we do know we can take precautions. Besides, you couldn't know what information we have unless someone tells you. There's no harm done. But I'm glad we know now."

Davata looked at Bear. The man's breathing was finally slow and regular. Somehow, she felt he would be okay-she hoped so at least. For some reason, she wanted to get to know him better.

When the door opened, Kyle, Sandy, Dr. Hamilton, and David entered the building. David carried a metal bowl in one hand, and Sandy was telling them the information she had just received from Davata. David listened as he pulled the blankets back and got ready to help the doctor put the powdered bone in the wound.

Dr. Hamilton prepared himself, David, and his patient for what could be a touchy operation.

246

CHAPTER TWENTY-ONE

Gabriel returned to the jail annex to see the two mutants. When he walked in, Bo once again locked his eyes on Gabriel. There was no change. The creature still hated the human with all its being.

Bo knew this man only wanted to use his kind to control the other humans in the city. Bo also knew the man would do whatever he could to achieve it. The game was afoot and he would use the human's greed against him. He and the other one in the cells were the leaders of over a hundred mutants gathered from various parts of the Texas Hill Country. There were still at least that many more still living in small bands out in the hills. Bo also knew of some living in San Antonio, one of which was, like him, of the intelligent type. He knew it might take some time, but he figured the pack in San Antonio would be the way he would eventually get free of Gabriel.

The mutants bore a natural hatred of humans, but this human had killed his friend and now threatened to kill his mate. She was the mutant in the cell next to him, and he knew if the human discovered this, he would use it as leverage. At the same time, he wouldn't let this Gabriel, hurt her if he could help it.

Gabriel pulled up a chair and sat in front of the bars of the cell. "Have you been fed?"

Bo nodded slowly and grunted. Gabriel had no idea the simple grunt meant the food tasted like shit.

Gabriel then asked, "Have you been treated okay?"

Again, another grunt came from the mutant. Bo knew the right question was sure to come up. All he needed to do was be patient and wait for it.

Gabriel continued asking questions for another ten minutes concerning his comfort and treatment. Then Gabriel asked, "How many mutants like you are there?"

Rather than making it easy for the human, he let out a long low growl. It actually meant nothing, but he knew Gabriel would think it did and push the subject.

Gabriel then asked, "Do you know how to contact other packs in the area?"

Bo slowly bobbed his head up and down indicating that he did.

"Would you be willing to contact them for me?" Gabriel asked.

Bo stared back.

"Don't make me do something to that one," Gabriel said pointing with his thumb toward Bo's mate in the next cell.

Bo looked in the direction Gabriel pointed then back at the man. He lifted his chin as he let out a series of grunts and growls. He returned his gaze back to Gabriel. This time though, he was showing no anger or aggression.

Bo knew his ruse was working. He could see the excitement in the human. He also knew he must take care not to slip up and show his true feelings. This might be the only chance he would ever have. If he blew it, the human would kill him and his mate. If he made it work, he could learn about the locations of all the humans in the city.

"Is there anything you need?" Gabriel asked.

Bo nodded, and at the same time, held both hands out cupped in front of him. He wanted to see how far this human was willing to go to get information.

"What do you need, more food, water?"

Bo continued to hold his cupped hands out for a couple of seconds then drew them up to his mouth as if drinking.

Gabriel stood and went to the door leading to a hallway outside. He told someone there to get two bowls of water and said something else Bo couldn't quite make out. Then he said a little more loudly, "... and hurry up. We need to show these two we mean them no harm."

Bo knew this action was only to get him to cooperate. This was okay. He would cooperate only as much as required to give him and his mate a chance to escape. It may take some time, but they would escape.

A few minutes later, a man brought two bowls of water. Gabriel took them and returned to Bo's cell. He set one of the bowls on the floor where a slot was located for pushing food through the bars. "Now if you will tell your friend there to stay away from the bars, I'll put this water down for her."

After a few grunts, the female backed away and sat on the bed attached to the wall. Gabriel placed the water outside the cell and backed away. "You can let her know it's hers," he said.

Again, after a couple of sounds from Bo, the female retrieved the water.

"See," Gabriel said. "I told you, all I want is for us to be able to work together."

Bo sniffed the water and then tentatively took a drink. The second mutant did the same and sat back down on the bunk.

"Is there anything else you need?" Gabriel asked.

Bo shook his head no. He knew he shouldn't push his luck too far. Right now, it seemed like he was getting the human to relax and that was what he wanted.

For the next hour and a half, Gabriel talked to Bo, who responded with some answers. The rest of the questions Bo answered with the best-puzzled look he could produce. He wanted the human to think they were making progress slowly because of a problem with communication.

Finally Gabriel, through frustration, decided they both had done enough. He rose from his chair and told Bo he would return the next day so they could talk more.

***

Gabriel left the cell room and entered the hallway outside. To one of the guards standing there he said, "Keep them both in water and food. Keep the water at the same dose you just gave them. Be sure and tell your relief what to do. Anyone screws this up, and I'll kill them myself, understand?"

"You got it boss. I'll take care of it personally."

Gabriel left the jail annex. He had some thinking and planning to do.

250

CHAPTER TWENTY-TWO

General Clark stepped from the bathroom, zipping his pants when his door burst open and the two men rushed in. "We've got a problem General," one man said.

The General looked at both of them and said, "It better be a big fuckin' problem for you to bust in here like that."

"The rest are dead. They killed every one of them," the same man said.

"Hold on now," the General ordered. "Slow down and tell me what you're talking about. Who's dead?"

"The rest of the scouting party," the man answered.

"Now look, Buck," General Clark said. "I don't have time to play twenty questions. Start from the beginning and tell me what you're talking about."

The man named Buck paused for a couple of seconds then said, "We were waiting for them to come back in the truck like you said. When they did, we followed them onto a back road. After a mile or so, they ambushed us. There must have been thirty or forty of 'em. They came from all around us and... "

"Hang on," the General said. "You mean to tell me they ambushed you out of the clear blue. None of you did anything to them to provoke it?"

"No, Sir General," Buck answered. "We were walking down the middle of the road. You can ask Al here. He'll tell you."

"Is that right Al?" General Clark asked. "Did they ambush you for no reason?"

"That's right General," Al answered. "It's exactly like Buck here says. They jumped us out of the blue with guns blazing. They were shooting from everywhere. We were lucky to get out alive."

"You mean to tell me they didn't make any demands before they attacked?" The General asked. "They didn't warn you or nothing?"

"No Sir," Buck answered. "They just started shooting. Before we knew it, we were the only two to get out alive. Even Marty Carpenter was killed."

"What about Captain Campbell?" General Clark asked.

"I don't know," Buck answered. "He wasn't with us. He and Sam Carson were coming to our location from the square. They must have been a mile or so behind us."

As if on cue, Captain Campbell and Sam Carson opened the door and walked in. Ron Campbell stepped forward and presented a salute.

General Clark returned the salute and said, "The rest of you need to pay attention. This is how to properly report back to your Commanding Officer." Then to the captain he asked, "Did you see what happened?"

"Yes Sir General, I did," he answered.

"Tell me about it," General Clark ordered.

"I'd like to speak with you in private if I may," Ron answered.

General Clark looked at the other men. "You men are dismissed for now. Wait outside."

***

When the others left the room General Clark said, "Have a seat Ron and tell me what happened."

After Ron Campbell settled into a chair he said, "General, Carpenter fucked up royally. He captured two of the men from the camp over there. They were both tied up and walking in the middle of our troops when they met two other men. Carpenter talked to the two men for a couple of minutes. I couldn't hear what was being said, but then he let one of the prisoners go. When the one he let go walked over to the other two, one of them gave him a rifle and pulled a shotgun out from under his coat." Ron knew this was against the militia's beliefs, but it was the truth.

"Wait a minute," the General said, holding his hand up motioning for the other man to stop talking. "Are you telling me he let a prisoner go and then let his friends arm him?"

"Yes Sir," Ron answered, "that's what he did. Then something happened with the one we still held prisoner. The next thing I knew Carpenter shot him, and all hell broke loose. There was shooting from all directions. They had surrounded our detail while they were talking. I didn't even know they were there until the shooting started."

"How many of the enemy would you say there were?" General Clark asked.

"Only ten or twelve," Ron answered and then quickly added, "but they were good shots, and we were in a cross-fire. There might as well have been fifty. There was no escaping. How Buck and Sam got away, I don't know. Believe me, they were lucky."

"Maybe, maybe not," General Clark answered. "They both stood here and lied to me about what happened. I can't have troops lying if we're to keep up discipline. Bring them both in here, Lieutenant."

***

Moments later both Buck and Sam stood in front of the General. General Clark was on his feet as he talked to the men.

"Gentlemen," he said. "Both of you stood in front of me and gave a false report. Whether or not it was because of cowardice, I don't know. I would rather believe it was to protect your team leader. Whichever it was, I will not tolerate any of my people lying to me. This also puts your dedication to our society in question."

The General paused and looked at both men. "Due to your actions and the possible impact they could have on our community, it's time for you both to prove your loyalty. Therefore, I sentence both of you to ten lashes in public. Should you decide you don't want to accept this punishment, you will be banned from our ranks for life."

Banishment essentially meant a death warrant. The Militia would have nothing to do with them, and most of the people around the area who knew of the Militia would kill any of its members caught out alone.

"It's time for you boys to make your decision," General Clark said, "What are you gonna do?"

Buck answered, "General I can only speak for myself. I want to stay here and will accept any punishment you decide."

254

Sam was looking down at the floor while the General made his statement. He now looked up. "General there's got to be some other way we can make up for what we did," he said in a pleading voice. "It's probable we won't survive ten lashes. There's got to be another way."

"I take that as a no," General Clark said. To Ron he said," Captain Campbell, take both these men out to the compound and gather the rest of the troops together."

"Yes Sir," Ron answered and ushered both men from the office. Once outside, he rang the bell used to assemble all the members of the militia.

It only took about five minutes for everyone to gather. Once all the troops were there, General Clark stepped on the porch of the house containing his office.

"Ladies and Gentlemen," he started. "There are two among us who have been found guilty of indiscretion. Both men are guilty of lying to their Commanding Officer. One man wishes to stay with us and face his punishment like a man. The other has chosen to leave our ranks-to skulk off like a coward."

General Clark turned to Ron and said, "Captain Campbell, lead the convicted man to the redemption post."

Captain Campbell led Buck to the post in the middle of the compound, where they stripped his shirt off and tied his hands together, attaching them to a ring high above his head. Another man stepped forward carrying an eight-foot bullwhip and positioned himself a short distance behind Buck.

The General then said, "Since this is a matter of honor, it is improper for a coward to witness the punishment of one of our people. Captain Campbell you will remove the coward from our midst."

Ron walked Sam to the front gate of the compound. Once there, Ron ordered the man to remove his weapons and drop them on the ground.

"You can't kick me out with no way to protect myself," Sam protested.

In a low voice, Ron said, "make this easy on yourself. Drop the weapons. If you don't, we'll strip you not only of your weapons but all your clothes too."

Sam looked at him a couple of seconds, and removed his pistol belt dropping it to the ground. He took his rifle off his shoulder and dropped it as well.

Ron stepped to the open gate and waited for Sam to approach. As Sam approached the gate General Clark said, "Kick the coward out."

Ron immediately executed a spinning heel kick catching Sam in the middle of his back. The man stumbled a couple of feet before slamming face first into the dirt. Immediately, two other men closed the two doors of the gate locking them. Outside, Sam cringed in pain, trying to regain his breath. Inside the compound, Ron turned and walked over to Buck where he then turned and faced General Clark on the porch.

The general scanned the group before him and said, "This man broke our laws and has been sentenced to ten lashes. However, through his willingness to face his mistake and uphold the beliefs of our society, I am going to commute his punishment. Rather than lashes, he will be a worker for a period of one month. Let this demonstration of compassion serve to show all of you I'm the kind of leader who has all of your best interests in mind."

He then called for Ron to follow him, dismissed the assembled group, and went into his office. Ron followed him and closed the door.

General Clark sat down behind his desk and said, "We're gonna need all the men, women, and guns we have. If those people in Rollingblock decide to fight us, we'll have a problem on our hands. Let Buck stay at home at night, but for the next week let him work right beside the rest of the workers. Also, I want you to intensify the training schedule. Our people have to be ready for whatever comes."

Ron saluted, turned, and walked out.

CHAPTER TWENTY-THREE

Spyder and Wind finished gathering the cattails and were on their way back to camp. It only took about five minutes to gather enough plants to fill a saddlebag.

"Is there any way to cut across to camp?" Wind asked.

"Nope, the camp is on the other side of those cliffs," Spyder answered indicating the vertical, one hundred-fifty foot cliffs to their left.

"You think Bear's gonna make it?" Wind asked.

"I don't know," Spyder answered. "But if he doesn't, I'll kill every son-of-a-bitch involved with his death."

There was no doubt in Wind's mind the man meant exactly what he said. They continued until they came to the trail used to get to Rebel's Revenge, which wound through what was once the Lazy R Ranch Resort. It only took them another five minutes until they reached the camp. As they dismounted, David met them.

"Were you able to get the cattail?" he asked.

"Got enough to have extra after we've treated Bear," Spyder answered.

"How's he doing?" Wind asked as he took the reins from Spyder.

"Better," David said. "We went ahead and used the dragon bone alone until you two got back. Looks like the bleeding has stopped."

He took a couple of the cattails from a saddlebag. The rest he returned to Wind and said,

"Take these to Ginny. She knows what to do with 'em. Wind took the plants and departed toward the cooking area to find Ginny.

"What does the doctor say?" Spyder asked.

"Well, barring any infections. He thinks Bear might make it," David said. "He also said if he recovers, it shouldn't take too long for him to be up and around. There wasn't too much damage, just a severe loss of blood."

"Knowing Bear, he'll be giving us all a bunch of shit within the week," Spyder said with a grin.

From the side a voice startled both of them. "Gents," Lynn said. "I think we should go to the health food store and do a raid on it."

The men turned to see the woman approaching them with tears streaming down her face. They moved quickly toward her. David took her in his arms and she began sobbing. "Kyle is dead, Rafe is lying in there dying and Carl is out somewhere following two of the bastards that attacked us. None of this makes any sense. The boys are now without their father, me without my husband and for what? So we can all be thrown back into the past? She was talking rapidly into David's shoulder. Then all we can do is join together and do what-have to fight other people? And don't forget the new kind of animal. We're gonna have a lot of fun with them." She pulled back, and the men could see anger had replaced grief.

"Come on," David said, his arm still around her shoulders. "You need some rest. It's been a long day."

"Don't patronize me, David Alexander," Lynn said. "I know what's happening. I'm going through a

259

grieving process. I'll be okay. Just give me time. I'll work through it on my own and in my own time." She shrugged his arm off her shoulder and walked away into the camp.

"A remarkable woman," David said turning back to Spyder as Wind walked up carrying two bags.

"She damn sure is," Spyder agreed. "She'll have a tough time for a little while, but she's gonna be okay."

They watched until Lynn disappeared around one of the tents. Then, David took the bags from Wind, and he and Spyder went over to the stage barn. Wind led the horses over to unsaddle and feed them.

***

Inside the building, Sandy and Davata sat talking to Dr. Hamilton. David mixed the cattail and dragon bone together according to the percentages in the book and put it in the wound the doctor created to access the internal bleeding. He could see very little blood oozing from the wound, and Bear looked like he was resting easy.

"Was Lynn doing okay when she was in here?" David asked.

"She seemed to be okay," Sandy answered. "Why, what's wrong?"

"Nothing really," David said. "I just want to make sure she's all right. I think Bear's condition has triggered emotions about Kyle's death and given her another reason to release 'em. She's one tough woman. So like I said, I think she'll be okay."

260

"I don't want to give anyone false hope," Spyder said. "But they said they only saw blood in the truck. They never saw his body. He could still be alive."

"Not a chance in hell," David answered. "Not with the amount of blood in there. It'd be a miracle."

"It could've been Melon," Spyder reminded him. "We don't know if any of it was Kyle's."

"True," David admitted. "But, I can't believe Kyle would have been taken alive. Plus, there's something we've been leaving out." He paused and looked at them. He didn't want to be too graphic. They didn't need to know all the gruesome details. "They could have been killed by one or more of those mutants."

"I doubt it," Spyder said. "The trucks were all lined up with one parked behind the other."

"There's something Davata told me," Sandy said. "I've already told Hal, but both you need to know too. If a person is bitten or scratched by one of the mutants, they'll change."

"What do you mean change?" David asked.

Davata stepped forward and said, "Andy, the man I lived with in Louisiana, was scratched, and in a couple of days started to turn into one of them."

"There's an enzyme in the sweat and saliva of the mutants, which reacts with humans," Dr. Hamilton explained. "In some way it causes a change at the cellular level and changes the person into one of them."

"Well I'll be, kiss my ass," Spyder said and leaned back against a support beam. "If that ain't some shit."

"Doctor," David said. "Are you telling us there are more of those things being made daily?"

"It's a possibility," Dr. Hamilton answered. "But it seems most of the time, the mutants use humans as food. We're lucky in that aspect. They don't appear to leave many people alive after an attack. Therefore, there aren't many people changed."

"We could be in deep trouble folks," David observed.

"It all keeps getting better 'n better," Spyder put in.

"Okay people," Dr. Hamilton said in a stern voice. "Who's staying in here with him?" He pointed at Bear.

"Sandy, you get some rest," Davata said. "I'll stay for a while."

Sandy smiled. "Let me know if there's any change. I'll be back in a couple of hours."

"Everyone else needs to leave," Dr. Hamilton instructed checking the wounds. "He needs to rest."

Once outside he said, "He's stable for now. It looks like he has a much better chance. The bleeding has stopped. Those herbs really worked fast." Shaking his head, he scanned the others he said, "I'm sorry about the voodoo comment."

"Don't worry about it," David answered. "I called it worse than that until I had it done to me."

The group dispersed throughout the camp to pass the information they had learned about the mutants.

***

Outside the gate of the militia compound, Sam was unaware of the commuting of Buck's punishment. All he wanted was to stop the pain now radiating across his back. It was sickening and he was barely able to breathe.

Sam stumbled to his feet, and after a long look at the compound, began staggering away. He mumbled to himself, "What the hell am I gonna do now?"

After Sam was out of sight of the compound, Carl stepped out in front of him. Carl pointed his rifle at the other man and said, "Put your hands where I can see 'em."

Sam raised his right hand. His left remained on his injured ribs.

"Both hands," Carl said and raised the rifle to his shoulder.

"I can't," Sam answered. "There's something wrong with my back."

Carl cocked the hammer on the weapon and said, "Both hands up or die. It's your choice."

Sam tried to raise his left arm, but the pain almost caused him to drop to the ground. "If you're gonna shoot me, then do it," he said. "But there's no way I can get my hand up."

Carl thought for a couple of seconds then said, "Okay, then you're coming with me."

"That's fine," Sam answered. "Just take it easy, please son."

"I ain't your son. The name's Carl and you deserve no mercy from me for what you did," Carl answered and motioned with his rifle for the man to start moving.

263

Carl and Sam slowly made their way toward Rollingblock. Sam was having a tough time traveling. He traveled stooped over and groaned with almost every breath he took. Every time he would stop to take a couple of breaths, Carl would force him on with the barrel of his rifle.

After traveling for a little over an hour, Carl realized there was no way they were going to make it back to camp before nightfall. They were going to have to either find a place to hole up or risk traveling at night. He knew they would have at least five miles to travel in the dark. He didn't know if this guy, the other man at the compound called him Sam, would be able to make it. Then, of course, if they stopped for the night, how was he going to keep an eye on the man?

"Let's take a breather," Carl said to Sam.

They both found a rock and sat down. "We've got a problem here," Carl said.

"Yeah, I know," Sam answered. "Night's coming on. The question is do we stop or go on."

"Right," Carl agreed.

"The way my side and back is hurting," Sam said. "I'm in for a lot of pain either way we go. But if it means getting to safety, I vote to keep going."

"Sure, we keep going, and you have a better chance to jump me in the dark," Carl answered.

"Man, you are in no danger from me," Sam said, looking Carl in the eyes. "I only want to get to safety before we become a meal for one of those animals."

"What animals?" Carl asked.

"Those weird looking ones. Look like a cross between a werewolf, ape, and some sort of reptile."

Carl remembered what Bear and the rest said about the thing they saw in the resort the other night. He also remembered how fast the men said they were. "Have you ever seen one?"

"Only from a distance and then only for a second, Sam answered. The damn thing was at a trot and moving as fast as a man can run."

It only took Carl a couple of seconds to make up his mind for them to keep going. "You've convinced me. Let's get going. But remember, one wrong move and you're dead."

"I'm having enough trouble making the right moves much less making a wrong one," Sam said as he walked in the direction of Rollingblock.

They made it to one of the paved roads as dark settled over the countryside and still had about six miles left to go. They just left Hanged man's Valley when Sam said, "You're not planning to go to the "T", then to Rollingblock are you?"

"I don't know any other way," Carl answered.

"If you turn left up ahead, there's a dirt road over there that runs to the edge of town. It'll cut off at least three miles."

Carl thought a second then said, "Lead the way."

Sam walked up the road a short distance then turned left. They were on a dirt road running down the side of a hill and into the floor of a valley.

"Keep your eyes open," Sam said. "There's a good chance we might run up on one of those creatures."

Two hours later, the men were at one of the low water crossings of the Buffalo River. They walked up the road beside the resort and Sagebrush and

265

eventually came to a large tree. Carl made Sam lay face down beside the road and then climbed the tree. Once up there, he found a small rope and gave it a hard pull.

***

The other end of the rope caused a bucket to fall out of a tree, alerting the person on watch one of their friends was on their way in. It was a system devised by Hal.

When the bucket hit the ground, Cindy immediately sent Deborah back to the camp for back up in case it was someone else who had found out about the rope. She took a rifle and moved into position to where she could see the person approaching in secrecy.

It only took a couple of seconds for them to come into view. Both men came down the path slowly. Sam led the way with Carl holding a rifle on him. "Carl, are you okay?" Cindy asked, almost giving her position away by rushing to the young man. Catching herself, she remained under cover and watched from her vantage point.

"I'm fine," Carl answered and pointed at his companion with the barrel of his rifle. "This here's Sam. He got run off from the militia camp," then as an afterthought he said, "... and he's injured. We're gonna need Dr. Hamilton."

From the other side Wind said, "Bring him on in, and we'll take a look at him." He stepped out of the bushes and joined Carl behind the other man.

Cindy watched them leave. "Lynn'll be relieved to see you back," she said as they walked away.

CHAPTER TWENTY-FOUR

When the power went out, and Gabriel began gathering his gang together, he knew exactly where he would set up his headquarters. A lawyer who successfully defended him on a murder charge once occupied the office. Gabriel was impressed by the man's office and even told him someday he would have an office exactly like it. The lawyer simply smiled. He shot the attorney when the man returned to his office a couple of days after the blackout. *Told you I'd have an office like this someday,* Gabriel thought as the lawyer hit the floor.

He now sat in the office thinking and one of the things that really pissed him off was when the people living here in Austin tried to challenge him. *They should know by now there's nothing they can do to me. I took on the police and won. Hell, it was easy. I started with three hundred members, and now I've got over a thousand under me. These idiots living around here have to learn that fighting me is useless. When Manny and his people get here, I'll have an army of twenty-five hundred, and if I can get those mutants working with me, it won't be long before I own the whole area of Texas, Oklahoma, and New Mexico. I think it's time to make believers out of these assholes.*

"Ross," he called to his assistant. The man entered the room. "Get Robert in here," he ordered the other man.

The man left and returned a couple of minutes later with Gabriel's second in command.

"Robert," he said. "It's time to put an end to this shit, once and for all."

"Which shit are you talking about?" Robert asked.

"Those assholes that jumped our security team last night. Did you find out anything about them?"

"They were all cops before the blackout," Robert answered.

"How many were there total?" Gabriel asked.

"Twenty-four left alive and eleven dead," Robert answered.

"Thirty-five cops and they couldn't even take our patrol of six," Gabriel mused.

"I figure the M16's and grenade launchers we got from the National Guard Base had a lot to do with that," Robert suggested.

"No shit," Gabriel said sarcastically. "The best part of is we have more coming in from San Antonio. Agular is sending everything he found at an Air Force bases there. But for now, I want you to send runners out to all our camps and bring people in from all over the city. I want these people to see what happens to anyone who opposes us. Have them all here by tomorrow night. As for the prisoners, I want them to be able to walk. I don't give a shit what they look like, but I want them to walk into the U.T. stadium on their own. Have all the people rounded up and in the stadium by five tomorrow afternoon."

"How many people do you want?" Robert asked.

"Bring in about five from every area of town. Search 'em, I don't want a couple of hundred citizens all together and armed. Put thirty guards around them all with automatic weapons. That should keep the cowards in line."

"I'll get it done," Robert answered and left the room.

***

There were three hundred-eighteen people herded into the U.T. stadium. They sat between sections four and five near the fifty-yard line surrounded by men and women armed with automatic rifles. In the center of the field, a long platform stood about four feet off the ground with wooden posts rising from it.

The only sound from the crowd was a soft murmur as Gabriel emerged from a tunnel in the end zone and walked to the platform. He stopped in front of the crowd-his witnesses, as liked to think of them. "I want all of you to witness what happens to anyone who is stupid enough to resist my people."

He waved to a man standing near the tunnel at the end of the stadium. The man turned, said something, and a line of men emerged from the tunnel. The men walked in single file, their hands tied in front of them, and their mouths gagged. They walked to and mounted the platform at the center of the field. Each man faced the witnesses and an escort tied them to a post.

"These men attacked one of our patrols the night before last," Gabriel said, having to shout to be heard. "... a patrol made up of only six men and women. When they attacked, there were eleven others with 'em. We buried those eleven assholes last night. The twenty-four men standing here were

269

police officers before the black out-all of 'em. Not only does this go to show you how totally useless the old authority is now, but I'll show you exactly how useless it is to resist us. In the future, anyone who doesn't do what they're told or tries to fight us, in any manner, will be handled exactly the same way."

He turned and faced the men on the platform. "You have been tried and found guilty of a conspiracy to overthrow our authority. You are all hereby sentenced to death."

Gabriel walked to the end of the platform. The escorts positioned themselves beside each of the prisoners. Gabriel ordered the execution squad consist of both men and women to prove both sexes were capable of upholding their laws. He wanted everyone to know there were no weak links in his army.

On his command, they all drew knives from their belts and positioned the points against each prisoner's stomach. On his next command, each stabbed a prisoner and then sliced all the way across their stomachs. Because of the gags, the men only issued muffled cries. After only a couple of seconds, he gave another command and they cut each of the prisoner's throats.

Many in the crowd tried to look away. But as they did, a rifle was jammed into their back and an order given to look at the scene before them or be shot where they sat.

It only took a couple of minutes for all the captives to bleed out. Gabriel returned to the center of the platform and faced the crowd. "Go back to your respective areas of the city and report what you've seen here. Tell everyone that failure to obey our laws will result in the same consequences for the each of them. If anyone breaks any of our laws, they and one member of their family will die the same as this. Obey our laws, and we will take care of each and every one of you. Anyone who turns a conspirator in to us will receive double rations for themselves and their family for one month. Anyone knowing of a conspiracy and not reporting it will die along with the conspirators as an accomplice."

Gabriel turned and abruptly walked out of the stadium. As he left the witnesses were ushered from the stadium and sent back to their homes with instructions to follow the orders given to the letter.

Back in his office, Gabriel said, "I think that should keep them in line, don't you?"

"Sure do," Robert answered. "I especially liked the part about the extra rations for turning someone in."

"Rewards, my friend, will produce more results than fear from a threat. I was serious about it too. If any of them turn someone in, we give them double rations for a month, and we do it quick. If this is going to work, the rewards have to happen as quickly as the punishments."

"I agree," Robert said.

"Now we have to figure something out with this mutant situation. They can either help us a lot or cause us a ton of trouble."

CHAPTER TWENTY-FIVE

It was a week since the run-in with the people in Rollingblock. Ron knew many of their workers were people from that area, and it only made sense they would cause trouble if they knew the militia was planning to wage war on the citizens there. Therefore, he instructed his troops to keep their mouths shut on the subject.

He intensified the training for everyone in camp. He could see there was a problem with trying to instill military discipline in civilians, even those who were previously in the military. Trying to make them work as a coordinated unit was proving to be a monumental task. They were too quick to let personalities get in the way. They had to be constantly reminded that, like the person or not, they must follow orders.

Ron took the problem to General Clark. The General told him people would come around the first time they had to rely on someone else to cover their ass. Then he increased the patrols of the area. Ron understood the patrols would probably teach them to work as a team. Especially since the night patrols were doubled.

Trying to teach maneuvers was an entirely different thing. They would all do as instructed but couldn't understand their part in the overall picture. They all wanted to argue about someone else having easier terrain to cross or having to wait on another unit while it moved into position.

Ron was impressed with Buck, however. The man took his punishment in stride. He was always early to assignments and worked harder than anyone else on the detail. Even though he was on work details, he also trained with the rest. Ron asked for and received permission from General Clark to make Buck a Squad Leader and Sergeant.

The general said if Buck kept it up, when his punishment was finished; he might even make platoon leader. This would show others even a person who made a mistake could still have a chance with the militia.

Buck was a good leader. He seemed to be the only squad leader who could get his people to work as a team. He was able to show, not only the importance of, but also how to make sense of their assignments. He didn't try to bullshit them. In some of the exercises, he told them straight out they were targets for the enemy-distractions so the other groups could overtake a position. With this knowledge, his squad was able to accomplish their goal. In one case, they even captured the objective. If Buck wasn't being punished through work details, Ron would have used him to train all the rest of the militia's leaders.

A messenger approached Ron, saluted, and told him the general had called a meeting of all officers. Ron was to report immediately to the General's office. He saluted the messenger and walked to the office.

Inside, General Clark stood before a wall map depicting the area around Rollingblock. Ron was the first one there and saluted as he entered the room. The General returned the salute, "Come over here Ron and look at this." Pointing to the map he said, "Here's where the ambush took place, right?" Ron nodded and kept looking at the map. "Well, if their camp is somewhere around here, then they can be boxed in. These cliffs run along the edge of town, and here's the road the attack happened on. Buck and Sam both said most of the attack came from their left. That would be toward the cliffs."

"Sure, unless they were trying to create a diversion," Ron suggested.

"I don't think so," General Clark answered. "They wouldn't have taken the time to do something like that. Not if we held their people prisoner. They would have taken the quickest cover possible in the time they had."

Makes sense," Ron agreed. "The only thing around the area is the resort ghost town. There on the map-it's Sagebrush. They could be anywhere on the ranch. They might even be living in Sagebrush. I suggest I take one other person and check it out. They never saw me. So they might be receptive to a man and a woman approaching the camp-especially if they're coming from the other way."

"I'm glad you said that," the General answered. "It's exactly what I'd like for you to do. Pick a female and head out tonight. You need to look like you've been traveling for a couple of days. Who are you gonna use to go with you?"

"I figured Barbara Wright would do okay. She's a good fighter, and she and I get along fine," Ron answered. "I'll let her know to be ready in two hours."

"Good," the General said. "Take as much time as you need with them. We need all the info we can

274

get. Location, size of their group, training and anything else you can find out. Don't rush anything unless they decide to move on us."

Ron stepped back, saluted and exited the room, which was now full of officers of the militia.

***

They left later in the evening and spent the night in a militia safe house. The next day, they traveled for six hours when Barbara saw a movement in the trees ahead of them. Both stopped and peered at the spot. Following another movement, a mutant stepped onto the road about thirty yards ahead of them.

It stopped for only a second before it began running toward them. As both people raised their rifles to fire, they heard an explosion behind and to their right. The mutant's head slammed back jerking the upper part of his body with it. It hit the ground hard and lay still.

As the animal hit the ground, Ron and Barbara spun around. Standing behind them was a strange looking man dressed in a long coat and brown cowboy hat lowering a .50 cal. black powder rifle from his shoulder. He looked as if he had walked out of a western novel.

"Don't ya hate it when they do that?" The man asked walking toward them. "Hal Sloan," he said, tipping his hat to Barbara and then held his hand out to Ron.

"Ron Campbell," Ron answered shaking the man's hand, "and this is Barbara Wright."

Barbara smiled and held her hand out. "Thanks for helping us out mister."

"Aw think nothing of it, ma'am," Hal answered reloading his rifle. The cartridges were on a bandoleer strapped at an angle across his body. When he pulled the long coat back, Ron saw he was also wearing a pistol on each hip.

"You live around here, Mr. Sloan?" Ron asked.

"Not far from here, and it's Hal," the man answered. His rifle reloaded, he held it across his body in the crook of his left arm.

"What about any towns?" Barbara asked. "Are there any safe ones around close by?"

"I'm not sure any town or city is safe anymore, ma'am," Hal answered. "People seem to be a might crazy since the electricity went out. Where are you folks headed?"

"No place in particular," Ron answered. "We met up on the outskirts of El Paso. I was headed to my brother's house over near Flat Butte. But when we got there, he was dead."

"A lot of it going around these days-damn near an epidemic," Hal commented. "Sorry to hear about that."

"Now we're trying to find some place safe," Ron finished.

"And warm," Barbara added quickly.

"You're gonna need that," Hal assured her. "There's been some nasty weather building for a couple of days."

"Is there some place around here you know of we could stay until it blows over?" Ron asked.

"There's a house about two miles down the road," he answered. "I have to tell you though; a

276

mutant was killed there not long ago. I imagine there's more around, especially since seeing this one." He motioned toward the animal on the ground.

"Anything would beat staying out in the cold weather," Barbara said. "Is it on this road?"

"I'll show you," Hal answered. "I can cut across to my camp from there."

"Your camp," Barbara said shocked. "You're welcome to stay with us if you want."

"I thank you ma'am, but I have a wife waiting for me back there, and if I'm too late getting back, she'll be worried sick." Hal was choosing his words carefully. Since the run-in with the militia people, everyone at Rebel's Revenge was careful when talking to strangers, and he really wasn't lying. Sandy was waiting on him. He just didn't mention how many lived back at the camp.

"Well, if you're ready to go," Ron said, "maybe we should be on our way."

"Hang on a minute," Hal said. "I have to get my horse."

"Horse?" Barbara exclaimed. "You have a horse?"

Hal was already walking off and over his shoulder said, "I'll be back in a minute."

A moment later Hal emerged from the trees atop a dapple-gray horse. Sitting on the horse, Hal, more than ever, looked like he was part of a western movie.

As he reached the two people, they turned and started walking. When they passed the mutant lying on the road, it tried to roll up on one elbow to sit up but collapsed to its back.

Ron shot the mutant in the head, and the animal lay still. When Ron looked up, Hal was putting his pistol back in its holster. Ron eyed the other man for a couple of seconds, then turned, and continued walking up the road.

When Hal and Barbara caught up with him, Ron appeared deep in thought. Shortly, he looked up at Hal and asked, "Doesn't it bother you to kill those things?"

"The thing bothering me is I can't eat 'em afterward," Hal answered. "I've seen what they can do first hand, and to answer your question, no it doesn't bother me."

Sensing where Ron was going with this, Barbara said, "We've seen a couple of them but never had to kill one before. They usually stayed away from us and seemed to watch what we were doing from a distance."

Hal was looking at her with a neutral gaze. After a couple of seconds he said, "I guess you've been lucky."

***

After about forty-five minutes, they came to the same house where Bear met Keith, Amanda, and Mike. "This is the house I told you about," Hal said. "It should be okay if the weather turns really bad. Remember though, some of the mutants have been around here. I'd stick around and help you get settled, but I have to get back to camp. It looks like it's gonna get cold quick."

"We thank you for all of your help," Barbara said.

278

"Are there other people around here we need to worry about?" Ron asked.

"None around here on a regular basis," Hal answered. "There's a group about twenty miles or so over near Lake Brazos that may come around. But I wouldn't think so. There's no reason for them to be here. Besides, I thought you were looking for people to settle down with."

"We're looking for a community to settle in," Ron answered, "but not just any community. We sure wouldn't want to be involved with those militia people. We want to be part of a group who wants to survive the situation we're in now and nothing else.

"Well, if you stay here you should be relatively safe," Hal said. "I've gotta get going. It's only a couple of hours 'till dark and I have to get back." He reined his horse around and was off before the other two could say another word.

Ron and Barbara slowly entered the house. Inside it looked like the owners were gone for only a couple of hours. Everything seemed to be in place. They checked the whole house, including all closets and a small basement.

There was a wood-burning stove in one corner of the living room along with a TV. "Well, at least we can keep warm," Ron said.

"Sure," Barbara answered. "Then we can pop some popcorn and watch TV."

"It hasn't been too long ago I used to do that exact thing," Ron said. "The weird part of it is I really haven't missed the TV or radio."

Barbara went into the kitchen and opened a cupboard. "There are some canned vegetables in here and some soup. Does that sound okay to you?"

"It sounds better than me having to go out and hunt something down. It really does feel like some bad weather is coming in,"

After Ron got a fire started in the stove, Barbara brought in a pot. "The only soup was tomato. I mixed some green beans and corn in, hope it tastes alright."

The stove proved to be excellent for warming the food. Barbara tended the stove as Ron walked over to the window and looked out. The sky was gray, heavily overcast, and the wind appeared to be rising. Ron opened the front door and stepped out on the porch. The temperature had dropped drastically in the last hour. He reached into his back pocket and brought out a packet of papers.

"Do you have any idea what day it is?" He called back inside to Barbara.

"I think it's still December."

He turned and reentered the house. "It's December the nineteenth. I've been keeping up with the days on this calendar. He held up the packet of papers, which was a pocket calendar. Christmas was always my favorite time of the year."

"I know what you mean. It has been for me too."

They both sat lost in their own thoughts, for a long time. Finally able to relax both dozed off. Then Ron sat up and asked, "Did you hear something outside?"

Barbara listened for a couple of seconds, "What did you hear?"

"I don't know. It sounded like muffled voices. There may be someone out there."

They listened for another minute as Ron quietly crossed the room and picked up his rifle. He went to the front door and slowly opened it. Standing there, in front of him, was Hal. Beside him were another man and a woman.

"Sorry to bother you folks," Hal started. "This here is David and my wife Sandy."

Sandy held up a sack and said, "We didn't know what supplies you have so we brought you this."

Barbara joined them at the door. Hal said, "This is Ron and Barbara. They're the people I told you about."

Barbara took the sack from Sandy. "Come on in," she said. There's plenty of room in here, and you can get in out of the cold."

They entered the house, now warm due to the radiance of the stove. "Feels good in here," David said removing his coat, revealing a pistol on each hip. He put his coat on the floor and then took Sandy's and put it on top of his own. Hal seemed comfortable to wear his.

Ron noticed Sandy also wore a pistol on her hip. "It seems like all of you travel well-armed," he said as everyone sat near the stove.

It's not as much by choice as necessity," David answered. "Things have changed, and we have to be ready for whatever happens. I figure it's the same reason you have yours." David indicated the rifle now leaning against Ron's chair.

"You're right," Ron said. "We've both got one with us. So far we've been lucky and haven't used either until today."

281

"I hope you don't mind me asking," Barbara said, "but why all the cowboy clothes? I mean the three of you look like you were caught in a time warp. You look like you just stepped out of the days of real cowboys-like the eighteenth or nineteenth century."

"It's simply because of how well they wear," Sandy answered. "There's a big difference between how long clothes last when washed in a washing machine compared to when they're washed in a river on a rock or on a scrub board. Plus this style is easier to come by around here."

"We were all members of a gunfighter's group before the blackout," David continued the explanation, "and we all owned these type clothes already."

"I guess we might look a bit different to someone else," Sandy said. "I never really thought too much about it. The only thing we care about is how functional they are. If you layer them properly, they can handle almost every kind of weather."

"So then, it sounds like there's a group of you here," Ron suggested probing for information.

"There's some others of the group scattered around the area," Hal answered. He was standing near a corner and all but forgotten by the others.

"Where are the two of you headed?" David asked.

"We're not sure," Ron answered. "We're just looking for a place to settle down. Someplace that's quiet and far out, away from the cities. All the ones we passed through are controlled by gangs now."

"What made you leave Laredo?" Hal asked. "That seems to be far enough away from any real large cities."

"We were in El Paso," Ron corrected, "and it was filling up with Mexicans from south of the border. Those people, along with the gangs already there, were going to make the place a very dangerous *hell hole* soon. There were a lot of people leaving at the same time as us. But most of them were heading west or due north."

A knock sounded at the front door. Ron stood and walked over to it. Looking back at the others he asked, "Are any of you expecting anyone?"

David stood and said, "It might be Ben. He lives around these parts and might have smelled your fire."

Ron opened the door and standing there was an old man. He had a beard and wore the same type clothes as the others in the room. "Ben, come on in here," Ron said. "There's no sense in you standing out there where it's cold."

Ben gave Ron a surprised look and then entered the house. "Folks, we need to get going," he said. "I just saw a pack of those mutant things moving through the trees about a hundred fifty yards out. I figure they're looking for the best way to approach the house."

Instantly, David, Sandy, and Hal were up and moving. David paused and looked at his friends. "Well, what do you think?"

"I think they're okay," Sandy answered.

"I always trust her judgment," Hal answered.

David turned to Ron and Barbara. "Here's the deal. We're members of a group composed of the

283

gunfighters we told you about and some others. We all live a couple of miles from here. If you want to join us, you're welcome to. If you decide you like us, you can ask to stay. Whether you do stay or not will be up to a vote of the group. But you need to make your minds up right now. We need to get going if we don't wanna tangle with the animals Ben saw."

Ron and Barbara looked at each other for only a couple of seconds. "I'll get my pack," Barbara said.

"... and your rifle," Hal put in, "you may need it."

A couple of minutes later, the group was easing out the door, looking for any movement in the bushes and trees. Barbara and Ron followed the rest to the right of the house where they noticed horses tied among the trees.

"We brought two extra horses," David explained, "just in case you came with us. Can both of you ride?"

"We can," Ron answered.

"Then, use those two," Ben told him pointing at two horses. "Get on them and let's get going."

David led the way with Hal pulling up the rear. They traveled through the trees at a trot, only slowing down for a steep downgrade. After a mile or so, David pulled his horse up. "Hal check our trail. We'll wait here for you."

Hal was gone for fifteen or twenty minutes before he returned. "There's no sense in going back there for quite a while. Looks like the mutants have taken it over," he said. "I couldn't see everything, but one was standing outside and the rest were inside."

Without warning, a freezing wind slammed into them, a mixture of frozen rain and snow followed immediately afterward. It almost felt like a solid wall as it pummeled them and the temperature dropped to what felt like the freezing level.

"We need to get back quick," David said.

"Then let's get moving," Hal answered.

CHAPTER TWENTY-SIX

It took them another hour before reaching Rebel's Revenge. They dismounted and moved their horses into a protected area behind the stage barn. After seeing to the animals, they went to a large tent in the middle of the camp. Crowded inside the tent was the rest of the community.

Spyder walked up to David who stood beside a wood-burning stove in the middle of the structure. "David," he said. "We've been talking, and most of us think we should move into the cabins over at the resort. It's been long enough since the blackout that there shouldn't any people around wanting to cause trouble." He handed David a map and continued. "We figure we can block the roads in these four places, and then set traps in the river. As for security, if we all stay in the cabins, we'll be in a central area. We'll also be inside buildings where there's a hell of a lot more warmth than these tents."

When Spyder finished, David gave him a confused look and said, "What the hell are you telling me about this for? I'm not the leader here. I'm simply another member. If everyone wants to move there, then let's move."

"We'll talk about the leadership later," Spyder answered. "For now, we can get the camp transferred in less than three hours. Actually, we can get moved into the cabins in less than an hour. Tomorrow morning, we can come back over here and get the rest of our personal belongings and the supplies."

"Let's do it," David said.

Spyder turned toward the rest of the people in the tent and called out, "Folks, let's get things packed up and get over to the main part of the resort."

It was obvious no one heard him since everyone was all talking loudly to each other. He yelled again and as before the voices inside the tent drowned him out. He reached into his duster pocket and pulled out a derringer. Pointing the small pistol at the smoke hole in the center of the tent, he pulled the trigger. The weapon wasn't as loud as the others he carried, but it was loud enough to silence the group immediately.

"Everybody shut the fuck up," he yelled. Everyone instantly stopped talking, and Spyder continued, "Now that I have everybody's attention, let's get all our things gathered up and move to the cabins. Pick your cabin and move in. I would suggest the cabins on the ends remain empty. We'll use those as guard posts. Every cabin has a wood burning stove and a gas oven. Take it easy on the gas until we can go out and get more. For now, only take what you'll need for tonight. We'll get together tomorrow morning and move everything else then. By now, most of you have wind-up watches. If you don't have one, ask someone with one to come and get you. Let's all meet at eight o'clock, in the Sagebrush Saloon. For now, let's move it out."

Everyone in the tent immediately started moving around. Some gathered personal items, while others, discussed, which cabin they wanted and the rest went on their way to gather what they needed for the night. Hal and Sandy left the tent and went over to the stage barn. Inside they found Davata and Dr. Hamilton standing beside Bear who was sitting up sipping a cup of soup.

"How's he doing Doctor?" Hal asked.

"He's doing fine," the doctor answered. "In fact, I'm having trouble making him stay in bed. He keeps wanting to get up and go hunting."

"Hell Doc," Hal said. "If I shoot him on the other side, maybe then he'll sit back and relax."

"I'm sure he would," Dr. Hamilton answered with a smile. "But, I don't want to have to fix him up again." Then turning back to Bear he said, "Mr. Edmonds, as I've told you, you need to spend at least a couple more days in bed to get your strength up."

"Doc," Bear said. "First of all, you're the wrong sex to be trying to keep me in bed. Second, if we're moving to the cabins like I think we are, I'll have to take care of myself. I know Sandy and Davata have been doing all of the nursing on me. But they have lives of their own and other duties to the group. They can't be expected to come over to my cabin all the time to see about me. Last of all it's Bear, Rafe, or in a pinch I'll even answer to Dr. Edmonds because, contrary to your belief, I am a doctor and can take care of myself"

"How about if I move into your cabin until you're back on your feet," Davata suggested. "Then I can find one of my own."

"Davata, I think you for the offer," he said. "But, I can't ask you to do that."

"You didn't ask," Davata snorted, "and I don't know why we're all standing around arguing with

288

this stubborn, mule headed, jackass. Let's just move him. What's he gonna do, fight us off?"

Bear started grinning, looked at Sandy and said, "Now that's my kind of woman."

***

There were thirty-five single story buildings situated between the river and the *ghost town* of Sagebrush. They were situated in three rows, placed end to end. The resort's office, a maintenance building, and a compound resembling a log fort (built by the Calvary of the old West) sat behind them. To one side of Sagebrush, four buildings or group lodges stood, each with a common area capable of holding up to fifty people.

It only took about twenty minutes to get Bear ready to move. Hal asked David to bring a truck to the front of the barn and help load Bear in it. David then drove toward the cabins with Davata and Hal to help get Bear in one.

Bear insisted on being in one of the cabins under the trees, near the end of all the others. They got him inside and settled quickly. Once inside, Hal and David assured Bear and Davata they would take care of moving their belongings for them.

After Hal and David left, Davata went in search of some type of light. Bear told her to look in the cupboards. He said he had a friend who once worked at the resort and told him one of the biggest problems for the maintenance staff was to keep the lamps filled with kerosene. Along with the lamps, she also found some candles.

Their cabin had a fireplace, and she could now see why Bear insisted on this particular one. There were trees to provide shade in the summer and everything needed to stay warm in the winter.

"Can I ask you a couple of personal questions?" Bear asked.

"Sure," Davata answered, "ask away."

"Well, first of all, just how old are you. You look like you're in your early to middle thirties."

"That's sweet of you," she answered. "I'm forty-seven years old and proud of it."

"Forty-seven," he exclaimed. "Not a chance in hell. That's almost my age.

Davata giggled and said, "I'm not gonna answer any more questions if you're gonna call me a liar."

"That's not what I meant" he said quickly. "I just find it hard to believe you're so close to my age."

"Okay," she said with a sigh. "What's the other question?"

"Where does the name Davata come from? I've never heard it before."

"It's the name of a goddess in Hindi. My mother liked it, and since my father wasn't around anymore to have a say, she made the decision."

"It suits you," he answered and lay back against a pillow. "It's a beautiful name."

"Why Mr. Edmonds, if I didn't know better, I'd think you were flirting with me," Davata remarked fluttering her eyes with a smile.

"Might as well," Bear answered. "I can't watch TV. I can't even go out and play."

"Well at least I'm the second choice," she said still smiling.

"Look lady," Bear said with a stern voice. "We've lost the ability to communicate with everyone out of yelling distance. The world has turned inside out and there is a new species of animal out there wanting to use us as snack food. Now, if none of that were happening, you would be so far ahead of any other choices. You would think you were the only choice." He smiled, and with a wink, said, "you're lucky I'm confined to this bed. Otherwise, you'd have your hands full with me. Believe me; flirting would be a minor concern for you."

"Wow!" Davata exclaimed. "That's the most I've ever heard you say at one time. I guess I should be flattered."

"I say what I mean and mean what I say," he answered still smiling. "You're a beautiful woman. That's no secret. Obviously, it's no secret I'm attracted to you, and it seems you're at least a little attracted to me. But, with our present situation, I have to keep everything in perspective."

"I understand," she answered looking down at the floor.

"I have a lot of friends out there-good friends." Bear explained. "Some of them are like brothers and sisters to me, and I couldn't stand it if anything were to happen to them." Davata looked up and saw a faraway look in the man's eyes. "I've been through a lot with 'em, and it looks like we're gonna go through a lot more together. You're now part of that group, and I damned sure don't want anything to happen to you either."

"Thank you," Davata said and placed her hand on his shoulder.

"Besides," he said his smile returning. "There's no one else to flirt with if anything were to happen to you."

Before she could answer, there was a knock. She rose and left Bear alone in the room. Hal, David, and Sandy were at the door. Just outside, with its rear backed up to the building was a truck carrying all of Davata and Bear's belongings. Along with everything else, they unloaded four M16s and about a thousand rounds for the rifles along with about twenty grenades. Everyone back at the stage barn had agreed to bring in enough weapons and ammunition for every person in each house. They figured it was unwise for the group to leave their weapons.

It only took a few minutes for them to unload everything. When they finished Davata asked, "Can I fix you folks some coffee?"

"None for me," David answered. "I've got to be able to sleep tonight. We've got a meeting early tomorrow morning."

"Same for us," Sandy agreed. "We also have to get back up to the camp and get our own stuff."

"Have you all picked a cabin out yet?"

They all turned at the sound of the voice coming from the side. Bear stood in the doorway.

"What the hell are you doing out here?" Davata asked. "You're supposed to be in bed."

"I know-I know," Bear answered. "I just thought I'd come out and thank everyone for what they've done."

"Okay," Hal said. "You've thanked us. Now lumber your decrepit, old ass back to bed."

"Fine thing," Bear said, "people come in my house and start ordering... "

"Our house," Davata corrected, "and they're right. You need to be in bed-now move."

As Davata went over to help Bear back to bed, the rest said goodnight and left.

Outside David said, "That woman's got her hands full."

"Maybe," Hal answered. "Then again, she might be exactly what the grumpy old fart needs."

CHAPTER TWENTY-SEVEN

Sam moved around the camp freely with only Mike to keep watch on him. Upon arrival, they questioned him about the militia and what actions they might take. Sam had answered all the questions truthfully. As a grunt in the militia, the leaders never gave him purview to any of the plans they made.

The questioning wasn't what he expected. There was no violence or threats. They simply asked him for any information he might have or was willing to give. Sam told them everything he knew. After the session, they said he could stay as long as he didn't cause trouble or attempt to sabotage any of the property of the camp. In the case of the latter, he would die, plain and simple.

Sam didn't intend to cause trouble, especially with these people. Because of Carl's report, they allowed him to stay at the camp, even if only a short time. Sam was never a violent person and only joined the militia as a means to survive. He didn't agree with their beliefs on slavery and the white race being superior. He only wanted a safe place to live.

When he told Spyder, David, Wind, and Hal about the militia's workers, all their reactions, with the exception of Wind, had surprised him. As expected, Wind was angry. David and Hal were visually upset, and both men had asked about the possibility of sneaking into the militia compound and releasing the hostages. Sam assured them of how well guarded the workers were, and such an attempt would only result in the death of those attempting it.

Spyder rose to his feet and roared, "This is a bunch of bullshit. Those assholes need to get the shit kicked out of 'em."

The viciousness with which he spoke those words surprised Sam and by the looks on their faces, the rest of the people there too. He had heard the man Spyder was once a member of the KKK, but had changed. But obviously none of them knew just how much he had changed and how strong his feelings were against the idea of slavery.

Spyder continued, "So I guess you think we should take Wind here and make a slave out of him. People like you make me sick," he said, pulling the pistol from his holster.

David quickly stepped between the two men and put his hand on the gun. "Hold on, Spyder."

Sam, his voice now shaking, said, "I didn't say I agree with what they're doing. I simply told you what is happening."

"Put it back in the holster, Spyder," David said. "Let's find out what's going on before we fly off the handle. There's no need to kill the messenger."

Spyder returned the pistol to its holster, but kept glaring at Sam as he sat down.

Sam knew he better choose his words carefully at that point. He damn sure didn't want Spyder any more upset than he already was. It took some time for Sam to settle the other men down and convince them he didn't follow all of the militia's beliefs.

After the questioning, Sam went to the doctor and had his ribs tended to. Inside the stage barn, he saw Bear lying on a bed and recognized him from the gunfight the day before.

Bear opened his eyes, saw Sam and said, "Don't I know you? You look like one of the men that took Hal and me hostage."

"Yes sir," Sam answered. "I'm sorry to say I was one of the men."

Bear nodded and said, "I remember you. You're the one who tried to stop those assholes from kicking the shit out of me."

"I'm sorry I wasn't able to do more. I know saying I'm sorry doesn't change anything, but I personally didn't mean you any harm."

"Don't worry about it man. You at least said something. That was risky enough, especially as fired up as the others were."

Sam sat on a barrel with his shirt off, a large bruise extended from his spine around to the front of his chest. Dr. Hamilton applied some salve to the area and wrapped it with a bandage.

"What happened to you?" Bear asked.

Sam explained how he came to be at Rebel's Revenge. He explained how he was run off, and when leaving was kicked in the side. He told how he and Carl finally made it back to camp.

When Sam finished, Bear said, "Well if there's anything I can do to help you around here just give a yell. I owe you one." He turned his head away and closed his eyes.

How the hell could he think he owes me anything? I was one of the members of the people who treated him like shit. Sam knew there was something different about the way the man thought.

He could see an acceptance in Bear he hadn't seen in anyone since his own mother.

***

Now, a little over a week later, Hal watched as everyone moved quickly around the camp, gathering the essentials needed to relocate in the cabins. The temperature was in the upper thirties with low-level clouds hanging overhead. The wind was out of the north, which said they were facing a severe storm.

On his way up to the half-empty camp, he met Lynn and her sons as they took all the extra horses down to the fort-like enclosure near the cabins. They had put saddles, blankets, and extra tack on the horse's back and hauled it to the enclosure. There were rooms around the edge of the area since it was originally for storage for the resort. As it happened, it made a perfect area for all the tack and the horses when they needed to be close to the cabins.

Hal met Sam and Mike stood in the main tent and informed them they had watch from midnight until eight the next morning. They would relieve Spyder and Wind keeping an eye on the personal items left at the camp. Sandy and Cindy would be on guard, at the cabins until midnight, and then Keith and Amanda would take over until eight tomorrow morning. With the storm coming in, no one expected any trouble. They were only to ensure nothing blew away if the wind kicked up.

It took the better part of two hours for everyone to pick a cabin and get the essentials moved, which left only Spyder and Wind to wander around the now deserted camp. Most of the tents, now torn down, were stored in the stage barn to keep them from blowing away. The only one left up was the large one located in the middle of the camp.

The only things they needed to worry about were the things left in the stage barn. Spyder and Wind built a fire outside the building's entrance in an attempt to ward off the cold. The stage barn, which allowed the warmth of the fire to drift inside, blocked the wind warming the area nicely. They then settled in for a long, boring watch.

CHAPTER TWENTY-EIGHT

Spyder and Wind made it back to the cabins as Keith and Amanda relieved Sandy and Cindy. "Is anything moving up at the stage barn?" Sandy asked as the other two walked up.

"Not a thing," Wind answered.

"Nothing but wind moving the snow around up there," Spyder told them. "We were able to start a fire in front of the barn door, and it works to keep the place warm. Sam and Mike should be fairly comfortable. What about around here, anything going on?"

"It's all quiet around here," Cindy answered. "Ginny is in cabin number twenty-one, Spyder." Then looking at Wind, she said, "Dr. Hamilton told us to tell you he would have a bedroom ready if you wanted to stay there for the night."

"Thanks," Wind answered. "I think I'll take him up on it. Are there any cabins left for me to get tomorrow?"

"Not too many," Sandy answered, "only about ten or fifteen."

"Good," Wind said. "Maybe I can find one for me to set up house in."

A picture flashed through her mind, and Sandy started to giggle despite the cold wind blowing around her.

"You find that amusing?" Wind asked.

"Sorry, I just had a vision of you standing in a cabin wearing a French maid's outfit and an apron and holding a feather duster."

The others joined her laughing.

"I'm glad all of you find it so funny," Wind responded.

"It really wasn't you," Sandy said, her giggles subsiding. "But I have to admit, you were real cute.

"Which is the doctor's?" Wind asked.

"The third one on the left," Cindy answered, pointing down the row of buildings.

He turned and walked away from them mumbling something, which was lost in the sound of the storm.

***

Bear lay awake listening to the sound of the storm. Davata had drifted off to sleep sitting in an overstuffed armchair a little over an hour ago. As he watched her sleep, he couldn't help but wonder about her strength. *Everyone has been through a lot, but since the loss of electricity, she seems to have suffered more loss than most. Before the blackout, she lost her husband and children. Then afterward, she lost two more children she had become attached to and the man she loved and relied on. Essentially, she lost her family and then almost immediately following it, a surrogate family. It seemed she's faced one catastrophe after another, and now here she's taking care of me.*

He climbed out of bed and went to where she slept. He gently shook her shoulder calling her name. He had to repeat the process a couple of times before she slowly opened her eyes and looked up at him.

"Come on sweetheart," Bear said. "You need to go to bed. You're neck and back are gonna be sore as hell if you sleep in this chair."

"Okay," Davata mumbled. She rose from the chair and walked over to the bed. Climbing onto it from the end, she crawled up to the head and collapsed on the side closest to the wall.

Bear figured she was asleep even before her head hit the pillow. *Well if she doesn't mind, then I don't*. He climbed into bed beside her.

PART THREE
DEVISTATION

I have felt darkness lead me by the hand over
the hill to greet the singing dawn...

Allen Tate (1899-1979)

If we are always arriving and departing, it is
also true that we are eternally anchored.

One's destination is never a place but rather a
new way of looking at things.

Henry Miller (1891-1980), U.S. author. "The
Oranges of the Millennium," Big Sur and the
Oranges of Hieronymous Bosch (1957).

CHAPTER TWENTY-NINE

There was a knock on the door. Gabriel looked up, "Come on in."

His second in command, Ross, came in the room, "Manny's here."

Gabriel jumped to his feet. "Get him in here!" Gabriel hadn't seen Manny for over a year and was looking forward to seeing his old friend.

The man that entered the room looked much older than he should have. He was thin, his face drawn and his left arm was in a sling. Gabriel walked quickly over to him and took the man's hand. "Damn," Gabriel said, "you look like you've been through a rough time."

"I have," Manny answered. "You wouldn't believe the bullshit happening over in San Antonio." He paused as Gabriel stepped back and motioned toward a chair. After sitting down he continued. "People all over the city have polarized and are at each other's throats. I pulled most of the other groups together and now have about thirty-five hundred men and women under me. Sooner or later, we will get it completely under control. Shit. There's even a group that took over the Alamo. There're about two hundred of them living in the Alamo and the museum. They stand guard around the walls of the enclosure and sometimes they even take pot shots at my people passing by."

"Why don't you just take 'em out?" Gabriel asked.

"Well, for right now, I know where they are. If we jump them, they might scatter throughout the city. Then we have two hundred troublemakers running around stirring people up.

"Makes sense," Gabriel answered. "What about the rest of the city? How much of it do you control?"

"About half," Manny answered. "I figure if I get it completely under control, then the rest of the area around it will be a lot easier. That is if there's anything left after the Neanderthals have finished."

"Neanderthals?" Gabriel repeated questioningly.

"Yeah," Manny answered. "Don't tell me there's none of those part man, part ape, and part bear things around here."

"Oh we've got 'em," Gabriel answered. "We call them mutants. In fact, I think I have one of the leaders in a jail cell right now."

"You've got what?" Manny asked.

"I think I've got one of the leaders," Gabriel repeated.

"What the hell for?" Manny asked. "Why haven't you killed the thing yet?"

"I'm trying to strike a deal with it," Gabriel explained. "I think if I can reach an agreement with it, I can own the entire area."

"Strike a deal with it," Manny exclaimed. "How the hell do you propose to strike a deal with an animal? It would be like trying to get your rabid pet dog to understand what you're saying."

With a sly smile, Gabriel said, "You're wrong. Believe me; they understand what you're saying. Their intelligence is frightening. They understand everything you say. They can't speak, but they understand."

"I think you're dreaming," Manny answered. "Those wild mother fuckers won't make, much less keep, any agreements."

"I think they will," Gabriel answered. "If we can supply something they want."

"What the hell do they want?"

"That's where I'm stuck," Gabriel told him. "I haven't figured out what they want or need."

"You say you're able to talk to it?" Manny asked.

"Well, I do all the talking." Gabriel explained. "He will explain the best he can with gestures, grunts, and simple drawings."

There was a knock on the door, and Lydia walked in carrying a tray with food on it and said, "Ross figured both of you would be hungry and told me to fix this." She sat the tray down and left the room.

"You hungry?" Gabriel asked.

Manny lifted the cover of the tray and saw ground meat, bread, and vegetables for the sandwiches. "Looks pretty good."

Both men fixed themselves a hamburger then continued talking as they ate.

"Have you figured out what they want or need?" Manny asked.

"Not yet," Gabriel answered. "But there has to be something."

"Well, what do we all want... " Manny thought aloud, "food, water, shelter, safety, things like that. If you can communicate with the thing, why don't

305

you simply ask it what it needs, or what he's willing to trade for?"

Gabriel looked at his friend-surprised. "The one thing I haven't done. It must have been too obvious for me to see it. Let's finish eating, and I'll introduce you to Bo."

"Bo?" Manny repeated the name.

"Bo is the mutant's name."

"The mutant has a name?"

"Yeah, and it knows the identity of at least one of the mutant leaders in San Antonio," Gabriel answered. "I'm not sure, but I think that might be information we can use.

"Maybe," Manny said. "Again, it depends on what they want or need."

Bo sat, eating food the guards had brought him. The confinement and inactivity was turning the hours into days. The only way he could tell day from night was by the light filtering through a window at the end of the hallway outside his cell.

Through patience and sheer willpower, Bo was able to do some work on the door of his cell, and now there was a surprise for Gabriel. He wanted to impress the human with his abilities and trustworthiness. He also knew that a surprise was the only way to get Gabriel's complete attention.

When the door at the end of the hallway opened, Gabriel and another man walked in. Both men came over and stood in front of his cell.

"Bo, this is Manny," Gabriel said motioning to the other man. "He's from San Antonio."

Bo looked at the other man, nodded, and moved over near the door of his cell. Manny looked nervous, and he could smell the man's fear.

"Hello Bo," Manny said hesitantly. He felt strange talking to the animal sitting behind the bars. He could see intelligence behind those red eyes, and briefly, a feeling of dread ran up and down his spine. With a shudder, he shook the feeling.

Gabriel stepped close to the cell door and asked, "Have both you and the other one"-he motioned to the other creature with his thumb and head-"been fed and treated properly?"

Bo turned toward his mate and uttered a couple of grunts. As she rose from her cot, Gabriel stepped to the front of her cell. Quickly, Bo swung his cell door open. By doing so, he completely separated Manny and Gabriel. Manny was near the door to the cellblock, but Gabriel was trapped on the other side of the cell door, in an area with both mutants.

Bo stepped between Gabriel and the open cell door. Gabriel pulled his pistol from his holster and pointed it at Bo.

***

It was then he looked down and saw his pistol was not only in front of him, pointed at the mutant, but it was beside a large outstretched paw. The creature was extending his hand in an apparent show of friendship. Gabriel looked at the hand and then back up at the mutant's face. Slowly, he switched the gun to his left hand. He then hesitantly moved his hand into the grasp of the mutant. Bo took his hand, gently shook it and immediately released it. He stepped back into his cell pulled the door closed behind him, allowing Gabriel a passage to the end of the hall and the exit door. Gabriel moved slowly to the end of the hall and safety, partially from surprise and partially from fear.

As Gabriel reached the exit door at the end of the hall, he turned watched as the mutant walked over to his bed, sat down, clasped his paws in front of him with his arms on his legs, and hung his head with his chin on his chest. He looked as if he had lost his last friend or something.

Both men left the cell-room and stood outside the door connecting it from the outside hallway. "What the hell just happened?" Manny asked.

"I don't know," Gabriel answered. "He had a chance to tear me apart and didn't."

"It almost looked like he was trying to show you something," Manny suggested.

"Now what the hell could he be trying to show me?" Gabriel asked. "How easily I can be trapped in my own jail."

"How about that he could be trusted," Manny answered. "He did have a chance to kill you and didn't take it. He might have been trying to show you he and his kind are willing to work with you and your people. He could have just as easily escaped while they were in there alone rather than trap you-and then let you go."

"You may be right, Manny. It makes sense. But the one thing that doesn't is why. Why would he do this? Does he simply want to escape, or is there something else behind his intentions?"

"I saw something on the mutant's face when he released you. I'm not sure what it was, but there was something there. I'm not sure if it was slyness, satisfaction or something else; but there was definitely something else there, and I don't like it.

"I know they're smart," Gabriel said, "but I think you're going a bit too far with the expression part. However, I think I may know how to test this. We'll have to do it a little at a time, but I think it'll work. Let's go back to the office, I'll tell you about it and we can set it up."

***

Leaving his cabin, David stepped between the two to three foot snowdrifts and headed for the camp to see how Mike and Sam fared during the storm. The wind had let up shortly before the sun rose, but snow still accumulated between the large drifts that formed overnight. With the rate the flakes fell from the sky, the snow would be over four inches soon. As far as he knew, this storm would be the worst one Central Texas has seen in past twenty years, and there was no electricity to protect people from its wrath. As he left the ghost town, he ran into Spyder who apparently had the same idea. The two men walked together across the new stable area toward the campsite. With no wind and the snow falling straight down, the area was beautiful.

"It's times like this I almost forget all the problems we have," Spyder said.

"I know what you mean. Even with some of the problems, there's times I prefer the way it is now over how it was. It may make finding and keeping food a little harder, and I think the summer is gonna be unmerciful; but this is a simpler way to live."

The men followed a bend in the rutted path now covered with snow and pulled up short at the edge of camp. The only structure left standing was the

309

stage barn. The large tent in the center was down and ripped apart, and the rest lay in ruins. Breaking into a run, the men hurried to the barn door. No fire burned in front of it.

"Something's wrong here," Spyder said softly, pulling two of his pistols. "Take care."

"Right," David answered and drew one of his.

A couple of steps later, they found out why the fire was out. Inside some bushes and partially covered with snow, they found the bodies of Mike and Sam, torn apart by some animal. There was no way a storm would have been able to do that to a person.

From the look on Spyder's face, David figured they both knew what had done the damage. David motioned to the entrance to the building, and Spyder nodded. They flanked both sides of the door. At Spyder's signal, both men stepped into the doorway with guns at the ready. There was no one inside.

The mutants had made a total mess of the barn. They took all the meat in the barn and some of the vegetables. Anything stored in a factory-sealed carton, box, or package was left behind, strewn all over the floor. Sorting and inventorying what remained could wait. Now, however, the two men needed to make sure there was no danger present. David realized they hadn't actually checked the area around the camp. "We've gotta check the place out. There may still be some of the creatures around here."

Spyder nodded and looked out the door. "You read my mind. This had to be done by those mutant creatures.

"There aren't other animals around here that could do something like this. A mountain lion could've killed those two, but it would have never made this mess."

After searching the area and confirming that there were no more mutants, they returned to the cafe. David knew neither of the dead men had close friends in the community, but they were members of the group and breaking the news of their deaths would come as a hard blow. When they finished, they could turn their attention to gathering what remained of the supplies.

Inside the cafe, people sat in groups talking excitedly, and with the Regulator's western get-ups, it looked like he stepped into a restaurant from the 1880's, especially now with the loss of electricity and the use of kerosene lamps throughout the place. David glanced around the room which was large enough for fifty or sixty people and wondered what else had happened to cause such a stir in the crowd.

David followed Spyder over to Ginny where he asked, "What the hell's going on?"

"Keith and Amanda returned from the camp and said both Mike and Sam was killed by mutants," she answered. "They also say everything has been torn apart."

"Yeah," Spyder said. "We saw it when we were up there."

"There were signs leading up a trail toward the Crystal Crossing area. People are talking about going after them."

"First things first," David answered. "We need to get the supplies down here before we do anything else." He stepped up on a chair at Hal Sloan' table,

311

held his arms up, and shouted for everyone to quiet down. Shortly, the talking stopped. "I know you all want to get revenge for Mike and Sam's deaths, but there are other things, which have to take priority. We have to get all the supplies from the camp. We also have to make sure we're all moved in, and this area is secure."

"The longer we take in tracking those mutants down, the better chance they have of getting away," Wind called out.

"You're probably right, Wind," Hal answered, rising, "but David has a point. Our immediate concern should be to get the supplies here so they're safe. I don't want to have to leave anyone else out there on guard another night."

There was a murmur of agreement following his statement. With the rumors going around, it was obvious none of them were anxious to spend another night up at the stage barn.

"We'll also have to dig graves for those men up there," Spyder said. We might as well bury them in the fake graveyard at the edge of Sagebrush. There's no reason it can't become a real cemetery."

From the side, Keith said, "Amanda and I'll dig Mike's grave since he came here with us."

"Carl and I will take care of a grave for Sam," Katy said, nodding at her son.

"Thanks folks," David answered. "We'll get the bodies to you in a couple of hours." Then looking around at the others in the room, he said, "We also have to remember we don't know how many of the mutants there were last night. If there was only one or two, we would be okay, but if there's any more, then we'd be in trouble."

***

From the door, a voice said, "You don't want to be out looking for any of those animals in weather like this."

"Nice to see you up and around," David said.

"Thanks." Bear leaned against the wall, partially supported by Davata. "It's been my experience that those things die hard. It takes at least a couple of shots to kill 'em. In bad weather with low visibility, it makes things a bit touchy."

"I agree," David answered. "That's what I'm talking about. We don't need to take any more chances than we have to."

"I've killed a couple of them," Ron said, "and anything short of a headshot with a rifle won't work immediately. They'll have enough left in them to do damage for a couple of more minutes."

Hal figured that explained why Ron used the rifle on the dying mutant when he and Ron first met. At the time, Hal thought of it as overkill. But now he understood why the man used the long gun rather than his pistol. It also helped Hal understand the look Ron gave him after firing the shot. The one thing Hal didn't understand was why Barbara told him they hadn't killed any mutants. It probably wasn't anything, but something about it bothered him. He also wanted to know how Ron knew the group near the lake was a militia.

David stepped down from his chair. "Once everyone has finished eating, we can go up to the camp and do everything we need to do."

313

"Glad to see you back on the floor," Hal said grinning. "You had me wondering if you were gonna step in my grits or not-thought you might deprive me of a meal."

"You don't look like you've missed too many meals," Bear said from behind David.

David held his hand out to Bear. "You noticed that too, huh?

"Bear, sit your ass down," Hal ordered.

"I will in a minute," Bear answered. "First, I want to get something to eat from the kitchen."

"Sit down," Davata restated the order. "I'll get the food."

Bear eased into a chair as Davata left for the kitchen.

"Looks like you're feeling better," Hal observed.

"A lot better," he answered. "I figure the more I move around, the faster I'll heal."

"Just don't overdo it," Hal said.

"Telling him that is like saying it to you, Hal," Sandy answered. "It does absolutely no good."

As Davata came back with two plates piled high with breakfast, Bear said, "One thing about it-she isn't about to let me starve to death."

The four of them talked, ate, and drank coffee for the next half-hour. For once, the conversation wasn't about survival. It was of past memories and hopes for the future.

"What do you think of the new couple, Hal?" Davata asked.

"They seem nice enough," he answered. "There's something off about them though. I can't put my finger on it, but something isn't right."

314

"He always thinks there's something wrong with every person he's around," Sandy said. "He even thinks there's something wrong with me."

"So do I," Bear answered. "In fact, I know there's something wrong with you, look who you're married to. Damn, how obvious does it have to be?"

"Enough of this shit," Hal announced standing up, "time to go get things from the camp."

Bear rose along with him. "I know I can't be much help, but I'll stay out of the way; and I need the exercise. So, if you don't mine, I'll accompany you."

"Doesn't matter to me," Hal answered.

"You'll have to stay in the truck while we're up there," Sandy informed him. "You can't be out in the cold for any length of time."

"She's right," Davata agreed. "I'm going to help up there all I can, and I won't be around most of the time."

"Damn people, I'm not helpless," Bear protested. "I can take care of myself. I don't have to have a babysitter."

"I'll remember that the next time you're complaining about having to get a snack or something from the other room," Davata informed him.

"Blew it again huh, dude?" Hal said through a big grin as he turned and walked toward the door.

"Dude?" Bear repeated. "Dude... who the hell's he calling dude? Hal, you asshole, come back here... " His voice fading as he followed Hal from the table.

The four went outside and climbed into one of the trucks they would use for the move. They

315

picked one with a crew cab so they all could fit comfortably with Bear there. It took a little over four hours to complete the move, dig the graves, and bury the two men. They conducted a short ceremony and placed crosses on the graves.

***

With the task completed, everyone met back at the cafe. It was lunchtime, and there was still business to conduct.

Ginny, Barbara, and Ben had remained behind and cleaned up after breakfast. Afterward, they set lunch out for everyone, consisting of potato soup, luncheon meat, and condiments for sandwiches. When there were over twenty people to feed with limited supplies, soup and sandwiches were the easiest and quickest meals to prepare.

When everyone finished lunch, Spyder stood and got everybody's attention with a yell. "There's some things we all need to take care of," he said moving to an open area near the serving line. "One of the main things we have to decide is who our leader will be. We need to know who'll be making the important decisions. We've talked about electing a leader for some while now, and I think it's about time to do it. If there are no objections, and since I'm standing up here, I'll chair the election."

Each member looked around at the others. With no objections from the rest, Spyder continued, "I don't think there's any secret who I think is best for the job. I'd be more'n willing to follow David Alexander. It's nothin' against any of the rest of you. I just think he's the best man for the job, and I

316

nominate him to be our leader. David, will you accept the nomination?"

"I'll accept the nomination," David answered, nodding.

"Are there any other nominations?" Spyder asked.

"I don't have a nomination," Bear said. "I do have something to say if it's all right."

"Sure it's okay," Spyder answered. "If nobody else cares."

No one voiced an objection.

Bear rose from his chair, "Now all of you know how well David and I get along. Hell, I've known him since he and his family moved here. He's probably got one of the better heads around. However, I do have a problem with what's going on."

He paused and looked around the room. He could see most of the people present were surprised at what he had said. Most of them knew David and figured his election was simply a matter of formality.

"Nothing against David, but I have no intention of allowing a single individual to make a decision on my safety or my way of living. No single person except me, that is," Bear corrected. "One of the things I liked about the Regulators was that we were run by five elected officials. Now, David happened to be the head of the group, and as far as I'm concerned rightly so. But there were four other people there to help make the decisions and throw in different ideas. Something like that is perfectly acceptable to me, but I don't agree with having a single person in charge." He looked around the room and sat down.

"An interesting point of view," Spyder said. "Does anyone else have any further discussion?"

Hal raised his hand and rose to his feet at the same time.

"Go ahead, Hal," Spyder instructed.

"I understanding what Bear's saying," Hal said. "Like him, I know and respect David and his ideas. At the same time, with things being the way they are, I don't think I want any single person telling me what I can and can't do either. It's not because I'm any smarter or know more than any other person here. I'm simply not willing to completely turn the decisions of Sandy's and my safety over to one person."

"I'm not trying to be responsible for everyone else's safety," David interrupted. "In fact, I agree with both of you. I think a committee the same as it was before the blackout should run the group. It worked well then and should now."

"Well, I disagree," Cindy said as she stood. "A committee is great when people's lives aren't on the line. I don't know about any of you, but I don't want to have to wait through a discussion to find out what *The Committee*"-she formed imaginary quotation marks in the air with two fingers of each hand-"has decided is the best way to protect us."

"What makes you think David can make the correct decision by himself when the pressure is on?" Wind leaned against a far wall.

"Obviously he knows how to be a director," Cindy answered with slight anger in her voice. "He and a friend of his formed a successful multi-state corporation before all this happened."

"Cindy," Sandy said from her seat. "I agree with Hal. Not because he's my husband-God knows I disagree with him enough as it is-this time, I agree with him and disagree with you because there is a big difference between directorship and leadership. As a director, you tell others what to do. As a leader, you tell people things needing to be done, then show or help them do whatever it is. I don't think there is any one person here capable of doing that in every circumstance. It can, however, be done by a group of people. There's something else we should keep in mind along this line. Right now, we are essentially the same group of Hays County Regulators as we were before, with only a few people added to our numbers. I honestly don't think it'll be too long before more and more people find us or hear about us and search us out. Then we'll definitely have to have our leaders in place and have procedures for accepting or rejecting others wanting to become a part of our group. Not to mention defending ourselves from some of them, or for that fact, anyone else." She looked around at the assembly and with a sheepish grin said, "Sorry folks, I tend to get excited. I'll shut up now."

"Excited or not," Spyder said, "You makes sense. What do the rest of you think?"

"I agree with her," Wind said. "I don't know which of you were on the committee, but think there's more strength in numbers. I think we should leave the committee in place and let them run things for a little while. If we don't like what they do, we can vote 'em out."

319

It appeared everyone in the cafe agreed with this last statement and began talking amongst themselves. Even Cindy nodded in agreement. Of course, it meant David would be head of the committee. Spyder banged a hammer someone had handed him on the railing he had been leaning against previously. "Hold it down," he said loudly. "Let's get on with this."

The rest of the people in the room soon quieted down, and David raised his hand.

"The floor recognizes David," Spyder said.

"I think we're all in agreement on what needs to be done. So, I hereby decline the nomination as leader and instead make the motion that the committee, as it was previously set up, be accepted as the ruling committee."

"I second the motion," Wind said in agreement.

"Point of Order," Bear called out over a few of the people that were mumbling.

"The chair recognizes Bear," Spyder said.

"We can't vote the committee back in as it was," Bear stated matter-of-factly.

"What's the problem now, Bear?" Cindy asked and sighed, irritation back in her voice. It was obvious she wanted this business over and done with. She also wanted her husband to be in charge.

"Kyle Jennings was on the committee. I hate to think that he may be dead, but it's a very real possibility." Bear looked over at the rest of the Jennings family and said, "Sorry folks." He then continued. "Also, if we're gonna vote a committee in then we need to vote them in because of abilities and not popularity."

320

"He's right," Wind agreed. "I know I may sound wishy-washy about this, but I was a little uncomfortable voting the group in without knowing who they were. I was willing to though, because they proved themselves before. Now, I agree with Bear, let's vote them in individually."

Without waiting for anything else to be said, Spyder banged his hammer again and said, "Nominations are now open for *Head of the Committee*."

"I nominate David," Cindy said.

"I second the nomination," Deborah called out.

"Will you accept this nomination?" Spyder asked. "Hey man, I have to ask," he said when David looked at him as if he were crazy.

"I accept," David answered.

"I nominate Hal," Bear said from the side.

"Do you accept?" Spyder asked Hal.

"Yeah I accept," Hal answered with a sheepish grin

"Are there any more nominations?" Spyder asked.

Davata raised her hand and asked, "Can I make a nomination?"

"As far as I'm concerned, you can," Spyder answered.

"I would like to nominate Bear," she said.

From where he was sitting, Bear immediately said, "Declined."

Davata looked at him questioningly.

"Not a chance in Hell," Bear said with conviction.

"Are there any more nominations?" Spyder asked. When he saw none, he brought his hammer down. "The nominations are closed."

When the vote was finished, Hal won with David surprisingly getting only two votes, Cindy and Deborah's.

Spyder turned to Hal and asked, "Will you accept the position?"

***

Hal, completely surprised by the outcome said, "I'll accept it." Under his breath he mumbled, "I damned sure didn't expect it, but I'll accept it."

Spyder handed him the hammer, "Your gavel of office," he said, grinning as he sat in Hal's empty chair.

To the group Hal said, "No big speeches-I'll just do the best I can. There are some things I personally think we need to take into consideration when we vote on the rest of the committee. As I see it, we need people in charge of the following areas: security and defense, weapons, supplies and food preparation, animal maintenance, construction or maintenance of buildings, and patrols and hunting. In most of the areas, we know who will be in charge, but we have to decide who will be responsible for helping."

When all the debates and discussions were over, the committee consisted of all the same people previous to the blackout, except without Kyle Jennings and with the addition of one. Hal was Head of the Committee and in charge of construction and building maintenance. David managed security, camp defense, and an armory and all its weapons. He was also in charge of training all members and any new members in the use and safety of personal firearms. Spyder had supplies and food preparation along with helping Hal with construction and building maintenance. Bear was in charge of self-defense, patrols and hunting, and Lynn was to take the care and feeding of all animals.

Every member of the camp would be required not only to receive training in the use and safety of personal weapons but also in the martial arts to the level of black belt or as high as their abilities would allow.

The Committee agreed to meet again at Hal and Sandy's cabin at seven o'clock that evening to set up guidelines for the entire group to vote on. Another meeting would be set up for a vote as soon as the committee could iron things out. They adjourned, and except for Sandy, Davata, and the members of the committee, most of the others headed out.

"We've got a hell of a job ahead of us," Spyder observed.

"More than most of us know," Hal answered. "I don't think the way we lived before will be enough to give us what we need to survive."

"There is something we need to face," Bear said and looked at all of them. "This group is going to have to be the final decision when it comes to right and wrong. We're gonna have to be willing make decisions, which very well may determine whether a person lives or dies. We're also gonna have to adopt a set of laws the entire group will have to live by, also what the punishments will be."

"And who's gonna be the sheriff or enforce the laws?" Sandy asked.

"Well, I see we're all here," Hal observed. "Does anyone have any objection to starting our meeting right now rather than tonight? I know we're scheduled for seven o'clock, but we have a lot of work ahead of us."

It was two-thirty in the afternoon, and everyone agreed they should all stay. Their first meeting continued until ten o'clock in the evening with only a short break once every hour. It would take two more meetings, of six hours each, before the committee completed their basic guidelines.

***

"It's not that we don't trust you," David told them. "It's simply because we don't know you, and we do know how everyone else, here in camp, will react in a given situation. Give us a couple of days and if you want to stay and the group is okay with it, then you can have the choice of any of the cabins that are left."

"We understand," Barbara answered. "With circumstances being the way they are, we're simply glad you're willing to allow us to stay here in camp."

"I think we've been lucky all the way around," Ron said. "Hal saved our asses when we met him... then the three of you with all those mutant things at the house. And now with it being so bad outside, Barbara and I could be in real trouble without all of you."

David and Spyder left Ron and Barbara in their new suite with a living room, kitchenette, and bedroom and food for their cupboards. Barbara busied herself putting the food away while Ron sat down in a chair at the kitchen table. "Well, what do you think?"

"They seem to be willing to help others," she answered, "and that's nice to see in this day and circumstance. They brought us in and gave us shelter and food very quickly and without asking many questions."

"You're right," Ron agreed. "We're gonna have to be careful and take our time finding out about these people. Damn, I'm tired." He ran his hand through his hair as he moved from the kitchen chair and sat in a large, comfortable, overstuffed armchair.

"I know exactly how you feel," Barbara answered. She sat down on a couch and pulled off her boots one at a time.

Ron stood and walked over to a potbelly stove standing near the far wall. He opened the front door, wadded up some pages of a magazine and placed them inside, arranged some kindling and two small pieces of wood, and then put a large piece on top of them. He lit the paper and closed the door, leaving it open a small crack to create a draft and fan the flames. He then returned to the comfort of his chair.

Outside, the snow coated the ground as well as the branches of the trees. It lay on the ground in smooth, even drifts around and on top of all the cabins within their view. It slowly wafted straight down adding to the complete serenity of the scene.

"Now I'd be willing to stay here forever," Ron commented, leaning back in his chair and raising the legs.

"Don't even tempt me. If we weren't on a mission, I wouldn't think twice about staying right here."

"Did you notice that Sam was one of the men we buried today?"

"I did," she answered. "I was wondering how much he told them."

"He couldn't have told them anything about us. I don't think he saw us when we arrived. I didn't see him until this morning, and he was already dead."

"What I meant was I wonder what all he told them about the militia."

"I tried to feel Hal out about it, and he wasn't very forthcoming," Ron said. "I didn't want to push it. I was afraid he might become suspicious. All he would say was Sam was once a member of a group believing in the ethics of the confederacy of the Civil War.

"It sounds like Sam told them about most of their beliefs," Barbara said, "which is no big secret, and that alone couldn't cause any problems."

The rest of the evening they spent stoking the fire, relaxing, and later having supper. With both of them worn out, they went to bed early. They'd have a long day ahead tomorrow.

***

The following two days was spent gathering supplies from the storehouse and learning their new temporary assignments. Barbara was to help Lynn

326

with the animals, and Ron would help Ben with the supplies. Barbara was glad she wasn't in the armory since she already knew how to break down and clean every weapon they had. She was sure the others would have discovered that if she were there.

The morning of the third day, Barbara awoke to the smell of coffee coming from the kitchen. As she slipped out of bed, she also noticed the smell of eggs and bacon. She dressed and went into the kitchen.

There she found Ron standing in front of the gas stove cooking eggs, bacon, and toasting bread in the oven. He looked completely comfortable making the food. He put two eggs on a plate along with two pieces of buttered toast. On another plate were six pieces of bacon along with more butter and strawberry jam. He placed both plates on the table, and pointing at the one with the eggs said, "That plate's yours. Go ahead and start while it's still warm, I'll be there as soon as I finish mine. It only took a couple of minutes for him to finish preparing his food and join her.

She ate as if she really enjoyed it. "I like to see a woman enjoy her food," he said with a grin.

"Believe me," Barbara answered, "it's worth paying attention to."

Spyder and Wind passed by the window with four strangers walking in front of them. Neither man held a weapon directly on the newcomers. However, they did have their rifles presumably as a matter of precaution, while they all walked toward the office area.

"Look there," Ron said to Barbara as they went by. "Who the hell's that?"

"I've got no idea," Barbara answered. "But I plan on finding out." She stood and quickly headed for the sink with her dish. To her surprise, Ron picked up his plate and the extra one and joined her. Ron grabbed the last two remaining pieces of bacon and Barbara the last piece of buttered toast as he put the plates in the sink. Both of them grinned at each other as they quickly pulled on their boots and jackets and left the suite.

They hurried to the office, and to their surprise, found Bear, there along with the strangers, Spyder, and Wind. Bear sat at the reception desk looking at some papers in front of him. As they walked in, Spyder was making introductions. "Folks this is Bear. Bear, these are some new folks Wind and I met out on the road. That good lookin' couple that just walked in the front door is Ron and Barbara." Then to the others, "You'll all have to introduce yourselves since I don't remember all your names. Sorry about that."

There were three men and one woman standing in front of Bear. One of the men stepped forward and said, "My name is Harry Sears." Turning to the others, he motioned to each in turn, as he said their names, "Larry Archer, Dale Schubert, and Maria Villegas." Harry turned back to Bear and said, "We've been traveling since the electricity went off or was lost or whatever it was that happened."

"Where do you all come from, Mr. Sears?" Bear asked.

"From up around the Baltimore, Maryland area," the man answered, "and please, call me Harry."

"Okay Harry, where are you headed?" Bear asked.

"We're on our way to the Texas Coast," he answered. "Larry was raised in Corpus Christi and told us it was a place worth looking at, with everything that's happened."

"What's the rest of the country like between Baltimore and here?" Bear asked.

"We can't tell you about all of the cities," Harry answered. "We mostly stayed away from them-except for Washington, D.C. Since we were there, we went by the Lincoln Memorial and Arlington Cemetery. We also went to the Tomb of the Unknown Soldier. Do you know there are still soldiers standing guard there? They're still pulling guard duty the same as usual. They said they had a job to do, and they would do it until they died or were relieved. Some of the most dedicated people I've ever seen."

"Doesn't surprise me," Bear answered. "They aren't called the *Old Guard* for nothing." Turning to Ron he asked, "You got any information about Corpus?"

All eyes turned toward him as he said, "It was being taken over by gangs when we went through."

"You were there?" Larry asked.

"I was only there a couple of hours," Ron answered. Then to Larry he said, "Believe me, it isn't a place fit to live in now. Do you have family there?"

"Not anymore," Larry said. "The last of them died a couple of years ago."

"Sorry to hear that," Bear said.

329

"It's okay," he answered. "I was only going back because of the climate and the abundance of food in the area."

The door opened and Davata walked in followed by David and Hal. Bear motioned to each person as he introduced them.

"No offense meant," Harry said. "But you mean there are people around here with real names?"

The three new arrivals looked at him questioningly.

"I mean, we've mainly met people named Wind, Spyder, and Bear," Harry explained, "I was wondering if anyone here had regular names." He was smiling in an attempt to show that he meant no harm and was only kidding.

"I know what you mean," Hal answered. "You're just lucky you met them like this. They can be mighty peculiar at times." He held his hand out.

Harry took his hand and shook it. "Again, not wanting to cause any trouble, but what's with the getups?"

"Seems like everyone we meet asks the same question," David answered and held out his hand. "I'm David Alexander." After shaking the other man's hand, he explained the reason for the clothes they all wore. He ended with, "... and it seems like everyone joining our group starts wearing this same style even though it's not required."

Bear stood up and asked, "What part of the military were you attached to?"

Surprised, Harry eyed him closely, and then answered, "U.S. Marines." Then after a pause he asked, "How did you know?"

"Look at your people," Bear answered. "They're either at parade rest or a relaxed attention. The hands are always a dead giveaway with them being in a fist and the thumbs along the seams. Not to mention that all of you were in step as you walked up the front walk."

"Is this a problem?" Harry asked.

"My name is Rafe Edmonds, SOC, USN Retired, and no, it's not a problem," Bear said. "There are other people who were members of the armed forces for various lengths of time who are now with this group. The United States Military is always welcome here."

There was a look of relief on all the newcomers' faces. It was obvious they were unsure of what would happen to them. It was equally obvious they were in service long enough to learn discipline and not long enough to know what to do with it.

"You can stay here with us for a while if you like," Hal told them, "or move on to some other place. It's up to you."

Harry pulled himself to attention, and in a sharp, crisp, military tone said, "If it's all the same to you, sir. We'll stay with your group for a while."

"You're welcome to stay with us for a little while, Harry," Hal answered. "But there are some things you need to know first."

"What would that be, sir?" Harry asked.

"First of all," Hal explained, "you won't be in charge of these people from here on. They'll be equal members of the group with an equal say, and they'll have to make decisions on their own. Secondly, all of you will have to assist the group in

331

all its activities such as gathering food, feeding animals, guarding the camp, and anything else that may be assigned. Thirdly, all of you will have to abide by the rules of the group and any rules, which may be passed by the committee previously elected. There's just one other small thing and it is, I'm not a sir, I'm Hal."

Harry grinned. "Is it possible for us to live here for a while so we can see what all the rules and tasks are? Then we can then make a more informed decision?"

"Not a problem," Hal answered. "In fact, we require you spend some time with us before making any permanent decisions to stay or leave."

"Sounds good," he answered. He held his hand out and said, "We'll stay for a while and see how things are."

"I don't think you understand," Bear interjected. "The decision isn't yours to make for all of them. They have to decide this for themselves."

"Without hesitation, the other three quickly agreed.

"Well, if you're all gonna stay at least for a little while," Bear said. "Then you might as well start meeting people right now." He stood and pointed to the two people behind them and said, "Those are two other new people named Ron and Barbara. If they are willing, they'll show you where you'll be living. It'll be near their suite."

They all greeted each other with names and handshakes after which Ron and Barbara led them out of the office toward the other suites near theirs.

It only took a couple of minutes for Ron and Barbara to settle the new people in two of the rooms near them. After telling the newcomers to make themselves at home, Ron and Barbara returned to the office to see what may have happened overnight.

CHAPTER THIRTY

In his cell, Bo sat eating his breakfast from a bowl. He looked up as Gabriel walked up and sat in a chair outside Bo's cell.

When Bo finished his food, Gabriel asked, "Are you being fed enough?"

Bo nodded.

"I've been thinking, Bo," Gabriel started. "I think there's something I can do to help you and all your kind."

Bo looked at the man knowing an attempt was about to be made to get his assistance. He expected some feeble offer, and that would be when the negotiations began.

"How many of your kind are there around here and near San Antonio?"

Bo picked up the pad and pencil, and scrawled *"100's,"* and then showed it to Gabriel.

Gabriel looked at the pad and asked, "How many will obey what you say?"

Bo simply turned the pad back so he could see the writing.

"Do you mean all of them?" He asked.

Bo nodded.

"What is the survival rate for infants born of your kind-or the survival rate of your kind who become injured or get sick from some disease?"

Bo stared steadily at the man.

"Show me with your hands."

Bo hesitated and then held his hands out, far apart. He only meant to demonstrate the death rate of the mutants. As far as he knew, there hadn't been any births yet. However, he didn't think Gabriel needed to know that right now. He had no idea if a birth among his kind was even possible.

"I'm not going to beat around the bush," Gabriel said. "I'm willing to put two veterinarians at your disposal full time. I'll set up a clinic on the edge of the city, and they'll spend all their time treating any of your kind willing to work with us."

Bo continued to look at the man. He knew there had to be something else to the proposal.

"In return," Gabriel continued, "you'll have to convince all the mutants to help us protect ourselves and expand our territory. If we cooperate with each other, we'll be invincible. I will make sure no one from Austin or San Antonio will harm any of you, and you can do the same for us. You can hunt anywhere outside of the city, or we can supply food from inside."

Bo understood what the man was saying, and on the surface, it sounded good. He also knew the man was a gang leader before the loss of power and not someone to be trusted. However, the opportunity for medical treatment and the possibility of living in buildings without the concern of hunters made the proposal worth looking at. He needed time to think about the offer and consider his options.

As if reading his mind, Gabriel said, "I know this is a big decision, and you may want to think about it. How about if you and your friend there get a little exercise while you're thinking?"

The last statement confused Bo until Gabriel stepped up to the door of the cell and unlocked it.

He left the key in the door and walked to the solid steel door leading out of the cells. "You have an hour or so to think it over," Gabriel said as he left the room. Through a slit in the door, he said, "Just follow the corridor to your left." The slit closed, and the two mutants were alone in their cells.

Bo stood, opened the door to his cell, and stepped out. After opening his mate's cell door, he slowly led the way down the corridor to their left. They followed the passageway to an exercise yard outside the building. The yard was a square, about fifty-yards on each side. A ten-foot high fence, topped with coiled razor wire, surrounded it. There was a second fence identical to the first one about ten feet beyond it. Bo could feel the ground consisted of hard-packed earth with a frozen layer. There was about four inches of snow coating the ground with drifts running up the corners. The sun shone brightly in a crisp, clear blue, cloudless sky.

Both mutants knew they could get out of the yard with little problem. However, at two corners, there were guard towers. In the towers, there were men armed with rifles. There was also a tower in the middle of a brick wall forming the fourth side.

Bo saw Gabriel and Manny walk up to the guard shack on the wall and begin talking to the two guards inside. From their vantage point, in the tower, the men could safely watch the mutants below.

The mutants slowly ambled around the yard, stopping every-so-often to lift their nose and sniff the air.

Bo communicated the offer to his mate. He also told her that he figured the offer would include her staying locked up until he returned with an answer from the other packs.

As much as she hated the confinement, she was willing to put up with it for a while longer if it meant help for others of her kind.

He figured it would take him a week to ten days to contact the leaders of the largest packs in the area. Each of those packs could in turn get the information out to other smaller ones or those further from the cities.

***

"It's hard to see them down there and think of them as intelligent," Manny said. "They look like a cross between a reptile, bear, ape and some kind of big cat. Shit, the sight of them alone is enough to give someone nightmares for a month."

"I know what you mean," Gabriel agreed.

"What's to stop the mutants from eventually turning on us when they are all healthy?"

Gabriel looked at Manny in mock surprise. "Why nothing," he answered. "Except that I'll have the doctors give them Lorazepam-in the correct dose, it doesn't make them high but will require another treatment within a couple of days. Once they're hooked, we can control 'em simply by the treat of withholding doses."

"Damn," Manny replied. "Remind me to stay on your good side, man."

Gabriel grinned and looked back down on the two mutants down below.

***

"Bear looks like he's getting better as each day goes by," Sandy said as she and Davata combed through the camp's supplies for books. They were looking for information helpful in teaching both the kids and adults' classes.

"He's getting better," Davata agreed. "The thing I worry about is whether he is feeling pain and not showing it."

"He probably is. But knowing him like I do, I don't think he'll go to the extent of causing injury to himself, he knows better than that. There are too many people relying on his talents. He won't let them down. That's just not the way he is."

"You really do care about him, don't you? This is the second time you've talked about him so fondly."

"Like I said, he's my brother," Sandy said matter-of-factly. "Maybe not by blood, but he's closer to me than any of my brothers or sisters who are of my blood."

"Well... you know Bear and I are sharing a cabin."

"Sure," Sandy answered, smiling. She knew what the other woman was thinking. "I hope it won't cause any friction or a problem between us. Nothing's happened. Don't get me wrong," Davata quickly continued. "I'm not saying anything will or won't. It's just that nothing has up to now."

"Davata," Sandy interrupted, holding her hand up. "I have to explain something to you. There seems to be a lot you don't understand about Rafe and me. Either that or you misunderstand our relationship."

She took hold of Davata's arm and said, "Sit down for a couple of minutes. Let me explain some things to you."

They both sat in chairs facing each other. Davata sat back in her chair and Sandy leaned forward with her elbows on her knees. She looked straight into Davata's eyes and said, "There seems to be some things you misunderstand about our relationship. Either that or I've misled you about him and I. He is my brother." She paused, waiting for this information to sink in. Then she continued, "Not really my brother by blood but closer than any of my real brothers and sisters are to me. He's much closer to me than any of them were ever willing or capable of being. He'll do anything I ask, and I would do anything for him."

"That's what I don't want to mess up," Davata said interrupting. "I don't want to come between you and whatever he might ask of you."

"Again you're misunderstanding me," Sandy answered. "There is nothing physical between us. Our relationship is completely spiritual. He lifts me up spiritually, and hopefully I do the same to him. There is nothing I'm willing to do with him I'm not willing for my husband to know. You have to understand, Hal knows everything between us. Not only that, but he has no problem with it. Rafe may not be as close to Hal as he is to me, but he would never do anything Hal would disapprove of-and I know and trust that. Rafe may not agree or approve of everything Hal does, but he will follow what is decided upon without question. The last thing is-there is nothing you could do to cause a problem between us. I don't mean to be harsh or insulting.

It's just that our feelings are on a different level, and no person alive could change it. In fact, I would love for something to develop between you and him. Like I said before, he needs someone in his life, and it seems you might possibly be that someone. Actually, it may be up to you to make something happen between you and him. Believe me, he may not look like it, but he's extremely shy."

"I guess I did misunderstand your relationship," Davata answered. "My only reference, up until now, was a physical one. Both of you have gone far beyond that and frankly, I'm not only surprised but very happy."

"I admit, he isn't the type to make you think he would be lent to more spiritual beliefs," Sandy said. "But he has never given me a reason to think otherwise. He has always been extremely considerate of what Hal may think about him and me and conducted himself accordingly."

"Okay," Davata answered. "I feel like a fool. I was worrying about something that was only in my mind."

"Not only in your mind, but probably in the minds of many others," Sandy said. "I'm sure most people don't understand what's going on with us. Next to Hal, he's the best friend I have-I love him. He would support my marriage to my husband and reject anything that would possibly make a difference between my husband and me."

"I said it before. You're a lucky woman."

"Yes I am-very lucky."

"What you said about him being spiritual has to be true," Davata said. "We talked when I first got here, and he explained some of his spiritual beliefs.

It was what I told you the other day about him and death."

"You're right," Sandy agreed. "He is very comfortable with an *existence after death,* and it all stems from his spiritual beliefs."

Both women sat in silence a couple of seconds, and then Sandy said, "Just do me a favor, please. Keep an eye on him and don't let him over extend himself for another week or so. He may look and act okay, but he's not fully healed yet."

"Don't worry. I'll keep an eye on him."

Both women rose, and Sandy reached out and gave Davata a hug. "You'll be good for him," she said. Then in her usual lively attitude continued, "Now let's see if we can find any more of those books you need."

They returned to work looking through boxes, plastic bags, and the numerous other containers containing all kinds of items.

***

Back at the stage barn and the site of the old Rebel's Revenge, David set up a series of targets and was checking people out on the use of the various weapons in the camp. He had set up an armory, inventoried, and categorized all their weapons. He also made a detailed list of every weapon, the number of boxes of ammunition, and amounts of powder and balls for black powder weapons.

At the target range, Ben, Hal, Bear, Wind, and Spyder stood in a row with black powder rifles to their shoulders pointed at the targets.

"Fire," David called out. An instant later, the quiet was shattered with the explosion of five fifty-caliber rifles. With almost no wind, a large cloud of blue smoke slowly drifted from around the shooters.

"Look around," David instructed. "Look at the smoke. Remember that you put out this much every time you fire one of these." He knew they could not only see the smoke, but smell it as well. The smell of burnt powder was unmistakable.

"Also remember that it will give you away," David said, "it and the flash of the muzzles. Unless you have a strong wind, the smoke is a finger pointing straight to your location."

He looked at each man. Except for Wind, all of them were previously members of the Hays County Regulators when they were putting on shows. Back then, the smoke was impressive to the crowds and reminded them of how much power the weapons possessed. Before the shows, one of the men would put an aluminum soda can down on the street and after warning everyone in the crowd about the power of the blast, put the end of the barrel against the can and pull the trigger. The blast would blow the can fifteen to twenty feet away and either tear it in half or leave the halves connected by only the smallest piece of metal.

David continued, "If there is no wind, and you are shooting at someone who will shoot back, then you have to move immediately. If you don't, there will be enough smoke to block them from view. All your enemy has to do is move a couple of feet to the side and saturate the smoke with lead. This is only one of the differences between these weapons and the modern, smokeless ones. Now look at the targets."

Every one of the gunfighters had put their bullets in the black center of their target. "That's the only good thing we have on our side," David said. "You're all good shots. Now pull your pistols."

David knew he was *preaching to the choir*, but this was the information he gave out to all members of Rebel's Revenge. Every man had already heard what he was saying, yet none of them took exception to the information. They knew their lives might depend on remembering it at any given time and were glad for the refresher course.

As the men each pulled out one of their pistols, David told them, "I don't want anyone trying a quick draw, That's only to be used in case of an emergency. Too many people have been hurt, shooting themselves while clearing the holster with the pistol. Now take your time and fire six shots at your targets when I say go."

The men aimed their weapons down range and waited. David checked the area around the targets and seeing it was safe, called out, "Fire."

***

Ron and Barbara were on roving patrol as the volley rang out in the distance.

"Sounds like the small arms training has started," Ron said.

"Sounds like it," Barbara answered. "They're definitely serious about defending themselves."

343

"We've been here a month, and I personally haven't seen any actions, which could be considered a danger to the militia."

"Neither have I. It seems like all they want to do is keep to themselves."

"True, but I don't think they would take kindly to anyone who keeps workers the way the militia does."

Barbara didn't say anything. She lowered her eyes to the ground as she kept walking. She wasn't crazy about the practice herself. The militia had been good to her, but the slavery thing didn't set right with her. However, she didn't think she could say anything to Ron-not yet anyway.

They walked along the edge of a cliff as they talked. A small rock landed about a foot from Ron. They stopped and looked around. Another rock landed on the other side of them. They brought their rifles up, held them at a ready position, and slowly turned in a circle searching the area. They were barely inside a grove of cedar trees extending away from the cliff. The rest of the area was a mixture of cedar and spruce trees with patches of grassy areas between them. Another rock landed nearby and they both squatted, unable to determine where the rocks were coming from. In couple of seconds, they heard someone laughing a short distance away.

"I'm coming in," the voice said. "Don't shoot."

Seconds later, Buck emerged from a group of trees.

"Buck," Barbara exclaimed. "What the hell are you doing here?" Then realizing one of the militia was here, she looked around to see if anyone could see them. There was no way they were visible from the lodge area, and they were the only ones on patrol right now.

Buck raised his hand to salute Ron. Instantly Ron punched him in the face, knocking him on his ass.

"Don't make that mistake again," Ron warned him.

"Sorry sir...uh, Ron," Buck said.

Ron held his hand out to help the other man to his feet. "Sorry to have to hit you Buck. But now you'll remember not to make that mistake again."

Rubbing his cheek, "You got that shit right," he said.

"Did you see anyone else around here?" Barbara asked.

"Nope," Buck answered, "only the two of you. I did hear some shooting a couple of minutes ago, though."

"It's only some of the camp doing target practice," Ron explained. "We should be able to talk safely."

"The General sent me to see if I could make contact with the two of you and see what's going on."

"I figured he'd do it sooner or later," Ron said.

"It's not that he doesn't trust you..."

"I know he trusts us," Ron interrupted. "It's smart to try and stay in contact. Shit, you may have to make two or three trips like this."

"Is there any information I need to take back?"

"There's nothing really to report," Ron told him. "Barbara and I are still on the outside. This patrol is the most trust they've shown us since we've been here."

"Can you tell if they're planning to make a move against us?" Buck asked.

"Like I said," Ron answered. "They haven't decided they can trust us enough to let us into their inner circle. We're not in on their planning right now."

"How about your cover? Do you think they suspect either of you?"

"I don't think so," Ron answered. "They're more interested in finding food and staying alive than anything else."

"What about you, Barbara? Have you learned anything?" Buck queried.

"Nothing other than what he's said," she answered. "As you can see, they pretty much keep us together. I can't go out on my own that much."

"When I talked to General Clark," Buck explained, "he said he was concerned these people might decide to try and attack our compound. Do you think there's any chance of that happening soon?"

"Not anytime soon," Ron answered.

Barbara shook her head agreeing with him. "They know there's a group around somewhere. They don't know where. Only that it's around in the area. They're strange, these people. They brought Sam here when we ran him out, and even though he was one of the men who attacked them, they were willing to give him another chance. They treated him much the same as they're treating us."

"Sam was here?" Buck repeated a look of concern on his face.

"Yeah, he was here," Ron confirmed. "He was here, but he didn't give them any information. He didn't even tell them he knew us."

"Is he back in the camp now?" Buck asked.

"He's dead," Barbara answered. "He was killed during the snow storm a couple of weeks ago. It looks like he and another man were killed by some mutants while on guard duty one night."

"Well," Buck said. "At least he's no longer a threat to tell what he knows."

"Not anymore," Ron agreed.

"How long do you think it'll take for you to get the information we need?" Buck asked.

"I have no idea," Ron answered. "It's gonna take a while. That is, if they're even planning anything. Look, there's a good chance-a very good chance-they won't do anything."

"How will you let us know if they do?" Buck was pushing for answers. "You know, we need to know as far as possible in advance when they decide to do something."

"If they decide to do something," Ron corrected.

"Okay, if they decide to do something," Buck said. "I don't mean to be pushy, but have to have something to take back to the general. "If I have to get information back to you in an emergency, I can get away for a day by going hunting or something," Ron explained. Otherwise, I'm sure we'll be back on patrol a number of times. We'll make sure to pass this way at least once every time we have patrol duty. Then you can catch us here on one of those rounds."

"Good idea," Buck said. "I'll get back and let the general know there isn't anything for us to worry about right now."

"Take care on the way back," Barbara said. "Evidently there are some of those mutants living in the area."

"I will," he assured her. "Good luck to both of you."

Both men shook hands, and Buck headed off the direction he had come. Ron and Barbara waited until he was out of sight, then Barbara said, "What was that about him possibly having to make two or three more trips before we know something?"

Ron looked at her, smiled and said, "I would imagine it's the same thing as you not being able to get away by yourself to scout out the camp."

Barbara looked at the ground and without saying anything else, started walking slowly off. Knowing not to push her, Ron stepped up beside her as they resumed their patrol in silence.

CHAPTER THIRTY-ONE

Gabriel released Bo from the jail annex after a couple of hours in the yard with his mate. Through a sort of sign language developed between Gabriel and himself, Bo told the human he would return within two weeks. In that time, he should be able to get to the various packs in the area and find out if they were willing to work with the humans.

Gabriel's proposal was almost more than Bo could believe. He knew he and the rest of the packs were being set up as a band of killers for the gangs in Austin. At the same time, he knew the medical care offered would be more beneficial to his kind than Gabriel would ever know.

Injuries in the various packs were the largest cause of individual losses, and Bo figured injuries would account for a loss of over fifty percent of a pack in a period of two years. With medical care, the losses would be around five percent instead. It could mean the saving of around two to three hundred of his kind. He was sure the rest would be willing to kill chosen humans and allow others live in order to receive that kind of help.

He left Austin, heading west and in about ten miles, he located a large pack. This particular pack, because of its size, had two of the intelligent type mutants. After communicating Gabriel's offer to them, it only took a short time for the first messengers to be on their way. The messengers were to bring other leaders back for a meeting within seven days.

Bo was southwest of Austin, north of where he knew another pack to be located. He would try to get them to scatter out west and south from there to cover most of the Texas Hill Country bringing mutant leaders in from all over the area. He also knew his mate's life depended on his timely return, and there was a lot to do. Unsure of how he could complete it all, he moved quickly toward the pack.

***

It only took Buck until nightfall to return to the militia headquarters for his report to General Clark. He was in the general's office, and General Clark signaled for him to sit in one of the chairs on the other side of his desk. "Did you have any trouble on the mission Sergeant?"

"None sir," Buck answered. "I had to stay around their camp two days before I saw Ron and Barbara though. I finally found them on a guard patrol."

"Guard patrol," the general repeated. "Sounds like their starting to be accepted."

"Not according to them," Buck said. "They said they aren't being let in on any planning over there."

"That's okay," General Clark answered. "If they weren't trusted at least a little, they wouldn't be allowed to patrol their perimeter. Remember, the camp's safety is always in the hands of the guards-the same as here."

"They both said that even though they weren't in on any planning, there wasn't anything to indicate a move against us. The group over there seems to be more interested in guarding their boundaries than doing anything aggressive."

"It's good to hear," the general said. "At least we have more time to train and plan what we're gonna do. Did you set up some way to contact them again?"

"Yes sir," Buck answered. "I'll be able to catch them when they make rounds on patrol."

"You did good, soldier," General Clark stood up.

As the general stood, Buck rose, gave him a salute, and left the office. General Clark turned his attention to the map on his wall. He knew there was a lot more planning to do if he was going to attack those assholes at the other camp. He also knew there was no way he could let them continue to live over there. It would weaken his command not to mention that it would allow an enemy to live virtually on their doorstep. There was no way he would put up with that.

He had two spies in the other camp and could eventually gather all the information he needed to take them completely by surprise. He would simply take his time and plan properly. He knew it would pay off in the end.

***

Bear, Davata, Hal, and Sandy were on a brief scouting patrol. It was the first for Bear since the shooting. The group planned to keep the patrol short due to his condition. At the same time, Bear was using the patrol to teach some basic techniques in scouting and stealth.

After an hour or so of practice, the group took a break. They sat around in a circle facing each other to talk and relax. Bear told them to sit back and relax, and he'd get the food for lunch from the bags on the horses. He had brought an MRE for each of them. He knew Hal had experienced C-rations from when he was in the military, but MREs were head and shoulders above them.

Bear took the food packs from some saddlebags and started back to where the others waited. On the way, he decided to sneak up on them and demonstrate what he had been teaching. He moved to the side where he would approach from their peripheral vision. About fifty yards out he moved very quietly forward, taking care not to make any noise. He also approached from downwind, not that he thought it would make any difference in this instance.

He came within twenty yards without detection when he heard a noise from his left. *Probably a deer*. Squatting down, he waited to see if the deer would come in close to the others. More noise from his left-but this time it seemed to be from more than one location. Taking slow deep breaths, he waited only a couple of seconds when he saw a mutant moving through the trees. Looking closer, he saw a second then a third and a fourth. They were traveling in a line, heading toward his friends.

As the mutants approached the humans, they split apart, clearly planning to circle Bear's companions. The mutants' speed increased from a fast walk to a trot. It only took them a couple of seconds to close in on the group, run by them, and head away almost as if they didn't exist.

Bear ran toward his friends with both pistols drawn as the mutants passed by the small clearing. They had approached and left with such speed and surprise Hal was only able to stand and get his weapon drawn as the animals departed the area.

Bear stepped forward and said, "Hold your fire."

Hal spun at the sound of the other man's voice raising his weapon to fire. Quickly realizing it was Bear, he uncocked and holstered his pistol. "What the hell was that?" "Beats the shit outta me," Bear answered.

"I counted four as they went by," Davata said.

"That's what I saw," Bear agreed.

"But they just passed us by," Sandy said. "They didn't even give us a second glance."

"You're not complaining are you," Hal asked, "because if you are, I can call them back."

"Kiss my ass, Hal," Sandy's answered as she held her middle finger up.

"We'd better get back to the resort," Davata said.

"I agree," Bear said. "We'll eat on the horses." He passed out the MREs and explained how they worked. As they rode, they ate and discussed what had happened.

Back at camp, they gave their horses to Ben. Sandy stayed behind to help him unsaddle and curry the animals. They would all meet in the cafe as soon as they finished. The rest dispersed to advise everyone of an emergency meeting.

The meeting ended two hours later. At the beginning, the scouting party had given all their information. After that, it went rapidly downhill

353

with wild theories and suppositions. The only positive thing to come from the meeting was a schedule proposed by Bear to set up watches for the next week.

There were to be three guards on horseback, roving the perimeter of the camp twenty-four hours a day. Adults were to always wear weapons, and for a while, everyone or at least one member of a family would report to Ben three times a day. This way, they would know if anyone was missing. Until they could find out what was happening, everyone was to stay close to camp.

CHAPTER THIRTY-TWO

The group at Rebel's Revenge had seen four more mutants traveling in various directions in the last two days. They had all acted the same. Each appeared to be going somewhere in a hurry and paid little or no attention to those watching them. Each person had reported them traveling in different directions, but all said they were traveling fast.

Hal, Sandy, Bear, Davata, David, and Keith were in the office of the resort. They met to discuss everything reported about the mutants. Maybe together they could figure out what was going on.

"There's no doubt something is going on," Hal said, "and since we have no idea what's happening, we've got to get ready for anything."

"Could you possibly be just a little bit more obvious?" Bear asked.

"Fuck you, Bear," Hal answered. "Other than you're ugly as mud, and dumber than a rock, not much."

Ignoring the insult, Bear said, "I'll need Spyder with me."

"What the hell for?" Hal asked.

"We're gonna find out where the mutant's are going," Bear answered and took a sip of coffee. "We'll also need a horse each and a week's worth of provisions. We need to leave as soon as we can, and I've got no idea how long we'll be gone. So we're gonna have to be sure we've got enough food. We won't be able start any fires while we're out."

"Not a chance," Davata stated. "You're not well enough to do all that traveling."

Bear turned and looked at her, "I understand you're concerned, and I appreciate it; but this is one of those times you're gonna have to listen to me and trust me."

Davata opened her mouth to protest, and Bear stopped her saying, "Sweetheart, I know you only have my best interest in mind. Again, I appreciate it, but Spyder and I are the best chance this camp has to find out what's going on. We're not gonna hunt 'em down or fight 'em. We're only gonna try and find out what's happening. This is one of those times I'm not willing to argue with you-Spyder and I are going if he's willing to go."

"Go where?" Spyder asked closing the door behind him.

It only took Bear a couple of minutes to explain what had happened and ask Spyder if he was willing to go see what they could find out."

"Hell yeah," Spyder answered emphatically.

"You're as stupid as he is," Davata said looking straight in Spyder's eyes, not willing to admit defeat. "He's not well enough to travel-it'll kill him."

Spyder looked at her and softened. He stepped up to her and took one of her arms in each of his hands. Gently he said, "Little lady, nothing's gonna happen to that man of yours. He's like a brother to me, and I'll bring him back to you in one piece. You can bet anyone or anything will have to kill me first, before I'll let 'em hurt him." Then to her surprise, this longhaired, bearded, eighteenth century holdover hugged her tightly.

She stepped back looking at the man. It was clear to everyone he meant exactly what he said. It was just as clear any argument was useless. Bear was going with him and returning safely if humanly possible. She relaxed a little knowing Bear was in the best hands possible considering the situation.

Sandy came in the door with her arms loaded. She left as soon as Bear said he and Spyder would need supplies. She carried two bags full of food and two bags with supplies for their weapons. "Both of you need to check both your bags and make sure I didn't miss anything."

The men looked over the supplies and found they had everything they would probably need.

"Lynn'll be here in a minute with a horse for each of you," Sandy continued. "She should have them here by the time you gather your clothes and get back."

Bear turned and headed toward the cabin he shared with Davata. About half way there, she walked up beside him and took his hand in hers. They walked the rest of the way to the cabin in silence. Once inside she said, "I'm sorry if I embarrassed you back there. I didn't mean to. I'm just worried about you and your condition."

Bear put his arm around her and said, "Don't ever worry about embarrassing me when you're showing concern for my safety. I would much rather that than for you not to care."

Bear took two changes of clothes out, and after folding them as he did for years in the navy, put them in a saddlebag. He was wearing his usual western wear with a down-insulated vest under his duster. His hat was a heavy duty, black, western hat with a stampede string.

He picked up his saddlebag and walked toward the front door. He and Davata entered the kitchen when someone knocked. Davata opened the door to see Sandy standing there.

Sandy entered the room and held a package out to Bear. "Here's some bandages to take with you. I also put some of your acupuncture needles in there in case you start to hurt."

"Don't know what I'd do without the two of you watching out for me," he said to the women.

He gave Sandy a hug and said, "Thanks for everything. I'll see you in a few days." Then he turned back to Davata. "Quit worrying. We're both gonna be fine. We'll be back as soon as we get the information we need. Hopefully, that'll make everyone around here safer."

He turned and walked to the door. "There's no need for the two of you to get back out into the cold. I'll just say good-bye here."

Davata hurried over to him and put her arms around him. They held each other for a couple of minutes, and then Bear pulled back, looked at her, and smiled. "I'll see you soon," he said, kissed her and then walked out the door.

***

Spyder waited for Bear back at the office, and Lynn brought their horses up and tied them outside. "There's feed in the saddlebags already on them," she said.

Bear gave her a hug. "Thanks, Lynn."

"Thank ya, darlin'," Spyder said and hugged her as well.

"You two take care and get back here safe." Hal shook hands with both men. They turned, left the room, and in a couple of minutes they were both mounted and riding away.

Both Spyder and Bear knew they had to depend on luck if they were to run into one or more mutants. Then they had to be lucky enough for the animals to be heading somewhere in a hurry-the same as the other ones were reported to be.

"They were all heading south or west," Spyder said as they rode along. "I don't know if you agree, but I figure we only follow one if it's in a hurry and heading north or east."

"I agree," Bear answered.

"Otherwise, we might just be out on a hunting trip."

"You'll get no argument out of me. We're gonna have to be damn lucky to find anything out. Not to mention to keep from getting killed. How many pistols are you carrying?"

"The usual," Spyder answered, "four-plus I have my Buffalo Gun."

"I've got two black powders on my hips and a 9mm in a shoulder-holster with four clips of fifteen for it. In the gun boot, I've got the Sharps. I've also got two Claymores in the ammunition saddlebag."

"A little nervous are we?" Spyder asked with a chuckle.

"As slow as I still move, hell yes. I figure, in my condition, I can move faster scared than they can blown up."

"Maybe," Spyder answered. "I've seen you move ¼"

"Kiss my ass, Spyder. Where do you want to set up and wait for those things?"

"I figure we can wait for them at the bottom of Satin's Spine Valley. It seems there were more seen over there than anywhere else."

"Sounds good to me."

Three trucks towing trailers appeared around the bend ahead of them moving slowly along the road. Spyder and Bear had no time or place to hide. As the trucks pulled even with them, Spyder recognized one of the men in the lead one. It was the men that had gone to gather what they could from the military bases in San Antonio and Corpus Christi.

The lead truck pulled to a stop and the driver climbed out. Bear and Spyder dismounted their horses and shook hands with the man. "We'd about given up on you guys," Spyder told him. "It's been a while."

The other man named Grant said, "We almost didn't make it back. Mobsters run San Antonio for the most part now, and Corpus Christi has some dedicated assholes on its Naval Air Station. There were only four, but they were dedicated to the end."

"Don't tell me you killed 'em," Bear almost growled at the man.

"No, not us," he quickly answered. "There was a group of people trying to raid the commissary there that got 'em. After that, we raided their armory and warehouse. We've got MREs, canned food, soap, weapons, ammunition, mortars, M72A2,

360

LAAWs, and a trailer load of claymore mines-plus some other odds and ends."

"You can bet we're glad to see you back," Spyder informed him. "You'll need to pull down to the resort area. That's where our headquarters is now."

"It's good to be back," Grant responded. "We'll get this stuff on down there. Where are you two headed?"

"Just doing a little scouting," Bear answered.

Grant waved to both men as he climbed back into the cab of the truck and moved the convoy on toward their camp. Bear and Spyder waved a greeting to each of the drivers in turn, as they passed.

"Good to have them back," Spyder said as he and Bear urged their horses on.

After a little less than two hours, Spyder and Bear found a place to camp. They could see everything moving below them for a quarter of a mile both up and down the valley. They were in a good location to see and remain unseen.

They tied their horses to stakes, on a wide ledge about twenty yards away and arranged the tack so they could saddle up in a minimum amount of time. Now, they knew it was time to settle down and wait. The perch where they waited was about ten feet wide and twenty feet long. There was also a shallow cave in the cliff to shelter them from the elements.

The wind was light, but the temperature must have been around freezing. "There's no way to light a fire without drawing attention to where we are," Spyder said. "You sure those horses will be okay?"

"They'll be fine," Bear answered. "They're used to this weather. They have blankets on, and they're protected from the wind. It's as good as if they were back in the corral at the resort."

It was dusk, and the sun was setting over the hills to the west when they saw the first mutant. It traveled north up the valley at a rapid trot. It made its way through the trees as easily as if it crossed flat plains.

"Heading the wrong direction," Spyder observed.

"Yeah, you're right," Bear agreed. "Besides, I don't think it would be too smart of us to try and track one of those things in the dark. A big cat, like a Mountain Lion or Lynx will double back on you and before you know it, you're the hunted."

Spyder knew this and watched with the other man as the mutant nimbly picked its way through the trees, never slowing or missing a step. In only a few minutes, it disappeared from view. "We're gonna have a real problem keeping up with 'em," Spyder commented.

"Look up there." Bear pointed to the same side of the valley where they watched. Further up the slop, the mutant they had seen in the valley quickly reached the top and disappeared.

"Think it's doubling back because it saw us?" Spyder asked.

"I doubt it," Bear answered. "Even if it is, there's no way for it to get to us without making a hell of a racket. There's a twenty-foot cliff above us for at least a hundred yards in each direction. Even if it were able to make it down, it would make enough noise to warn us well in advance."

362

They both waited and listened. The only sound for the rest of the night was the wind blowing gently through the trees high above and below them. Only a half moon hung in the sky, which made the chances of seeing one of the mutants through the trees below virtually impossible. The two men agreed they should keep watch in shifts and act as a listening post for anything approaching from along the ledge.

***

Spyder was on watch as the sun rose across the valley from him. About thirty-minutes after the sun broke the horizon, he saw a movement in the trees. He quickly reached into one of his saddlebags and pulled out some binoculars. He put them to his eyes and adjusted them. Partially hidden by the trees, what appeared to be a mound of dirt moved. Spyder reached over and punched Bear in the butt.

Sleeping on his side, the other man grunted, spun on his back, and sat straight up. Wide awake and alert, he whispered, "What's going on?"

Spyder handed him the binoculars and in a muffled voice said, "Look out there just to the left of the clearing." He pointed to an area about two hundred yards away and below.

Bear took the glasses. It took him a couple of seconds to locate the movement. As he looked, a mutant stood up as if rising out of the ground. "That son-of-a-bitch has been there all night."

"Sure looks like it."

The animal below turned, looked straight at where the two men were located, and began trotting away, up the valley.

"He looked at us," Bear exclaimed, turning to look at Spyder. "You don't think he knew we were here, do you?"

"Beats the shit outta me. If he did, then why didn't he come after us?"

"I've got no idea, and the way they've been acting lately, there's no telling."

"You think we should follow him," Spyder asked.

"He's not heading the same direction the first ones were," Bear commented.

"True. But it's the second one we've seen heading in that direction in two days."

"Let's wait and see what happens."

"Fine with me," Spyder answered. "I ain't got a hell of a lot else to do."

Bear grinned and said, "I'm glad. I'd hate to interrupt your busy schedule."

"I'll let you know if you start to. My time is expensive, you know."

"Expensive?"

"Hell yes. You never know when I have to put someone's electricity in or program a computer or some such thing. Shit, people need me to do all kinds of electrical hook-ups in their houses all the time."

"Electrical hook-ups," Bear repeated. "What the hell are you talking about?"

"Man, I thought English was your primary language?" Spyder said and held a serious look for about five seconds before breaking into a wide grin.

"Asshole. I thought, for a second there, you had lost what's left of your feeble ole mind."

Both men sat back, opened an MRE, and ate breakfast as they watched the mutant appear and disappear, through the trees, off in the distance. About ten minutes later, the animal went up the side of the valley, the same as the one before.

"There it goes," Bear said pointing. "He is heading up the same way as the other one did."

"Looks like they're coming back," Spyder observed. "There's no way we can tell if they're the same ones, but they probably are."

"Exactly what I was thinking," Bear answered. "But where are they returning from."

"Well, some of them are supposed to be intelligent," Spyder said.

"So... " Bear said, waiting to see what Spyder was thinking.

"Is it possible they're messengers of some sort?"

"Messengers," Bear said softly. "For that to be true, we would have to accept they're at least close to the intelligence of a human."

"Whether we accept it or not," Spyder stated, "doesn't change facts.

Bear looked at him and raised his eyebrows questioningly.

"Look at it this way," Spyder explained. "Do you believe in God?"

"In my own way."

"So do I, but what if there is no God. Because you and I believe in him doesn't make it a fact. The fact then would be that there is no God, and all the beliefs in the world wouldn't change it being a fact.

I figure most people would rather believe the mutants are less intelligent than humans are because we're supposed to be the most intelligent animals. In the same way, their beliefs wouldn't change the facts as they truly are."

"So you believe they're as smart as we are," Bear suggested.

"Not necessarily. But I don't disbelieve it. I'm simply trying to keep an open mind so I don't underestimate them and get caught in a surprise."

"For an old fart who looks like a *Mountain Man*, you're pretty sharp," Bear commented.

"Don't let my looks fool you. My appearance is because of my past." Spyder figured Bear would remember his past included growing up in the country, over in East Texas and Louisiana, being in a motorcycle club and several brushes with the law.

"I've always known you were smart. I just didn't realize how much you think things out. I figured you were more of an off the cuff person."

"Like they say, never judge a book by its cover." As Bear looked back down to the valley below, Spyder stood up and said, "I'm gonna check on the horses, be back in a little bit."

Bear settled back to watch out for any mutants that might pass by as Spyder made his way around the bend in the ledge. When Spyder reached the horses, they were grazing on the sparse grass in the area. He took some grain out of one of the saddlebags and poured it on the ground for them, took out a cigarette, lit it, and leaned against a rock to smoke.

When he was about finished with his cigarette, he spotted another mutant traveling along the floor of the valley. He ground the smoke out under his boot and headed back to where he left Bear. As he rounded the corner, Bear was looking at the animal through the binoculars.

"What do you think about us saddlin' up and following the next one we see?" Spyder asked. "I wanna know what the hell's happening."

"I'm with you," Bear answered. "We'll need to get to the top of this hill and wait there. It looks like they're all climbing up to the top at the other end, and we'll never keep up with them if we have to climb the hill with these horses."

The two men cleared their camp and then saddled and packed their horses. Spyder knew a way to the top of the hill and led Bear up the trail. At the top, they climbed off the horses to watch the valley below.

***

About forty-five minutes later, Bear nudged Spyder and pointing across the valley said, "Look over there."

Spyder looked where the other man pointed. Three men on horseback traveled in single file as they wound their way along the opposite ridge. They didn't seem to be in any hurry. Below them, a mutant crossed the valley floor. The men above seemed to be unaware of the animal below them.

Spyder and Bear allowed the mutant to get a short distance in front of them before moving. They followed along the edge of the valley until the mutant started its climb up the side of the hill. The two men allowed the animal to reach the top before falling in behind it. It traveled at a medium trot for the horses, which both men knew could be a problem if they had to go too long, especially since they didn't want to be seen or heard. They also had to keep an eye open for the other riders.

About six miles later, the animal trotted into a clearing. Bear reined his horse back and stopped it. Spyder was beside him in a couple of seconds. "Whatcha got?"

"That's the clearing where I met Amanda, Keith, and Mike," Bear answered. "There's a big, two-story house over there." He pointed to the left. Pointing to the right, he said, "There's a big barn over there. We'll have to go on foot from here."

Both men climbed from their horses and cautiously made their way to an area at the edge of the clearing. Bear stopped suddenly and motioned for Spyder to as low as he could. Spyder like his namesake crawled up beside Bear before him he saw five of the mutants standing on the porch that ran across the front of the house.

The animals there grunted and growled to each other as if holding a convention. Both men watched the scene amazed. It was obvious they were communicating to one in particular.

"I guess that answers the question about their intelligence," Spyder whispered.

"It does for me," Bear whispered back.

After another five minutes, a large bag was brought out. Alternately, two of the mutants reached into it, pulled something out, and ate it.

"Looks to me like those two are planning to leave," Spyder said, nodding at the group on the porch.

"I think you're right," Bear answered. "Let's get the horses."

As both men started to move from their positions, Spyder grabbed bear's arm. "Look over there," he pointed across the clearing.

The three riders they had seen across the valley watched the scene from the other side.

"I think we'd better stay clear of them too," Bear said and crawled away from the clearing.

Spyder nodded and followed him.

When the two men were sure they couldn't be seen from the house and after making sure there were no mutants wandering the area, they hurried to where their horses were tied.

"We can only guess which direction they'll head," Bear said.

"Not necessarily. Follow me." With Spyder leading the way, they went to an area where they could see the three men lying in the bushes. They could also see where their horses were tied. "I reckon all we need is to follow them boys," Spyder said, grinning.

"Damn son," Bear said, "you're almost as smart as one of those mutants. Just the same, check your weapons. This could get tricky."

While both men checked their guns, they saw the other men go to their horses and mount them. They then circled around the clearing of the house, obviously keeping out of the sight of the animals there.

Once clear of the ranch area, their horses assumed a trot the same as Bear and Spyder used to follow the mutants before. After about a mile, one of the men peeled off to the right. He stayed even

369

with the other two but steadily moved away. A few minutes after he moved out of sight, another rider slid into view.

"An outrider," Spyder said barely above a whisper.

"Then there's four of 'em," Bear answered.

"At least," Spyder said. "There may be one on the other side.

"Stay with 'em Spyder," Bear said and started to edge to the left. A few minutes later, he disappeared into the trees.

Bear made his way slowly away from the trail the main group traveled. After a couple of minutes, he heard voices. Carefully, he moved closer until he could see two more riders ahead of him. Looking to the side, he could barely make out the main group of three. Looking back, Spyder was invisible.

He slowly pulled his horse to a stop so as not to cause the animal to make any noise. Then he made his way back and joined Spyder. He approached from behind Spyder, hoping to keep out of the sight of the others. "There appears to be two outriders on each side of the three ahead of us. I suggest you move to the right so you can see the main group and the two outriders. I'll do the same over here to the left. Maybe it'll cut down on the chances of them surprising us."

Spyder simply nodded, turned his horse, and headed to a position where he could keep both groups in sight. Bear went to a similar location to the left.

***

Bo knew there were riders behind them. He knew they could be from Gabriel but didn't think so. They hadn't come to the house where he and the others were staying the five days since he left Austin. The last of the pack to return reported humans followed her for a while. She also reported one of the packs wouldn't be returning because of an ambush while on her way to the great cave.

She did however know where the humans lived. She had accidentally run close to the walls of the enclosure. Bo grunted an assurance to her the time to kill the humans would come. She snarled back at him, which was simply a show of anger.

The great cave was a location near San Antonio with a large pack of at least one hundred mutants. The female had taken a message to the leader there to contact the other packs in the area and have them meet him at the small cave. The small cave was once a tourist attraction in San Marcos. However, now packs used it from time to time for shelter when they wanted to hunt humans or other game in the area. The packs knew the humans were so scattered and unorganized there was little danger from them there.

Bo knew it would be near dark by the time he and his companion reached the outskirts of Austin. However, he was determined to make it there today. He wanted to make sure his mate was okay. He was also interested in whether Gabriel would keep his word or not. If he did, many of the mutants would live when they would have certainly died before. He, like the rest of the mutants, didn't like making a pact with the humans. However, he also knew he must do what was best for all the packs, and this was definitely the best thing for them.

He looked at his companion and grunted for him to speed up. Bo was anxious to get back to Austin.

***

The mutants passed two streams without breaking stride. At the third they stopped. One at a time, they went down on all fours and drank directly from the stream and then continued at a trot. They seemed to be super-human and lacked the need for much food or water.

Behind them, the group from the militia had to pause a couple of minutes to let their horses drink. Each of the men drank from their canteens or flasks and talked about how the animals in front of them were able to keep this pace up. They were also gaining more than a healthy respect for the mutants.

Behind them, Spyder and Bear paused to give their horses a drink at the previous two streams alternately. Bear stopped at the first one, and Spyder kept the other group in sight. At the second one, it was Spyder's turn.

While the militia group paused to let their horses drink, Bear and Spyder were able to climb down for a couple of minutes and let the horses graze without their riders. By the time the group ahead of them resumed their trot, the horses from Rebel's Revenge were breathing normally. They weren't totally rested, but they had caught their breath.

Bear and Spyder kept up their pace until about thirty minutes before sunset. Both men saw the group ahead of them stop suddenly. They circled to their left until they could see both the militia group and the mutants.

When they reached the edge of Austin, the mutants slowed their pace and cautiously approached a house. As the mutants approached the house, an armed man stepped from the front door. One of the mutants held up both hands above his head. He dropped his hands to his side and just stood there looking at the human.

The man at the door said one word, "Bo?" He called out loudly. The mutant nodded, and the man motioned him toward the house. The mutant turned its head and grunted. The other mutant followed him inside.

"The mutant answered him," Spyder said so surprised, his mouth hung open. "That son-of-a-bitch nodded to answer a question"

"Did the guy call it Bo?" Bear asked. "Did I hear him right?"

"That's what I heard," Spyder answered, "and it responded to the guy." What the fuck's going on here? An open mind's one thing, but... "

"You're asking me? I know as much as you do."

The back door opened, and the two mutants and two men went to a truck. The animals, along with the men, climbed inside. The vehicle started rolling down a hill then fired into life and disappeared around a building.

CHAPTER THIRTY-THREE

Bo and his companion arrived as the sun sat in the west and went to Gabriel's headquarters. Escorted from the pickup to the gang leader's office, they found him sitting behind his desk and Manny occupied a chair to the side.

As the two mutants entered the office, Gabriel stood and said, "Damn, Bo, I was starting to worry about you." He motioned for Bo to take the other chair.

Bo looked at it and squatted where he previously stood. The other mutant did the same where he was.

"If you're worried about the other one that stayed here, she's doing fine," Gabriel said. "We tried to have the doctor take a look at her, but she became violent so we left her alone until you could tell her it was okay."

Bo kept his gaze on the man behind the desk. He was sure Gabriel would do nothing aggressive, but he didn't want the man to think he was coming over to his side too fast. Bo also knew there was still a game to be played here.

"I don't want to seem insensitive to your position," Gabriel said, "but I have to ask if you were successful in contacting the other leaders?"

He nodded.

Gabriel grinned and clapped his hands together. "Outstanding. I trust they were agreeable with my proposition?"

He shook his head no.

Gabriel went quiet. He looked at Bo, and hesitated.

"If I may," Manny interjected. "Did you give them Gabriel's proposition?"

He looked at Manny and shook his head no.

Then Gabriel asked, "Did you see them at all?"

Again, he shook his head no.

Gabriel was beginning to understand. "Did you send for them to meet you somewhere?"

This time he nodded.

"It only makes sense," Manny said. "There's no way for him to get all of them together in so short a time and get back here with an answer. He wanted to make sure to get back in time to keep his friend in the cells safe."

Bo looked at Manny and nodded. This human was quicker to understand his communications than the one named Gabriel. He wondered how it was that Gabriel was in charge of Manny. This was something he would have to think about later. It might be something he could use in the future.

"Makes sense," Gabriel said. "Are they willing to meet with me somewhere?"

Again, Bo nodded.

"Where-where and when are we to meet?" Gabriel asked the mutant.

Bo stood and walked to the maps on the wall. Another one of the Texas Hill Country hung beside the map of Austin. He pointed to the location of the caverns in San Marcos.

Gabriel looked at the spot and asked, "When?"

He went to a hand-made calendar on the wall and pointed at a date ten days away.

Bear and Spyder made their way back toward Rebel's Revenge as soon as the pickup truck departed with the two mutants. Their plan was to travel for at least three hours before making camp. When they reached a deserted indoor/outdoor restaurant they had done a Wild West show at a couple of years before, the sun was down, but the three-quarter moon made moving around in the dark much easier. They removed their saddles and packs from the horses and set them out to graze. Bear went inside and began organizing his items so he could get a good night's rest, while Spyder took care of the horses.

Bear heard the sound of voices outside. Since Spyder wasn't in the habit of talking to himself, and the voices seemed to be coming from at least three people, Bear quietly went out through the front door of the building.

A couple of yards away, he found four men talking to Spyder. There were two women with them, their wrists tied together and a rope running from them to one of the men. Obviously they weren't there of their own free will.

Before stepping out, Bear unhooked his pistols from their holsters. He now stood beside the group of men at a ninety-degree angle from Spyder. "Is everything okay here?" He asked when he knew he had a clear view and shot if needed.

"No real problem, Bear," Spyder answered. "These gents here are on their way up to Dallas."

"Dallas," Bear repeated, "it's quite a ways from here." Then to the men he asked, "You men planning on walking all the way, or do you have transportation?"

"Nah," the leader answered, "we had a truck but it ran out of diesel some miles back. Figured we'd find another one to use somewhere along the way."

"What about them ladies," Bear asked, "you planning on taking them all the way with you?"

"Not sure," the man answered. "We heard there's a group around here 'bouts that'll possibly take them off our hands for a price, since they're..." These last words he slurred with an obvious distaste.

"Then you're gonna sell 'em," Spyder said.

"It's about all their good for," the man answered. "That n something to fuck."

With that statement, the women took a step closer together. It looked to Bear like they were recently taken. Both wore pants and a shirt, their shirts were still tucked in and neither appeared to be too dirty. One looked to be about her mid-twenties, the other was probably a teenager.

Bear noticed each of the men carried at least a pistol and rifle. A couple wore two pistols, and one of them appeared nervous. By the way they handled themselves, it was clear they had been in a number of scraps and were willing to kill if they thought they needed to.

"How far are we from Austin?" the leader asked.

"About twenty miles," Spyder answered. "If you follow this road, it'll take you into the southern part of the city."

377

"You know anything about this militia group I was talking about earlier?"

"I know they're around here somewhere," Spyder answered. "Don't know where for sure. The only thing I'm really sure about is, unless my friend over there feels differently, I can't really see me letting you take those women anywhere, whether you're gonna sell them or not-doesn't seem like they want to be with you boys."

Bear relaxed all the muscles in his body, took a couple of deep breaths, and waited to see what the other men would do. He knew speed and accuracy would be of paramount importance here. Spyder had issued the challenge, and Bear was sure these men wouldn't back down without a fight. He could feel death permeating the air. The feeling came crashing in on him as it did many times before, when he was still in the military. The air was so thick with it you could almost taste it. Men would die here tonight. Now, it was a matter of how many and whom.

"You don't think the two of you are gonna do anything about it, do you?" The leader asked.

One of the other men stepped to his right, away from Bear.

"Stand where you are," Bear told him. The man stopped and turned slightly toward him.

"Look gents," Spyder said, "there don't need to be no killin' here tonight."

"You don't seem to understand," the leader said. "We're gonna take these bitches with us, and there ain't a damn thing you can do about it. You and your friend may dress and look like cowboys, but you don't scare us. Your problem is that you

378

seem to have started believing in all that cowboy shit and don't know when to get the hell outta the way. But I'll tell you now, it's time for you and your friend to move out. Let us go, and we'll leave you alone."

"Can't do that," Bear answered.

"On the other hand," Spyder said, "If you let the ladies go, we'll let you go on about your way with no problem.

The three men took a couple of steps away from each other putting a short distance between them.

Both Spyder and Bear knew there was no way to stop this thing from happening. Now, it was time for them to try to stay alive and if possible, keep the women alive as well. Bear allowed his hand to slide into position so he could draw his pistol quickly. Spyder's hand was in the same position. Both men waited for the inevitable.

The leader of the group was the first to move. He quickly reached for the pistol in his holster. Two of the other three reached for their weapons a split-second later. The third was carrying a rifle with the barrel pointed toward the sky and swung it down toward Spyder.

Before the rifle was level, Bear pulled his pistol and fired. The bullet caught the man in the left shoulder, spinning him around. Bear fired his second shot at the man standing closest to him, and the bullet hit the man in the chest, immediately below his neck, instantly dropping him to the ground.

Spyder's shot was less than a quarter of a second behind Bear's and caught the one beside the leader above the right eye, killing him when it hit. The last of the bunch had just gotten his pistol out when Spyder's bullet hit him in the middle of the chest. The man with the rifle turned back toward Bear and raised it with only his right hand. Both Spyder and Bear fired at the same time. Both forty-four caliber bullets hit the other man in the chest and threw him backward where he landed with a dull thump.

Bear looked around trying to see in spite of his night blindness. The difference between the black powder weapons they primarily used and modern weapons was the muzzle blast. Black powder weapons would spit out a ball of fire along with its lead. At night, the fire from a pistol was more than enough to cause temporary night blindness. Bear had remembered this and closed his eyes with each shot except for the last when both men fired at once. After a few seconds of standing dead still and listening to the now quiet night, his vision slowly started to return.

"Can you see?" Spyder asked.

The question scared the hell out of Bear. He didn't know if Spyder was hit or like himself, blinded from the muzzle flash. "I can't see a damn thing," he answered knowing they were both in trouble if any of the others were alive and able to shoot.

"Me neither," Spyder said.

A few seconds later, Bear's vision returned enough for him to see the other four men on the ground before them. He looked at the women and both seemed to be unharmed. "The ladies seem to be okay."

380

Spyder's head turned toward Bear and asked, "You all right, man?"

"Yeah," Bear answered.

"How about you ladies?" He asked the two women.

Neither of them answered immediately. Eventually the oldest said, "I...I think we're okay."

"You sure?" Bear asked. "Were you hit by anything?"

"No," one of the women assured him. "We're okay.

"We weren't shot or anything," the other said.

With most of his night vision back, Bear was able to see that each of their enemy lay dead on the ground. Both men walked over toward the women, who took a couple of steps back, away from the approaching men. Both men stopped and Spyder said, "Take it easy ladies. You're safe now. No one here's gonna do you no harm."

"We only want to untie you and get you inside, out of the cold," Bear explained.

Spyder stepped up to them and pulled his knife. Before they could react to its size, Spyder flicked his wrist and cut the rope holding them. He turned as he put the knife back in its sheath. "We'll get you to inside, then clean up out here."

They led the women into the building. Inside, Spyder said, "I'm Spyder and this here's Bear. We're part of a group of people over in Rollingblock. Like I said, you're safe for now. Most people don't travel at night, so we shouldn't have any more trouble tonight." Then looking at Bear, "Why don't you get a fire started in the fireplace while I get rid of those four out there?"

"I'll help you with the bodies," Bear answered.

"Nope," Spyder answered. "You need your rest. I'll take care of it."

"Not a chance in hell," Bear said. "Now let's go."

"We can make a fire," the older of the two women interjected, "if it's okay with the two of you."

"That's fine, ma'am," Bear said with a tip of the brim of his hat. He turned and walked out the front door with a scowling Spyder behind him.

"I don't think we should've left them alone in there," Spyder said as he grabbed the shoulders of one of the dead men.

"It's exactly what we should've done," Bear countered carrying the man's feet. "They have to feel like they're back in charge of themselves. You know like they have choices again. They also need some time to see that we trust them. I figure some time to themselves will let them see that they could sneak out if they want to-and don't be surprised to find out they've armed themselves with something when we get back inside."

"Makes sense," Spyder answered. "I was just thinking of making them feel safe. I imagine you're right. This'll probably make them feel even safer. Now, where we gonna put this asshole?"

They found an outbuilding where they put all the bodies. Upon finishing, they gathered all the extra weapons and went inside the restaurant where the women had indeed made a fire in the large rock fireplace. The room around the fire was warming up nicely. They also lit some kerosene lamps located

382

on the walls. The light from the fire and the lamps gave a warm and friendly glow to the large room.

Both women sat at a table close to the fire. Bear walked over to the table and laid one of the pistols down next to the oldest of the women. "Hang on to this," he said. "You shouldn't need it, but if for some reason you do, you'll have it.

Spyder walked over to the table and laid another one on the table for the other woman. "Do you know how to use it? The youngest woman picked the weapon up and looked it over.

"Yes sir," she answered and ejected the clip from the handle. The weapon was a 9mm pistol, and she handled it as well as anyone Spyder had seen. After inspecting the pistol, she put the clip back in and released the slide. She then put the safety on and laid it in her lap.

"Our father was in the National Guard," the other woman said as she did the same with her 9mm. When she finished she said "I guess we haven't properly introduced ourselves. My name is Libby Chen and this is my sister, Kai. It's spelled K-A-I, but pronounced like the American name Kay."

"Nice to meet you both," Spyder answered.

"Ladies," Bear said and tipped his hat. The room was getting warm, and Bear removed his duster revealing that he was carrying two side arms and a knife as large as the one Spyder used to release the women.

It was Kai who asked the inevitable question. "Why do you two look like you come out of the old west?"

With a grin, Spyder explained the reason for the clothes. Both women seemed to understand as if it made perfect sense to them.

"I'll fix some coffee if you ladies would like," Bear offered.

"It would keep me awake," Libby answered. "But I did see some bottles behind the bar. Would either of you like a drink?"

"Now that's a woman who knows what a man likes," Spyder answered.

Libby got up and went over to the bar. "We have Gin, Bourbon, Rum, Tequila, and warm beer," she said.

"Hang on a minute," Spyder answered. Before anyone could say anything else, he was up and out the front door.

"What is he doing?" Kai asked.

"I have no idea," Bear answered. "He seemed to have some sort of idea or something. Of course, he could have heard something outside." He pulled a pistol from its holster, went to the door to check it, and waited.

Two or three minutes later, Spyder came in carrying a sack. "Just the thing to go with drinks," he said. Bear holstered his pistol as Spyder sat the sack down on the bar. "Be careful with those," he said as he dumped a bunch of canned sodas out. "They're a little shook up, but they should be cold. They've been outside for a long time."

After finding out what kind of soda everyone wanted, he put the rest back in the sack and set them outside the door.

"Kind of strange what's really appreciated now since we don't have all the luxuries we used to," Libby observed.

"Ain't it the truth," Spyder answered.

"Not to bring up a touchy subject," Bear said. "But how did the two of you wind up with those yahoos?"

After a few seconds, Libby explained what happened. "We were at home on the other side of Marble Falls when those four came up to the house. Actually, there were two more then.

"My father and five other men, neighbors, went out to see what they wanted. They said they were going to Dallas and needed water. They said they had plenty of food but were running low on water. We should have known something was up since there was a stream no more than a mile from the house the way they had come. But in these times, you want to help others as much as you can... My father said there was as much water as they wanted out back at the windmill. It produced water in a tank even without electricity. That's when Kai and I walked out on the porch. It only took a couple of seconds for the men to look at each other and obviously decide they would take us." Libby's eyes began to tear up.

"It's okay, missy," Spyder said. You don't have to say anything else.

"No," Libby answered. "I have to tell someone."

The men waited for her to continue.

"Before any of us knew what was happening, the men pulled their guns and started shooting. They caught my father and his friends by surprise but not

385

totally. Each of them was able to shoot at least one shot. The fight lasted at least five minutes. None of them got back in the house, but they fought back and shot two of strangers. One was dead and the other severely wounded. When the fight was over, they captured us. One of the strangers noticed another group of men coming up the road from the valley. The leader said the wounded man would have to be carried and instead shot him. He cussed afterward and said the man was his best friend. That's the kind of men they were. We later found out all of them broke out of some prison in New Mexico.

We traveled about five hours before we came up on you two. You know the rest." She hesitated a couple of seconds, and then added, "There's no telling what would have happened to us by now if you hadn't saved us."

As the tears flooded from her eyes, Bear reached across the table and laid his hand on it face up. He knew he could offer her support but was careful not to invade her space as she cried. Libby's sister was crying too. There was nothing he or Spyder could do but allow the grieving process to happen.

As the two women held each other and cried, both men sat back and let them work it out between themselves. After a remarkably short time, considering the story just related, the girls pulled away and tried to compose themselves. "I'm sorry," Libby said.

"Don't ever apologize for having feelings, li'l lady," Spyder answered. "I'm not sure I could handle this situation as well as the two of you have."

The four sat and watched the fire for a long time before Bear said, "Why don't the three of you get some rest. I need to take a walk, and we need someone on watch."

"I'll take the watch," Spyder answered.

"No, let me take the first watch," Bear answered. "Once I go to sleep, I'll be out for the rest of the night. I won't be worth a damn to anyone from then on. Besides, I need to take a walk."

"You be sure and wake me up in a couple of hours," Spyder said.

Bear nodded as he rose to go outside.

"I'm serious, Bear," Spyder said. "This ain't the time for the tough guy act."

Again Bear nodded. "I know-just a couple of hours."

As Bear walked out the front door, Kai asked, "What was that all about? What do you mean the 'tough guy act'?"

"Bear was shot a few of weeks ago," Spyder answered. "We figure it was the group those four guys were looking for. He almost died and hasn't fully recovered yet. Still, there's no telling him what to do. He'll do what he thinks is best no matter what the cost to him physically. He spent over twenty years in the Navy and doesn't understand someone who doesn't pull his weight. He's one of the few men alive you can trust-and I mean trust your life with."

"He sure proved it tonight", Kai said softly and then to Spyder she asked, "Please don't get me wrong. We're grateful, but what made the two of you do what you did out there? I mean both of you could have been killed, and you didn't know anything about us. Yet, you stood up to those men and saved us."

Spyder rose and went to where his things rested. He was laying out a blanket to sleep on. He paused in his work and said, "Missy, some things just ain't right." He tossed a pile of blankets over to the women and lay down on his side, using a saddle as a pillow. "It's up to you, but I suggest both of you get some sleep."

"I guess we don't need these anymore," Libby said as she pulled the knife from behind her. They each took a blanket to lie on and another to cover up with before choosing the two couches to sleep on.

The night was quiet, and all seemed well inside the restaurant. The people inside were safe and warm. They would be able to get a good night's rest for whatever would happen the next day.

***

Almighty Architect of the Universe, please forgive me for what I've done, Bear prayed. He felt it was wrong to kill, even if it was to save another life. He simply couldn't have allowed the kidnapping to continue-it just wasn't in him. He had to protect innocence. *When will this craziness end? Maybe I need to leave the others. It seems like I'm only causing death to the people I meet. There has to be more to all this than killing. There has to be a reason for all this to be happening.*

He was on watch for about two hours when he heard a sound from his left. He froze and waited.

388

There it was again-the sound of someone or something walking. He stepped behind a tree, pulled his pistol, and waited. He was downwind from the horses so he couldn't rely on them to raise an alarm even if they were still alive.

In a couple of seconds, he saw a figure coming toward him. It moved slowly, and clouds were covering the moon so he couldn't make out who or what it was. Unable to see around the tree he was hiding behind, he waited several seconds until the sound of the movement seemed to be only a couple of yards away. He stepped out, pointing the weapon at the figure. Standing in front of him was a startled Kai.

She stopped and froze in her tracks as Bear appeared in front of her. Kai started to smile until she heard the click of the hammer as he cocked the pistol. Before she could make a sound, bear fired, producing a blinding flash of light. Kai screamed and crouched, leaning against a tree as Bear continued firing at the mutants behind her.

Bear heard four more shots in addition to the five he fired. Then he heard the pop, pop, pop of a 9mm firing. He rushed to Kai and squatting down, pulled her close to him. He held her there with his gun ready to fire.

Shortly, the firing stopped and he heard Spyder's voice calling his name.

"Over here," he called back.

"Is Kai with you?" Spyder asked.

"She's here. I've got her," he answered.

"We're at the front door," Spyder called back.

Bear helped Kai up, and they both headed for the door of the restaurant with her clinging to him for dear life.

"You two okay?" Spyder asked.

"We're all right," Bear answered as he and Kai approached the door. "What the hell's going on?" He asked as they all stepped inside.

"Beats the shit outta me," Spyder answered. "We shot those three mutants out there, and there were three more that got away and headed over toward Austin.

"We killed two of 'em out there," Bear said.

Spyder looked at Libby, "Keep a look out for us," he said, and both men went over to where Bear laid out his "possibles" bag on a table.

"I'm stealin' some of your balls and powder," Spyder told Bear.

Bear looked up slowly at Spyder and started to grin, "Now I've told you about keepin' your hands off my ... "

"Drop it," Spyder said quickly and then mumbled about having to watch what he said around the goofy son-of-a-bitch.

Both women looked at each other smiling. "The two of you together make a good team," Kai observed.

"We do all right," Bear answered.

"You should've seen Libby," Spyder said. "She opened up with her pistol and took one of those things down at a dead run."

"You're kidding," Bear said in surprise, "while it was on the run?"

"Yup," Spyder answered, "and with no hesitation."

"Damn good shootin', girl," Bear said. "I'm impressed.

"We may just have to keep her around," Spyder said. "Of course, that's if she and Kai are willing to stay."

"Speaking of Kai," Bear said, "how are your eyes doing?"

"I'm okay," Kai answered. "I'm starting to get some of my sight back."

Spyder was looking at Bear. "She was about eight feet away and facing me when I had to shoot over her shoulder at the first of the mutants," Bear explained. "I didn't have time to warn her to close her eyes."

Spyder nodded and to Kai said, "You're lucky young lady, he could have set you on fire with you that close." To Bear he asked, "You got any idea of what's going on? That was a large group of mutants out there."

"No idea whatsoever," Bear answered. "But you can bet your ass something's happening. We've seen more of those things in the last few days than the whole time since the world went to hell in a hand basket. Plus, they've started acting strange. By what you said, some attacked us, and the others kept on traveling. They've never done that before. Before it was all or nothing; they either all attacked or left us alone."

"One thing's for damn sure," Spyder said. "We gotta keep our eyes open from here on in." He stood and continued, "I'll take the watch from here."

"It'll mean you're on watch the rest of the night," Bear answered.

"Not a problem," Spyder said. "I got a couple of hours, and we don't have that far to travel tomorrow. We'll be home by noon."

"Well, I ain't gonna argue with you," Bear replied. "I'm beat."

"You get some sleep," Spyder said and walked out the door.

Bear made himself a bed, and after lying down, was asleep in less than five minutes.

***

The next morning, after eating and packing, the women said they wanted to go to Rebel's Revenge. They climbed on the horses behind the men soon after sunrise. It was a little after noon when the group made their way into Rollingblock, and it took them less than an hour to get to the resort area. As they approached, Ben came out of the bushes, stepped in front of the horses, and in a loud voice commanded, "Who goes there friend or foe-what business do you have here-what's your names where do you come from-and answer any other questions I might have forgot to ask, and you think I should have." Having said everything in one long sentence, he took a deep breath and stood stoically before the new arrivals.

Spyder looked at Bear and said "Bear, shoot that crazy ole bastard and shut him up, will you?"

"I'm not about to waste lead on him," Bear answered.

Ben immediately reverted to his impersonation of a young child and said, "Did I do it right? Did I say the right thing? Huh? Huh?"

"You done good," Bear answered.

With that Ben wiggled around and dug the toe of his boot in the dirt and said, "Aw, thanks, mister. I knowed I could do it."

Shaking his head, Spyder said "Ben, it's good to be back."

As quick as he reverted, he was back to normal and answered, "It's good to see the two of you again. People were starting to worry. Not me, of course, but some people."

"Of course not you," Bear answered. "Is Hal in the office?"

"Yeah, him and some others-they'll be glad to see you. Go on through. I gotta get back on watch. By the way, who are these pretty ladies you have with you?"

Spyder introduced the two ladies to Ben and added, "The best entertainer in the area even before the loss of electricity."

Ben tipped the brim of his hat and said, "Ladies, you're welcome here, and if there's anything I can do just let me know."

The men walked their horses toward the corral so they could unsaddle and feed them. To their surprise, Lynn was at the entrance gate and took the animals.

"I'll get Carl to take care of these, you all head on over to the office. I'm sure they'll want to hear whatever you have to report. She briefly introduced herself to Libby and Kai as the four of them walked off toward the resort office.

At the office, they found David, Hal, Sandy, Davata, and Dr. Hamilton. They all stood, grinning, when the four travelers entered the room. There were hugs and handshakes all around.

"He's gone a couple of days, and he's already replaced me," Davata said smiling.

Bear put his arm around her and squeezed. "No ma'am, it would take more than two to do that."

Bear introduced the two new women to the group then they all settled down to discuss what he and Spyder had discovered.

***

Lynn and Wind joined those already in the office. They all sat listening to Spyder and Bear as they gave their report. Following their introductions to the group, Libby and Kai sat along a wall trying to draw as little attention as they could to themselves.

Spyder related what happened when they followed the mutants to Austin. He told how they found the two women and repeated the story Libby and Kai had told them. Bear told of how the group of mutants attacked them. When the report ended, he added, "If it hadn't been for the courage of these two young ladies, Spyder and I both could have been killed. They earned their keep as far as I'm concerned."

"Me too," Spyder agreed. "They both proved themselves last night."

There was a short silence then Sandy said, "Well, I think I speak for the rest when I say thank you. You brought these two back to us safely. They may not be much, but they're ours."

"Not much?" Spyder quickly repeated with a grin. "Did you hear her? She said we're not much."

"It's okay, Spyder. I know what she was saying," Bear answered. "She meant you may not be much, but I belong to them; and you had to come along."

A short but loud discussion broke out with everyone talking over each other and only ended when Hal started banging on the desk with the side of a book. "I think Libby has something to say," he said when the others quieted down.

"I only wanted to say thanks to Bear and Spyder once again for saving our lives. I can see the rest of the people here think very highly of them, and I can understand why." She took a deep breath and asked, "Is it possible that Kai and I could stay here for a while? We really have no place to go, and I don't know what we should do next."

It was obvious the request was hard for the young woman to make. The request was also a surprise to the members of Rebel's Revenge. They had already accepted that the two new women were going to stay. They simply forgot to tell them the fact.

Again, Sandy was the one to speak up. "Young lady, you and your sister have a place here for as long as the two of you want."

"In fact," David suggested. "I think it's time for us to have a meeting. We can have dinner tonight and let the rest of the camp get to know our new members.

The front door opened, and Ron and Barbara walked in. They noticed the smiles on everyone's faces then saw Spyder, Bear, and the two new women. Ron grinned and extended his hand to Spyder. "Welcome back you two," he said and shook hands with Bear.

"It's good to have both of you back," Barbara said giving both men a hug.

Then Hal got serious and said, "Ron, Barbara. You both need to pack your things up."

Ron and Barbara both turned toward him with questioning looks. The rest of the group wore solemn expressions. "Did we do something wrong?" Ron asked.

"It's time for the two of you to pack up and move out." He paused, then giving them a big grin continued, "We've got two new people here we need to keep in close. The two of you can take any of the empty cabins and stake your claim. You've both earned it."

Ron and Barbara both visibly relaxed. "You scared the hell out of me," Barbara said. "I thought we'd done something wrong."

"Me too," Ron agreed, "thought we were being kicked out."

"Not a chance," Hal answered. "You've both shown us you're a part of us for as long as you want to be."

Hal introduced Ron and Barbara to Libby and Kai. "They'll be taking your suite when you've moved out."

Ron tipped his hat to the two ladies and said, "We'll be out in an hour or so."

Barbara greeted Libby and Kai. "You couldn't be taken in by better people," she said.

"We're gonna have a get-together this evening, and we'll do a formal vote then," David said.

***

Ron and Barbara took a cabin near the east end of the camp.

Sandy and Davata helped Libby and Kai move into their suite. Afterward, the sisters went to the camp's stores where they received clothes, food, diesel for their lamps, and other supplies they might need to establish a home for themselves.

They sat in the cafe, meeting the citizens of Rebel's Revenge as they arrived. Sandy and Davata made the introductions and told the two girls the various jobs of each person.

"It seems like everyone here has two or three jobs," Libby observed.

"Most do," Sandy confirmed. "Those not already knowledgeable about what is needed are being trained by whoever has the job as a primary task."

"I don't understand," Libby answered.

"Everyone here is assigned a primary task or job and at least one secondary one," Davata explained. "The primary one is something you already know how to do-like me, for instance. I am, by trade, a schoolteacher. It was natural for me to teach here. In addition, I am also learning to be an assistant to Bear and his alternative medical treatments. I've been learning about the use of plants, animals, and minerals for medicinal purposes. Amanda, the other teacher, is learning to be a nurse for Dr. Hamilton. Spyder and Wind are our principal scouts with David and Bear backing them up as needed. In other words, we try and have

397

one person thoroughly trained in an area with at least one back up to help or take over if needed."

"Impressive," Libby answered, "very impressive."

"I'm not sure there's anything I can do to add to the group," Kai interjected. "I'm not trained in anything that would be helpful here."

"That's hard to believe," Sandy answered. "You'd be surprised what you can do to help. We'll just have to take a look at it and figure out where your interests lie. You may be surprised exactly how helpful both of you will be."

"I'll be very surprised," Kai answered.

"Look at David," Sandy said. "He's in charge of keeping all the weapons working here in camp, along with making any new ones we may need. He's also one of the scouts and one of the main people to schedule the watches and set up defenses around the camp. Now, what do you think he did before the electricity went away?"

After thinking about it a while Libby guessed, "Something like car repair-fixing cars up after wrecks."

With a grin Sandy said, "Nope. He was a computer specialist. He could make a computer do anything you wanted it to do. He was a master at it. Working with guns was only a hobby. He was actually a gunsmith at one time-again as a hobby. He can also make about any kind of stringed musical instrument you want."

"A computer programmer," Libby mused. "I never would have thought that."

"Spyder was an electrician," Sandy continued. "He's done a lot in his life, but that was what he made his living as."

The cafe was almost full now. Davata rose and said, "Let's take the two of you around and let you meet the rest of the people here."

The other three women stood and followed her around the room, meeting the people of Rebel's Revenge.

After everyone finished eating, Hal rose and gaveled a meeting to order. "Can I have your attention, folks?"

Everyone quieted down and looked at him.

"As you all know, we have two potential new members with us. Libby, Kai, please stand up."

Both women rose and looked around to the applause of the group. They were both surprised at the reception. Neither of them expected the group to be so outgoing in their response to new people among them.

Both women returned to their seats as Hal continued, "We also need to get a formality out of the way. Would Ron and Barbara stand please?"

Both Ron and Barbara stood looking around at the people sitting at the tables surrounding them.

"Ron and Barbara has been with us a couple of weeks now and have proven that we can trust them with keeping our camp safe as lookouts. Neither of them has given any of us reason to question their loyalty to our way of life or to any of us. So as the head, elected official, I'm asking for a formal vote to accept them as official members of Rebel's Revenge. Do I hear a motion?"

399

"I make a motion Ron and Barbara, both, be accepted as members of Rebel's Revenge," Ben said rising from his seat.

"I second the motion," Lynn said standing.

The vote unanimously carried. Ron and Barbara were now official members of the group of survivors known as Rebel's Revenge.

"I know this may seem a little strange to an outsider," Hal said. "But to the original members of the group, this is an important step." Hal paused a moment, looking around the room. Then he continued, "If you will allow me to go back before our current situation, I'll explain."

He shifted from one foot to another and looked down at the notes in front of him. Then continued, "Back when we started the group known as 'The Hays County Regulators', we were run by Kyle Jennings. It was his idea, and he had done one season of performing shows with other people. The second season, he recruited Bear, Spyder, Ginny, Lynn, Ben, and Carl. In the middle of the season, he met David and Cindy who joined us. We followed strict rules about our weapons. Anyone who asked to could look at any other member's gun to make sure it was safe before a show. No one took exception to this-it was a matter of safety. We practiced and planned how every show would go on. Each person had a place to be at a certain time and a certain time to shoot-again for safety. Now we're living under a similar set of rules. Every member of the original group knows they can rely on any other member to keep their safety and survival in the forefront of their minds. We now task the people voted in tonight with the same sacred trust. All of us that are members of Rebel's Revenge trust you with our lives. Welcome to our family."

As Hal sat down, a thunderous applause broke out with many rising to their feet. It took a full five minutes for the assembled group to settle back into their seats.

When they finally sat back down, Ben remained standing. "I'm not sure what to call you, but for now I'll say, Mr. President, it comes to my attention that not everyone here has been voted into the group. We've accepted many people without officially voting them in. I therefore make a motion we accept everyone present as members of the Rebel's Revenge unless they choose not to accept."

There was a cheer from the crowd. With the events of the past few months, some of the people present were simply accepted as members of the community and not formally voted in. Spyder seconded the motion, and again the vote was unanimous. The community of Rebel's Revenge now boasted over sixty members not including any of the thirty to fifty people who had come and gone since they established the camp. It did, however, include everyone living in the camp itself and some living close by, in the surrounding area. This last group was actually thought of more as friends of the core group. They would help with hunting and agreed that if an emergency arose, they would move into the camp and help defend it.

CHAPTER THIRTY-FOUR

In their cabin, Bear had his feet propped up on a kitchen chair beside him, while Davata cut deer meat to use in a stew for dinner. She had taken over the cooking and especially the coffee making with instructions to Bear that he should do no cooking unless it was an emergency. As for the making of coffee, she would rather him not touch the pot unless it was for him to pour some coffee into a cup. If the pot was empty, he should ask someone, anyone else in the camp to make more.

Speaking over her shoulder, she asked, "Would you like a beer to drink while you wait?" She started for the door anticipating his acceptance.

"Do you think you should be doing that in your condition?"

After only a slight hesitation she answered, "It's not too cold out. I think I can handle it for a few seconds."

"I'm not talking about the cold, and you know it."

"Then, what condition are you referring to?" she asked, turning back toward him. She had taken care to cover up the fact she was pregnant by wearing bulky clothes and continuing her daily tasks. She was barely showing and sure no one could tell the difference yet. She wore bulky shirts around the cabin and knew Bear couldn't yet feel the difference in her stomach when they lay together. They hadn't even made love yet so maybe-hopefully-he was teasing her about something else.

"Oh," he said looking out a side window, "I was just wondering if a pregnant woman should be doing all that bending and toting. Now don't get me wrong, I enjoy being served. I was only wondering if it was good for you."

"Pregnant, what makes you think I'm pregnant of all things?" Davata asked pretending exasperation.

Bear held her gaze. "There've been a number of things pointing in that direction."

"Like what?" Davata demanded and crossed her arms across her chest.

Bear smiled. "Like the two mornings and one afternoon you left the house to be sick. Morning sickness doesn't only strike in the morning. Like the other day when you complained about being tired more than usual, and I took your pulse and looked at your tongue. Using Traditional Chinese Medicine, your pulse and the coating on your tongue told me it. The other indication was when I found the remains of a peanut butter and cheese sandwich with mayo and jelly on it. I don't know a lot of people who eat such a gourmet type of sandwich."

Davata let out a long sigh. This was the one thing in their relationship she was unsure of. She knew she loved Bear, and she thought he loved her. However to add a child to the equation, especially with things as they are, was something that could ruin even the strongest of relationships. They hadn't even made love yet. Then for her to be having another man's child was almost too much to ask any man to accept. She refrained from any sexual advances toward him because of his physical condition and the possibility causing further injury.

403

She figured he held back for the same reason. Either that or he didn't really feel as strongly about her as she thought he did.

She wasn't going to lie to the man, so she said, "You're right. I'm pregnant. The baby is Andy's. He's the man the mutants killed when I met Dr. Hamilton and his group. I didn't want to bother you with this until I began to show, and I damn sure don't want anyone to treat me any different." She lowered her head and softly said, "I also wasn't sure how you would take the news. I know it may be too much to ask-for you to put up with me and a baby. "

Bear rose from his chair, walked over to and opened a drawer on the far side of the kitchen. Davata was still talking..."If you want me to move out I will. There are some other cabins not in use, and I don't want to be an additional burden on you." It was as if she was a battery-operated doll who finally ran down. She simply stood with her eyes looking at the floor and her shoulders drooping. She looked to Bear like a prize-fighter who just lost a world championship fight.

He reached in the drawer and as he pulled a container out said, "You need to be taking prenatal vitamins for you and the baby."

When she looked up in surprise, he was holding a bottle for her to see. "Can't have any kids of mine born any way but healthy," he said and stepped toward her.

Davata almost sprinted across the kitchen into his arms. They held each other close for a long time then he said, "Since I'm a doctor and know that some exercise is good for an expectant mother then

404

you need to get your cute little ass back over there and finish fixing my dinner wench.

She reached up kissed him. "Thank you."

As he stepped away, he said, "Think nothing of it ma'am." Getting himself a beer from outside the door, he returned to the kitchen, sat back down in the same chair, and watched Davata work.

They made love for the first time that night, and Bear believed better things were to come even in this dark time.

**

It took Bo over an hour to convey to Gabriel what the mutants who arrived two days ago told him. With Manny's help, Gabriel finally understood the need for immediate action. If he were to keep the alliance of the mutant packs and the humans intact, he would have to act now.

Bo squatted in the office, and Manny sat in a chair in front of his desk. "Is there any way you can send some of your pack out in groups of two or three and find where the other humans are?

Bo bobbed his grizzly head yes.

"Good," Gabriel said. "Do you want any of my people to go with them?"

This time Bo shook his head no. He was sure the humans would be unable to keep up with his scouts and couldn't guarantee any of them would return alive. In their current state, some of the less intelligent of his kind might get frustrated and take it out on any human in close proximity.

Gabriel seemed to understand and nodded back to him. "Tell your scouts to find the location of the humans only. I don't want them to kill any of them yet. They should report back to you so you can tell me where they are. Then we'll make plans for you and me to coordinate an attack on them. Can you get your pack to do that?"

Bo nodded and stood. He uttered a low growl then turned and walked out of the room, leaving both men surprised behind him.

"I still can't get used to him," Manny observed. "Sometimes he acts human enough; you can almost get by his appearance. Then, he does something like this. I wonder if his growl meant he would do it, or if he didn't like but would do it; or he was hungry and left before he ate us."

"You're guess is as good as mine," Gabriel answered. "As long as he does it and there's no trouble over it, then I'm satisfied. If he's hungry, you're the hors d'oeuvre."

***

Hal, Spyder, and Bear entered the office of the resort to see David, Ben, and Wind waiting on them. It was six in the morning, and they were gathering to go hunting. It was a long time since the group did anything together just for fun. The administration of their new community took priority over everything else.

Two days before, they decided they would all like to go hunting. Each of them was taking along a couple of flasks of their favorite drink. They carried food for lunch and supper and were serious about killing more drinks than animals. The only thing they agreed upon was that none of them was to shoot another member of the party or any of their horses. The men mounted their horses and headed to the river. Once there, they turned and went downstream along the bank until about ten o'clock, when they found a clearing. Here, they dismounted, unsaddled, and staked out their horses where there was grass for them to graze.

David walked over near the river, sat down with his back against a tree, and placed his pack beside him. "Now if all of you will keep the noise down, I'll sit here and hunt."

"You gonna hunt with your eyes open or closed?" Hal asked.

Spyder reached over and pushed the front brim of Hal's hat up. "I can't get used to you wearing a cowboy hat the right way. You don't look like the old sidekick that way."

Hal reached up and pulled the brim back down. "Sun's bright today. Besides, I don't plan on shootin' my rifle out here-might bring unwanted company."

"Some hunters you guys are," Wind observed.

"I'm a damn good hunter," Spyder answered holding up a leather flask. "Lookey here, I hunted and found my water bottle."

"What's in your water bottle?" David asked.

"Tequila," Spyder answered and took a drink.

Ben stood in front of all the others. "I now christen this area The Rebel's Rest and Recreation Area."

"I'm resting," David responded.

"I'm recreating," Spyder said drawing the words out.

"Well, this gonna do both," Wind declared.

Immediately, every head spun toward him in surprise. None of the other men expected to hear that particular word used-especially by Wind. "Hey," he explained, "I'm among friends. I've called each of you a shitheaded, red-necked jackass at one time or another. I'm an equal opportunity bigot."

"I don't know what the rest of you are surprised at," Spyder said, "I call him it all the time. Let's face it. You boys and me's the only people around here that's worth a damn." After a couple of second's hesitation, he added, "... and I'm beginning to wonder about alla you."

"You've been awfully quiet, Bear," Hal observed.

"I'm just listening to you red-necks pick on this poor up-standing black man in the most unmerciful way," Bear answered. "If the ACLU was still around, you boys would be in deep shit."

"Don't make me shoot you," Wind said to Bear.

"I'll load your gun if you want," Ben offered.

Bear shook his head and said, "Now you see why I haven't said much since we got here."

The men sat back and relaxed for a couple of minutes. Each of them lost in his own thoughts.

It was David who broke the silence. "Any of you remember the time Kyle fired his gun to open one of the shows, and that deputy sheriff almost shot him?"

"Almost shot him?" Wind asked.

"Yeah," Hal took the story up, "the deputy didn't know we put on a show with loaded weapons. In fact, he didn't know there was a show. Kyle shot up in the air to get everyone's attention to give the safety lecture we did every show. Before anyone knew it, he had drawn his pistol and was telling Kyle to get down on his knees. He had his gun pointed at Kyle who was as surprised about it as the audience was about him shooting in the air. Before the deputy knew it, there were eleven cowboys and cowgirls converging from all directions to calm him down."

"It took ten or fifteen minutes to explain to the deputy that there was a show, and Kyle was part of it," David explained. "Even after we told him everything, he insisted on inspecting all of our guns."

"The only good thing to come out of it," Ben said, "was when we passed the hat, we took in almost two hundred dollars."

"Passed the hat?" Wind questioned.

"We used to literally pass one or two of our hats to collect donations," Ben explained.

"Did you make much money?" Wind asked.

"We made enough to keep us in powder and supplies," David answered. "Eventually, we turned professional and charged five hundred to seven-fifty a show depending on who it was for and what we did. We did shows for professional football players, weddings, corporate parties, town and city celebrations, and even with other organizations."

"Damn, you guys must have been good," Wind praised. "It must have taken a lot of organization and a lot of work."

"You're looking at the organization right here," Bear said. "Except for Kyle, we were it. Kyle was the founder of the group. It was something he always wanted to do. He ran it for two years, then we appointed a governing committee made up of all of us here and ran it for another five or six years before the current circumstances changed it."

"Speaking of which," Ben said, "does anyone have any idea about what happened to cause this?"

"I've been thinking about it," David answered. "I figure some government might have set some kind of bomb off, and this was the result."

"Who would want to cause this to happen?" Wind asked.

"This wouldn't have been the intended result," David explained. "Maybe something on a smaller scale but not this. The U.S. had the neutron bomb, which did something along this line. I simply figure they went a step farther."

"From what I understood, the neutron bomb was only supposed to affect a small area," Hal said. "This seems to be at least nationwide-probably worldwide. I'd say that's more of a giant leap than a step."

For the next couple of hours, the men talked about whatever came up. Each of them was careful not to drink too much, knowing they could possibly have to defend themselves at any time. Twice, they saw deer passing by the clearing, but none of them raised a weapon to shoot it.

Finally, after the sun crossed the sky and hung low in the west, Hal said, "Well gents, I reckon it's time to head back."

The other men slowly started to move around and gather their food and drink into their packs. Bear rose, walked to the edge of the river, and looked into it.

"What the hell are you doin', Bear?" Spyder asked.

Without answering Bear quickly pulled one of his pistols and fired. The other men were instantly up with weapons pulled, searching the area around them. It was then they apparently collectively realized Bear had shot the water in the stream.

Why the hell' did you shoot the river?" Spyder asked. Then grinning he added, "It never done nothin' to you."

Bear bent down and pulled the body of a fish out of the water. "I never go home empty-handed from hunting," he answered, "and this is easier to clean than a deer."

The other men chuckled with some of them shaking their heads. "Finally find something you couldn't face down, so you shot it," Hal said.

"Awe hell," Spyder said, "he's just a bully, that's all."

Bear looked at David and Ben, "You two are sure quiet. Don't you have anything to say about me shooting a fish?"

The men looked at each other, grinned, and shook their heads with innocent looks on their faces. It was Wind who asked, "Say Bear, you bring an extra horse with you to pack that critter back?"

"Nope," Bear answered. "I figured Hal would carry it. Then if one of the mutants attacks us for food, it'll go for the fish and get him while we get away."

"Kiss my ass, Bear," Hal said.

"There he goes getting romantic again," Bear answered. "Looks like I'm gonna hafta tell Sandy to start taking better care of you sexually. It's gettin' to where you're not safe to be alone with in the woods."

Again, the group chuckled and continued getting ready to leave. In another couple of minutes, they saddled and packed the horses, and then the group headed out toward Rebel's Revenge. Their moods were light, and it had been a good day.

***

Unknown to Hal and the rest of his group, two mutants watched and followed them at a distance. They were two of the scouts Bo sent to find the militia headquarters. As instructed, they remained out of sight and didn't attack the enemy.

They related their story to Bo through grunts, growls, and gestures of their giant arms and paws. They could tell these humans didn't intend to cause trouble. They sat in a clearing by the river and made noises. Eventually, the humans got up to leave, and one fired one of their killing things, into the river. It reached down, picked up a fish and carried it away.

Some of the sounds coming from the humans were familiar. Even though they couldn't understand the exact meaning of each word, deep inside, something told them the idea of the conversation. The sounds were happy sounds-unlike the ones they usually heard from most of the humans they encountered.

Bo knew they described a pistol, and the sounds were happy ones.

The mutants remained behind the men until they returned to a group of buildings. Once there, the men paused and made sounds at each other, and then each went to a different building and disappeared inside.

The mutants scouted the perimeter of the buildings to see what else they could discover. They encountered three other humans keeping watch. These, they avoided with little effort. After learning all they could about the camp, they returned to report their findings to Bo.

A couple of hours later, the last of the scouts Bo sent out returned to the caves. It took him a few more hours to assemble all the information they brought him. It seemed there were two large groups of humans. One was almost due west of them, and the other was close to the large lake south of there. High walls and wire surrounded the one to the south, obviously built for protection. The one to the north of that was in a group of buildings beside a river.

He knew Gabriel would want to know about both groups. However, he spent the night in the cave with his mate. Somehow, he knew it would be his last peaceful period for a long while.

He and two of his best scouts arrived at the edge of Austin about eleven this morning. Now, in Gabriel's office Bo conveyed to the human what he had learned. Looking at the map in Gabriel's office, Bo was able to show him where both camps were.

"What do you know about the people in the camp by the river?" Gabriel asked.

Bo grunted, shook his head from side to side and wrote, *"Nothing ~ I find out."*

"I appreciate that," Gabriel said. "Are you willing to take a look at it today? I realize it's short notice, but they might be a problem for us."

Again, Bo nodded. *"Take 3-5 days."*

"I understand," Gabriel said. "I don't want you to take any chances. Be careful and don't get caught. I have some of my men checking the other group out, and we'll plan our strategy when you both return."

CHAPTER THIRTY-FIVE

General Clark gathered his top officers around a large table in the center of the room. He was laying out his plan to destroy the community over at Rollingblock. He knew those assholes were a threat to him and all the people here at the compound. There was no doubt he could handle all those cowards living in the immediate area. It was the group over in Rollingblock that was a problem.

On the table before him was a detailed map of the area. It showed the area around their compound and the terrain between them and Rollingblock. It was rugged country. However, if they were to attack the resort with anything more than rifles, his people would have to stay on the roads, which made them vulnerable to attack at any one of a thousand different places along the way.

"What we'll do," he told his officers, "is have ten people in front of the column and ten behind with out-riders to the side. Their job won't be to defend the main body, but more importantly, to sound the alarm in case of an ambush." He looked around the room and realized all the people present were taking this thing way too lightly. Many times, he had heard people say they were the strongest, most invincible entity in this part of the country. *Of course they're right. At the same time, that type of thinking is what leads to defeat. It's a sure road to a good, old-fashioned ass kicking.*

"Folks," he said, "I can see by the look on your faces, you figure this will be a simple mop up kind of operation." He paused and looked around the room, making sure he had all their attention before he continued. "You can bet the people of ours they killed earlier would disagree with you. It's obvious they're military trained. I figure their leaders all have strong military backgrounds. Even if we are able to hit them by surprise, you can bet they will have contingency plans to regroup and counter our attack. Plus it's obvious they're trained in skirmish fighting. They'll use snipers, mines, and anything else they have. If you want to win, then don't underestimate 'em. It would be a grave mistake." The General noticed a young lieutenant standing at the back of the group. The young man seemed to be distracted as he shuffled some papers in his hands.

"Am I boring you son?" The General bellowed. The rest of the people in the room turned and looked where General Clark's gaze froze the young man.

"N-No Sir," the man answered and snapped to attention.

"You think this is some type of game?" The General asked. "Or maybe you already know everything I'm going to say."

"No Sir," the man answered, "my apologies, sir."

"Don't apologize. Just pay attention. The rest of these people will be depending on you to do your part. And you can believe me-if I see you cause one death because you have your head up your ass here, I'll blow your shit away myself."

Still at attention, the lieutenant answered with a sharp, "Yes Sir."

General Clark knew the incident would drive home to everyone in the room exactly how important this meeting was. He also figured the young lieutenant would quickly snap back from the ass chewing. With this in mind, he continued his briefing.

He laid out the rest of the plan on how he figured they could circle the resort area on the south, west, and east. "We'll drive them to the northwest where the cliffs are. Once we have them there, all we have to do is keep pressing, and they will either surrender or die. The secret to success is once the attack starts, we have to maintain pressure and not allow them time or a place to regroup or escape." He paused and looked at his officers, then continued. "Other than hand-held weapons, the only other armament we'll have is ten mortars. There'll be enough ammunition to sustain a fight for three days without replenishment."

***

The next day General Clark assigned eleven people to Buck to take as a scouting party. The group was now about two miles from the area of Rollingblock. Their plan was to get as close to the resort area in town to see the layout of the place.

"We know from maps where the resort is," Buck said. "Our mission is to learn about the guards, and if possible, locate any armament they may have. We're to avoid any contact at all costs. This is a covert operation, and discovery could cause problems for The General and the militia. We'll go through the main part of town and then cut

417

across to the resort and approach it from the opposite end of the cabins. Stay off the road beside the resort to avoid any guards. "Keep an eye out for anyone hunting or gathering items from the homes or businesses," Buck instructed.

They found a place to tether their horses on the south end of town and continued on foot through the empty houses and businesses. They made it through the square then to where the road formed a "Y." Taking the left branch, the scouting party continued about a mile and then turned west so they would come out about a half-mile north of the resort.

They were successful in their travels, remaining unseen as far as they could tell. They stopped around two o'clock and ate food previously prepared so they didn't have to build a fire. After eating, they rested for an hour, and then Buck ordered them to move out.

Buck was determined there would be no repeat of what had happened the last time he was here. People died, and the residents here found out about the militia's presence. The General wanted this to be done quietly, and he would make sure that is how it happened. Now, moving along the north end of the resort property, the guards would probably be rare since it was over a mile from the main area and the rentals. It was the best way to avoid contact and still achieve their objective.

***

Spyder, Bear, Hal, and David were saddling their horses when Davata and Ginny arrived with food and extra water for the men to take with them.

"Damn," Spyder exclaimed. "My little Teacup has done it again. Would you look at the grub she and that sweet young thang there have put together? We're gonna hafta be sure and bring back at least enough food to make up for what they're feeding us. It's fer sure, with the two of them, we never have to worry about going hungry.

"You just be sure and bring yourself back," Ginny told him.

"See that?" Spyder answered. "She's even worried about my safety. The rest of you fellers eat your heart out."

"If you don't come back," Ginny said, "then all the food I gave you'll go to waste, and you know we can't have that."

With a big grin, Spyder reached over and hugged her. Everyone knew there was a bond there more than simple friends. With Ginny's husband considered dead, the two of them were almost inseparable.

Bear leaned over to Davata and gave her a hug. "You take care of yourself. I want you here and in good condition when I get back."

"Nope," Davata answered. "I'm not gonna do it."

Bear grinned and opened his mouth to respond when she cut him off.

"If it's okay with the rest of you, I'd like to come along. I know this is usually when you men get together, and one lies and the others swear to it; but I'm pregnant and would like to go out one more time before I become too big to do so. I'll try and not hold you up too much, and Lynn has a horse saddled for me in the corral."

419

Bear was about to protest when each of the three other men spoke at once, "Sure, fine, that's great, glad to have you along," they said over each other.

Bear looked around and then at Davata, "Are you sure you're up to this?"

"I am today," Davata answered. "But, I don't know how much longer I'll be able to, so I'm going today-especially since these wonderful gentlemen agree." She smiled demurely.

"She'd better be able to," Ginny said. "I packed food for her too."

Bear sighed, removed his hat with his left hand and ran his right through his long hair. "Well," he said, "You'd better get your horse out here before I come to my senses and say no."

Davata went into the corral and emerged with a horse barely taller than a pony. After she climbed on, Ginny walked up to her and in a low voice said, "Keep the trotting to a minimum and take care of yourself." She then patted the other woman on the leg and walked away.

"I'll take lead," David said. "Bear, you take drag with the others between us." He turned his horse and headed north where a number of deer were seen in recent days. Everybody fell in line, with Bear taking the last position and Davata in front of him.

***

Buck and the rest of his scouting party gathered along the north end of the property, and he was drawing an outline of the resort on the ground when one of his guards came hurrying up. There're some of those mutants moving around over there," he pointed to the southeast.

"How many?" Buck asked.

"Only two that we saw," the guard answered.

"How far away?" Buck asked.

"About two hundred yards and their moving slow. It's like their scouting the area the same as us."

"Don't be ridicules," Buck snorted. "There's no way those things are scouting. They're probably avoiding the people there," he paused to think a minute then continued, "which will make it easier for us to kill those fucking things."

"But The General said..." Another man started.

"I know what General Clark said," Buck cut the man off. "He said to avoid the people here at the resort. He didn't say anything about not killing any of those mutant things if we got a chance. Now, spread out and form a line so when they move into position, we can get rid of those pieces of shit."

The men around him hesitated for a couple of seconds. "Move," Buck growled.

The men spread out in a line, being careful to stay low and in the bushes so the mutants about fifty yards away couldn't see them. The creatures walked in graceful, easy strides. They didn't seem to hurry, but by their movement, he could see how they were able to travel from place to place without being seen or heard.

Buck waited until the animals were in the middle of the men he had spread in ambush. He took sight on the one in the lead, took a deep breath and slowly let it out. As he did, he squeezed the trigger until his weapon fired.

**

Spyder saw the men as they came running from the woods and bushes. Everyone on horseback pulled a weapon except Davata. Thinking she was safe with the men carrying weapons and not planning to hunt herself, she was unarmed.

A bullet whined by Spyder's head and was all it took. He fired two shots before dismounting. A fraction of a second after Spyder flew from his horse, the others did likewise.

Bear ran up to Davata and forced her to the ground beside a tree. "Stay here," he ordered and scrambled to the other men.

David was using an M16, and two men hit the ground as Bear reached his position. Bear, using a lever action 30-30, began firing. Spyder and Hal moved to their right trying to flank the men now firing at them.

The men on the other side must have seen what they were doing and forced Spyder and Hal back to Bear and David's location. Bear immediately moved to his left to try the other side. He only went about fifteen yards when he had to stop. David had followed him and was putting another clip in his rifle.

Bear motioned to a mound of dirt ahead of him, and David nodded. As one, both men hurried to the mound. The air seemed full of flying lead as the men made it to the mound. To their surprise, they found it wasn't a mound of dirt but a mutant laying there. Without hesitation, David opened up with the M16 on automatic and sprayed the trees in front of them. There was a lot of movement where David was shooting. Bear took aim at one of the men there and squeezed his trigger. The man threw his arms out wide as the bullet caught him square in the middle of the back. Another man turned to shoot in time for David to spray him with four bullets. The man went down without firing a shot.

With no more movement in front of them, they both rose and moved into the trees to see if they could locate any survivors.

Hal and Spyder both carried M16s and fired on semi-automatic. There were four men on the ground about twenty-five yards ahead of them. The rest of the group seemed to have scattered to their left. Both Hal and Spyder slowly rose and started to where the fallen men lay.

They only took a couple of steps when a sound came from behind them. Both men spun and raised their weapons to their shoulders. Neither seeing anything there kept turning with their rifles ready to fire until the sound came again.

It was Davata, and she was groaning. Both men sprinted to where she lay.

"Go get Bear," Hal said to Spyder.

Spyder looked down at the Davata lying on the ground before him. Blood ran from three bullet wounds in her stomach and chest. He quickly turned and sprinted into the woods looking for the other men.

***

423

Bear and David found the bodies of the three men they had killed. Since the men were previously carrying M16s, they relieved the bodies of their rifles and extra magazines. As quietly as possible, both men moved on in the direction the others had run. About three minutes later, they heard someone moving around a short distance away. Both men stepped behind a tree and waited.

Seconds later, they heard someone call out, "Bear-David."

Bear recognized the voice and answered. "Over here, Spyder."

Spyder hurried to them. "Bear, you gotta get back to Davata. She's been shot."

Not caring that other men might be in the vicinity, Bear sprinted to where he left Davata. When he found her, she was lying on the ground with her head on a rolled up blanket. Hal looked up as Bear ran up. He stood and blocked the other man's approach.

"Comfort her," was all Hal said, his eyes locked with Bear's, and the man knew instantly she was in a bad way.

He knelt beside her and bent low so his head was slightly above hers. "You hang in there sweetheart," he whispered.

Her eyes fluttered and then opened. He could see how much pain she was in by gazing into them. Her breathing was shallow and ragged. She opened her mouth to speak and then closed it.

"Just relax," he said. "We're gonna get you help."

She looked straight into his eyes, smiled, and slowly let out her last breath. She quietly slipped

424

away looking into the eyes of the man she cared for more than anything else in this world except for maybe the unborn child that now left with her.

Bear witnessed death many times before and knew when she went. He bent down and kissed her one last time. "I love you," he said and slowly rose.

"Can you men take her back to Rebel's Revenge?" He asked the others.

"What are you gonna do?" David asked putting his hand on the man's shoulder.

"I've got some killin' to do," he answered and turned toward where his horse was now grazing.

"You can't go alone," David said. "You need to come back to the camp with us."

"Can you take her back or not?" Bear answered.

"I won't let you go alone," David told him.

Bear looked directly into his friend's eyes and asked, "Do I have to start with you?"

"Let 'em go," Spyder said. "You can't stop him, and we need you alive. We'll take care of her Bear."

"What the fuck?" They all looked at Hal who was pointing to the west.

The mound of dirt David and Bear previously hid behind was moving. It was the mutant both men thought was dead. It was obvious it wasn't dead, but it wasn't going anywhere on its own anytime soon.

Bear looked in the direction the men ran. He looked back at the animal struggling on the ground. Something deep inside him said this animal was important. In addition, it was the first they ever had a chance to examine while it was still alive.

He went to his saddlebag and retrieved two syringes of morphine Dr. Hamilton had given him in case of injury. "We'll take both of 'em back," is all he said as he strode over to the mutant lying on its back. Unceremoniously he plunged both needles into the creature and watched as it slipped into unconsciousness.

***

Buck and two other men ran through the trees, heading toward their horses on the far side of Rollingblock. Upon reaching the animals, Frank, the man left on guard, challenged them as they approached.

Buck was in clear sight of the man and said, "Get the fuck out of the way. Get on your horse and let's get outta here."

"What's going on?" Frank asked as Bill and Wilbur ran past him for their horses.

Without answering, the three men climbed on their animals and headed south with the horses at a run. A mile or so later, they slowed enough for Frank to catch up. "What the hell happened back there?"

"There was an ambush," Buck answered. "When we attacked some mutants, we were attacked by the people from the compound over there.

"I don't think so," Bill cut in. "They seemed to be firing at both them and us."

"I think he's right," Wilbur added. "It looked like those other men were shooting at anything that moved."

"How many people were there?" Frank asked looking from man to man.

"Must have been eight or nine," Bill answered. "Bullets were coming from all directions.

"That's wrong," Buck said as he stopped and turned his horse toward the others. "I only saw four people. Two were using automatic weapons, and two used regular guns."

"Not a chance," Bill argued. "There's no way only four men could have been firing that many shots."

"He's right," Wilbur said and looked from man to man. "They're good. They fired deliberately and made every shot count. We're looking at trained people over here-very well trained."

Buck and the rest looked a Wilbur. There was no doubt in the man's expression. He was sure of what he was saying and understood the implications asserted by his agreeing with Buck. They had severely underestimated the group of people living over here. It was going to take more resources and people than General Clark figured.

Silently, Buck turned his horse and headed southward toward the militia compound.

CHAPTER THIRTY-SIX

Hal returned to Rebel's Revenge and rounded up some men from the camp to help carry the mutant and Davata's body back to the cabins. They put the mutant in a cabin used for medical purposes and strapped it to one of the beds from a doctor's office in town.

Dr. Hamilton kept the mutant sedated while he tended to its wounds. He sutured three deep lacerations in the animal's chest and one on its left shoulder. Its other wounds proved superficial and only required him to clean them with disinfectant. He gave it antibiotics intravenously and morphine to keep it calm and passive.

Spyder insisted this mutant was the one he and Bear had followed into Austin. He claimed it was one of the *smart ones,* and there was a good possibility they could garner information from it. "If it's the one I think it is," Spyder explained, "and we show it that we don't consider it an enemy, then there's a chance we may be able to lower the instances of having to kill them. I know if I don't consider someone an enemy, I won't bother 'em."

"I think you may be giving them too much credit," David said. "I know some of the new people think there are mutants smarter than others, but I doubt there's any way we could communicate with them."

"Shit!" Spyder exclaimed. "We communicate with you."

428

David even laughed at that. Before the snickering stopped Spyder continued, "You may be right. It may be a load of crap. But if it's not, I think it's worth taking a chance."

"Anything that'll keep us any safer has my vote," Hal said. "I think we need to, at least, give it a try."

***

Bear sat in the cabin he had shared with Davata. The lamps remained unlit. He sat in the dark and silence and let his mind wander. He and Davata had become as close as two people could in the time allowed. He thought back, going over the incident earlier in the afternoon. *There were other men there. The other men set up an ambush for the mutants. The animals hadn't done anything to anyone. They were simply traveling from one point to another. The humans were in a group and probably searching for the mutants. But if that's true, then why didn't they stop by and let us know they were in the area?* The more Bear thought about it, the less sense it made. *Not only had the other men shot at the mutants, but they shot at us as well. Most of them are dead, and Davata's in one of the other cabins being prepared for burial. There's no way to ask...*

There was a knock at the door, a pause, and then another one. Bear finally got up to see who was there. Opening the door, he found Hal and Sandy there. "You okay man?" Hal asked as he and Sandy stepped inside.

"I'm alive," he answered running his hand through his long hair and going back to the easy chair.

"Mind if I light a lamp?" Sandy asked.

"No, go ahead," he answered.

Sandy lit two lamps, and Hal removed his hat and sat on the couch. She sat beside him and watched Bear carefully. She knew most of his moods and searched for anything out of place. Hal fiddled with the brim of his hat, clearly wanting to say something but not knowing what to say. Bear was comfortable with the silence in the room.

"We talked to the others about burying her tomorrow if that's okay with you," Sandy finally said.

Bear looked up at the woman who was still his best friend. "That'll be fine," he answered. He could see how much pain she was in. Not only had she lost a friend, but also, at the same time, the woman her *brother* loved.

"Spyder thinks the mutant we brought back is one of the two of you followed to Austin," Hal said

Bear thought of when he and Spyder followed the animals to the house on the outskirts of the city. In his mind's eye, he could see the mutant nodding and grunting to one of the men there. Concentrating on the animal, he could remember what it looked like but couldn't bring up the image of the one they brought back to the camp today. "I don't know," he answered, "it's possible. I can't even remember what this one looks like."

"That's okay man," Hal answered. "I wasn't asking you to make an identification. Just letting you know why so much was done to keep it alive after what happened."

Bear looked up at his two friends. "I want it alive. There's been enough killing. Smart, dumb, or otherwise, it has as much right to live as we do. It did nothing to any of us. Those assholes out there are the problem. They're the ones that killed Davata-and those motherfuckers'll pay.

Both Sandy and Hal knew the last sentence was anything but an idle threat. Bear wouldn't rant and rave about the injustice of it all. He would simply not forget and sooner or later, they would pay a high price.

After a couple of minutes of silence, Hal said, "Spyder is going to do the service if it's all right with you."

"She wouldn't have had it any other way," he answered.

Getting up, Sandy asked, "Whatcha got to eat around here?"

"I don't want anything," he said.

"I know you don't," she said, "but Hal and I do."

"I don't want anything," Hal said.

"Yes you do," she argued, "you just don't know it."

"I really don't... ," Hal started.

"You'd better hush up and go along with her, or she's gonna hurt ya," Bear said after seeing the look Sandy was trying to convey to her husband.

Hal looked at Sandy and started to grin, "I'll have pheasant-under-glass, with a salad and freshly baked bread, maybe a white wine... "

"Hal Sloan," Sandy started, "if you weren't my husband... "

"You'd marry me," Bear interrupted.

Back to rummaging around in the cupboards, Sandy said, "I'm not so sure. I'm not that hard up yet. After all, you men are all alike."

***

The levity felt good to Bear, but he was unable to hold on to the moment. He slipped back into feelings of loss, despair, and guilt. Even though he knew better, he couldn't help but feel he should have been able to do something to change the afternoon's events. A tear slipped from the corner of his eye and ran down his face as he thought of the woman he had lost-the possibility of future love, being a husband, being a father, and having a family. Though they never spoke of it, Bear had thought about it. With things the way they were, he figured he was lucky to have this chance. He also believed it was his last chance for this type of happiness.

***

That night while Bear, Sandy, and Hal ate supper, Dr. Hamilton prepared Davata's body for buried the next day. Bo was kept sedated and tied on his treatment table. The four men from the scouting party made their way back to the militia compound, and Rebel's Revenge was quiet except for the rustling of the wind through the trees. No

432

one could even dream of the horrors, which lay
ahead for man and beast.

CHAPTER THIRTY-SEVEN

The next morning, the sun rose in a cloudless sky. The temperature was in the lower fifties, the air was fresh and even though most of the trees were leafless, there were a few that withstood winter and kept at least part of their foliage. The air smelled of cedar wood burning in fireplaces of the cabins-it was a beautiful day.

They scheduled Davata's funeral for ten o'clock in the morning. Everyone agreed the tradition of having a body lie in state for a couple of days was a thing of the past. Due to the lack of medical preparation, it was better to get the burial over with as soon as possible.

Inside his cabin, Bear dressed in the best clothes he owned. They were clothes made by Sandy and consisted of a black long coat, with a white western shirt, black vest, bow tie, and black western trousers with suspenders. To top it all off, he wore a black hat.

No more good guy *for me,* he thought as he put it on. Instead of wearing his total armament, he tucked a 9mm pistol in the back of his pants. Squaring his hat, he walked out of his cabin and came face to face with nearly every citizen of Rebel's Revenge and the surrounding area.

They quietly assembled outside his cabin and waited to walk with him to the cemetery for the burial service. The community continued to grow over time, and there were almost three hundred people waiting outside to show their respect for the gentle soul taken from them.

The service started with a hymn, and then Spyder read from the Bible. Many of the community stepped forward to say a myriad of kind things about what Davata had done for them, or what they had seen her do for others. At the end of the service, Kai stepped from the assembly and began singing. She sang for a soul she had known but for a short time, a soul who quickly came to mean so much to her. Her voice was sweet and clear as it rose and mingled through the trees in the haunting verses of Amazing Grace. From the crowd, her sister, Libby joined her, singing harmony. They sang it *a capella* in the tongue of the Native Americans as it was on the *Trail of Tears* more than a century before.

As the familiar tune drifted through the trees and countryside, time stood still for Rafe. A choir at his father's funeral had sung this song. Until now, he thought it was the most beautiful version he ever heard. Now his situation finally hit home-all was lost. He had lost everything with any meaning to him in his life. He and his wife had divorced, his father passed away, and now his last chance for happiness was about to be lowered into the ground. All of this driven home by a song sung in the words of his ancestors.

Rafe lost himself in the song even though the words themselves were foreign to him. He knew their meaning and was thankful for these two young women, their message of hope and of better things to come. When the song ended, he leaned over to Sandy who had refused to leave his side and asked for she and Hal come to his cabin. He walked a short distance to Spyder who stood with Ginny and asked him to do the same. He immediately turned and walked off. Something inside said he needed his closest friends with close by today.

***

Buck stood before General Clark's desk. He and the three other survivors of the scouting party were in the office to report. The general sat quietly as Buck told of the attack on his troops as they ambushed the mutants.

"Are you trying to say those people over there are protecting those animals?" General Clark asked.

"No Sir," Buck answered. "It seemed more like they simply happened to be there when we started shooting. The WNs came from the east, and the people from the south."

"WNs?" The general repeated. "What the fuck's a WN?"

"Walking Nightmares," Buck answered. "It's what everyone's calling them."

The general looked at the man hard for a couple of seconds and then decided the name was as appropriate as anything else. "How many do you think attacked you?"

Buck hesitated obviously knowing his leader wasn't going to like his answer. "I counted four, sir."

"Bullshit," Bill mumbled under his breath.

"What did you say trooper?" The general asked looking at the man.

"That's bullshit, sir," Bill said, coming to attention and squaring his shoulders to the general. "There was lead flying from all directions. There's no way only four people would have been able to fire that many times from that many directions."

General Clark looked at Wilbur and asked, "What about you son, how many do you think there were?"

"Four, sir-Exactly like Buck, uh, Sergeant Johnson said." He answered, correcting himself for his familiarity.

"What about you?" General Clark asked looking at Frank.

"I wasn't there, sir," Frank answered. "I was back guarding the horses."

"If I may, General," Bill started. "Lead was flying everywhere. There's no way just four of them could have done all that damage. We were lucky to get out alive." Looking at Buck he finished, "He got some good men killed."

General Clark rose from his chair and looked at each man in turn. "Is that so? Tell me trooper, what did he do wrong? What would you have done differently?"

Bill opened his mouth, but nothing would come out. He looked like a deer caught in headlights.

"Well?" The general demanded.

"Just look at his record," Bill finally said. "Damn near everything he's done has wound up being a cluster fuck. We've lost a lot of good people because of him. I, for one, don't think he should be in charge of anything"

General Clark looked at the men for a long time. "I agree there's been a mistake made here-a big goddamn mistake." He scanned the men again, "Sergeant Johnson, give me your sidearm," he said holding out his hand.

Buck slowly pulled his pistol from its holster, turned it around and handed it to the general.

Looking at Buck, General Clark said, "I gave you another chance when you survived the first encounter with those people over there. Now you come back after losing eight people to another ambush. What have you got to say for yourself?"

"With only a slight hesitation Buck said, "I have no excuse, sir. They were under my command. I alone am responsible for what happened, sir."

General Clark raised the 45cal pistol and aimed it at Buck's chest. "You're right. They were under your command."

Buck closed his eyes and braced himself. If he were to die, he would do it as a warrior and not as a coward.

General Clark turned the pistol on Bill and pulled the trigger before the man knew what was happening. The bullet struck him slightly above the right eye, killing him instantly.

Buck flinched as the gun fired and waited for the pain but there was none. He opened his eyes and looked to his left where the general pointed the pistol. There, on the floor, lay Bill's body. He hadn't heard the body hit the floor after the deafening roar of the pistol in the confines of the office.

The two guards from outside the door burst in at the sound of the gunshot. The general held his hand up indicating everything was okay. "You two take that piece of shit outta here," he motioned to the body on the floor, "and have it buried."

438

The guards grabbed the body by the shoulders and feet and carried it outside.

General Clark let the hammer down on the pistol, turned it around and handed it back to a stunned Buck. "I can't abide stupidity," the general said. "Every mission I've sent you on carried a high probability of failure. That's why I gave them to you. You're a good man, Lieutenant. You have more to learn, but you're a good man-and I don't need some asshole questioning my decisions."

Buck was staring at the general, "Lieutenant, sir?" He questioned.

"Consider it a battlefield promotion," General Clark answered. "Now tell me what you found out while you were over there."

The general sat behind his desk and motioned to the chairs in the room for the other men.

After sitting Buck said, "General, I think we might be underestimating the group over there. Two of them were using automatic weapons, while the other two had regular guns. Almost immediately after we started shooting at the WNs, they started shooting at us. At first, they were all in one group. It only took them a couple of seconds to fan out into a skirmish line. They're trained-well trained. They not only shot us, but they shot the WNs also. Their tactics were military precise. I'm afraid it's gonna take all our people and resources if we plan to get rid of 'em." After a couple of seconds thought he added, "I wouldn't count on *any* of them giving up. They really don't seem the type. I figure we'll have to kill every last one of them before it's over."

General Clark sat back in his chair, obviously contemplating the news. "Guards," he called out.

Both of the outside guards entered the room. "Have every officer assembled here at 0800 hours tomorrow morning. You two can go," he said indicating Frank and Wilbur. "Lieutenant, you stay behind." Both guards saluted and turned to leave the room, the other two men rose from their chairs, saluted and followed the guards out.

***

As Bo slowly regained consciousness, he was aware of a human presence in the room. His body was sore, and he knew he had been injured. He couldn't tell how bad, but it was severe enough that it hurt when he breathed. He could also tell there were straps holding him down, but even more than that, his muscles felt weak. He also felt groggy; kind like everything around him was a dream. He realized the humans had drugged him. Somehow, they captured him and then drugged him and strapped him to this bed.

He looked around the room and saw there were three humans with him. One was wearing a white doctor's smock. The other two were dressed in western wear and carrying guns of all types. One was dressed in black and the other in natural colors of shades of brown and tan. Of course, these revelations were pictures in his mind, concepts-ideas as sophisticated as any human thinking process.

He wasn't sure, but he didn't feel like he was in danger. The humans around him didn't appear menacing. They merely looked curious about him and his condition.

The one in the white lab coat was telling the others about his injuries-he was obviously a doctor. Bo listened as close as he could to what the human was saying.

"There's nothing life threatening with his injuries," he said. "He'll be well enough to do whatever it is he does in a day or so."

"When will he be fully conscious?" The human in brown asked.

"Ten or fifteen minutes," the doctor answered.

"Will the restraints hold him? The man in black asked.

"I can't say for absolutely sure," the doctor said, "but they should be strong enough. I added four just in case."

Both men in western gear turned their attention to the table where he lay.

"If he actually is one of the smart ones," the man in black was saying, "maybe we can convince him we're no threat to him or his kind."

"Maybe," the other answered, "but I wouldn't count on it. Smart or not, they may be nothing but animals and be guided by nothing but instinct."

The door to the room opened and a black man entered. "How's it going guys?"

***

"It's just coming around, Wind," the man in black answered.

"You okay, Bear?" Wind asked.

"As okay as possible, I guess," Bear answered.

"Then he's still no problem," Wind answered and looked at him lying on the table. "Hell, he's not

441

totally black, but he's close enough to be a brother."
Wind stepped up to the table.

"Careful," the man in brown warned his friend.
"Even drugged he still has enough strength to put a
hurtin' on ya."

"Take it easy, Wind," Bear said stepping
forward.

Wind looked at the man in brown, smiled and
said, "Spyder, if I can make friends with you, this
guy should be no problem."

Noticing Bo's hand was positioned slightly off
the table with his palm up, Wind gave it a slap as if
giving the mutant a *low five*. Almost instantly, as if
on reflex, the hand turned over.

Wind looked at the animal astonished. "Did
you see that?" He asked. "He tried to return it."

"Wind," Spyder almost shouted as the other
man reached toward the mutant. "Don't. We've got
no idea what's going on. Besides, I doubt that he's
friendly enough to return a low five. He would
probably rather just tear your arm out of its socket."

"Look at his eyes," Wind said. They're honest.
There's no malice in 'em. I know you may think I'm
crazy, but what he did was a reaction and not a
premeditated thought. If it's true, and these animals
came from humans, then this had once probably
been an African-American."

Bo turned his hand back over resuming its palm
up position. Again, Wind slapped his palm, and he
immediately turned his hand over. Wind then raised
his hand slapping his palm again. Immediately, the
mutant's hand closed into a fist.

All four humans in the room stood transfixed in
place, staring at Bo strapped to the table.

"He knows what's going on," Wind exclaimed.

"Now just hold on there," Spyder said.

"You saw that," Wind countered. "He returned the slap."

"Wind," Bear said, "I admit it's weird that he turned his hand over, but it's all he did."

"Bullshit," Wind argued, "he responded to what I did. Let his arm loose, and I'll prove it."

"We'll have to have more proof than him simply turning his hand over before we let him loose. If we did, he could probably get free before we could stop him," Bear said.

"Can I say something?" Dr. Hamilton asked.

The other three men looked at him and waited.

"I agree the movement was strange. On the other hand, it wasn't a normal movement. The hand turned palm up. It had to do that on purpose. That isn't a natural position for the hand." He looked at the men, hesitated, then said, "Honestly, there may be a chance it was responding to Wind and not simply doing something to impress us."

"Are you saying we should free its arm?" Spyder asked.

"I can readjust one of the straps so it can only move its arm from the elbow down," the doctor offered. "Then if it turns aggressive, we can strap it back down before it gets loose."

Bear looked at Spyder.

"Go for it Doc," Spyder said. "Let's see what happens."

Bear and Spyder maneuvered themselves so they were close enough to the mutant's arm to restrain it if necessary. Wind stood by its shoulder.

With everyone in position, Dr. Hamilton slowly released the strap.

Bo remained still even when the strap was completely released. He waited, knowing what the humans were waiting on. Wind moved a little closer to the table and as he did, Bo raised his arm from the elbow down and held it vertical. Wind held his hand up with his palm the hand of the mutant and waited. In just a second, Bo slapped his hand and immediately turned his hand over. Wind returned the slap and looked at the animal.

Without looking at the other men Wind said, "There's no way you motherfuckers can deny that.

Bo immediately bent his arm at the elbow and holding his fingers together with his thumb out, moved his open hand toward Wind. Before the others could stop him, Wind took the animal's hand in his in a grip similar to an arm wrestler. Bo shifted his hand into another grip and then with a snapping motion, pulled his massive paw-like hand from Wind's.

The other men stood staring in amazement. Not only had Wind put himself in extreme danger, but the mutant on the table made no aggressive move toward him. He seemed to know what the man was doing and responded accordingly.

After a minute's hesitation due to confusion and disbelief, Spyder stepped up to the other side of the animal. He bent over and looked directly into the mutant's eyes. Obviously uncomfortable and a little embarrassed with what he was about to do, the man asked, "Can you understand us?" His voice shook slightly as he asked the question.

444

Bo stared back intently at the man and slowly nodded, indicating he understood what Spyder asked.

Spyder raised up, "Son of a Bitch." He said softly. "It understands what we're saying to it".

"It looks like what we heard about at least some of them being smart is true," Dr. Hamilton said.

"Not after just one question," Bear said and stepped closer to the table. "Do you know where you are?" Bear asked.

Bo looked at him and again nodded in the affirmative. It seemed this was the man he needed to convince.

"Come on man," Wind insisted. "Doesn't that prove it understands us?"

Bear ignored Wind, and still looking at the animal asked, "When we caught you, were you here to harm us?"

Without hesitation, Bo shook his head from side to side indicating no and made a soft grunting sound.

***

It was clear to Bear the mutant on the table before him could understand what it was being asked. It answered in the affirmative and negative. He didn't think the answers were lucky guesses. The mutant had to know they were questions to answer either way.

"Let him up." It was Wind speaking now. "He don't mean to hurt us."

445

"Bullshit," Bear quickly answered. "All we know is that it can understand us. Nothing indicates it doesn't mean to try and kill us."

Again, from the table came a soft grunt.

When the men looked at the mutant, it was shaking its head no.

"See," Wind exclaimed, "He's friendly."

The young man reached for the restraining strap on Bo's arm, and Spyder shouted, "No!" Wind hesitated above the strap. "What we've seen is incredible I agree, but all we have is it shaking its head. Even if it could talk, I wouldn't be convinced yet."

The men moved to the other end of the room to the outside door. "Wind, go and get Hal. I want him here. He needs to know what's going on."

Wind started to protest, but then looking at the other men, thought better of it, opened the door and left the room.

"We need to keep it quiet," Dr. Hamilton said. "Its wounds are healing, but they could easily be torn open and cause a problem."

Both men nodded and turned back to where the mutant lay on the table.

As they turned, it sat up and swung its legs over the edge of the bed. He stopped moving and looked at the shocked men.

Instantly, Bear and Spyder pulled their pistols and cocked them. The mutant raised both arms in the international symbol of surrender and softly made a sound like the cross between the mewing of a cat and the growl of an alligator.

"Hold it," Dr. Hamilton ordered. Slowly, he moved two steps closer to the table. "Gentlemen," he said, "I don't know if this means anything to you, but it tells me that this animal is willing to be submissive right now at least."

Bear and Spyder both understood what the doctor was saying. The creature was obviously willing to remain quietly on the table.

"Put your guns away," the doctor ordered. When the men hesitated he said, "If he had wanted to do anything, he could have already done it."

Bear looked at Spyder who nodded and slowly uncocked his weapon and returned it to its holster. Bear follow Spyder's example and put his gun back on his hip. Both men stood there cautiously watching the mutant there before them.

Dr. Hamilton stepped closer to it and asked, "Were you human at one time?"

It nodded yes.

"Can you speak?"

It shook its head no.

Dr. Hamilton looked at the other two men and said, "This is going to take a long time if all we can do is ask yes and no questions."

When he looked back, it pointed at a chalkboard hanging on one of the walls of the room.

The doctor looked where it pointed. "Do you mean you can write?"

It again bobbed its head up and down.

"Be my guest," Dr. Hamilton said motioning toward the board with the sweep of his hand.

As it rose from the table, Bear and Spyder tensed. If this thing made one wrong move, they would gun it down without a second's hesitation.

When the door opened, the mutant was writing on the board. Hal, Sandy, and Wind started into the room. The three people froze as they saw the mutant standing before the chalkboard.

"It's okay," Bear told them. "Come on in."

They entered the room, and Wind closed the door behind them.

On the board, it had written, *"my name is Bo."* He held the chalk in his fist with it sticking out under his little finger. The writing was large and looked like the scribbling of a child, but he was obviously able to communicate this way.

"You let him go," Hal said in astonishment.

"Nope," Spyder answered. "When Wind left we turned around, and he was free and sitting on the table just looking at us."

"I told you he was safe to let loose," Wind said.

Bo was again writing on the board. When he finished the words, *"i no hurt"* were there. He erased them with his arm and wrote, *"i no speak ~ i understand."*

"Bo," Hal started, "why were you near here when you were attacked?"

Bo wrote, "look for food."

"But there were more than one of you," Spyder argued.

"food for pack."

"Then there are more of you around," Bear said, the sentence more a statement than a question.

Bo nodded.

"How many?" Bear asked.

"Many," Bo wrote. He would communicate with these humans, but there were things he wasn't willing to tell them.

"Are you hungry?" Dr. Hamilton asked.

Bo nodded. He was extremely hungry, but didn't want to give these humans anything to hold over his head.

"Do you want meat?" The doctor asked.

Again, Bo nodded.

"Sandy," Hal started, "Will you get our guest something to eat?"

Sandy looked at Bo, "Cooked or raw?" She asked.

The men looked at her as if she were crazy.

"Well," she said responding to the looks, "I make a hell of a home cooked steak, and I want to give him what he wants."

The men started to snigger until they turned around and looked at the board where Bo wrote, *"cooked."*

Looking back at the humans, he hesitated and then added, *"please."*

Sandy looked at the men. "Now you can all kiss my ass," she said and left the room.

"Of course you can have it cooked, Bo," Hal answered. "We're sorry to have been laughing. It's just that none of us would have thought you would have wanted it cooked."

Bo turned to the board, erased it with his arm and wrote, *"may look like monster but not one."*

"Looks like we owe you an apology, Bo," Hal said. "We seemed to have misjudged a book by its cover."

"Not entirely," Bear interrupted.

Bo looked at him.

"Some of your kind has attacked some of the humans around here. I've even had a couple attack me without being provoked."

449

"hunters," Bo wrote. *"no think ~ feelings only ~ not leader."*

"That must mean you're a leader," Hal said.

Bo hesitated. He had given information he didn't intend to. Slowly he nodded.

"Do you have any influence over the others?" Hal asked.

Again, he nodded slowly.

"Then you could tell them to leave us alone, and we'll leave them alone?"

Bo nodded and turned to the chalkboard again. After erasing the previous writing he laboriously scrawled, *"would leave alone but not tell you from others near lake."* After the men read this, he erased it and continued, *"kill us for fun."*

It seemed obvious to the humans these animals were only defending themselves. It seemed equally as obvious there was a possibility of developing a peace between the two groups.

Bo's legs seemed to give way slightly and without hesitation, Spyder and Bear were at its side. They took hold of both arms and started guiding him back to the table. The mutant gave no resistance, as it appeared to realize what the men were doing.

He sat on the table and then swinging his legs up, lay down.

Dr. Hamilton quickly moved up beside his patient. "You're going to have to let him rest now. He's had enough questions for a while."

As the other men moved toward the door, Wind ignored the doctor and stepped up beside Bo. Solemnly Wind asked the mutant, "Do I have your promise you'll stay here and not try to escape?"

450

The rest of the men stopped dead in their tracks. They simply took for granted the actions of the mutant. The young man showing so much trust before brought them back to the reality of the situation.

Bo nodded and uttered a soft growl.

"We'll see you in a while," Wind said. "Sandy will be here soon with something to eat. You rest and mend. You're safe here-I give you my word on it."

Wind joined the others as they left the room, leaving Dr. Hamilton and Bo behind.

Outside the door, Hal turned to Wind and said, "You astound me sometimes young man."

"How's that?" Wind asked.

"You were the first to trust him, back before and just now you were the one to make him promise to do something."

"If nothing else," Wind said, "he'll follow what he agrees to. His animal instinct makes him true to himself even if his human side would lie. If nothing else, I think we'll always be able to trust him to do what he promises."

"I hope you're right," Spyder said, "I hope you're right."

The men walked silently back to their headquarters. Once there, Hal said, "I need all of you to go out and explain to the others here what's happened. I don't want any accidents if for some reason Bo walks out of that treatment room."

The other men agreed and left to tell the others what had happened while Hal went to his cabin to see if he could help Sandy prepare a *home cooked meal* for their guest.

***

The morning of the second day Bo was in the treatment room and restless. His present form allowed him to heal exponentially faster than a human. He was ready to go outside, exercise his legs, and smell the fresh air. He didn't like having to stay in this room even though he understood the human's desire to restrict his movements.

It was around noon when Dr. Hamilton, Wind, and Hal came in. Bo was sitting on the treatment table picking at one of his wounds, which was now only a scab.

"Stop picking at that," Dr. Hamilton said. "You could still cause an infection."

Bo gave a grunt and lowered his hand obeying the order even though he didn't think there was a problem.

Wind approached him and said, "Bo, I need your promise that if we go outside with you, you won't try and run off.

Surprised at this proposal, Bo grunted and nodded.

"Sorry, that's not good enough," Wind said and pointed at the chalkboard.

Bo looked at the board then back to Wind. He got up, went over to the board, picked up a piece of chalk and wrote *"promise I not run."*

"Good enough," Hal said. "Let's get you out of here and get a little exercise. He opened the door and stepped to the side to allow Bo to exit the room.

Bo stepped outside, looked around then held his head up and sniffed the air. It was sweet and clean.

452

He could smell the aroma of the trees and bushes of the surrounding area and of the water in the river down the hill. He could also smell the odor of humans from all around him.

Hal started walking to his left, and Bo followed. He recognized the two rows of buildings from when he was human. They were two dwelling places put together. There was smoke coming from almost all of them, and the smoke stirred feelings, comfortable feelings he hadn't felt since he changed.

Hal led him between two rows of duplexes and then turned left between the office and the enclosure where the stable was located. When Bo walked beside the stables, the horses started to whinny and moved to the far end of the enclosure. It was clear they considered this animal passing a danger. Bo could feel their fear and understood it. Under other circumstances, he might consider them food.

Past the stables, the group turned left and entered the facades of the mock-up town of Rebel's Revenge. There were over a hundred people standing at a distance watching the group. No one there ever thought they would see a mutant in their midst, being treated with kindness. A short block later, Hal turned toward a building and opened a door.

Bo saw this and hesitated. "Don't worry," Wind told him. "It's okay. We've got something to show you."

Bo turned and walked through the door and into a short hallway, where Hal stood waiting. Wind stepped around Bo and facing the mutant said, "Wait here for just a minute. There're a lot of people in the next room. Don't let it bother you. We've told them all about you, and they want to meet you.

In the next room, Hal was telling the rest of Rebel's Revenge that Bo was about to come in. He also told them not to make any loud noises or sudden movements. He then leaned back into the hallway and motioned for the others to enter.

As Bo walked in, he saw over seventy-five people sitting at tables scattered throughout the room. The rest filled the cafe to capacity standing around its edges. All the members of the community wanted to see the mutant when it moved around the camp. Bear stood beside the opposite wall. He wore both his pistols, but in addition, he carried a rifle.

The committee agreed Bear was to keep both sides from clashing. He told the people in the room he would shoot the first one of them making an aggressive move toward the mutant. He also assured them he would shoot Bo if he thought for even a millisecond the animal was going to harm any of them.

Bo walked into the room, which served as the main cafe for the resort. He looked at Bear and slowly walked over to the man. Slowly, he placed his hand on the M16 that Bear held and gently pushed it down. He guided it to where it was resting on the counter next to him. Bear looked at Bo who slowly shook his head from side to side. Bear released the rifle and left it lying on the counter. Bo looked around the room and saw another chalkboard. It was the one used to write the day's specials on. He walked over to the board and picked up a small piece of chalk and wrote one word "*friends*."

After only a slight hesitation, Libby rose from her seat. Bo noticed the movement and turned toward her. The young woman, softly at first, then with a growing strength began clapping. Only seconds later, others joined in. Soon everyone was on their feet, applauding the mutant standing before them.

Before reverting to a time without electricity, a time where the flip of a switch produced light, warmth and the feeling of security, some people might have seen this as trite or corny. However today, with the situation as it was, it was a possibility of hope. The main thing, everyone left in the world, was short on-hope. Hope for a future of safety-and for peace.

***

Three days had passed since Bo left to scout out the settlement over at Rollingblock. Gabriel didn't expect him back any time before tomorrow. Still, he wasn't completely comfortable relying on an animal for information even if it did what it promised before. As well, he no longer held the other one in the cells.

Another of the intelligent mutants had turned up looking for Bo. Gabriel and Manny were able to establish a type of communication with it much the same as with Bo. It appeared the other mutants were falling in line and had been a considerable help in gaining the trust of this new mutant leader. She brought a group of about twenty with her and it was clear she exercised complete control over them.

"I'm glad you trusted us enough to come here after meeting some of Bo's mutants," Gabriel said.

The mutant simply nodded.

"Would you like to eat?" He asked.

The mutant nodded again.

"Robert," he called to a man in the outer office. "Take this friend of ours and give it some food and water.

The mutant left the office to follow the human.

Manny was looking at a map of the area surrounding Rollingblock. There were a number of roads in and out of the town, which would make it a lot more difficult to contain the people there once the attack started. Even with the help of the mutants, there were numerous escape routes for anyone to use if they were trying to get away.

Manny pointed this out to Gabriel who smiled and said, "What do you think the mutants are for?"

"But look at all the roads they can use," Manny argued. "There's no way we can cover them all and still take the town even with two thousand people."

"Besides the two thousand humans, we have over two hundred mutants at our disposal. Those two hundred mutants are equal to at least a thousand humans. If we didn't have them on our side, there's no way I would even attempt this right now. If we had to worry about them as well as try to take the town, it would be entirely too risky. Also, what about that help from San Antonio you talked about the other day?"

"I wasn't going to say anything until they got here, but I've got about a thousand coming in tomorrow," Manny told him.

"A thousand!" Gabriel exclaimed. "Manny, you're outstanding. That makes over three thousand humans along with all the mutants, there's no army in the country that could resist us."

"What about all those tanks over at Camp Mabry?" Manny asked. "Have you been able to train people to drive them as well as operate the guns?"

"I think you mean Camp Manny," Gabriel answered. "I just renamed it in your honor. You gave us the edge we needed. The answer to your question is yes. I do have people trained on the tanks and the Armored Personnel Carriers. The problem with using the tanks is the terrain, and you can hear the goddamn things five miles away."

"Thanks man-my own military base and I wasn't even in the military. Makes me feel like I've done something to help out, and I think you're right. The sound could be a problem," Manny agreed. "Since there are only a couple of vehicles that might be moving around in the area, the tanks would definitely be a giveaway."

"I think we'll use mortars instead. We can lob them in from a distance and cause a hell of a lot of havoc. That ought to demoralize those assholes enough for our people and the mutants to go in and wipe 'em out."

"Wipe 'em out?" Manny questioned. "Aren't you planning on taking any prisoners?"

"Hell yes," Gabriel answered. "We need to keep gathering as many people as we can. We'll indoctrinate those we can and kill the rest. I don't want anyone left to cause us problems in the future."

Manny's people had encountered the same problem on the outskirts of San Antonio. Some of the locals formed small groups and conducted hit-and-run operations until Manny ordered his people out to perform a complete sweep of the area and kill anything that moved. Immediately, the place quieted down.

"When do you expect Bo back?" Manny asked.

"Tomorrow or the next day," Gabriel answered. "Just depends on how long it takes him to get all the information we need and then get back here. It still astounds me how far those mutants can travel in a day. They don't ever seem to get tired."

"Have you figured out the best approach to the town without being seen?" Manny questioned.

"I think so," Gabriel answered and turned toward the map to explain what he thought were the weaknesses of the town.

CHAPTER THIRTY-EIGHT

Wind accompanied Bo walking around the camp. As they strolled along, some of the residence cautiously approached them and tried to communicate with the mutant. He could only grunt in response to their greetings. Wind would tell them Bo was saying hello. Bo was really conveying that he meant no aggression toward them. It was what his kind did to let the other know there was to be no challenge over food or a mate or anything along those lines. He even had a child come up to him and offer him a flower. He knew the innocence of the young and accepted it with a sigh. Wind thanked her for him, and they continued their tour.

Wind had shown Bo almost the complete area. At the same time, he was careful not to get close to where the extra weapons and ammo were stored or where the members of the group trained in shooting or martial arts. He knew these things should remain secret for the time being.

Eventually, they made their way back to the headquarters office. Hal, David, Spyder, and Bear were all sitting around a large table talking. Hal stood when Wind and Bo entered the room and motioned to a couple of empty seats around the table. "Have a seat, gents."

The chalkboard from the restaurant laid on the table. "Do you feel like writing or answering some questions?" Hal asked, looking at Bo.

Bo shook his head yes. He figured this was what all the good treatment was leading to. Now he would find out what these humans really wanted.

"Do you remember where you lived before this change happened to you?" David asked.

Bo shook his head yes again.

"Where was it?" David again spoke.

He took the piece of chalk lying on the board and wrote, *"marble falls ."*

"Marble Falls," David read the name aloud. "Then you're from this area."

He nodded.

"Do you have family around here?" Hal asked.

He shook his head no and wrote, *"dead."*

"All of them?" Wind asked.

He nodded.

"Damn," Wind responded. "Sorry to hear that."

"Where have you been living since the world and you changed?" Bear asked.

"Near Austin."

"Bo," Spyder started, "Bear and I were over near the south side of Austin a couple of weeks ago, and we saw two of your kind meeting with some men at a house over there. Was that you?"

Bo knew these humans had seen him, and the one with him when they returned from contacting other groups. He also knew they were sure it was him; otherwise they wouldn't have asked the question.

He shook his head yes and wrote, *"treat my pack good too."*

Then Hal said, "We've heard gangs have taken over most of Austin. Do you know if it's true?"

460

He nodded. *"Most parts."* He waited for the inevitable question-was he a part of them, but it didn't come.

Instead, David asked, "Do you live in Austin or outside the city?"

"Outside"

"Is there any way us humans and your kind can live without fighting and killing each other?" Hal asked.

Bo was shocked at this line of questions. These humans weren't trying to gain information about his pack. Instead, they wanted to live in peace. He wrote, *"maybe."*

Spyder was the next to speak, "If we leave you and your kind alone, will you leave us alone?"

"My pack yes others don't know." He then erased the writing and wrote *"must go soon."*

Hal read it and asked, "You must go soon?"

He nodded.

"When," Hal asked.

"Tomorrow."

"You have to leave tomorrow?" Wind asked.

Again, he nodded. Now he would find out if he was a prisoner or not.

Hal looked at Wind. "Go get Dr. Hamilton and ask him to come here please."

Wind got up and left the room.

"Would you like a beer?" Spyder asked Bo.

Bo shook his head and wrote *"water."*

Spyder went over to a bottled water dispenser and poured Bo a glass. Then realizing what he was doing asked, "Not to insult you, but can you drink from this glass?"

461

Bo nodded and took the glass. He leaned forward and put the glass almost completely in his mouth and leaning back, poured the entire contents down his throat in one move. With this done, he sat the glass on the table as Wind returned with Dr. Hamilton.

"Doc," Hal called out. "Just the man we're looking for."

The doctor sat in an empty chair. "What can I do for you?" He said as he settled in.

"Our friend needs to leave tomorrow. Is he able to travel without causing himself damage?" Hal asked.

Dr. Hamilton looked at Bo and then back to Hal. "I don't know much about their physiology, but as far as I can tell, he can travel as far as any human. His healing abilities are remarkable."

"That's what we needed to know, Doc." Hal said. Then to Bo, "Is there anything you need from us for your trip?"

Bo was astonished with this development. After a moment's hesitation, he wrote *"home cooked meal, Sandy?"*

Hal started laughing, "She's a good cook, isn't she. I think we can talk her into fixing something."

"Seriously, isn't there anything we can do for you or supply you with?" Bear asked.

After thinking a moment Bo wrote, *"many rolls gauze."*

"You've got 'em," Dr. Hamilton assured him. "I'll have them ready for when you leave tomorrow.

Night was descending on the valley, and all the humans agreed it was time to go to their respective homes.

462

"Bo, you come on over to my house, and we'll see about a home cooked meal for you. You too, Bear," Hal said. Then, after agreeing to meet the next morning, he, Bear, and Bo said good night and left.

The next morning a small group led by Wind came to the medical treatment room at eight o'clock in the morning. Sandy brought an extra steak she cooked the night before. Dr. Hamilton had previously brought in about fifty rolls of gauze in a sack, which he gave to Bo. He opened the sack, took out one of the rolls, pulled a long strip of it out and tore it from the roll. This he put on and tied around his neck. Except for its width, it looked like a white bandana.

Seeing the gauze around his neck, David grinned at Bo and said, "Looks good on you man."

Bo grunted and nodded. Sandy gave him a sack with the steak in it along with some vegetables she had. "Just in case you want something to eat on the road."

Wind approached the mutant and patted him on his shoulder. "You're welcome here anytime."

"I agree," Hal said. "I hope you'll remember you have friends here. We'd all be happy for you to come back any time."

Bo looked at each of the small group and nodded as he gave a series of grunts and growls. His gaze rested on Wind and he took a step forward. Raised his massive right paw of a hand and placed it over his heart. Then he reached forward, placed it over Wind's heart, and gave a ferocious growl.

Wind nodded. "Brothers," he said.

463

The mutant turned and trotted away. The group watched him leave secure in the idea they had made an important friend. A minute later, he disappeared over a hill heading toward Rollingblock, and the humans returned to the office.

CHAPTER THIRTY-NINE

It was ten days since Bo returned from his scouting trip. Almost immediately upon returning, he met the leader of the new mutant pack who arrived during his absence. After a series of grunts, woofs and hoots, Bo wrote, *"Gail,"* on presentation paper Gabriel had on an easel.

"She from TX Panhandle ~ no food ~ come here."

"She came here from the Texas Panhandle?" Gabriel asked.

Bo nodded and wrote, *"packs send her here."*

Bo preferred the chalk and board he used at the other location because his tendency was to rip the presentation paper with the point of the pencil lead. This, he kept to himself. He hadn't made up his mind about these two separate groups of humans. He still had things to think about and consider.

When Gabriel started asking about the group of humans at Rollingblock, Bo told him about how many lived there. He wrote that they were armed and well protected. When he heard about the report from Gail about the militia compound, he warned Gabriel this group seemed to be more of a threat than those at Rollingblock.

When questioned as to why he thought this, he took a long time writing on the paper. When he finished Gabriel read,

"Humans stay in area don't travel not looking for fight lake humans looking for fight sound like army"

"He's got a point," Manny said.

Gail stepped up to the easel, and when she picked up the pencil and started writing, both humans were shocked.

"I never thought of trying that with her," Gabriel said.

"Me neither," Manny agreed. "This could have made things a lot easier."

The two humans looked at what Gail wrote. It said, *"big guns there trained army problem for you soon they worry about other humans kill now."*

"Do you mean they're planning on attacking the humans at Rollingblock?" Manny asked Gail.

She nodded yes, following Bo's actions.

"Do you know when?" Gabriel asked.

This time Gail moved her head from side to side indicating she didn't know the answer to his question. She wrote, *"very soon."*

"How soon-a week?" Gabriel asked.

Again Gail shook her head no, added *"er"* to the word *"soon"* and erased the word *"very."*

"Sooner," Gabriel read.

After only a couple of seconds, hesitation Gabriel said, "Get all my group leaders in here-now."

*** *** ***

Gabriel had all his group leaders around him. "Get your people ready to leave tonight. I want all the ammo each person can carry. I want at least two mortar teams with each group and no less than twenty mortar rounds with each team.

466

We'll leave around nine o'clock tonight." Moving to the large map on the wall, he said, "The group we're after will be coming from the south. They'll be heavily armed and trained in combat."

Looking back at the leaders he asked, "Each of your troops have the gray vests to identify them-right?"

Each of the group leaders nodded. Each of the troops wore a gray bulletproof vest over green coveralls, which identified the members from their enemies.

"We'll take pick-up trucks to this road," Gabriel indicated an intersection about ten miles south of Rollingblock. "We'll wait here until they pass by and fall in behind and to the east of them. I want a truck loaded with ammo and a truck with MREs with us.

Bo and Gail squatted in the corner of the room, watching as Gabriel held the briefing. He turned to the mutants and said, "Can one of you send two of your pack over to the compound where they are?"

Bo nodded, and Gail stood up.

"One should stay and watch them as they move out; the other will come and tell you when they start moving. That way we'll know when to look for them. I want no surprises."

Bo nodded and this time grunted. Then he gave out a series of guttural sounds, and Gail walked out of the room.

Gabriel returned to his group leaders. "Have everyone at the southern city limits on Interstate thirty-five at eight o'clock tonight. Load them in every vehicle we have so we can run a convoy through San Marcos and over to the staging point."

He looked at all the group leaders, nodded, and said, "Dismissed."

Manny looked at Gabriel, "I'll get going and meet my people coming from San Antonio and meet you at the city limits."

"Good," Gabriel answered. "Stop by the warehouse and get enough of the vests to pass out among them. We don't want to be shooting each other."

Bo went to where the packs waited. Gail had sent two of her pack with instructions for one of them to return with news of the enemy's movement and for the other to follow them as they proceeded. Bo issued a series of vocalizations imparting exactly what he wanted all the mutants to do.

CHAPTER FORTY

Hal and Sandy were sitting in their recliners and eating off wooden TV trays when they heard a soft thudding on their front door.

"Wonder who that is," Sandy said looking at Hal.

"There's one sure way to find out," Hal answered grinning.

"Kiss my ass, honey," she said as she got up to answer the door.

"There she goes, getting all romantic again," Hal said, his grin even bigger.

Sandy held her middle extended toward him as she opened the front door and let out a screech.

A mutant stood in the doorway with a piece of white gauze tied around his neck.

Immediately, Hal was up and grabbed a rifle sitting beside his chair. Even though he couldn't see what the problem was, he knew something was wrong by Sandy's actions and her squeal.

She backed up toward the center of the room, and the mutant slowly followed her in. Hal raised his rifle and aimed at the animal in front of him.

The mutant slowly raised his hands in a sign of surrender. That was when Sandy overcame her surprise enough to notice the gauze around its neck. "Hold on Hal," she said and pointing she continued, "look."

Hal didn't recognize the mutant, but he saw the gauze and lowered the rifle to his hip, still keeping it pointed at the creature.

The animal slowly lowered its arms and held out one hand. In it was a folded piece of paper. Hal took the paper and unfolding it, found a note. Judging by the scrawl, it was from Bo. *"attack in morning from south and east will help"*

Hal looked up at the animal before him. He could tell it wasn't comfortable being here with humans and was getting antsy. He turned the note over and wrote *"Thanks, will be ready."* He refolded the note and gave it back to the mutant. As he did, he patted the animal on the shoulder. This action seemed to surprise it, and it flinched away from his touch.

"Open the door," he told Sandy.

She opened it and stepped back.

Without ceremony, the mutant left the cabin and disappeared into the dark.

"We're about to be attacked," Hal said. "You get David, Spyder, and Wind. I'll get the rest. We have to hurry. There's not much time.

In less than fifteen minutes, the leadership of Rebel's Revenge along with Ron, Barbara, and Keith were in the office. Ron, Barbara, and Keith were at David and Cindy's cabin when Sandy knocked at the door and informed them of an immediate meeting at the office.

"We've got a serious problem," Hal said. "Bo sent a message saying we were going to be attacked tomorrow."

"Bo sent a message?" Barbara questioned.

"It was written on paper and carried by another mutant," Hal explained. "It said we were going to be attacked tomorrow from the south and east."

Ron and Barbara looked at each other. Both were sure who the attackers were.

"Are you sure it was from Bo?" Wind asked.

"It was either from him or a five year old who has a mutant with a gauze neckerchief for a pet," Hal answered.

"We need to get everyone moving," Bear said.

"It's probably the militia over by the lake,"

Everyone looked at Barbara.

"We were sent here to spy against all of you here," Ron added.

Before anyone knew what was happening, Spyder and Bear had their pistols out and pointed at Ron and Barbara.

"Hang on Spyder-Bear," Hal ordered. Then to Ron he asked, "What did you tell 'em?"

"Nothing," Ron answered. "After a couple of weeks here, both of us knew there was nothing back there for either of us."

"When our contact met us, we told him we weren't coming back, and if we ever saw him here again, we'd shoot him," Barbara answered.

"Bullshit," Spyder answered taking a step forward.

"It's not bullshit," Ron argued. "Neither of us could condone their practice of slavery. We decided to stay here, hoping to have a quiet life."

"Why didn't you tell us what was going on?" Spyder asked still not convinced they were telling the truth.

Bear holstered his weapon and nodded.

"Now I understand your story when we first met," Hal said. "There were some things that didn't make sense-some things simply didn't go together."

471

"We're not proud about how we got here, or what we did," Barbara said. "But we're willing to help any way we can.

"Okay," Bear said, "I understand loyalty to those you have lived with before and moved away from-that's admirable. Now, what can you tell us that will help in this situation? We can talk about all the other stuff later. Now we need information about how to defend ourselves."

"They have automatic and semi-automatic rifles, side arms, hand grenades, and mortars. There are around fifteen hundred of them and God only knows how many slaves or workers, as they call them. They may even run the workers ahead of the troops-use them as fodder."

"The note said we would be attacked tomorrow. We need to figure out what we're gonna do?" Hal said no one in particular. "I'm open to suggestions."

"How many claymores do we have?" Bear asked.

"Dozens," David answered. "We can circle the camp with them fifteen to twenty yards apart."

"That's enough to run a strong line along the south and east sides of the camp," Hal said.

"I've got a question," Spyder said.

The others looked at him and waited.

"If the message was from Bo, then what makes us think this militia is the ones attacking us? Bear and I saw Bo as he walked up to some armed men in Austin. Isn't it possible it could be someone from there?"

"Actually, it doesn't really matter who it is," Bear said. "Our actions will be the same if we're to survive. We need to set up skirmish lines behind the

472

claymores and everyone should be completely supplied with ammunition and hand grenades."

"We only have until sunrise to get ready," Hal said. "Start getting all of your people out and set them up. Get them ready to defend the resort area. Set the claymores up along the river so they can be set off with tripwires and since we can't use the hand triggers, run some lines back so we can set them off by pulling the wire. Place the others along the far side of the road beside the area and set them up the same way."

Everyone started moving. Soon people were out getting the message to everyone in the resort area.

In less than an hour, every member of the community was quietly and cautiously setting up perimeter defenses.

CHAPTER FORTY-ONE

As the sun peeked over the range of hills to the east, a red flair popped high into the sky. Immediately, all the gang's mortars erupted, taking the militia by surprise. There were two lines of explosions running north and west of a point located outside the village of Rollingblock.

Gabriel's orders were that the mortars were to start with the first red flair and continue firing as rapidly as possible until the second flair went up. He figured this would more than soften their enemy up. Then every man and woman was to charge the militia lines. When the battle was over, they could return and retrieve the mortars and extra ammo left behind. If, for some unforeseen reason, they were forced to retreat, they would have supplies when they moved back.

Before they knew what was happening, the militia had deadly explosions erupting all around them. Not only did the mortars hit their targets but flying rocks, branches, and falling trees took their toll as well. After the initial mortar attack, it only took a couple of minutes for General Clark's subordinate commanders to regroup and fight back.

In some areas, the militia was able to use their mortars in return before the gang members moved too close for them to be effective. In those places, they tore the gang members to shreds only to find them replaced by people from beside them. Even outmanned, the militia was better trained for combat situations. They also had comparable weapons to their attackers. The militia fired automatic and semi-automatic weapons along with their mortars when possible.

Buck knew General Clark focused the main contingent of his force on the east-west line where he had placed about a thousand troops. The general wanted the people in the resort to experience the most force from a frontal attack by approaching across the river that ran along the southern end of the area. This way the defenders were more apt to draw their own forces from the sides to reinforce the fight there. However, the attack wasn't from the resort. It came from beside them.

Unlike the scouts, those at the river were simply ground personnel. They were good fighters but had shown no special abilities. They were trained in combat situations and proved a formidable force but would be in the open and stood no chance of winning the battle. The general positioned himself near the center of his command, where the two lines met, and his personal guards formed a perimeter around him.

***

Buck and his platoon of scouts found themselves surrounded as the militia troops on both sides were massacred by the gang from behind. Much as with the fighters at the river, they were four hundred ground troops and proved little trouble for a force twice their size.

Buck had his platoon in the line running north and south. They had only been able to regroup and fire their mortars a couple of times before the gang members were too close for the weapons to be effective. He and his scouts were the best trained militia members in close combat. Each man and woman in the unit worked as if he or she were of one mind. Because of this, they were here to perform a flanking maneuver and close the door behind the target area while a frontal assault happened.

Buck looked where Major Jenkins and the second platoon were. The major directed his squad leaders where he wanted their fields of fire. As if one, three explosions erupted around the group of men huddled behind a rock ledge. When the smoke and dust cleared, Buck knew he was in charge of the platoon-the Major and his group lay dead with pieces scattered in the immediate area.

He ordered a squad to cover the area left undefended by the explosions. In front of him, he saw the movement of troops among the trees. Even though he couldn't make out individuals, he knew his people were outnumbered.

"Watch your shots," he barked, "Make every one count." Then as a second thought, he called out, "Fix bayonets."

Every man and woman of the scouts carried bayonets on their belts and knew how to use them. As well, they carried a second knife on their belts or strapped to their legs. Each also carried four grenades and a garrotte as part of their combat uniforms. These were the best fighters of the militia.

Realizing there was no chance for success and unwilling to surrender, Buck passed the order for all the scouts to charge their attackers. If they were to die, they would take as many down with them as possible. When the fighting was over, the scouts had taken at least four of the enemy for every one of them as they went down.

Buck ran out of ammunition. After breaking the stock of his rifle, while using it as a club against a gang member, he used his knife. He took four more of the enemy down before a bullet slammed into his chest. As he died, he saw the enemy moving toward General Clark's headquarters.

***

Gabriel, Manny, and their elite fighters were also in the center position of two lines. Their plan was to do all the damage they could from a distance before having to encounter the militia in close combat. They knew the more damage they could inflict from a distance, the fewer casualties they would suffer in close.

Both of the gang's lines charged when a second red flair went up. The east west line only held about thirty minutes before the members of the militia either ran trying to escape, or dropped their weapons and surrendered on the spot.

The standing order from Gabriel was there was to be no prisoners. The militia members were killed where they stood or as they surrendered or attempted to escape.

Gabriel and Manny positioned their elite fighters moving just ahead of them as they met General Clark's personal guards. Here, the fighting was almost equal on both sides until gang members converged on the location from both sides. After almost an hour of fighting, General Clark had one of his officers' hold up a piece of white cloth tied to a long tree branch.

Gabriel called for a cease-fire and waited to see what the other man was going to do. With the officer still holding the flag, General Clark walked out of the house he was using as a headquarters. Both men looked around them at the bodies of both sides lying around them.

"My name is General Roland Clark of the New South Militia," General Clark held himself at attention.

"So," Manny asked, "is that supposed to mean something to us?"

Gabriel put his hand on Manny's shoulder. "Let the man talk," he said facing the general.

"I wish to discuss terms of surrender," General Clark informed the men.

"Surrender or die," Gabriel responded. "There's nothing difficult about it."

"I need to know if my people will be allowed to live upon surrender," the general said.

"I can tell you that you will never get back to that house alive if you don't surrender now," Gabriel told him and then lit a cigarette. "The choice is yours."

General Clark thought about what the man said for a few seconds, then to the other officer said, "Go back and tell everyone to lay down their weapons and come out."

"Smart move, General," Gabriel said as the other man left to deliver the message.

Gabriel nodded at Manny who followed the messenger.

All the people in the former headquarters slowly walked out of the building with their hands on their heads. When the last prisoner exited the building with one of the gang members following her, Manny yelled, "Fire". Immediately, a squad armed with M16s opened up. In less than three seconds, all the prisoners lay dead.

CHAPTER FORTY-TWO

While the confrontation between the commanders of the two forces took place, Bo and a large group of mutants entered Rebel's Revenge from the north.

A contingent of defenders, headed by Keith and Amanda lay scattered among the bushes and trees forming a defensive line along the north end of the resort. Before them lay a large open area, which was formerly cleared as a recreation area within the confines of the stagecoach trail.

Two mutants emerged from the bushes and trees on the far side of the open area. Both walked slowly with their arms raised and wore white bandanas.

"Is that Bo?" Keith asked Amanda.

"I don't know," Amanda answered. "I'm not sure. It looks like it."

Keith rose and took a couple of steps toward the animals moving toward them. "Stop right there," Keith ordered.

Both animals stopped and dropped their arms to their sides.

"If one of you is Bo then raise your hand," Keith instructed.

"Raise your hand?" Amanda questioned.

"If it's Bo, he'll understand. If not, then something's wrong."

One of the mutants raised his right arm in response to the order.

"Stay where you are, Bo," Keith told him. "There are mines in front of you."

Bo grunted, then turned around and issued a series of growling and whooping sounds. When he finished, he and the other mutant began walking toward Keith and Amanda.

Keith started to protest. At the same time, Bo turned directly to his left, walked a couple of steps and then turned again. The other mutant followed his lead exactly. It was obvious they were able to find their way through the anti-personnel mines with no problem.

A small army of mutants emerged from the trees, every one of them wearing white gauze tied around their necks. It looked like there were at least a hundred of them now all making their way past the mines.

Keith looked back to find all his people rising to their feet. None of them had ever seen this many mutants in one place, and it was obvious none of them were comfortable with what they saw.

When Bo reached their location, he handed a folded piece of paper to Keith. Looking up the young man grinned and said, "Follow me." To the humans he said, "Stay where you are, I'll be back shortly-Amanda, you're in charge."

In a couple of minutes, all the mutants except for two traversed the mines and now trotted to follow their leaders and Keith through Sagebrush and into the main area of Rebel's Revenge. Two of the animals remained on the other side of the minefield. In a couple of seconds, they drifted back and disappeared into the woods.

Keith instructed Bo to leave the other mutants in the *ghost town* and to follow him to where Hal was.

Bo conveyed to Gail she was to keep the rest of the mutants on the main street until he returned. When he turned to follow Keith, she was wailing orders to the rest of the mutants who now almost completely filled the street.

When Keith approached, Hal's jaw dropped as he saw the mutant accompanying him. "What the hell's going on?" He asked.

"Bo and some other mutants just arrived from the north," Keith said with a grin, "a lot of mutants-all friends of Bo's." Keith was obviously excited and speaking rapidly.

"Now hold on Keith," Hal said. "Calm down and tell me what's happening."

"I told you," Keith answered. "There must be over a hundred of 'em back there in Sagebrush." Then remembering the note, he held it out to Hal.

"Here to help," the note said. Hal continued reading, *"where u want us in case."*

A big grin spread across Hal's face. "Do you know where they will attack us?" He asked.

Bo nodded and moved a map of the resort lay on a picnic table. With his finger, he traced a line along the river to the south and along the road to the east.

"Do you have any idea how many of them there are?"

The map was covered with plastic and Bo picked up a grease pencil lying beside it. He wrote,*"2000+."*

Hal turned to the four messengers he used for communications. He directed them to contact Spyder, Bear, David, and Ron and tell them reinforcements would be arriving soon and to hold their fire. They were mutants and friends of Bo's, and they would already know what to do. The messengers left with the instructions.

"Keith you're gonna have to hold your position in case they try to come at us from the North," Hal said.

"No problem," Keith said and turned to leave.

Before he could go, Bo grabbed him by the arm and growled.

"Where will you put your... ," Hal hesitated. He didn't like calling them mutants, and he damned sure didn't want to insult the creature before him. "Friends," He finished.

Bo traced lines running along the north, south and east of the resort. He also pointed at the corral where all their horses where. He pointed at the cliffs to the west running his claw in a line along them.

Hal nodded. "How many of your friends are here?"

Bo picked up a grease pencil and wrote on the plastic covered map, *"200+ another reads."*

Hal looked at the animal in confusion. "I don't understand," he said.

Bo continued writing, *"understands like me."*

"He must be talking about the other one that came up with him," Keith surmised.

Bo slammed a large paw on the young man's shoulder almost dropping him to his knees and nodded.

"There's another one of your kind, here with you that can understand us?" Hal asked.

Again, Bo nodded.

"Go get him," Hal told Keith.

"It's a *her*," Keith informed him.

"I don't give a shit," Hal answered, just bring it here. Besides, how you know if it's a *her*?"

"She has bumps," Keith answered with a smile, holding his cupped hands up as if supporting two breasts. Without waiting for a reply, he trotted away toward the Sagebrush area.

Hal shook his head in disbelief when Bo nudged him. Hal looked up to see the mutant nodding in the affirmative and holding his cupped paws up to his chest.

Hal grinned, "Shit, not you too," he said and turned back to the map.

***

Gabriel gave the order for his people to go and gather everything they left behind when they charged the militia. He wanted all the weapons and ammunition they had left brought to their present location and equally distributed. Then he gathered his key members around him where he spread a map before him.

He looked at the people around him. They had won a hard fought battle. He recognized the mixture of fatigue and excitement on each of their faces. Even though tired, they each yearned to get back in battle and achieve their goal. They also knew the battle before them would be twice as hard as the one they just fought.

"I think this General Clark had the right idea," Gabriel explained, "except, we need to hit them from three sides. We'll hit them from the south, east, and north. There are cliffs to the west, and there's no way to get at them from there." Pointing to the map, he continued, "The first flair starts the attack from the south, the second flair from the east, and the third one means come in from the north. Now, there'll be a long time between the second and third. I want all their attention on those two areas before we move in from the north."

"Excuse me, Gabe," Manny interrupted the briefing, but you need to hear this."

"What, Manny," Gabriel answered plainly irritated at the intrusion. "I'm in the middle of a strategy session."

Manny motioned him over and whispered something in his ear when he got there.

Gabriel stepped back with an astonished look. "All of them?"

Manny nodded in confirmation, "All of them," he repeated.

"Goddamn," Gabriel said in a hushed voice. Recovering his composure he asked, "Where the hell are they?"

"Almost all of them are simply gone," Manny answered. "There are some that have the tubes crushed."

"Crushed?" Gabriel repeated. Then after a second's hesitation, "Where the hell are all those fucking mutants?"

"Gone," Manny answered, "Looks like they either wrecked or carried off all but three of the mortars while we were fighting the militia."

"We still have three working?" Gabriel asked.

"Yep, that's all," Manny answered. "However, there's one part that's not so bad."

"What would that be?" Gabriel asked.

"All they carried off was the tubes of the mortars. They left the base plates. They're no good like that." Manny explained. "They can't be used by the enemy."

"How many people do we still have?" Gabriel asked.

"At least twenty-five hundred," Manny estimated.

Gabriel thought for a couple of minutes. "This changes nothing," he said. "We still have three mortars and all the rest of our weapons and ammunition. It may take a little longer, but we can still get the job done."

He turned back to his Group Leaders and the map.

***

Keith returned with Gail and one other mutant. Hal looked at the animal but didn't question his presence there. He figured the other leader had a good reason for it being there.

Hal asked Bo a few questions while they waited for Gail to arrive. He found out what Gail's name was, and it was an organized gang out of Austin, which attacked the militia. Bo also wrote the words *"yes"* and *"no"* in the top corners of the map they were using. Hal figured it was a faster and easier way to answer some of his questions than having to write the answer each time. There was no doubt; he

486

was gaining a greater respect for this ally before him.

Hal faced the female mutant and said, "Gail, we're glad to have you here with us. You and your pack are welcomed allies."

Gail opened her right paw, raised it to her mouth and then motioned toward Hal with it.

Hal looked at her and said, "I don't... I'm sorry, I don't under... "

"It means *thank you* in sign language," Bear said from the side as he and Spyder approached the group.

Hal looked at Gail who nodded.

"I didn't know you could sign," Hal said.

"I can't," Bear answered. "I just know a couple of the most common signs."

Hal looked back at Bo and asked, "Do you know if they will attack us the same as the others were going to-from the south and east?"

Bo pointed to the word no on the map and shook his head. Then on a blank space on the bottom he wrote, *"maybe north too."*

Gail took the grease pencil from Bo, erased the word *"maybe"* and wrote below the other two words, *"saw plans."*

Hal looked at Gail and asked, "You saw their plans, and they're coming from the north too?"

Gail nodded and pointed to *"yes."*

"How many mines do we have out there, Keith?"

"About thirty," Keith answered. "But by watching all the mutants when they got here, they must not be very well hidden. All of them came

487

through the field like they were sitting on top of the ground."

Hal looked at Bo for confirmation.

Hal thought for a second then asked, "Do you think a human can see them?"

Bo grunted twice, shook his head and pointed to *"no."*

Gail snapped her head to the left and looked across the river from their location, paused a couple of seconds, then quickly scrawled, *"Fight now."*

Bo gave her a series of vocalizations and she turned and ran toward Sagebrush. The mutant accompanying her stayed at Bo's side and Hal figured he was a messenger between the two animals.

Bo could see the movement of humans across the river. He moved to near the left end of the cabins. The other humans tried to mass in the trees, about fifty yards on the other side of the road there.

Bo returned to Hal, Bear, and Spyder. On the map he pointed where the other force was.

"About fifty yards from the claymores," Hal said.

Bo heard three thumping sounds in the distance, let out a growl and stepped behind the nearest cabin. In a couple of seconds three explosions erupted short and wide of the resort. Bo pointed to three locations on the map and growled. Hal quickly called to three messengers. He gave each messenger a different set of map coordinates. Each of the messengers, in turn, went to a location where three mortar crews waited for instructions.

In a couple of minutes, each of the mortars fired two shells in return. Since Hal had no people forward of their location to direct fire, he was forced to wait and see if they possibly hit any of the other locations.

After a few seconds, three more shells landed. Again, they were wide and short of the area-but getting closer.

***

Cindy, Deborah, and three other adults had all the children of the camp with them, crammed in the small chapel near the center of the occupied area. Each carried two rifles and two side arms and stood guard at the windows. Deborah was to keep all the weapons loaded, and the older children were in charge of taking care of the younger ones, including trying to keep them calm if possible. The camp would have to be overrun and defeated before an enemy could approach the chapel. Inside, the occupants could hear the noise of the mortars as the enemy adjusted their fire.

Keith re-joined Amanda and explained what was happening when the two mutants again appeared on the far side of the minefield. They stepped out of the trees and waited until Keith stood up and waived to them. Immediately, they turned back and waived at the trees and another group of mutants emerged.

Like the ones before, all word white gauze tied around their necks. This group was considerably smaller than the first. There were only about fifteen or so this time. Like the other group, they passed through the mines with no trouble.

By the time they reached Keith, Gail joined him. She made a series of noises at one of the beasts and listened as it communicated with her in a long series of grunts and growls. She issued a series of sounds of her own, and all the other mutants except three departed in different directions.

Gail turned to Keith and after she grunted, pointed to herself and with the other hand pointed toward the front of the resort.

"You're going to see Hal?" Keith asked.

She nodded and growled. She again pointed to herself and pointed at the ground at her feet.

Amanda smiled, "Then you're coming back," she said.

Gail nodded and held the young woman's gaze a second before she left.

"I knew that," Keith said.

Amanda looked at him and smiled.

***

"What's taking so goddamn long?" Gabriel asked.

"We have to relay the information from the front lines back to where the mortars are," Manny answered. "Because of the hills, if our people get close enough to see the compound, those assholes over there shoot 'em-not to mention they have mortars too. They almost hit one of our teams a little bit ago-they're just as blind as we are, and we're lucky for it."

A man walked in the door to speak to Gabriel. "We finally hit one of the buildings," he said.

490

"We're relaying the coordinates to the other two mortar teams."

"Now we can blow them out of existence," Gabriel said.

The mortar crews received the information and made their adjustments when the first of mortar rounds hit. They were followed by five or six explosions at each mortar site. It appeared the resort had also zeroed in on them. Only one mortar fired in return, hitting another of the cabins.

Again, another rain of shells came in to all the locations, and which spelled the end of the mortar use by Gabriel and his army.

Gabriel stepped out of his headquarters and even before the messenger reached him, he knew what had happened. He looked at the only mortar not used to bomb the enemy.

"Send up the flair," he ordered. "We'll get killed if we sit back here and wait."

The second red flair went up and swung under a parachute when the gang to the south and east rushed forward.

***

Bear, Spyder, Wind, and David stood with Hal at their headquarters when the first wave of humans rushed from the trees and approached the river screaming.

"Take your places, men," Hal said.

Before the men turned to leave, Bear said, "Gents, it's time to get mean-I'm serious. Take a lesson from our mutant friends. Do what you have to do, give no quarter-you'll get none. You're gonna get bloody, now get right down mean-junkyard dog mean."

Each of them gave him a grim look and quickly ran to their assigned location. When Bear looked at Bo, the mutant stared hard at him. It growled, nodded, and headed to where Spyder and Wind had gone.

Bear looked at Hal who held his hand out, "We'll see you later man," Hal said.

"Count on it," Bear answered and headed off.

Some of the members went out the night before and set claymores on the far side of the river. When the gang members set off the trip wires, they tore gaping holes in the lines of the aggressors. Reserves, from behind and to the side of the front line, quickly filled the holes in the lines. It became clear very soon there would be nothing easy or quick about a victory-whichever side won.

On the east side, one of the mortars continued lobbing rounds. The enemy was too close in front of it for it to be effective there, so it was dropping rounds out on the troops trying to advance across the river. The Rebel's Revenge's mortar crew there saw what the other was doing, and using hand signals with a spotter at the end of the cabins, did the same thing in reverse. Both mortar crews were effective with their deadly crossfire.

CHAPTER FORTY-THREE

As mortars hammered Gabriel's lines, he knew the only thing they could do was get close enough so the mortars were useless against them. "Keep 'em moving," he ordered. "We've gotta overrun the bastards."

Both he and Manny relayed orders through messengers to the group leaders who pushed the people under them as hard as they possibly could. The invading group to the east was close enough to cause the first mortar to stop. As soon as the shelling stopped, the *rebel's* of Rebel's Revenge opened up with their personal weapons.

By the time the groups of gang members made it through the claymores and close enough to stop the other mortar, they were reinforced by the last of their reserves. The rest of the reserves were where the two lines met. This was the location Bear and his scouts defense. From a defensive standpoint, they could best defend the location by the use of hand grenades as the enemy exited the trees running along the east or the trees on the far side of the river. They would use rifles if the enemy got near the base of the small hill the resort sat on, and then use everything they had if they were in danger of being overrun.

This location was the easiest to defend of the entire perimeter even though it covered a large area. Bear was sure his scouts could handle anything short of armor coming at them. He also placed claymores on the slope of the hill with instructions they weren't to be tripped until the enemy fought their way there. He wanted the side of the hill coated with enemy hiding from his people's fire before they pulled the wires and set off the claymores.

Spyder and Wind had the largest and most difficult area to defend. They were along the eastern perimeter with Bo and about seventy-five mutants. The area was long with trees close to the opposite side of the road about fifty yards in front of them.

The humans were in fighting holes surrounded by sandbags, their ammunition and grenades with them. The mutants were behind some of the resort buildings where they waited in case the gang members got close enough the rebels had to fight them in close combat. If it came to hand-to-hand fighting the mutants were to circle the gang members trapping them between themselves and the rebels.

Approximately one hundred mutants covered the northwest corner and west side. They were to kill any human coming near them. Only another mutant was to approach the area, and the humans of Rebel's Revenge knew to stay away. If needed, another mutant could go get them.

When the gang to the east started their attack on Rebel's Revenge, they had approximately five hundred members, but when they finally made it through the mortars and claymore mines, their numbers were reduced by half. Now, only about two hundred fifty faced troops in fighting holes, which knew how to fight and knew the terrain.

On the southern end where Gabriel put a little over a thousand of his troops, the blood bath began.

Gabriel had two working .50cal machine guns and moved them to where he could spray the area with deadly fire.

Bear heard the familiar sound of the machine gun and motioned his long-time friend Ben over. He told Ben of his plan to defend the area. He also told Ben it would be up to him to trigger the claymores if they were in danger of being overrun. Bear patted the man on the shoulder then, staying low, ran behind a cabin and went to retrieve a weapon from his house. Meanwhile, the scouts kept shooting every one of the enemy presenting themselves in their line of fire.

Bear retrieved the M40A1 sniper rifle from the cabin along with the fifty rounds in a pouch. Making his way behind some of the buildings, he climbed a ladder to the roof of the headquarters building. Using the peak of the roof as a support and lying along the slope away from the enemy, he sighted in. His first shot snapped the machine gunner's head back, dropping him instantly.

He sighted in on the second machine gun emplacement. This shot took the man just below his nose. Turning back to the first location, he saw they had replaced the man and the machine gun was again spraying the area. Bear sighted on his target and was again deadly accurate.

As he returned to the second location, he felt a tug on his leg. Looking down, he saw David who carried an M79 grenade launcher. "Can I reach 'em with this?" David asked.

"I don't see why not," Bear answered.

David crawled up beside him, loaded a grenade in the weapon and took aim. The first grenade went past its mark. "It's been a while," he said grinning.

"If you got this here," Bear said, "I need to get back to my people."

"Go on," David answered. "When I finish here, I'll check on Spyder. The river must have been too deep for 'em. No one has come at us over there."

"See ya later," Bear said and scrambled to the ladder leaving the sniper rifle on the roof with the bag of shells. He didn't need it down on the ground.

When he got back to where Ben lay, holding a bunch of wires he asked, "How's it going?"

"Just about to set the claymores off," Ben answered.

"Not yet," Bear said. "Let 'em bunch up some more on the side of the hill first."

Only ten or eleven of the gang had been able to avoid the deadly fire and made it to the slope of the hill. Bear could no longer hear the machine guns firing. "David got 'em."

"Got who?" Ben asked him.

"The machine gun emplacements," Bear answered. "He was using a grenade launcher."

***

David fired, and it looked as though he almost hit the machine gun itself. When the smoke and dust cleared from the explosion, he saw two more men working to put the weapon back into operation. He fired another grenade with deadly accuracy. This time when the smoke and debris cleared, the

496

weapon itself was gone. It looked like both guns were out of commission.

He scanned the area and noticed a group trying to circle their defenses where his people were. Still carrying the grenade launcher, he climbed off the building and hurried take control of his people.

His troops took the gang by surprise, and it only took a couple of minutes to send them back from where they came. He handed Amber, the leader of his weapons squad, the grenade launcher. "Keep your eyes open here. Just don't let anyone get by. I've gotta get over to Spyder's location. That's where the main push is."

"Don't worry boss, Amber said. "We'll take care of it."

David arrived beside Spyder in time to hear a massive explosion from Bear's location. "There went the claymores," Spyder said.

"I wouldn't have wanted to be in front of that shit," David answered.

Both men were firing at the now rapidly advancing gang members. Spyder grabbed Wind by the shoulders and shouted in his ear, "Go tell Bear we're about to be overrun here. Tell him to watch his six. When they get through us, he's vulnerable from the back."

"I know you're just trying to protect me," Wind said, "but I can hold my own here."

"I know you can," Spyder answered, "but Bear has to know about the problem here if he's to avoid an attack from the rear."

Wind started to protest, but Spyder gave him a push and yelled, "Go."

When Wind sprinted off Spyder mumbled. "I hope he stays safe."

***

As Wind approached the new position, he saw human body parts scattered across the entire area before them. He gave his message to Bear and an instant later, two to three hundred people, rushed forward toward their position. "Everybody back," Bear yelled out. "They're breaking through behind us."

Bear was standing and waving to his scouts for them to move back to a line along the cabins, when a bullet hit him in the left shoulder and spun him around, dropping him to the ground.

Almost as quick as he hit the ground, Wind and Ben hauled him to his feet and half dragged, half carried him to where he ordered the scouts to regroup. As they rounded the end of a cabin, Ben grunted and pitched forward, face down.

Bear pulled away from Wind, pulled on one of Ben's arms, and turned him over. A bullet had entered his back then tore a giant hole in his chest as it exited. There was no way the old man would survive the wound.

Bear looked down at his long-time friend. Ben smiled and said, "Give 'em hell, Hoss." His body relaxed and this talented, gentle old soul departed. As memories flooded through him, Bear thought of happy times, being on stage together, having a hamburger on the square and being with the man when he survived a death sentence of cancer years before. He let his friend slip slowly to the ground,

498

picked up a nearby M16 and began firing. It was now time to get mean-*"junkyard dog mean"* as he had told the others. The rage inside him created a calm, which seemed to bring everything into crystal clear perspective.

To Wind he said, "Go tell Spyder Ben's dead." Wind started to leave, and Bear grabbed him by the arm and looking into the young man's eyes and added, "... and I'd better not see one of those bastards behind me."

***

The look of the other man scared the shit out of him. Wind shuddered; he had never seen that look on another person's face. There was absolutely no give in it. There would be no quarter-no mercy given this day. The man had become feral.

As Wind made his way back toward Spyder and David, the battle forced him closer to the center of the camp. The gang's forward advance forced the defenders back. Wind crawled to Spyder and David's fallback location.

"Down," David ordered, placed his hand on Wind's head and pushed him to the ground. Explosions erupted across the area before them. "That's what happens when someone jumps into a fighting hole we have to leave in a battle. Claymores make a hell of a mess in a small space like that."

The gang faltered and pulled back across the road to regroup for another push. They had lost another fifty or so people in the blink of an eye.

Wind grabbed Spyder's arm, "Ben's dead," he said, "and Bear says he'd better not see one of those assholes behind him."

Spyder looked at the other man, blood traced its way down the side of his face from a cut above his eye, "Ben's dead?" He repeated.

Wind could only nod in answer.

It was as if watching Bear all over again. Through his beard and long hair, Spyder's face hardened and became emotionless. He moved a couple of yards away to David. "Ben's dead," Spyder told him. "Make these sons-of-bitches pay."

***

At David's original location, the gang members massed against the defenders of Rebel's Revenge causing them to retreat deeper into the woods behind them.

Hal and his people also gave ground due to the sheer numbers of attackers. Every time they blew holes in the ranks with the claymores, the gang simply filled in the line with new people from one side or the other. Hal received reports from messengers about the situation on all sides of the camp.

Hal took a bullet in his side. It was a clean shot going all the way through with very little blood and his adrenalin almost completely negated the pain of the wound. He stuffed a rag in his shirt and continued fighting. When he yelled for his people to pull back, he had lost almost a quarter of them. Still firing, they retreated to a line behind the cabins. They were almost back into Sagebrush, when he saw the two other lines from the east and southwest backing up toward him. It looked like a black day for Rebel's Revenge.

Keith and his people could see what was happening behind them and pulled back to keep any of the gang from slipping between his troops and the other defenders. He ordered his defenders to form a line along the north end of Sagebrush. Many of the defenders had moved into the buildings of the ghost town and provided cover fire for their comrades still in the open.

Lynn and her small band were firing through gun slits cut in the walls of the mock fort. Their only way of escape now lay through the western end of the structure. If the gang advanced much farther, she knew they would have to abandon the horses and pull back into the main part of Sagebrush. Her sons proved to be deadly shots with the M16s as they fired through the slits.

**

From where Gabriel and Manny were, it sounded like World War III was well underway. Gabriel's messengers informed him all their troops were now committed. They had no idea how many defenders were in the resort, but his troops were dwindling. It was now a do or die situation. He felt he must keep his people pushing forward if they were to win. If he gave the defenders any breathing room, they would probably find some other way to fight him-he had already lost more people than expected. It was time to direct this war personally.

All the defenders of Rebel's Revenge were now inside Sagebrush, some in the buildings to the east and west, and the rest defending the open spaces to the north and south. The town was completely surrounded when Gabriel arrived. He received a brief report from two of his group leaders.

"I want you to leave a small contingency to the west and east-just enough to keep their attention there, Gabriel instructed. "Then divide the rest in half and put them to the north and south. When you see a red flair, you hit them from the north and south with everything you have there. There're no buildings there for them to hide behind."

"Send the flair up," Gabriel ordered when he received word that his troops were in place. The mortar just off to his left thumped. A couple of seconds later, there was an explosion from the corral area of the compound. The man at the mortar had put the wrong projectile in the tube.

A flair flew high into the air over Gabriel's headquarters.

Inside the corral, everyone stood together, reloading clips for their weapons. A few seconds later, a shell hit not ten feet from them. Neither Lynn nor any of any of her boys knew what hit them. Ginny was on the other side of the area getting water and food for them when the shell exploded-she was dazed but not injured.

**

Gang members rushed wildly from the south and north toward the main street of Sagebrush. The walls built by the defenders at the end of the street gave them good protection until the enemy was on top of them.

There was no time for either side to reload and the battle became hand-to-hand. Keith and Amanda, their guns empty, used Sais. Keith was deadly with the Okinawa farm tool and had taught Amanda to use it well. The Sais came in pairs and looked like a straight gardening fork with the middle tine extended beyond the others. Both people stabbed and slashed causing serious injury and death to the enemy around them.

Spyder produced a ten-inch bowie knife and used it with ferocity. A rifle, used like a baseball bat, slammed him. He staggered backward two steps, knowing at least a couple of ribs were broken. When the man swung the weapon again, Spyder stepped forward positioning himself at the man's hands negating the impact of the swing and immediately buried the knife in the side of the man's neck. Catching a movement to his left, Spyder spun. As he did, the knife tore the front of his enemy's throat out. The man dropped to bleed out in the street.

Hal was using an M16, which had a shattered plastic butt, as a bat. He never hit any of the aggressors in the torso but always in the head and neck. Therefore, he wouldn't have to waste time hitting them again. The action proved very effective as bodies piled all around him. When the rifle was totally useless, he dropped it to the ground and went to work with the machete on his hip.

David used two machetes of his own, which were razor sharp and used them to cut and slice everything around him. With one swing, he disemboweled two gang members. His training from Keith with the katana was paying off. He completely or partially removed arms and heads with almost each swing.

The rest of the defenders of Rebel's Revenge each took their toll as well-their combat training was paying off. Bodies from both sides lay all around. Clubs, guns, and knives became slick with blood and hard to handle. None of the defenders did anything fancy, only basic, straightforward, vicious self-defense.

When the three 9mm pistols Bear carried were empty, he pulled his eleven-inch bowie knife and went to work with it. Seconds later, he received a slice across his chest with a machete. He thrust his knife into the abdomen of the other man and twisted. The man grabbed his stomach and dropped to his knees screaming. Bear silenced his screams by pulling his head up, placing the knife under his neck and pulling upward, slicing his throat open.

Bear saw another of the gang members moving from him. He grabbed the man's head, lifted his chin and twisted the head around as hard as he could. The man wore a surprised look on his face as his head swiveled one hundred eighty degrees to face Bear.

He spun to his left and partially avoided a rifle butt to his head. The impact still took him to his knees. When he looked up, Spyder's knife emerged from the man's shoulder. It retracted and then appeared again slicing across the man's neck.

Looking around he could see the defenders were now fighting in every part of Sagebrush. They were in every building and crowded onto the main street. The sounds of a riot raged all around him.

Above the din, he heard a new sound of different screams of not only pain but fear as well. There was a change in the pitch of the battle. Something was different. Then among the rest, he heard growls, catlike screams and howls. He realized Bo, Gail, and all their mutant army had arrived.

They waded into the battle like a stampede of cattle destroying everything in its path. Gang members tried to withdraw but there was no place for them to run. The mutants came in from all directions. They poured into the main street from the buildings as well as both ends pressing the enemy against the defenders.

The gang members found the least resistance to the north and retreated there. As Bear watched, he noticed it wasn't the human's decision. The mutants seemed to be herding them toward the north. The animals were doing nothing to the inhabitants of Rebel's Revenge but would kill or chase everyone in a gray vest northward.

As the gang left the town, they fled straight into the minefield to the north. The mines detonated when people stepped on them. With the human defenders behind them, mutants appeared in front and to both sides. In confusion, the gang members tried to escape in all directions setting off the mines. The ones surviving the mines faced painful deaths from the mutants including dismemberment, beheading, and disemboweling. The final massacre lasted only a few minutes.

Strangely, Bo stood in a line of mutants across the north end of Sagebrush. When the mutants finished with the gang members, they turned toward the town and the remaining members of Rebel's Revenge.

A cacophony of animal screams, growls, howls and other ungodly sounds erupted from both sides of the opposing creatures. There was pushing and shoving along with a few blows, however, there was no bloodshed, and after a couple of minutes, the sound and activity slowly subsided. The mutants from in the final battle gave control back to Bo and those with him. It seemed even the animals were capable of battle rage.

The surviving members of Rebel's Revenge looked around unsure what was next. The condition wasn't new to Bear. People weren't sure if it was really over. Of course, the mutant's presence added to the strangeness of the situation. Only time would allow any semblance of normalcy.

Bear saw Hal standing a little ways away from him. As their eyes met the same thought struck both men like a bolt of lightning. "Sandy," they both said at once and headed for the chapel at a run.

As they approached the building, they found bodies strewn all around the building and the front door of the little church stood open. It was dark inside, and both men knew better than to go charging into a possible trap.

They slipped into position with one on each side of the door. Hal looked at Bear who nodded; Hal nodded in return and called out, "Sandy?"

There was no sound from inside, and he repeated her name, a little louder this time-again, nothing but silence. Hal held his fist up for Bear to see. Then in order, he raised one finger, then two and then three. Both men burst through the door and immediately each went to opposite sides. Both crouched behind a bench pew, bracing themselves for what they might see.

There were no sounds from the front of the chapel. Both men looked up and scanned the room. It was empty-there was no one there.

"Where the fuck are they?" Bear asked.

"Let's find 'em," Hal answered. "We'll get a search party together."

As the men hurried from the chapel, they saw a group of people coming toward them from the northwest. It was all the children and the adults previously in the chapel. Leading them was Sandy and two mutants. She was talking to Cindy, and the animals alternately as if each of them were old friends and could understand her.

Seeing Hal and Bear, she ran forward, grabbed her husband and alternated between crying and telling him how much she loved him.

"Is David okay?" Cindy asked Bear.

"He's kinda beat up," he answered, "but he's in one piece.

Cindy and Deborah quickened their pace and the others followed them up the slope toward the main street of Sagebrush.

Bear turned to leave and give Hal and Sandy some time together when she grabbed him by the hand, pulled him back said, "Oh no you don't. You're staying right here." She put one arm around each man and hugged them both.

When she finally pulled back, Bear asked, "What the hell happened? Where did all of you go?"

She smiled, "Immediately after I got here, Gail came and got us. She took us over near the cliffs. There were a number of mutants over there, and I guess she thought we would be safer with them- looks like she was right."

"Damn glad she was," Bear said as they headed back to re-join the others.

***

Unknown to the survivors, Gail and a contingent of twenty-five mutants sneaked off to the west and encircled Gabriel, Manny, and their group of ten personal guards.

"It's been quiet for too long," Gabriel said. "There's no way we could have won and not had a messenger report to us by now."

"It doesn't look good," Manny agreed. "I think we need to get our asses back to Austin. Anybody who escaped away will probably head back there themselves."

When the mutants attacked, it only took about three minutes for them to destroy all the humans except the two leaders. Even though short lived, it was a bloody encounter. Seeing what was happening, Manny put the muzzle of a pistol to his head and pulled the trigger. Gail spared Gabriel until the last. He was kneeling on the ground in front of Gail when she decapitated him with one swipe of her claws.

EPILOGUE

Only about seventy-five people of the population of Rebel's Revenge remained. The assault on the community happened yesterday and lasted over four bloody hours before the defenders killed or drove the attackers off. Bodies not only littered the resort grounds, but the surrounding area as well. The survivors of the onslaught had no idea how many died-only that it was nearly their demise.

Bo, Gail, and all the rest of the mutants disappeared as mysteriously as they had appeared. Most of the survivors were disappointed they weren't able to thank them properly. Still there was nothing they could do unless they happened to see the animals in the future. These creatures, these mutations of humanity were ultimately their means of survival and never received or felt the community's gratitude.

Almost no one slept last night. It would have been like sleeping in a morgue. As a group, they mended wounds, cleaned, and patched people up. These things were done not only to keep infection and disease down, but because no one knew what else to do.

Fifteen men volunteered to stay a day or two and bury the dead residents of the now defunct community. The rest they would leave to rot in the coming summer's sun.

The survivors of community of Rebel's revenge would move elsewhere. Some were moving on separately and some figured out other places for groups to live together. None wanted to stay here even if all the bodies were buried or disposed of. The memories were too painful.

"David, Cindy, and Deborah loaded a pick-up and headed out this morning for Colorado," Hal said. "They had family up there and wanted to see if they could find them. With David's parents gone, there was nothing to hold them here."

"It makes sense," Bear said.

"Spyder and Ginny loaded one of Lynn's horse-drawn wagons with provisions and were heading for East Texas," Sandy said. "Wind was riding along with them. He planned to continue on and see if he could find some of his family up in Tennessee."

"So you're going back to Tyler," Bear said to his two friends.

"Yeah," Hal answered. "According to Gail, there aren't many humans back there. I figure we'll go back to Sandy's mother's old house-maybe grow a garden. There's plenty of game around there. We should be okay."

"No doubt in my mind you will be," Bear answered as he adjusted the saddle on his horse Dusty. Both his packhorses stood patiently waiting to the side fully packed with supplies, ammunition and other necessities of the trail.

"Now just where it is you're heading?" Hal asked.

Bear looked up from his work on the saddle and toward the trees eastward. "Over there," he said, nodding. "I've got no family to hold me in one place. So, I thought I'd look around some."

"You've got us," Sandy said. "You know that."

510

"Yes, ma'am, I do," he answered. "I'll come back around sometime. I know where you'll both be."

"I love you, bro," she said and putting her arms around his neck, hugged him tightly. "You take care of yourself," she concluded and stepped back.

"I love you too," he answered.

"Like she said," Hal told him and held his hand out. "You've got family with us."

Bear shook the man's hand. "I know, and I'll be back. You take care of the both of you."

Tears stung his eyes as he mounted his horse. He tipped his hat to them, turned Dusty, and departed eastward.

THE END

THE END